HIGHEST PRAISE FOR
HOMESPUN ROMANCES:

"In all of the Homespuns I've read and reviewed I've been very taken with the loving rendering of colorful small town people doing small town things and bringing 5 STAR and GOLD 5 STAR rankings to the readers. This series should be selling off the bookshelves within hours! Never have I given a series an overall review, but I feel this one, thus far, deserves it! Continue the excellent choices in authors and editors! It's working for this re-viewer!" —*Heartland Critiques*

We at Jove Books are thrilled by the enthusiastic critical acclaim that the Homespun Romances are receiving. We would like to thank you, the readers and fans of this wonderful series, for making it the success that it is. It is our pleasure to bring you the highest quality of romance writing in these breathtaking tales of love and family in the Heartland of America.

And now, sit back and enjoy this delightful new Home-spun Romance . . .

FAMILY RECIPE

by Pamela Quint Chambers

Home is where the heart is . . .

JOVE
HOMESPUN
ROMANCE

Don't miss these stirring tales of
true and tender love from
the Heartland of America . . .

MAKE BELIEVE
by Teresa Warfield
MAY 1995

HOMEWARD BOUND
by Linda Shertzer
JUNE 1995

FAMILY RECIPE

PAMELA QUINT CHAMBERS

JOVE BOOKS, NEW YORK

FAMILY RECIPE

A Jove Book / published by arrangement with
the author

PRINTING HISTORY
Jove edition / April 1995

ISBN: 0-515-11589-4

A JOVE BOOK®
Jove Books are published by The Berkley Publishing Group,
200 Madison Avenue, New York, New York 10016.
JOVE and the "J" design are trademarks
belonging to Jove Publications, Inc.

PRINTED IN THE UNITED STATES OF AMERICA

10 9 8 7 6 5 4 3 2 1

1

MID-MICHIGAN—FRIDAY, APRIL 13, 1883

Balancing a stack of parcels against one hip, Katherine Augusta Bradshaw exited Tubman's Mercantile, pulled the door closed to the faint jangle of the howdy bell, and stepped onto the plank sidewalk in front of the store directly into the path of a thundering stampede.

Before she could gather her wits to retreat from harm's way, Katherine and two child-sized human forms collided. Packages scattered to the four winds. Katherine's reticule flew out of her hand. Her bonnet slid sideways over one ear, taking with it most of the neat coil of hair beneath, as the smaller figure attached itself like a burr to the folds of black cashmere draped over her bustle. The other circled in relentless pursuit, shouting "Dang it all, hold still!" while the child clinging behind yanked Katherine around in tight revolutions, staying just out of the pursuer's reach.

Caught unprepared, Katherine could only exclaim, "Oh, my!" then, "Good gracious!" as she clamped one black-gloved hand over the bonnet bouncing against her cheek. Dancing a clumsy two-step, she somehow managed to stay on her feet, with no thought in her head except that this folly must end before she and her dignity suffered irreparable damage.

"Children!" she gasped against the constriction of steel corset stays. "Stop! Please! Children! Cease this mischief . . . immediately!"

As if they had not heard a word she said, the pair continued to pull and whirl, the boy by turns cajoling and chiding the small figure attached to Katherine's skirt. Images of street and store and sidewalk came and went like scenes from upon a merry-go-round. Just when Katherine was certain all was lost, and she surely must topple, thudding footsteps vibrated the worn plank boards under her unsteady feet.

"Thomas! Celia!" a booming masculine voice bellowed close at hand. "Release that lady at once, or there'll be the devil to pay."

On the next turn around, a male figure, little more than a mountainous blur, captured the nearest perpetrator, restraining the offender securely by the scruff of a coat collar. The revolving came to a merciful stop.

"Da, I was only . . ."

Katherine scarcely heard the boy's explanation or his parent's sharp retort. Her head swam as if still in motion; spots danced before her eyes. Fearful she would add the indignity of fainting dead away to all the other indignations of the last few moments, Katherine forced a couple of steadying breaths, her hands fanned out high against her bodice.

Through a veil of flyaway hair and black netting, she surveyed one of her two assailants, a ragamuffin of no more than seven years in too small a coat and tattered knickers. Under an unkempt thatch of straight brown hair, he regarded her with resigned hazel eyes in a pale, narrow face. The lad, who no longer posed a threat to life and limb, appeared a good deal less menacing than Katherine had imagined. In fact, standing unresisting in the hands of his captor, he seemed quite contrite and somewhat forlorn.

Swiveling her upper torso against the restraint of her garments, Katherine then scrutinized the second child, a tiny female individual, still clinging to her bustle. Filthy red-gold curls all but concealed wide, unblinking eyes of cornflower-blue in a grubby, cherubic face.

An unexpected and heretofore unexperienced emotion tugged at Katherine's maiden heart instead of the anticipated reaction to her fright. She gazed upon the obviously needful, frightened babe, then regarded the scruffy urchin once again, finding the resulting odd, compassionate stirrings both confusing and dismaying. She knew little of children, had never desired to learn more. Seen and not heard seemed a prudent motto as concerned her acquaintances' offspring. But here before her were an entirely different sort of progeny altogether, clearly lacking the most rudimentary necessities, and just as clearly starved for both physical and emotional nourishment. Against her will, Katherine experienced a momentary responding pull deep within to fill those needs before coming abruptly to her senses.

Quickly concluding the boisterous giant pursuing the pair was to blame for the distress in the poor children's eloquent eyes, Katherine faced the bear of a man with self-righteous zeal and ire. She refused to quell at his sheer size and obvious foul temper as he towered, and glowered, over her, as formidable on closer inspection as upon first glance. Dressed in knee-high moccasins and gray woolen pants held up with suspenders over a red-plaid flannel shirt unbuttoned to reveal woolen long johns, his notorious costume showed him to be every inch the rough and rowdy logger. An untamed coppery mane curling about his unshaven face and flowing unfashionably long to his massive shoulders brought forth the image of some mythological beast of herculean proportions. His features, hewn as if by an ax wielded in the hands of a craftsman, presented to her an unyielding, weather-browned visage. Tilting her chin a notch higher, clasping her gloved hands against her waist, Katherine stared back, although trepidation pulsed against her tight, boned collar.

"Sir, what is the meaning of harassing these poor, helpless waifs?"

Thick brows became one over fiercely glaring black eyes sparking amber.

"Waifs? *Waifs?*" the brute roared, jutting his chin belligerently. "I'll have you know, madam—"

"M-miss. *Miss* Bradshaw," she interrupted, with only the faintest quaver in her voice.

"Miss Bradshaw, then." A melodic Irish inflection belied his ominous tone. "I'll have you know that this is my son, Thomas." He thrust the boy forward by the collar, all but lifting the child off his feet. "And the little lass there, hidin' behind your skirts, is my daughter, Celia." He paused expectantly, glowering.

"Oh! *Your* children?" she murmured, chastised but unbowed. Clearing her throat, Katherine squared her shoulders, gave her hat a single ineffectual shove, and leveled her opponent with an accusing gaze. "May I ask, then, sir, why you were pursuing them so relentlessly and conspicuously down the main street of town?" She maintained a tone she considered both calm and reasonable, though in truth she believed the man deserved a verbal trouncing. "Someone might have been seriously injured . . . property destroyed. Not to mention . . ."

Daniel Sean MacCabe, Dandy to all who knew or knew of him, groaned inwardly and ceased listening to the irate female staked out squarely in front of him, her voice buzzing through his already aching head like a swarm of angry bees. Saints have mercy, wasn't it abuse enough having to chase his kids from one end of the town to the other for all to see without the likes of her descending on him besides? *Hellfire and damnation! Another dad-blasted, self-righteous do-gooder!* Were it not for the unrelieved black of mourning she wore—from her fluffy bit of a veiled bonnet now resting on one flushed cheek to the once-shiny tips of her high-buttoned boots—he'd a good mind to give Miss Prim-and-Proper Whosits the full benefit of his most colorful vocabulary. Still, considering Miss . . . Whatever's run-in with his little terrors, he could afford to be more charitable.

Dandy swallowed his fury, fought for control, partly succeeding. Running a free hand through his forelock in exasperation, he shrugged, offering a halfhearted grin.

"The lad and myself were attemptin' to give the lassie a bath, and she bolted."

Indeed, now that their father mentioned it, Katherine's nose picked up odors reminiscent of soiled, wet woolens and privy vapors. Merciful heaven, they were both in dire need of a thorough scrubbing from crown to sole. Then it occurred to her just who planned on bathing the little girl.

"You certainly cannot intend to perform ablutions upon this . . . female child . . . yourself?" Katherine's tone rose sharply as her indignation flared anew.

Whatever considerations Dandy had planned on giving the pretentious little prude in view of her bereavement went right out of his head. He watched her pull determination around her like a protective cloak, then saw one well-defined eyebrow arch skeptically high upon her fine, fair brow. Dandy didn't hold with anyone who could do that . . . seemed unnatural somehow. Besides, her all-too-familiar type, with her up-tipped, aristocratic pointy chin and condescending gray eyes flashing holier-than-thou high dudgeon from behind a curtain of honey-colored hair, brought out the pure, cussed devilment in him.

"Ablutions, you say? Ablutions? Why, Miss . . . ah . . . Whatever-you-call-yourself, I most assuredly am goin' to give my own girl child a *bath*," he barked for emphasis, "seein' as how there's none but me and Thomas to manage it. Unless"—he leaned his intimidating bulk toward her until they were nearly nose to nose, the boy, Thomas, all that separated them—"unless you're volunteerin'."

Distressed by his intimate, broad-shouldered proximity, Katherine illogically found herself noticing the faint but pungent scents of pine pitch and wood smoke upon his clothing. Not an unpleasant combination. Katherine's insides quivered uncomfortably nonetheless. If he thought such bullying tactics would intimidate her, he was sorely mistaken. Refusing to give in to a sudden rush of weakness in the knees, flustered but undaunted, Katherine looked upward from his broad, flanneled chest into snapping chestnut-brown eyes and held her ground.

"Most certainly not. I merely thought, Mr . . . Mr.—"

"MacCabe," he supplied gruffly, rocking back on his

heels, smug in the face of uncertainty warring with propriety in her expression.

"Mr. MacCabe, then. As I was saying . . ." She swallowed. "It would be . . . far from proper for a single young lady like myself to . . ." She paused, highly embarrassed that she should be forced to explain.

"To . . . ?" he encouraged with a questioning quirk of a smile that drew deep creases down his cheeks in a most disconcerting way.

Katherine refused to be swayed by his questionable charms. There was more to the issue at hand than could be resolved by such an obvious ploy.

She inhaled a steadying breath. "Mr. Macabe, one of the *matrons* from the Ladies Aid Society—"

He snorted his derision. "Preserve me and mine from that high-minded bunch of cacklin' biddies—"

"Mr. MacCabe!" Indignation flared in her tone.

"I'd as soon let my children take root and grow grass in the dirt upon their small persons as allow those—"

"Mr. MacCabe!"

"So, Miss . . . ah . . . er—"

"Bradshaw!" she snapped.

"If that's all you have to say on the subject, we'll just be leavin' you to go about your business." His voice grew thick with a brogue seaped in sarcasm. "My apologies and those of my children for their misbehavior." He tipped an imaginary hat with exaggerated gallantry and grinned without humor. "A good day to you, then, Miss . . . Bradshaw. Come along, Thomas. Celia."

He plucked his daughter off Katherine's bustle, lifting her against one shoulder, caught his son's hand in his own large, thick-knuckled paw, and, children firmly in tow, strode away down the board sidewalk without a backward glance.

Damned blasted, hard-nosed, prissy, too good old maid! If I never again encounter the likes of her, it'll be too damned soon, vowed MacCabe. Since the day he returned to town to bury his wife and see after his kids, some overpious, mealy-mouthed, marriage-bent female had been trying to advise or reform him, or both. Not a one had succeeded thus far, and if he could help it, neither would her highness, Miss Proud-and-Haughty Bradshaw. Thanks to her, the throbbing ache behind his eyes now thundered in his ears; his rage-agitated stomach rolled and settled uneasily. Beneath his red woolen union suit, he was hot enough to have just crawled out of one of the camp cook's boiling stewpots. Damn her and her endless, interfering prattle. Damn them one and all. It was no one's dad-burned business but his own how he saw to the raising of his kids, and the quicker he dusted the silt of this sanctimonious one-horse town off his shoes the better.

Katherine watched father and offspring retreat until the trio turned the corner beyond the brick bank, appalled at the uncomfortable emotions she had absolutely no desire to feel thudding beneath her breastbone. Most disconcerting had been this startling, distressful interruption in her well-ordered day. The MacCabe trio, especially the man himself, had left her shaken and distressed.

Churlish, ill-mannered, ungrateful, insufferable lout! He had no idea whatsoever how to tend to the needs of those two poor children. She had half a mind to . . . *To what?* She silently brought herself up short. A chance encounter lasting only minutes at the most, and she was ready to defend the pair . . . and against their own father! Preposterous! However barbaric he seemed, Mr. MacCabe had not treated his runaway youngsters with undo harshness once he caught up with them, and obviously had their well-being in mind, however misguided his demonstration of that concern. Their relationship was none of her business. None whatsoever. If only the man had not had the audacity to behave as though *she* were in the wrong, Katherine would have given no more thought at all to the incident. He was nothing but an uncouth, bad-tempered . . . woodsman, and, given the opportunity, as likely as blasphemous and intemperate as others she had observed. Were it not for his children, the brute would have no redeeming qualities at all. Should she be forced to gaze upon him again in her lifetime, it would be far too soon.

She fought the impulse to stamp her foot and won.

"Well, I never! Oh, Miss Bradshaw, are you all right? Such rudeness! Such despicable behavior!"

Katherine struggled out of her disturbing musings as if from a fog. Etta Kimball, the milliner, had exited her shop next to the Mercantile unnoticed, and now flitted from one to another of Katherine's scattered parcels like a small brown wren, twittering indignantly. Arms laden, she thrust the retrieved packages at Katherine without pause.

"Oh, my dear Miss Bradshaw, look at you. Those horrid, horrid children have soiled and rumpled you. But never mind. Come inside. A little brushing, a little straightening, and you'll be right as rain, never fear."

Chattering and fluttering, as was her way, Miss Etta ushered Katherine into the tiny, crowded shop—a cozy feminine sanctuary faintly perfumed with lavender, indicative of Miss Etta herself—past cluttered display tables directly to an orderly workroom behind a green velvet curtain.

Katherine allowed herself to be led, then fussed over, for she felt as rumpled within as without after her confrontation with Mr. MacCabe and his children. A few moments of privacy in which to regain her normal self-command was precisely what she required.

Setting her packages on a nearby shelf, she turned toward a freestanding, oval mirror. Her appearance had fared worse than she imagined. In addition to handprints in two sizes scattered in profusion against the unrelieved black of her best walking suit, her black straw hat—in spite of her earlier efforts—lay rakishly over one eye, entrapped by the hat pin snared in black veiling. The tight knot in which she normally restricted her fine-textured tresses had completely disintegrated. Her hair, the bane of her existence, having gone its usual willful way, fell in long straight strands to her waist both front and back.

"We'll have you all in order in no time, dearie," Miss Etta chirped. "You just apply yourself to your coiffure while I brush down your skirt.'' The milliner set to work at once, clucking over small, grubby prints that refused to whisk away. "I just wish I'd been in time to rescue you from that terrible, terrible man. I saw the whole thing from my window. It's shameful, his treatment of those poor motherless babies of his. If you ask me—'' The howdy bell over the front door jingled. "Coming . . .'' Miss Etta lifted the green curtain. "Good afternoon Mrs. Bixby, Mrs. Clayton. Be with you directly.'' Returning to Katherine, she looked her up and down, checking her handiwork. "Why don't I try a damp cloth before those smudges set permanently?''

"Mrs. Tillit will see to a more thorough cleaning when I return home,'' Katherine assured the birdlike woman while positioning her hat over a once-more precise twist of hair at her nape. "Thank you so much for—''

"Tsk, tsk. It'll only take a minute. Let me moisten a nice soft piece of toweling.'' Miss Etta flew deeper into the shadowed recesses of the storeroom.

Katherine waited for the milliner's return, resisting the temptation to tap her foot with impatience. Miss Etta was doing her best to be helpful; and, in truth, the more time she spent composing herself the better. Especially with the most relentless gossips in town—Mrs. Bixby and her daughter, Mrs. Clayton—in the next room.

The voices of the two women in verbal competition rose and fell. Katherine easily dismissed the snatches of conversation concerning Widow Wilson's arthritic knees and Missy Cooper's latest in a string of beaux—until her own name caught her attention. Then she edged closer to the curtain.

"Did you see Katherine Bradshaw enter the Mercantile this afternoon, still dressed in full mourning? Such affectation. It's been over a year since her parents passed on—''

"Perhaps she has nothing fashionable to wear, Mama,'' the daughter interrupted. "They say the Bradshaw wealth is all but depleted and Katherine's been forced into genteel poverty.''

"Really? Are you certain?'' asked Mrs. Bixby in a hushed, scandalized voice. At her daughter's murmured assent, she continued. "Well, well! The only hope for the poor thing now is to marry suitably if she expects to maintain her parents' position in society. One always assumed Katherine and that nice young Mr. Howard would someday wed—"

"Then he just up and left town. Jilted her, they say," Olivia confided in a stage whisper.

Katherine's face burned hot. Angry words of rebuttal rose to her lips, forcing her to clench her teeth to keep from voicing them. Jilted by Braxton—so that was the tale being bandied about. Thank Providence the gossipy pair had no real knowledge of the truth. The good Lord willing, no one would ever need know. Katherine felt certain neither she nor her father's memory could endure the subsequent scandal. Unwilling to make herself known, Katherine stood silently behind the curtain and listened.

"Katherine's a bit . . . umm . . . mature to anticipate making a good marriage now, don't you think, Mama? Well on her way from elderly girl to spinsterhood." Though Olivia Clayton giggled like a foolish schoolgirl, it was a smug laugh, rooted in a successful marriage of some five years or more. The girl's mother agreed.

"Too old, and far too straitlaced besides. And if what you've heard being said is correct, as poor as a churchmouse."

A brief, gentle pressure touched Katherine's arm.

"Oh, my. Oh, dear. Oh . . . oh, my!" Miss Etta twittered in her ear. "Oh, Miss Bradshaw, I'm sure the ladies have no idea you're here." Her bird-sharp features mirrored her great agitation.

Katherine took a steadying breath, offering a small, tight smile.

"You are correct, Miss Etta. I'm certain as well that neither Mrs. Bixby nor Olivia are aware of my presence, for they would not dare voice such slanderous gossip with the victim so close at hand." It felt good to speak her mind, if only to Miss Etta.

The milliner gasped, murmuring "Oh, dear" as Katherine, head high, parcels once more in arms, brushed through the curtain, determined that no one, especially these relentless tale-bearers, would see signs of emotional weakness in Miss Katherine Augusta Bradshaw if she had a say in the matter.

As alike as twin peas in a single pod, except for gray at the temples marking Mrs. Bixby the elder, the two short, plump matrons recognized Katherine with identical gape-mouthed, wide-eyed alarm.

With a pointed glance and a curt nod for each woman in turn, Katherine acknowledged, "Mrs. Bixby. Olivia." To her great satisfaction, she watched their surprise turn to red-faced embarrassment. With a short "Thank you for your assistance, Miss Etta" and a brusque "Good day, *ladies*" to mother and daughter, Katherine exited the shop to the deceptively cheery tinkling of the bell and absolute silence from the occupants within.

A dismal April shower greeted Katherine, pungent with the roiled earth of the roadway and animal offal churned therein, but also scented with the promise of springtime blossoms and lush, verdant grass. A moist breeze brushed her flushed cheeks, cooling them if not her sorely tested sensibilities. In one short hour she'd been both physically and mentally tried almost beyond endurance; yet it was with grim satisfaction she congratulated herself on having come out the winner in this last confrontation, if not in the first.

Retreating under the mercantile's canvas awning, Katherine stepped to the edge of the boardwalk, raising one gloved hand. At her signal, her man-of-all-trades, Andrew Tillit, pulled the enclosed carriage with a roofed driver's seat up before her. A man beyond his middle years, yet normally spry, Andrew Tillit climbed down from the meager cover of his high seat as though the damp and cold had penetrated through the heavy brown wool of his coachman's coat to his very bones. Water ran in dreary rivulets off the rim of his top hat and dripped from the tips of his salt-and-pepper-colored handlebar mustache. Mr. Tillit spoke not a word as he handed Katherine into the carriage, but his rheumy blue eyes glared volumes; she knew he'd favor her with a surly silence for many hours to come for having kept him waiting in the rain.

Andrew Tillit and his wife, Hannah, had been in the Bradshaw employ for so long they were like family. As Hannah had learned to live with her husband's dour moods, so had Katherine from an early age. Little good it would do to chide Mr. Tillit for his disgruntled behavior now, she concluded as she settled herself inside the relatively dry comfort of the rockaway, dropping her packages beside her. He'd come around in his own good time, as always.

Chin up, her back ruler-straight, she glanced neither to the left nor to the right as the carriage pulled away from the sidewalk, lest someone be watching. She strongly suspected the occupants of Miss Etta's Millinery were doing just that. Well, let them. They'd find little impropriety in her demeanor to prattle about now she was gone, whatever else they might uncharitably comment upon. Thank fortune, Mrs. Bixby and Olivia had not observed the appalling altercation with that Mr. MacCabe earlier. What fodder for gossip the pair of them would glean from such an incident! Katherine inwardly shuddered to think of the social repercussions.

Rain sheeting against the glass obscured her view. Katherine's thoughts turned inward upon the encounter with that boisterous beast of a man and his two fugitive offspring which had shaken her far more than she cared to admit. Now she found herself pondering and, surprisingly, fretting. How were the motherless children faring once again in their father's questionable care? Had the pair been bathed at last? Dressed warmly and fed? More importantly, by whom? And who, pray tell, would teach them proper decorum and social graces? Certainly not their loud, loutish father. Katherine felt aghast anew at her maternal urgings in response to thoughts of the little ones left in the care of a man who clearly had no concept of how to raise his own precious progeny.

More disturbing still was her reaction to the barbaric Mr. MacCabe himself. She reluctantly admitted to herself that she had not been totally immune to his physical attributes. With rugged features more than tolerable to look upon, from his untamed russet crown to his roughshod moccasined feet, he was indeed a virile specimen of manhood. Were it not for his despicable disposition, he might even have set her maidenly heart aflutter. Katherine caught herself up short, suddenly uncomfortably warm, and somewhat breathless, chiding herself roundly for her gullibility where men were concerned.

Her association with another such well-formed male, Braxton Howard, had left her virtually penniless, sore of heart, and firm in her conviction that a personable, charismatic man was nothing but trouble. Uncalled-for memories surfaced of those terrible last few months before her parents' untimely passing. Where once she'd suffered heartbreak, surprisingly now there remained only shame for the folly of her heart, and anger over Braxton's ultimate betrayal.

The son of her father's deceased partner, and a junior partner himself as well, Braxton had seemed the most suitable match; he'd had her father's complete trust, and her own. Neither knew of the young man's compulsion for gambling and for borrowing company funds when it was his misfortune to lose. Had he not fled when those funds ran out, he would be languishing in jail by now, which he most rightly deserved. Were she a man, especially one of Mr. MacCabe's obviously unprincipled caliber, she'd have hunted down and confronted Mr. Howard, forced him to pay dearly for the charade he had perpetrated upon her father and herself. Since she could not follow through on that, the past best remained buried, certainly not to be dwelled upon any longer today.

As for Mr. MacCabe, clearly he and his children were none of her concern. Katherine quite concurred with the man's pronouncement that they were not. All thoughts to the contrary—especially those of a fanciful nature—should be banished from her mind. She had difficulties far more pressing with which to cope, concerning her dignity, her reputation, and her position in the social community.

The carriage rolled down Main Street toward the outskirts of town and home. Katherine at last allowed herself the luxury of leaning back against the horsehair-upholstered seat. She massaged the bridge of her nose with two gloved fingers. Eyes closed, she recalled the cruel words "elderly

girl'' and ''spinster'' spoken so readily by Mrs. Bixby and
her daughter, and their smug, rather self-satisfied tone. More
heartless still, and more socially deadly, their choice in using
the phrase ''genteel poverty''! So lightly had they spoken
those words; how little they understood the real implication
of their meaning.

With hands clenched into determined fists in her lap,
Katherine vowed to put an end to the rumors—however
correct—of her reduced circumstances. By the time Mr. Tillit pulled the rockaway up under the carriage porch,
signaling their return home, she had conceived an idea of
exactly how to accomplish the task.

2

"Mrs. Tillit. Mrs. Tillit. Hannah, where are you? I need you."

Katherine briskly paced the central hallway from front door to stairs, her heels beating a staccato on the polished parquet flooring. She found no one in the cozy, crowded back parlor, though an inviting fire burned in the hearth. Pocket doors to the remaining rooms were closed; none had seen any use since her parents' passing. Indeed, to expose them and others to observation would only prove the truth to the pitiful state of Katherine's finances. So many beautiful things, including her own precious Beatty parlor organ, had been spirited away by Mr. Tillit for sale in another town to keep food on the table and a roof over their heads.

Katherine stifled a sigh, resisting the temptation to let her shoulders droop. There were times, such as this, when she wished she could unbend and permit herself to indulge in a good, cleansing cry. If nothing else, however, the trials of the past year had taught her just how futile tears were in solving the problems at hand. A stiff spine and head held high served far better.

In her own good time, Hannah Tillit appeared from the doorway beyond the stairs, drying her hands on her voluminous bibbed apron. Unremarkable in either plain face or plump form, her voice was calm, as the middle-aged woman herself was unflappable.

"You wanted me, Miss Katherine?"

Pulling off one black kid glove and then the other, Katherine responded, "Here you are at last. I will require your assistance, Mrs. Tillit. I have decided a year's mourning sufficiently honors Mama and Papa's memory. It is well past time I reenter society." She removed her hat, laying it on the hall table beside her gloves. "Therefore, tomorrow I shall resume morning calls upon friends and acquaintances and—"

"Tomorrow is Saturday, Miss Katherine," Hannah interjected placidly, little moved by her employer's abrupt decision.

Katherine gave an impatient wave of her hand. "Monday, then—"

"It's the middle of the season, Miss Katherine."

"A fact of which I am well aware, thank you, Hannah. Nevertheless, I am all but certain there is no impropriety involved."

"And what do you suppose the book has to say in the matter?" Hannah asked, a bit tongue in cheek, for she herself set little store by the volume in question. "Perhaps you had best look into it, just to be sure."

"The book. Of course."

By virtue of its title and content, *Our Deportment, or the Manners, Conduct and Dress of the Most Refined Society; Compiled from the Latest Reliable Authorities,* commanded a prominent place on the shawl-covered table in the center of the back parlor. Regrettably, nothing appeared therein regarding entering the social season midway. Closing the blue-covered volume with disappointed finality, Katherine frowned.

"I always did feel your mama set far too much store by what was written in those books and far too little on plain common sense," commented Hannah mildly. "She raised you to be just the same way, more's the pity, Miss Katherine."

"Nonsense. It would simply seem that if one does not

find the rules for a specific set of circumstances, perhaps there are none. And with that resolved, the next decision is what to wear. Certainly not this old thing.'' She gingerly held out a fold of her soiled skirt.

"Whatever happened to you, Miss Katherine?'' demanded Hannah, circling her mistress to more easily assess the damage.

"Nothing with which to trouble yourself as I have no intention of wearing this sorry garment again. Come upstairs with me, Mrs. Tillit, and we will see if there is anything left in my wardrobe which is not severely outdated . . . or black.''

Monday, shortly after one o'clock, Katherine nervously attended to her toilette, dressed in a mauve brocaded wool walking suit trimmed in plum velvet, and was not at all sure the outfit would do. What if someone recognized the fabric as having been taken from one of her mother's promenade dresses? Her mortification would truly be more than she could bear, for surely then it would quickly become common knowledge that Miss Katherine Bradshaw could not afford new garments of her own.

"Such foolishness!'' Katherine muttered. She had every confidence in her skills with a needle, and in her ability to pluck a design from the pages of a latest issue of *Godey's* and reproduce it flawlessly. The draped and bustled two-piece suit trimmed with complementary braid—once curtain tiebacks in a spare bedroom—bore not the slightest resemblance to the original garment.

"The color brings out the blue in your eyes, Miss Katherine—''

"My eyes are gray, Mrs. Tillit,'' Katherine interrupted Mrs. Tillit and sought her gaze in the dressing-table mirror. Her hands automatically twisted her waist-length hair into a fresh knot at the nape of her neck.

"And,'' continued Hannah as if Katherine hadn't spoken, "your hair is such a lovely honey color. It shines like silk.''

"This hair is nothing but a very common shade of brown, Mrs. Tillit.'' Katherine sighed. Her fingers explored the twist at the back of her neck, tucking in stray wisps. "And as unbecomingly straight and willful as ever."

"Miss Katherine Bradshaw, you're a . . . a handsome young woman. With a little more primping, and you could be pretty as well."

"Pretty? Really, Hannah." She sounded bitter, a surprise to them both. "Plain is plain. There's little point in attempting to make a silk purse from a sow's ear, in any case."

Braxton Howard, the only man ever to express more than a passing interest in Katherine, had never so much as alluded to her physical attributes. Perhaps he saw none to extol. Had she appeared plain to that overbearing Mr. MacCabe as well? Katherine wondered. Likely while trying to regain control of his children, he'd not given her a second glance, though a small, secret part of her wished he had. *And why should he?* she asked herself, pushing aside the vain and silly notion. Plain she most definitely was, that fact clearly reflected back at her from her mirror. No sense desiring it to be otherwise.

"Harumph! Well, there's no talking to you when you get something set in your mind. You just go on your way to your calls. Maybe someone will take notice of how nice you look now that you're not wearing that awful black . . ." Hannah continued a running narration as she shooed Katherine out of her bedroom and down the stairs to the front hall.

Adding the finishing touches of bonnet and gloves, Katherine opened the drawstrings of her reticule to check that the mother-of-pearl and silver case contained cards enough for the calls she intended to make. "Has Mr. Tillit readied the rockaway?"

"Ready and waiting for you under the carriage porch, Miss Katherine." Hannah stood back and observed her mistress from polished toe tips to black-veiled crown. "You look mighty fine and you just remember that when you step into those other ladies' homes. No one needs to know about your temporary reversal of fortunes, Miss—"

"Nor need we mention it now, Mrs. Tillit," Katherine reminded her.

Hannah took no offense; she never did. Instead she smiled encouragement, shooing her charge through the vestibule to the front door. "Just keep in mind what I said, and for goodness' sake, have a good time."

Milder weather prevailed today than on her last venture into town, Katherine noted as she crossed the wide veranda to the carriage porch at its side. Perhaps Providence, like the sunshine slanting between billowing white clouds, would smile on her undertaking and make her return to society both a pleasant and an easy one. She gave her gloved hand to the dour Andrew Tillit and stepped into her carriage, settling back against the upholstery.

"Never could understand why they call it mornin' calls when they don't begin 'til the middle of the day," he grumbled into his enormous mustache. Not waiting for her comment, he climbed upon his perch. The rockaway rolled on down the drive.

The soft breeze against Katherine's cheek carried the scent of rich, moist soil. Frequent April showers would soon give way to May flowers. She should place an order from her Peter Henderson and Company plant and seed catalog, as well as direct Mr. Tillit to spade and fertilize both kitchen and ornamental gardens. The bounty of homegrown fruits and vegetables was now a necessity, yet it was a vision of mimosa, heliotrope, larkspur, and periwinkle in bloom that rose before her mind's eyes. A certain buoyancy of spirit lifted the last of Katherine's winter doldrums as she looked forward to the growing season and her social reentry with eager expectancy.

Beyond her carriage window rural expanses gave way to streets lined with pleasant homes and prosperous businesses. As the carriage slowed before her first port of call, Katherine smoothed her gloves over her fingers and slipped her reticule over one wrist, sliding forward slightly in her seat.

Mr. Tillit gave a warning shout. Something smacked hard against the street-side carriage door. Katherine strained forward to see out the far window.

"Mr. Tillit? Mr. Tillit, what is it?"

The carriage rocked as he jumped down, but Andrew Tillit neither answered her nor came around to assist her. Anxious to discover what calamity had occurred, Katherine exited the rockaway unattended, lifting her skirt and circling around behind the carriage where the cluster of people stood amassed in the roadway.

"What has happened?"

"An accident . . . I saw it all—" came a disjointed voice from the small crowd, with other contributions overlapping in fragments of sentences.

"Ran right into the side of your carriage—"

"Not looking where he was going—"

"Just like them MacCabe people—"

"Trouble ever since that Dandy Dan MacCabe come back to town—"

"Mr. MacCabe has run into the side of my carriage?" Katherine interrupted the deluge of words. "Was he injured?"

"Not Dandy Dan . . . his son—"

"Thomas? Merciful heaven . . ."

Pushing through the gathering, Katherine pressed forward. Clutching her collar with one gloved hand, her other fisted against her skirt, she prepared for the worst, only to find Thomas standing, apparently unharmed, with Mr. Tillit holding him fast by the arm, dusting off the small boy's trousers with a hand that visibly shook. The poor man looked more the worse for the experience than the child.

"Is he all right? Thomas, you aren't hurt, are you?" Her voice scarcely reached around the lump in her throat.

"I ain't hurt," the boy piped up, the expression in his hazel eyes indignant. "I just wish he'd stop poundin' on my backside so hard. I didn't mean to run into his dang ol' buggy."

Mr. Tillit immediately ceased his ministrations and released his small charge. Katherine clasped her hands together at her waist to keep from pulling the child into her embrace to reassure herself of his well-being. Such action would embarrass them both, and she could only assume profound relief prompted the impulse in the first place. Instead she chided gently, "Thomas, such language. You should be apologizing to Mr. Tillit for scaring him so.''

She paused, but no words were forthcoming.

"Very well, then. Climb into the carriage, and we shall take you home. Your father should be informed of this incident at once. Where do you live?''

His thin face under a brown shaggy thatch went pale, his expressive hazel eyes fearful.

"Oh, m'gosh, oh, m'gosh. I 'most forgot . . .''

"You forgot where you live?''

"No, ma'am, no, ma'am!'' Words tumbled out one after the other. "Number Five Wicker. But . . . everythin' was happenin' so fast . . . I was runnin' like blue blazes, never saw yer buggy 'til it was too late. Gotta go. Gotta fetch Ol' Doc Wilby—''

He would have darted off once more on his errand had not Katherine placed a restraining hand on his arm.

"Is someone sick? Your sister?''

"No, it's my da. He's awful bad sick. I done all I knowed to do . . . but it weren't enough . . . so I come for Ol' Doc . . . an' clean forgot. . . .''

Tears of remorse welled in his eyes. Katherine patted his arm reassuringly, if awkwardly.

"Do not fret so, Thomas. Mr. Tillit and I will see what help we can be, then he can go for the doctor if necessary. Everything will be just fine, I am certain. Climb into the carriage, now.'' Hoping her words were true, Katherine directed, "Mr. Tillit, number Five Wicker Street, if you please. And hurry!'' Katherine followed the boy into the rockaway, offering up an earnest prayer for Mr. MacCabe's full recovery, whatever ailed the man.

For his children's sake, of course.

Identical rows of like houses with steep-pitched roofs and two-step stoops, small enough to fit in one of Katherine's parlors, hugged both sides of a road little better than a two-track lane. Number Five Wicker was distinguishable only by the small, forlorn figure hunched on the front steps. Celia's dirty face bore traces of tears from cheek to chin. The first two fingers of her right hand were thrust into her mouth, while the forefinger of the left made corkscrews of the red-gold curls at her temple. Beneath the shredded hem of a faded, ill-fitting cotton dress poked two scabby bare feet; she wore neither coat nor shoes. Katherine wondered if the child owned either, for surely it was too cool as yet to go without.

Thomas climbed over Katherine's feet and was out the door before the carriage came to a stop. "Celia, what're you doin' out here? I tol' you to stay by Da an' watch after him."

The little girl merely stared at her brother with large, sad eyes and held her silence.

"Celia, dag-nab it, sometimes you're so . . . so . . . dumb." Thomas threw up his arms in exasperation and headed into the house.

Katherine stepped into a gloomy, narrow hallway behind Mr. Tillit. Thomas stood in an open doorway to the left, clearly reluctant to enter the room beyond. As reluctant as the boy, Katherine remained at his side, while Andrew Tillit pressed past them to have a look at the patient tangled in the covers upon the bed, no longer the blustering brute of the other day, but a helpless victim of his illness.

After a cursory examination Mr. Tillit returned to report, "Burning up, and out of his head. Looks like the grippe. Reminds me of when your mama and papa were so sick, Miss Katherine."

Thomas trembled at her side. Katherine fought back her own growing dismay, recalling her parents' illness and subsequent demise from influenza within days of each other in spite of her most strenuous measures. Mr. MacCabe appeared both sturdy and robust, however, and Katherine resolved he would not expire as her parents had.

"Quinine is needed for so high a fever, Mr. Tillit. You must go fetch Dr. Hiram Price . . . ask him to please bring sufficient for a possibly long siege of *la grippe*," she directed matter-of-factly, removing both hat and gloves as she spoke.

Andrew Tillit's expression registered shock. "Miss Katherine, I can't leave you here alone with this man—"

"I won't be alone. Thomas is here to assist me." Neither word nor demeanor gave leeway for argument.

A disgruntled Mr. Tillit left the house, muttering dire predictions into his enormous mustache.

With a hasty prayer and one steadying breath, Katherine forced confidence into her voice, asking the boy at her side, "Have you been seeing that your father drinks plenty of liquids?"

Thomas shook his head. "He don't want nothin' to drink or eat neither. Said his innards didn't feel so good."

"Well, we must force liquids upon him whether he wants them or not. Dehydration is one of the body's greatest enemies in an illness such as this."

Resolute, Katherine stepped into the sickroom and moved toward the bed dominating the small dimensions of the cubicle, Thomas trailing at her heels. Though Mr. Tillit had pulled the covers up to the man's chin before he left the room, Mr. MacCabe's fevered tossings had since dislodged both sheet and blankets. The unconscious man upon the bed was without clothing to the waist, a broad, heavily muscled expanse of . . . of torso exposed to the discomposure of Katherine's maidenly sensibilities. A blush rose to her cheeks and her pulse quickened uncomfortably.

Then Mr. MacCabe groaned and ran his tongue over dry, cracked lips. Beneath his russet stubble, flushed skin that followed the angles and planes of his craggy visage was stretched taut with delirium and pain. In view of such suffering, practicality overruled modest reluctance. This man was seriously ill; her flustered embarrassment certainly had no place in his sickroom.

Katherine took the cup of water from the bedside table in both hands. Leaning against the edge of the bed, she then pressed the cup to Mr. MacCabe's lips. He thrashed and turned his head away, spilling most of the water on his bedding and down the front of Katherine's newly remodeled dress.

"Mr. MacCabe!"

Moisture could not seriously damage wool, but the plum velvet trim was likely spotted beyond repair. She glared down at him for one furious moment, but he was neither aware of her nor of what he had done. How could she feel anger against someone so ill? she chided herself. His state of dehydration was severe, the fever in his body giving off heat that could be felt without touching his flesh. She looked up to find his son staring at her with a fear that was close to panic.

Sensing her self-control was vital to the boy's own, she told him, "I'll need more drinking water, a clean towel for an apron, as well as a basin of tepid water and a cloth with which to sponge your father to cool him down."

"Is Da going to die?" Thomas bit his lower lip to still its trembling, and he blinked rapidly to keep from crying.

Katherine did not believe in telling falsehoods. Still she could, in good conscience, offer the frightened lad some hope. "I will do my utmost to see that your father makes a full recovery, Thomas. Now, if you will bring me the items I've requested, I will proceed."

Waiting for the boy's return, Katherine gingerly placed a palm on Mr. MacCabe's forehead. He was burning up. Until Dr. Price arrived with the proper medication, there was little to do but sponge him and force as much liquid into him as possible. She straightened his covers as best she could, tucking them in tightly under the mattress while, with some reluctance, leaving his chest bare. She noticed his broad shoulders and how muscled he was—obviously a man used to much hard physical labor. Even in delirium his slightest movement sent ripples undulating across the expansive display of rises and hollows from shoulder to waist in the most fascinating manner. Despite her conclusions after their altercation some days before, Katherine caught herself studying the subtle, mesmerizing movements demonstrating his sheer masculinity. Propriety warred with a strange, not unpleasant stirring deep within her midsection, until propriety won. Katherine turned her head away, red-cheeked and over-warm, to examine the small, crowded bedroom.

A tall, narrow dresser on the far side pressed close to the head of the brass bed, its top invisible under a clutter of personal possessions. Beside her, a scarred-top nightstand held only an oil lamp and a framed, mounted photograph of a beautiful young woman with long, light curls. Katherine concluded this to be Mr. MacCabe's deceased wife and the children's mother. Celia obviously favored her, with her own perfect features and fair complexion. Odd that Thomas resembled neither parent.

As if bidden by her thoughts, the boy appeared in the doorway, his arms full. Everything was as she had requested; Katherine praised him for his competency.

"Took care of my ma 'til she died," Thomas reminded her. "Awful sick she was. Consumptive."

Now he must watch his father suffer, too, with a possibly fatal illness. Pity and compassion swelled in Katherine's heart.

"Thomas, there is much to do," she commented with forced confidence, wrapping a dish towel around her middle and tucking it in her waistband. "While I attempt to bring down your father's temperature, would you be so good as to take care of your sister? See she's fed and put to bed on time? The poor child seemed most distressed when I saw her earlier." When he appeared about to protest, Katherine quickly added, "If we each perform our own task efficiently, I am sure we will have your da on his way to recovery in no time."

Thus reassured, Thomas offered a tentative smile before slipping out the door to go in search of his sister. With a sigh of relief, Katherine rolled up her sleeves and set to work over her patient with renewed determination. Her earlier embarrassment compared little with her resolution to spare Thomas and Celia the loss of their remaining parent, blustering brute that he was.

He fought her ministrations at every turn, bucking and flailing until they were both soaked to the skin. Not once did he open his eyes to acknowledge her presence as she alternatedly sponged his skin and forced water down his throat. She lifted his head, his copper-colored hair curling around her fingers at his nape; his stubbled beard and mustache scratched the back of her hand most intimately when she applied the rim of the cup to his parched full lips. Katherine never hesitated, determinedly ignoring the tiny chills traversing the length of her spine.

Sliding the wet, cooling cloth across his body proved difficult beyond measure. How like a caress was the gesture, for her touch must be both firm and gentle. From shoulder to shoulder her cloth-covered hand journeyed, then down a broad expanse of chest, matted with rust-colored curls, to the edge of the covers, just above his waist. Then dip into the basin and return to lift and bathe first one arm from muscled shoulder to blunt-nailed fingertips, then the other. It would have been best to bathe his extremities below the waist as well; however, that was not possible. Simply imagining what lay beneath the covers concealing his lower limbs brought Katherine's cheeks to a flame as feverish as Mr. MacCabe's. Mortification all but took her to her knees with fervent prayers of forgiveness for her wantonness. Instead, she continued as before, alternately sponging and coaxing, while attempting to overcome her distress and curb her imagination.

Long shadows crept through the single small window and across the foot of the bed. When Katherine could scarcely see her hand before her, she stretched, arching, her fists at the small of her back. Lighting the bedside lamp, she resumed her labor, while Thomas curled up and slept at the foot of his da's sickbed. The house grew dark and quiet and isolated with the singular silence of nighttime. Hour after hour ticked slowly by to the rhythm of a clock somewhere in another room. She worked without ceasing, though her back felt as thought it were breaking in two, and she trembled with weariness, more determined with each passing hour that this man would not expire in her care.

For an indeterminable length of time, it seemed as though there would never be any change in Mr. MacCabe's condition, but slowly he grew less restive, more accepting of the proffered cups of water. Finally, when she was certain she herself could not go on a moment more, the fever broke, a healthy sheen of perspiration blossomed on his skin, and he slept, his rugged, handsome face unlined and peaceful.

Quick tears of relief and gratitude prickled behind Katherine's eyelids and she offered a heartfelt prayer of thanks to the Heavenly Being to whom she'd been praying both consciously and unconsciously throughout the long, lonely night. With some small self-satisfaction, she gratefully acknowledged that Thomas and Celia would not be orphaned after all, in spite of her earlier doubts. Mr. Dandy Dan MacCabe would live to bluster and bully for many more days and years to come.

Now that the crisis had passed, Katherine gave a moment's pause to wonder what had become of Mr. Tillit with the doctor, but found herself too weary to dwell upon their absence. Pulling a straight-backed chair out of a far corner, she placed it at the bedside and sank down gratefully, determined to keep a watchful eye on her patient through the remainder of the night. Soon, though, her head nodded, her eyes closed of their own accord, and Katherine slept as well.

A persistent pounding broke into her deep repose. Groggily Katherine lifted her head from her arm resting on the mattress, disoriented until her gaze fell upon her soundly sleeping patient, his slumbering son nearby. Daylight streamed across the blankets. Morning had dawned some time ago.

The knocking resumed. Katherine's first intelligible thought was that Mr. Tillit had finally returned with the doctor, and she staggered to her feet, acknowledging with a soft groan all the muscles that ached in her back and arms and legs.

The narrow hallway was gloomy even in daylight. No light penetrated from the equally dismal parlor across the way. Stumbling to the front door, she opened it wide.

"Mr. Tillit, I . . . Good gracious . . . Mr. Grissom? Whatever are you doing here?" What, pray tell, would bring her attorney, Gilbert Grissom, to Daniel MacCabe's front door?

Instinctively her hands went to the nape of her neck where her neat coil of hair should have resided; in its place a matted tangle snarled her fingers. Running both palms down the front of the damp bodice and skirt of her ruined morning suit, she felt the sodden towel encircling her waist and drew it off, twisting a knot into it with nervous fingers.

Mr. Grissom cleared his throat. "I might ask you some-what the same question, Miss Bradshaw." His rather high-pitched voice rang with reproof.

Drawing himself to his full height, he looked down a narrow, bespectacled nose with weak, all-but-colorless eyes full of accusation. Everything about Mr. Grissom was long, narrow, or disapproving. Though he, and his father before him, had always been the family's attorneys, Katherine found little to praise in the man. With only a scant hour or two of sleep, she was in no frame of mind to spar with the likes of him this morning.

"Mr. Grissom, why are you here? And at this early hour?" Katherine repeated with all the patience she could muster.

"Ahem, Miss Bradshaw . . ."

At a slight sound behind him, the attorney stepped aside to acknowledge his companion. A matronly woman of tall stature, generous proportions, and obvious wealth sailed past both him and Katherine into the center of the hallway. An ebony brooch nestled on the generous bosom of her Worth original, and the matching earbobs fairly quivered with the woman's self-righteous ire. Katherine knew well what sort the stranger was, rich enough to both defy all opposition and to issue overbearing, preemptory commands, expecting obedience. Nor was she mistaken when with a distinct Bos-ton accent, the dowager demanded, "Young lady, I must request that you explain your presence here at once."

Ever mindful of her disheveled appearance, Katherine straightened her weary shoulders, asking, "And to whom would I be offering an explanation?" To the flustered law-yer, she proposed, "An introduction is in order, if you would, Mr. Grissom."

Turning his hat round and round with both hands on the brim, the attorney cleared his throat, stammering, "This . . . this is Mrs. Beatrice Stewart, Katherine. Miss Katherine Bradshaw, Mrs. Stewart."

"*Miss* Bradshaw? You are a single young woman, then?" The dowager's nose rose a notch higher. "May I ask what you are doing in the home of my grandchildren's father?''

"Your grandchildren?''

"Yes, Miss Katherine. This is Thomas's and Celia's grandmother,'' Mr. Grissom parroted. "Please answer the question. What are you doing here? I had no idea you even knew Mr. MacCabe.'' His displeasure rang clear.

It had not occurred to Katherine while nursing Mr. MacCabe that she might be required to face questions concerning the impropriety of her presence in an unattached man's home, that anyone would discover she'd even made the man's acquaintance, let alone spent the night with him. Such was a breech of etiquette second only in severity to an out and out public dalliance, as she well knew. But to be accused of wrongdoing after having saved the man's life? How dare they presume? Katherine's exhausted state only served to stoke her anger as she glared from one to the other of her accusers.

"There has been no misconduct here. I cannot believe you would both be so quick to judge me thus without hearing the truth of the matter.''

The imperious Mrs. Stewart took a step in her direction, causing Katherine to take an instinctive step back. A look of grim triumph crossed the older woman's face.

"Explain, then, Miss Bradshaw. Pray begin.''

"Yes, tell us how you came to be here, Miss Katherine. Perhaps you may yet save your good name,'' Mr. Grissom added his somber request.

From behind them came a wavering, though commanding male voice.

"Dammit, Grissom, get that old crone out of here until I'm not feelin' like death warmed over, and leave off badgerin' my bride-to-be.''

3

"Mr. MacCabe!" Katherine spun toward the sound of his voice. One glimpse of her patient sent his ridiculous pronouncement out of her head. "Good gracious, Mr. MacCabe!"

He sagged in the doorway to his bedroom, leaning heavily on a muscled bicep against the jamb, his head pillowed on bare flesh, looking decidedly the worse for his illness. He clutched a sheet to his waist, draped like a toga around his torso. Even so, his limbs protruded, exposed nearly thigh high for one and all to see.

"Such indecency, Mr. MacCabe. Have you no shame?" demanded his mother-in-law, aghast, turning her gaze away.

"Cover your nakedness, sir," Mr. Grissom insisted. "And remove yourself from the presence of these ladies."

The attorney took a single step forward before Dandy stopped him with a threat. "Make another move, Grissom . . . and unless it's out the front door with your client, I'll drop this sheet and give the *ladies* a real eyeful."

Sputtering, Gilbert Grissom backed away, pausing at the front door. "This is not the end to these matters, MacCabe. Concerning the children, that is . . . and your so-called engagement to Miss Bradshaw. Mrs. Stewart and I will return, never fear, as soon as you are up to conversing with us in a more civilized manner.''

The indignant lawyer exited with an irate dowager on his arm. Silence descended in the shadowed hall like an ominous pall.

Outrage tangled Katherine's tongue, but she managed to sputter out, ''Mr. MacCabe, how dare you—?''

''If you've any mercy at all,'' he interrupted in his weary Irish brogue, ''you'll put off whatever you're meanin' to say 'til I'm not feelin' off my feed and windbroke.''

Dandy raised a palsied hand, then let it fall, clinging weakly to the jamb, fuzzy-minded thoughts forming no clear pattern in his head. He vaguely recalled declaring before witnesses that this woman was his intended wife—the same interfering, self-important, blue-blooded spinster of a couple of days ago. How she'd wormed her way into his house without his knowledge and put him in this predicament was beyond him. The most important thing right now seemed to be making an all-out effort just to stay on his feet while spots danced before his eyes and the furious female's trim little figure swam in and out of focus. Her sharp words pierced him as effectively as the point of his peavey.

''Mr. MacCabe, really, I must protest your—''

The front door opened, admitting both Andrew and Hannah Tillit. Spying her standing in the center of the hallway, Mr. Tillit began, ''Sorry about the delay, Miss Katherine. Had a bit of trouble on the road and—''

''A bit of trouble?'' his wife interjected mildly but firmly. ''The poor man is lucky to be alive, what with the wheel of the carriage coming off and . . . Oh, my, Miss Katherine, look at you.'' Hannah tsked, taking in water-and-perspiration-stained morning dress, disheveled hair, reddened hands, and dark circles of sleeplessness under the younger woman's eyes.

Struggling with the need to give Mr. MacCabe his due and to reassure the Tillits, Katherine insisted, ''It is nothing, Mrs. Tillit, do not be alarmed. I—''

''Excuse me,'' intruded a weak voice from the bedroom

doorway, "but would one of you mind helpin' me back to
bed before I pass out?"

Mr. Tillit reached the sick man as his knees buckled, and
supported him into his room, slamming the door behind him
with a kick of his heel. From the muted rise and fall of a
solitary voice, Katherine fervently hoped Mr. Tillit was giving the indiscreet Mr. MacCabe a large piece of his mind,
as she herself longed to do.

Bride-to-be, indeed! Of all the preposterous pronounce-
ments! She'd have a few pointed remarks to make on the
subject once Mr. MacCabe sufficiently recovered and had
clothed his . . . his self in more than just a drapery of a bed-
sheet.

Recalling Hannah Tillit's presence, Katherine asked,
"Where is Dr. Price? I sorely missed his services and the
quinine during the night."

"Not coming."

"Not coming?"

"Dr. Hiram Price made it perfectly clear to Mr. Tillit that
he was not about to make house calls in the vicinity of
Wicker Street—"

"Well, I never . . ."

"Me neither, miss, but he was most insistent. So Mr.
Tillit went in search of Old Doc Wilby. Turned out Old Doc
was delivering Mrs. Barton's baby over in the valley and
expected to be a good long while at it, too. Mr. Tillit headed
out after Old Doc . . . for the medicine, you know. Only the
rockaway threw a wheel before he made it. Took the rest
of the night and the better part of the morning to get on his
way and stop home to fetch me." With a deep breath Hannah added, "That's the long and the short of it, Miss Katherine."

Katherine smiled wanly, placing a hand on Hannah's arm.
"I am just grateful no serious harm befell Mr. Tillit with
the carriage, and that you are both here now. Though Mr.
MacCabe's fever broke during the night, he is yet in need
of further attention . . . him and the children—"

"Children, miss?"

"A son, Thomas, and a daughter, Celia. Both of whom

should be arising soon, I would think.''

"That being the case, I'd best whip up breakfast for them, and us. Brought along a few supplies." Hannah patted the large hamper draped over her arm. "You know me, I always come prepared with enough victuals to feed an army."

"Thank you, Hannah, I can always count on you to do what is needed. While you attend to breakfast, I should look in on Mr. MacCabe." *And give him a well-deserved dressing down for his outlandish fabrication,* she privately added.

"Mr. Tillit is seeing to the man's needs just fine, Miss Katherine. Perhaps you should attend to your own," Hannah chided gently. "I brought you one of your everyday dresses and a change of underpinnings. I'll warm some water so you can freshen up."

"Bless you, Mrs. Tillit, you think of everything."

"I certainly do try, miss." All the same, Hannah Tillit's plump cheeks reddened under such praise. She headed toward the back of the house, Katherine following her and looking forward to a wash and change of clothes.

An all but bare and decidedly musty pantry beyond the kitchen afforded Katherine the privacy to strip off her ruined jacket and skirt and sponge-bathe with the warm water Hannah supplied. Also provided were her own hairbrush, underclothing, and one of her serviceable black dresses. How Katherine hated the ugly thing, and all the other black garments she'd been forced by propriety to wear this past year. It would take time, and endless hours of sewing, to rebuild a fashionable and more colorful wardrobe. Thanks to the ungrateful rogue, Mr. MacCabe, she'd never again wear the mauve and purple suit. With a shove of her booted toe, Katherine kicked the yards of spoiled fabric out of her way and set about working the snarls out of her hair. With every tangle painfully pulling at her scalp, she thought of another scathing argument to launch at the infuriating Daniel MacCabe.

As ruined as her morning suit was her reputation, should it become known Miss Katherine Bradshaw had spent the night in the home of Dandy Dan MacCabe. Even so, what in the world had possessed that man to announce a fictional engagement between them in such a precipitous manner? He must offer Mr. Grissom and Mrs. Stewart a full retraction of his hasty, foolish words. The sooner the better. By the time she'd twisted her hair into a tidy roll at her nape, Katherine was ready to debate Mr. MacCabe to the last word, determined to prevail the winner.

Her ablutions completed to her satisfaction, Katherine returned to the shabby, sparsely furnished kitchen, accepting a proffered cup of tea from Mrs. Tillit with a grateful "Thank you!" She then greeted Thomas and Celia, already seated and eating their breakfast. Thomas mumbled " 'Mornin'!" around a mouthful of hotcakes, while Celia continued to eat without so much as lifting her gaze from her plate.

"Thomas, are you aware you must not speak while eating?" chastised Katherine.

"Ain't got time to stop. Hannah makes 'bout the best flapjacks I ever et!"

"Surely they teach you better grammar than that at school," Katherine declared, appalled.

Thomas shrugged, unperturbed. "Ain't been to school yet. Ma needed me home to take care of things 'til she died. An' I ain't never seen my grammers. One lives far away across the ocean, an' Da don't like the other'n. Won't let her in the house." He stuffed half a pancake into his mouth.

Rather than encourage his bad habit by soliciting another response, Katherine turned to Celia to ask, "Are you enjoying your breakfast as well?"

Celia did not so much as glance up from her plate.

"No sense talking to that little lass, Miss Katherine," said Mrs. Tillit from her position beside the stove.

Katherine's eyes silently questioned Hannah over the rim of her cup.

"Little girl's not right in the head," Hannah responded to the unspoken query, "or at least so it seems. Won't speak, doesn't even listen when I talk to her. She just wanders off. And, miss," Hannah said, lowering her voice, "the poor mite can't dress herself, or even take herself to the privy. Thomas, here, says she's three years old, yet the child's still in nappies. Can you believe it?"

"Ma tried teachin' her them things before she took sick," offered Thomas amiably, "but Celia couldn't learn a one. Ol' Doc Wilby figured there's somethin' missin' inside her head." He chewed contemplatively on a crisp strip of bacon. "Ma said she guessed Ol' Doc was right. Sure made Ma sad, though. She used to cry when she looked at Celia sometimes, when she didn't think nobody was watchin'." His voice took on a sorrowful tone before he stoically resumed eating.

"Why, that is dreadful." Katherine turned her attention to the small girl sitting so quietly across from her. "She appears so intelligent. Look at her, watching us and listening."

"Oh, but she doesn't understand though, miss. I've spent the better part of half an hour trying to make conversation with the poor little dear." Hannah spoke resignedly. Then, rousing herself from her troubling thoughts, she shrugged. "Be that as it may, I have biscuits in the oven I'd best see to. And dishes to wash, and scrubbing to do before the kitchen's clean enough to serve another meal in. You can surely tell by the looks of this place that a couple of males've been keeping house. It's hardly habitable for the family of mice I chased out of the cupboards, let alone for Mr. MacCabe and his children. Ah, there you are, Mr. Tillit. Your breakfast's ready and waiting for you. How's our patient?"

Declaring he could use double helpings of everything, Andrew Tillit reported the patient much improved and resting comfortably.

Good, thought Katherine. Now she could confront Daniel MacCabe with his outrageous lie and demand to know his reason for voicing such a prevarication in the first place. She set aside her empty cup and, sliding her chair back, stood.

"Can't I get you a little more tea, Miss Katherine?"

"No, thank you, I have had enough. There is something to which I must attend, a matter that needs resolving immediately."

* * *

The bedroom door stood ajar, and when Katherine pushed it open with some trepidation, she saw Mr. MacCabe propped upon a pile of pillows, blankets drawn to his waist, long johns covering his former nakedness. Beneath a couple days' growth of russet beard, his face looked pale but peaceful. His eyes were closed. Unsure whether or not to disturb his rest, Katherine fell to studying the man whose life had become so completely entwined with hers in a few short days, and whose very existence, truth be known, might well be due to her ministrations. Even at rest his features appeared rough-cut and rugged, the golden bronze of weathered skin evident under a pallor of illness. Waves of unevenly cut hair hung over his forehead, and others clung to the corded column of his neck and trailed unfashionably long to his shoulders—the broad shoulders she vividly recalled bathing only hours before. In her mind's eye, Katherine again saw the expanse of his bare chest from shoulder to shoulder, down through a tangle of soft, springy curls to his waist.

An unsettling warmth spread from the region of her middle both upward and downward as she brought the scene to mind, a sensation that became so unnerving Katherine tore her gaze away from the man in the bed, glancing elsewhere, anywhere, struggling to recover her composure.

What utter nonsense, she scolded silently. *He is merely a man, not unlike any other.*

Yet he was not like any man of Katherine's acquaintance. He was bigger and louder, rougher around the edges and so vigorously alive, surely the only reasons she felt peculiar in his presence. After a moment's reflection, common sense came to her aid. Recalling her purpose in seeking him out, Katherine again focused her attention on the sick man in the bed, and to her consternation found him openly staring at her.

"Mr. MacCabe, I must have a few words with you. Now." Katherine spoke without preamble to cover her discomposure. She sounded self-righteous and prim to her own ears.

"I don't suppose you could be keepin' those words kind

and charitable, Miss . . . er . . . Bradshaw, in view of my invalid state?'' His lyrical voice came out rusty; reluctance
laced his words.

Dandy's regret grew keen as he saw the thoughtful softness leave her expression to be replaced with prudish disapproval. He'd been studying her for longer than she
suspected, under half-closed lids when she first came in,
then openly when she glanced away. He'd watched the play
of emotions across the soft surface of her face, surprised to
discover she was not the plain and parsimonious spinster
he'd taken her to be at first meeting. Her dainty, regular
features appeared formed from fine porcelain. Though her
honey-colored hair was once again drawn back into a tight
bun, he held an earlier image of it hanging like rich silk
about her shoulders to her waist. Along with that memory
Dandy suddenly recalled what he'd said in the presence of
Gilbert Grissom and that witch, Beatrice Stewart. Inwardly
he groaned, knowing full well why the formidable Miss
Bradshaw now regarded him with sparks of anger shooting
from her lovely gray eyes.

She took a single step toward the bed. ''Regarding your
statement . . . in the hallway . . . before—'' she began.

He lifted himself onto one elbow, facing her. ''As fuzzy-
minded as I was, I distinctly recall tellin' Grissom and that
old witch I'd taken you for my bride-to-be . . . if that's what
you're talkin' about,'' he injected bluntly and saw the pink
in her cheeks turn scarlet, though she stood her ground, her
gaze locked upon his own. ''What the *hell* were you doin'
in my house in the first place?'' His words cracked like the
snap of a whip.

Startled, incredulous, Katherine lifted her chin, informing
him, ''Merely saving your life, sir, though *why* at the moment escapes me, especially in light of your monumental lie
before witnesses.'' Taking his silence to mean she'd left him
speechless with shame, ignoring his thunderous expression
that was anything but contrite, she continued. ''I can only
blame the blatant falsehood on your lack of clearheadedness
due to delirium. May I ask how you propose to correct the
misunderstanding? That slip of the tongue regarding an . . .

engagement between us must be corrected at once. I have a position in this community that must be protected—''

"Damned be your position," Dandy blurted, speaking over her indignantly sputtered objection to his profanity. For a second or two he'd almost fooled himself into believing she understood what she'd done. Her pretentious prattle told him otherwise. "Your buttin' your way into my household means more than just a few turned-up noses to me and mine. Thanks to you, I could lose Thomas and Celia."

"L-l-lose your children?" Katherine took another step toward the bed, then paused. "But why?"

"For your information, Grissom and the old lady weren't just after makin' a friendly call." In his agitation his accent grew thick. "That unholy pair was checkin' up to see what kind of da I'm provin' to be. Mrs. Stewart wants custody of her Annie's kids—"

"Custody?" Katherine echoed just above a whisper.

"That's the word, Miss Bradshaw. Complete, entire, no visitin' rights custody. All she's got to do is show I'm not makin' a good home for the pair of 'em, that my bein' a shanty boy off in the woods six months out of the year makes me unfit to be their father." He fell back upon his pillows. "The old lady's surprise visit was nothin' more than an attempt to catch me failin' on the job, and by the looks of things, she succeeded." He heaved a heavy sigh; his eyes glittered as he threw her a furious glance. "Havin' an unmarried woman in the house through the night just might've lost me my kids for good and all." His strength sapped, his voice faltered. "So, now do you have some understandin' of why I said what I did, Miss Bradshaw? There was nothin' else I could be sayin'."

Withholding her sympathy for his exhausted state in favor of more pressing matters, Katherine responded emphatically. "I believe I do, Mr. MacCabe. As you well know, however, you were unconscious throughout my rather . . . extended stay. Nothing untoward happened, a fact I am certain can be explained to both Mr. Grissom's and your mother-in-law's satisfaction at the first opportunity. I am surprised at your lack of gratitude. Were it not for me, you might have died.''

''As it is, I'll be dyin' by inches if they take my babes from me. Don't underestimate Old Lady Stewart's ruthlessness. She wants my kids. She'll take them if she can. Face it, Miss Bradshaw, we've no choice but to make truth of my lie and marry.''

Dandy closed his eyes, turning his head away in dismissal, inwardly cursing the fates. *What a damned mess!* How the hell was he supposed to endure a lifetime of marriage to the likes of this one when he couldn't tolerate more than a few minutes in the same room with her without his temper besting him? *Blasted uppity, straitlaced prude!*

Katherine observed the play of dark emotions upon his face with growing distress. How in heaven's name had her life become so entangled with a man such as the likes of Daniel MacCabe? Their first encounter occurred by mere accident; Thomas's running into her carriage, accidental as well; and an act of charity had placed her at his bedside to nurse him away from death's door. Fate, it seemed, had played a cruel, heartless joke on both of them, and now Mr. MacCabe expected that they would marry? *Ridiculous. Outlandish. Utterly impossible.*

''I believe we had best finish this conversation when you are more up to it, Mr. MacCabe, and more in control of your faculties,'' she suggested pointedly. ''Apparently we have much more to discuss—''

He roused himself briefly. ''As far as I'm concerned, time for talking's over. There's only one way to stop Old Lady Stewart and save my kids from her evil intentions—''

''Evil?'' Katherine scoffed, latching on to the word. ''Surely not. She would care for Thomas and Celia as her own certainly. With her position and wealth—''

MacCabe snorted. ''Money's not the most important thing in life, Miss Bradshaw, in spite of what you might believe, though I'm learnin' a bitter lesson just how much the old lady's power can buy. There's only one thing to be done to stop her. You know what it is as well as I do.'' He turned his head away in dismissal, his features set and grim. He threw her a quick glance, his brown eyes black with emotion. "But first, a sick man needs his rest. Close the door on your way out." As she backed out of the room with a final glance, he added, "Just keep in mind, the minute I'm on my feet again, we're gettin' hitched."

Resisting the urge to point out to him how wrong he was, Katherine did as he bid. In fact, she slammed the door—hard—then stood in the hall, every fiber quivering with indignation, responding under her breath, "Not so, Mr. MacCabe. You are most grievously mistaken!" *Marriage to a man such as you would be . . . would be . . .* Words failed, and she shuddered.

"How's my da?" asked a small voice at her elbow. "Is he goin' ta get better?"

Thomas stared up at her, his eyes large and misty with concern. Seeing the worried expression on the boy's face, Katherine forced a tight, artificial smile. "Your father is feeling decidedly better already, Thomas, and should be up and about in no time."

As if an invisible weight had been lifted from his shoulders, he let out his breath in one gust, relief relaxing his sharp, pinched features.

Compassion swelled within Katherine's heart. How much this child had borne in his short life. How much sorrow and responsibility. That it should be so seemed grossly unfair. The boy and his sister deserved more. Struggling with an uncomfortable, frighteningly maternal flood of emotions, Katherine asked, "You love your da very much, don't you, Thomas?"

He nodded vigorously. "Course! Da's all the family I got now Ma's gone."

"There's your grandmother Stewart." Katherine considered all the material blessings the obviously wealthy woman could bestow on the children, despite her abrasive personality. Belatedly she recalled Thomas had earlier mentioned he'd never met his grandmother.

His face puckered with disgust. "Hah! She don't care about me an' Celia. Never paid us no attention, livin' off out East somewheres 'til Ma died. She just don't want our da to have us. Tol' him he was a bad . . . influ . . . influ . . . says he don't know how to take care of us right. But Da does take care of us, real good, now he's around. Come right home when Ma died, didn't he? Even though the loggin' season wasn't goin' to be over for more'n a month. That proves he loves us an' wants to be with us, don't it?'' Thomas became agitated once again, and Katherine could hear that he was close to tears.

She awkwardly patted his shoulder. "I know for a fact, Thomas, that he loves you as much as you do him.'' The man was even willing to marry a woman he couldn't stand and who could not tolerate him to protect his children. Dandy Dan MacCabe went up in her estimation as her own anxiety mounted.

Thomas, an optimistic soul, it seemed, brightened appreciably at her words. "You bet,'' he agreed. "An' there ain't a chance in . . . in heck Da'll let the old lady get her hands on us. She ain't goin' to send me off to no ol' military school . . . no, ma'am, or Celia to an asy . . . asy . . . hospital for dumb people just 'cause she can't talk like other kids her age.'' He ran out of breath, but his determination was clear. He stood with feet widespread, a sturdy lad despite his slight build.

Shocked into silence by Thomas's revelation, understanding now his father's reference to Mrs. Stewart's evil intentions, Katherine digested this new bit of information. She found it incomprehensible that Beatrice Stewart could have such monstrous intents for her own grandchildren, especially the sweet, innocent toddler, Celia. Asylum. That was the word Thomas was unable to say. An insane asylum for that precious, pretty child simply because she was slower than most? Unbelievable. The mere idea of it sent Katherine's heart fluttering.

In the small, shabby parlor across the way, Katherine glimpsed Celia seeking the warmth of a sunbeam penetrating the murky glass of the single, narrow window. The child stood with both hands upraised, fingers opening and closing, as she attempted to catch tiny, dancing dust motes, her beautiful blue eyes in a rosy-cheeked face mirroring pure joy, her concentration totally upon her task—neither the expression nor the actions of an idiot child, to Katherine's way of thinking.

Every instinct told Katherine this child was intelligent, with capabilities as yet simply undiscovered. The thought of this darling little one being banished to a hospital for the insane—probably for the remainder of her life—was more than Katherine could bear. There was nothing she wouldn't do to keep such an atrocity from happening. Nothing. And there was definitely something she *could* do. Her decision made, she reached for the knob to the bedroom door before her courage failed her.

"Mr. MacCabe."

He started up out of sleep, blinking myopically, rubbing his eyes with his fists.

"Since my reputation has indeed been compromised, and as these children of yours are obviously in desperate need of a mother's care . . . I shall accept your offer and do you the honor of becoming your wife."

In four days time, on Saturday, April 21, Miss Katherine Augusta Bradshaw and Mr. Daniel Sean MacCabe exchanged vows before the Honorable Clinton Meyers in the judge's chambers. Andrew and Hannah Tillit signed documents as witnesses. Thomas stood up with his father, and Celia clung to Katherine's hand, two fingers in her mouth. To say that this wedding was a somber occasion was clearly an understatement. A resigned groom, a reluctant bride, two bewildered children, and the disapproving hired couple confronted a judge, who, had he not been Katherine's father's lifelong friend, would never have undertaken to join the unlikely pair. But rumors had already begun to circulate about poor Miss Katherine and the rogue, Dandy Dan. Little would salvage her good name short of marriage to the man with whom she had spent a night alone. His duty done, Judge Meyers watched the newlyweds depart, wishing them a long and happy union he was certain only a miracle could possibly bring about.

4

Her first name was Katherine, Dandy learned by the time they exchanged vows. Katherine. A good Irish-sounding name. Went well with MacCabe. A proud name—strong and stubborn—much like the lady herself. He might've known she'd have a name like that.

Feeling one hundred percent like his old self, Dandy's spirits rose accordingly. He figured fate had a way of flinging unexpected circumstances at a fellow one way or the other; it was up to him to handle them for the bad or good. No sense expecting a jam just because the water ran high and wild; the trip downriver might be the ride of a lifetime. And, he thought wryly, looked like he had a lifetime with Katherine Augusta Bradshaw MacCabe at his side to find out. Thank the Saints for small favors, she seemed to genuinely care for his kids, and that said a lot for the woman. Dandy could tolerate just about anything for his kids' sake, even his new bride.

He had yet to see where his wife lived. She stood firm in her insistence that they take up residence at her place rather than his own, claiming hers was bigger. Dandy couldn't argue with her reasoning; he was well aware his rented house on Wicker left a lot to be desired in more than its size. So now he drove Katherine's rockaway, herself, and the chil-

dren behind him in the enclosed seat, following Andrew
Tillit and his wife in a wagon rented from Bayer's livery
loaded with all the MacCabe worldly goods, few and modest
as they were.

Thomas jabbered endlessly, a happy, carefree sound unfamiliar to Dandy's ears. The boy's life had been a hard one
'til now; Dandy hadn't the heart to dampen his enthusiasm
over this turn of events with a reprimand. Celia, as silent as
ever, looked to be taking everything in stride all right. How
the heck would anyone know if she didn't?

Their procession moved through town, passing the business district, then modest homes set in trimmed, fenced
yards. Houses became sparser, bigger, grander. Dandy grew
more and more uneasy as a mile, then two, rolled away
under their wheels. He wondered what kind of path his bride
was leading him down.

A glance at her over his shoulder showed him Katherine's
set, impassive face that was all but unreadable. Hands
clasped tightly in her lap revealed her distress. She'd looked
much the same ever since she burst into his sickroom and
announced they would wed. He'd figured she'd warm up to
the idea of marrying him once preparations were under way.
Then she'd gone and worn black to their wedding, with a
trim black bonnet all but hiding her crown of honey-brown
hair and a black veil concealing the expression in her cool
gray eyes. *Black, dammit. Like a widow in mourning. Wish-
ful thinking on her part, likely.* Annabella—his Annie—was
no less hesitant a bride than Katherine, but at least Annie
had the good sense to dress for a wedding instead of a . . .
a blasted funeral. Even if Annie's gown had had to be let
out a couple of inches at the waist, her being four or five
months gone with child. Twice wed, and neither time for
love. Where was the luck of the Irish when a lad from Eire
needed it most?

While he was on the subject of wedding finery, who'd
she think she was, turning up her nose at first sight of him
like she was smelling something bad? So he wasn't wearing
a fancy dude's suit. So what? He'd given a pretty penny for
a serviceable new flannel shirt in a solid, respectable dark

shade of blue; his pegged pants bore a pressed crease; and his mocs he'd wiped clean of mud. Hell, he'd even slicked down his unruly curls, the best he could do, having spent close to his last cent on the shirt just to please her, with nothing left over for a trip to the barber. Dammit, if his preparations weren't good enough for his bride, that was her problem.

So preoccupied was Dandy, he nearly missed the turnoff when up ahead Andrew Tillit left the road for a long gravel drive between two wrought-iron gateposts. Ornate iron fencing stretched into the shrubbery and disappeared on either side. A structure of mansion proportions became visible at once, rising three stories high, with dormers, porches, and turrets protruding in all directions. Behind the house stood a large stable. Off to the left a formal garden—not yet awakened with spring—spread far and wide across a spacious lawn, an elaborate gazebo at its center.

The entire village of Ballywae in which he was born and raised would just about fit on Katherine's piece of land; and the little house where his own offspring had taken a first breath would likely be suitable for nothing more than an outbuilding were it to be plucked from Wicker Street and transplanted here. He and his didn't belong in Katherine's fancy house any more than pigs in a palace! Now what the *hell* was he supposed—?

"Stop here, Mr. MacCabe, if you please." His new wife spoke for the first time since reluctantly whispering "I do."

"Whoa!"

The rockaway rolled to a stop under the carriage porch, while the Tillits' wagon passed on and headed around back. Dandy and Thomas jumped from the carriage onto the front porch, but when Celia would have automatically followed, Katherine detained her with a gentle hand on the child's shoulder.

"Mr. MacCabe, we wish to disembark." His bride held out a small, black-gloved hand and simply waited.

Still reeling with his first view of her place, Dandy wasn't thinking as clearly as he'd like, but he figured the new Mrs. MacCabe would sit in the buggy, his daughter beside her, until Hades froze over to spite him unless he did as she bid.

She regarded him patiently, with a tight, closed expression that made him wonder at his eyesight for mistaking her for pretty. Beside her, little Celia squirmed, as eager to be out of the carriage and into the house as Thomas. *Oh, hell!* Bending low before his wife, Dandy took her gloved hand in his, offering his widest, friendliest grin and deepest, most courtly bow.

"Here we are, then, Mrs. MacCabe. Home Sweet Home!"

Her new husband's lack of social graces proved alarmingly apparent, not to mention his outlandish mode of dressing for the formality of their wedding. After grudgingly assisting both her and Celia to alight, he silently stalked ahead of her to the front door, a mood upon him as dark as his stormy eyes. Following at a slower pace, Katherine experienced an unexpected twinge of guilt for making such an issue of being handed from the carriage. While she felt certain in her mind that it was her place as his wife to correct the errors in his manners, she wondered—in view of his obvious anger—if perhaps a more subtle approach might have been beneficial.

The oval-paned front door stood wide open. Thomas and Celia repeatedly ran the length of the hall and back again, setting up a clatter with their hard shoes upon the polished parquet flooring. Katherine bit back a scolding, watching their eyes grow as large as china butter pats, their mouths fall open in awe. She was certain nothing in their short lives had prepared them for their first glimpse of her house, which might indeed appear quite grand to their inexperienced eyes. Seeing the richness anew herself, Katherine felt a surge of loving pride. Everything sparkled and gleamed from all the spit and polish the Tillits had expended between the event of her engagement and the wedding day itself. Hers was indeed a magnificent, elegant home, though many lovely things had had to be sold. For the children to observe—and hopefully appreciate—its tasteful beauty to the fullest, they must be allowed to explore to their heart's content. Time enough for deportment once Thomas and Celia became more familiar with their surroundings. She dared not make the mistake of being too severe with them, as she had with their father, and incur their ill will as she obviously had his.

Mr. MacCabe stood in the center of the hall beside the round, marble-topped table, which held a calling card tray and a few other trifles. He turned on a heel in a slow circle, hands locked behind his back, saying nothing, his expression sober. He threw her a questioning glance, then followed his children from one room to another, opening and closing pocket doors, making a full circle from front parlor to back, across to the dining room, disappearing from a time into her father's study, while the children clattered their way upstairs.

Katherine assumed, a bit smugly, that he was as overwhelmed as his children. Almost immediately he rejoined her in the hall; and judging from his fierce expression, she could see he was far from pleased; rather, he was unequivocally furious.

"Kath-er-ine," he bellowed. "Kath-er-ine Augusta Bradshaw MacCabe!"

Must he always make so much noise?

"My name is pronounced Kath-rine, not Kath-er-ine," she amended distinctly as he abruptly halted before her. "What is troubling you enough to warrant such bluster, Mr. MacCabe?"

Brought up short, disgruntled, yet with hard-gained restraint, he managed stiffly, "First, call me somethin' a little more friendly than Mr. MacCabe. Dandy or Dan would do. We *are* hitched together for life now, you know."

"Daniel, then, as you wish. And, yes, I am all too aware of our marital status."

He muttered an expletive under his breath, which Katherine chose to ignore. At another time she would have to have a lengthy discussion with him about his—

"And *second,* I thought you told me you were sufferin' from a reversal of income, usin' your words."

She flushed that he should remark on it so crassly. She stiffened her spine, folding her hands together at her waist. "I am, indeed."

"Then how the hell do you manage the upkeep on this mausoleum?"

"Mr. MacCabe—"

"Daniel," he ground out.

"Daniel. To answer your question, the Tillits and I have managed very well thus far. And now with the addition of your income—"

"My income? *My income?*" He fisted both hands high over his head in exasperation, then let them fall to his sides. "For your information, *Katherine,* just about every cent of a year's wages went to bury my wife and put food on the table for me and the kids." Taking a deep breath, fighting for control, he added, "I won't be earnin' any more cash until the fall loggin' season begins come November, Kate. And that I can't collect 'til the season's over in the spring."

"Oh . . ." Her voice was very small. She cleared her throat to speak, but nothing else came out.

"And while we're speakin' about income, it looks to me like there was money aplenty around here not so long ago. What became of it all, Katie?" he demanded, his brogue thickening.

Cheeks flaming, she stubbornly tilted her chin into the air. "That is a matter I have no wish to discuss either now or in the future, Mr. MacC . . . Daniel. Suffice to say, what has been lost cannot be retrieved."

Her husband paced away from her, five steps down the hall, five back. Rubbing the nape of his neck as though it pained him, he said, "We should've stayed on at my place then, Kate. The rent was cheap. Now someone else is movin' in, and we're stuck with this . . . this . . ." Words deserted him.

"I beg to differ . . . Daniel. We are *blessed* with these spacious accommodations. Why, in that little house of yours, where would the Tillits—"

"Hell's bells, Kate, we can't afford servants," he shouted. "We can't even—"

Without a rise in voice, her tone commanded his full attention. "Andrew and Hannah Tillit are far more than servants. They are almost family . . . my family." Her lower lip began to tremble. She turned her back to him so he couldn't see the telltale signs of her distress. This, her wedding day, far from being as she long imagined, was quickly disintegrating disastrously, thanks to her groom.

Dandy reached out a hand to touch and console her, then pulled back, knowing his friendly, comforting advances would be unwelcome, and angry with himself that he'd brought her to this state. A quick tongue and an Irish temper were often his downfall, and this time was no exception. But his words, though bluntly stated, were God's own truth. He studied her stiff, black-clothed back, totally bewildered as to what to say or do next.

"Da! Miss Katherine!" Thomas came thumping down the stairs from above, Celia trailing at a slower pace, clinging to the rail. "Oh, Da, we found our rooms . . . Celia an' me . . . an' they're grand. There's a baby doll an' a dolly's house in Celia's . . . an' you oughtta see the sets of toy soldiers in mine." Thomas came skidding to a halt at his father's feet. "We found your room, too, Da. Mr. Tillit's puttin' our stuff in it. There's doors goin' from my room to Celia's to yours so's we won't have to feel lonely in them great big rooms . . . an'—"

"Whoa!" Dandy exclaimed, overwhelmingly grateful for his son's interruption. "You'd best take a breath in there somewhere before you explode."

Thomas grabbed his father's large hand in both of his, tugging hard. "You gotta come up an' see for yourself. Come on, Da, come see."

"That I will, Thomas, that I will, and help Mr. Tillit with our belongin's."

Dandy let himself be hauled to the stairs, where Celia still struggled downward, two feet to each step, short, plump legs barely stretching from riser to riser. She watched them pass her going upward, then resignedly turned to follow, slipping two fingers into her mouth for comfort.

Dry-eyed once more, Katherine watched their ascent. Taking pity on the child, Katherine climbed the stairs to her, and when the little girl acknowledged her presence with a glance, Katherine first spread wide her arms, then picked up

Celia, nestling her against one hip. At a slower pace she followed Daniel and Thomas upward, relieved that the boy's interruption had given her time to regain her composure. That she should allow her emotions to shatter her control was almost as unsettling as the disagreement between her new husband and herself. Especially after her silent vow of the night before that she would make the best of her circumstances and try to get along with the contrary man. If this was an example of married life, however, it certainly was not proving amiable. Never before had her sensibilities been so severely, and so frequently, tried.

The three bedrooms in question stretched from corner to corner across the front of the house, Celia's in the middle and Thomas's and Daniel's to the left and right respectively. Daniel's was, in fact, the master bedroom, in which her parents had formerly resided; and Celia's had been an infant nursery, then invalid room, thus the doors connecting it with the other two. Katherine believed the arrangement to be a perfect solution for housing the three new family members, and felt justifiably proud of herself for having outfitted them accordingly.

In Celia's she had placed her own former playthings; in Thomas's the armies of toy soldiers that had been her father's as a boy; and in Daniel's she had laid out her father's satin robe, warm felt house slippers, and a toiletry set of finest ivory-appointed implements, hoping each new resident was as pleased as she with the results.

Joining them now, Katherine was first startled, then appalled, at the disarray that had come to her parents' former orderly room. Boxes and suitcases spread far and wide, some still closed, most opened, with contents scattered on bed, chairs, and floor. Thomas dug deeply within the largest trunk, intently searching for something, flinging items to the wind.

"Goodness!" Katherine set Celia down, and the child promptly joined her brother in his quest, though she likely had no idea what she was looking for.

Dandy, himself occupied with a suitcase on the bed, glanced her way briefly, apologetically. "Don't worry, Kate.

We'll have this mess cleared out of here in good order. By the time you've gathered up your finery and frippery, there'll be plenty of places to store it.''

"My finery . . . and . . . and . . . frippery?''

Her husband squatted before an open crate, his back muscles straining against the navy flannel of his shirt until Katherine was certain the seams would give way, and spoke over his shoulder.

"Your dresses, and notions, and night things. You know, all that stuff women require about them to make themselves so irresistible to us men.'' He favored her with a cajoling, rakish grin, dimples creasing deep; but his chestnut-colored eyes said he wasn't joking, not entirely. There was a hungry, eager look about them as well.

It quickly came to her what Daniel was taking so for granted.

"I will not be sharing this room with you, Mr. Mac-Cabe,'' she told him most emphatically. "I have my own quarters, as they have always been, just beyond the connecting dressing room over there.'' She gestured with a curt nod.

He rose slowly, turning toward her, hands fisted on hips.

"You'll not be sharin' your husband's room, *Mrs.* MacCabe?'' The Irish lilt made his voice appear friendlier than his expression gave evidence to. "You have your own quarters, *Mrs.* MacCabe?''

Clasping her hands at her waist to still their sudden trembling, Katherine forced herself to look him squarely in his brown eyes, grown black and intense.

"Why, certainly, Mr. MacCabe. Our agreement was that we marry to save my reputation and to provide a mother and a good home for your children. Was it not?''

"Our marriage vows, spoken for whatever reason, made us man and wife, Kate, not man and nursemaid. If you had no intention of carryin' out the full extent of the promises you made before myself and the children, and in the eyes of the law, then those words are little more than lies.'' At the last, his voice dipped to a more reasonable level, in fact, fairly purred with persuasion.

He'd come out of a long winter in a camp full of men straight to Annie's funeral and hadn't had the time, or the energy—or the cash—to seek out companionship of the female gender. Now he was again wed, no matter the reason, and it was his privilege, nay his right, to pursue the fulfillment of some very real needs with his brand-new bride, despite her prudish sensibilities to the contrary.

"I feel, Mr. MacC . . . Daniel, that such matters are best discussed in private," she responded primly, with a pointed glance toward the children rummaging through boxes, blissfully unaware of the turmoil around them. "Perhaps this evening, after the children have gone to sleep?" Scarlet cheeks spoke of her embarrassment.

If she needed that bit of time, Dandy magnanimously decided to give it to her. In truth, he desired no unwilling bedmate.

"All right, Kate, have it your way. A few hours to think things over will surely bring you to your senses. A husband and wife share their bed. That's the way of it, and that's the right of it. But if you need to take a little more time gettin' used to the idea . . . my kids generally hit the hay about eight." Impulsively he gave her flushed cheek a proprietary little peck and went back to his unpacking.

Hands fisted in the folds of her skirt, Katherine made no move to honor his dismissal.

"Daniel . . ." More distinctly, "Daniel . . ."

He gave her a smug grin over one broad shoulder. "Yes, Katie?"

She ground her teeth. "You will please do me the courtesy of addressing me by my proper name and not one diminutive after another."

His wicked grin widened. He winked. "Have it your way, Kath-er-ine."

"My name is . . ." She saw he was teasing and found it hard to stand firm. With effort, however, she did. "Oh, Mr. MacC . . . Daniel, will you never grow up?"

His brows rose quizzically high, his grin intact. "I sure as . . . as . . . heck hope not, Katherine. There's not much pleasure in a life without a little well-meaning fun now and again, especially between man and wife." He came to stand before her and placed one large hand on each of her slender shoulders, his eyes serious. "Let yourself take some joy from life, Kate. It can't hurt, and you might even grow to like it."

His hands rested heavily, yet not uncomfortably so, their warmth penetrating the fabric of her gown beneath his gentle grasp. His nearness had her quaking in her high-topped, patent-leather shoes. This large, rugged logger, with a wild mane of coppery hair barely contained in the short queue into which he'd restrained it for the wedding, terrified and exhilarated Katherine in a manner she dared not acknowledge, even in the darkest recesses of her private thoughts.

Stepping back, she broke his light hold upon her person, tipping her chin upward. "I derive great pleasure from the balance of order in my life, Daniel, and find satisfaction in the knowledge that my social skills allow me to both speak and behave properly in most every given situation. And I believe it prudent to restrain ourselves from discussing either personalities or proprieties until we are alone later this evening."

She turned and walked sedately, though briskly, out of the room before he had the opportunity for some uncouth rejoinder. Still, she distinctly heard him mutter a single syllable. "*Damn.*"

Dinner proved as disastrous as the day had been thus far. The festive touches to the table for the wedding dinner, from snowy linen to formal place settings replete with cut-glass goblets, polished silver, and delicate bone china, went totally uncomplimented upon. As the first course was offered, Thomas wrinkled his nose most unbecomingly, demanding, "What's this awful-smellin' stuff?"

Katherine replied, "Oyster stew. And indeed, Thomas, there is nothing foul-odored about it. Were there, however, one should not breech good manners by commenting upon it."

"Hunh?"

"Don't complain about the food," Dandy intervened. To

Hannah, who was serving, he suggested, "Maybe you'd just better get to the meat and potatoes."

Hannah threw her mistress a questioning glance, then responded, "Yes, sir. As you wish, Mr. MacCabe."

When Hannah, with Andrew's assistance, reappeared with a platter of roasted beef surrounded by potatoes and carrots, as well as a bowl heaped with fluffy mashed winter squash and a napkin-covered basket of fragrant, yeasty rolls, Dandy chortled, "Now, this is more like it. This is a meal a man can sink his teeth into."

He forked generous portions onto his plate and onto those of his children. He ate with voracious relish, offering no dinner table conversation, but cleaned his plate, including second helpings, and third, with silent concentration. Thomas followed suit; Celia picked and ate what she wished.

Katherine, aghast, could scarcely manage to swallow the first bite of her beef. After sopping up the last bit of gravy with the last piece of his fourth—or possibly fifth—roll, Dandy wiped his mouth with his linen dinner napkin, demanding, "What's for dessert?"

"Flan and rhubarb tarts." The errors of his ways were so vast and numerous that Katherine was left once again in her husband's presence without rejoiner.

"Well, then, ring that little bell of yours and let's get on with it."

After dinner Katherine and Dandy retired to the back parlor across from the dining room, its stove glowing with welcome warmth on a cool April evening, Hannah having taken two tired children off to bed. The bridal couple fell awkwardly silent in their newfound companionship, especially with the inevitability of discussing their sleeping arrangements hanging silently between them.

Katherine chose her usual place, a lady's brocade-upholstered slipper chair, a basket containing her embroidery at her feet. Instead of her usual needlework, however, she retrieved *Our Deportment* from the table in the center of the room, her intent to arm herself with proper rules from chapters headed "Home Training" and "Table Etiquette."

A subheading, "Courtship," caught her eye. To herself, she read of the proper conduct of gentlemen and ladies toward each other during this properly romantic period, the requirements of an acceptable suitor, and the unlikelihood of falling in love at first sight.

Of that fact both Mr. MacCabe and I are most painfully aware, she thought without humor.

Pausing, Katherine chanced a furtive glance in her husband's direction. In the shadows of a far corner, reclining in her father's favorite leather chair, he sat with his head thrown back, eyes closed, thankfully oblivious to her presence. Rubbing the throbbing ache out of her temples with the first two fingertips of both hands, Katherine continued reading, having now gone on to "Chapter XVII: Wedding Etiquette," detailing everything from the choice of ushers to the planning of the bridal tour. All so lovely, so grand . . . so wonderful, magical. And so unlike her own hasty and pitifully utilitarian event.

Were she the weepy sort, she might have been sobbing by now. As it was, not a single tear slid down her cheek. Tears were a weak individual's solution, not Katherine Augusta Bradshaw . . . MacCabe's. Mrs. Daniel Sean MacCabe! Incredible that her life had taken such a swift and irrevocable turn. Katherine absently twirled the plain gold band on her left ring finger. A week ago her steps traveled a path she seemed destined to follow forever—spinsterhood. And now . . . this! Married and the mother of the man's children. How would she manage? How would they all? She glanced toward her husband once more, only to find him now leaning forward, elbows on knees, watching her intently.

Kate moved her lips when she read. That little quirk made her seem more human, more vulnerable somehow. She was upset, Dandy could tell. Probably shouldn't have got back at her by behaving like an unschooled shanty boy at the table. His mother would've been sorely ashamed of him after all the manners she drilled into him time and again.

He'd watched his new wife reading for a long while, no

more eager than she to take up their disagreement where
they left off, before she looked up from that damned deportment book of hers. It surprised him to realize he enjoyed
watching her; all and all she was pleasant to look upon. Not
a beauty, mind you, not like Annie. But then Annie's looks
had gotten her nothing but trouble, so maybe it was just as
well. Now, if only Kate would do something to improve her
disposition, they might get along all right together.

"Why so glum, Katherine?" he asked at her glance.

She placed a palm against the surface of the page.

"Enlightening reading, Mr. MacC . . . Daniel. Food for
thought. Would you like me to read an excerpt aloud—?"

"I think we've had enough sober thoughts for our wedding night. How about a little entertainment?"

Katherine's heart began thumping erratically at his suggestive comment, but her husband merely reached down beside his chair, retrieving a musical instrument of a warm,
polished wood, with the appearance of an elongated violin
without a neck. At her expression of inquiry, he offered,
"Mountain dulcimer." Dandy placed the instrument across
his knees and lovingly spread his hands over the strings.
"Handcrafted by a loggin' friend of mine, Moonshine Jim-
mie Jacobs."

"Does every man in your occupation require a . . . a . . .
descriptive name in addition to that given him at birth?"

"Seems like. Usually someone hangs it on him by the
time he's spent his first month in the woods. In Donovan's
camp, we have Blueberry Bob and Three-Fingered Ole,
Whiskey Bill, Crosshaul Paddy, and a dozen more I could
mention. I was a greenhorn kid of seventeen when I got
mine." Dandy settled more deeply into his comfortable
chair. He grinned, remembering. "Fresh off the boat from
Ireland and thinkin' to make the best possible impression
on the foreman of the camp, I duded up in my Sunday-go-
to-meetin' suit, shined my shoes, and slicked back my hair."
The creases in his cheeks deepened. "Then I went to stand
in line with a bunch of seasoned loggers wearin' mackinaws,
stagged pants, and caulked boots. They called me Dandy

Dan from the moment of my hirin' . . . and Dandy Dan it is to this day.''

Katherine found herself smiling at the picture his words conjured up in her mind, and her husband's appellation no longer seemed quite as ridiculous to her.

He began strumming softly across his instrument's strings; his hands sought out and played a beautifully haunting, rather melancholy melody.

The sound pulled at her heartstrings as no music ever had. ''I cannot recall having heard that air before,'' she said softly around the swell of emotion blocking her throat as the last note died away.

''Probably because it's of my own creation . . . just a few chords strung together. 'Tis nothing—''

''Oh, but it is. It is lovely,'' Katherine protested. ''You should put words to your music.''

Dandy shrugged. ''Maybe on down the line, when I've time to spare and the mood's upon me. In the meantime, how about something with a little life to it?''

His talented fingers picked and strummed familiar, lively tunes, from ''Turkey in the Straw'' to ''Comin' Round the Mountain'' and ''Liza Jane.'' Katherine could not keep her foot from tapping, even while dread filled her heart for the moment when the music must stop. She knew that time was fast approaching when, almost absently, he began to strum the opening cords to a hymn Katherine well knew, ''Sweet Hour of Prayer.'' Played softly on the unfamiliar instrument, the tune took on a soulful, heartrending sound. Katherine gloried in the beauty of it, marveling at her new husband's talent, surely a gift from God, so great was his skill. Contentment settled over her. Perhaps marriage, though different by far from what she had read, would not prove so bad after all.

Dandy set the dulcimer aside, standing and stretching. ''I'd say it's time we went up to bed, wouldn't you? It's been a mighty eventful day.''

Bereft of the magical beauty of her husband's music, Katherine panicked; her words came out in a terrified croak. ''I suppose we must.''

The affability vanished from Daniel's face.

"You don't have to look scared out of your skin, Kate. I'll not be requirin' anythin' from you you're unwillin' to give." His voice held a quiet bitterness.

Relief swelled that, by his words, he was promising not to enforce his rights as her husband. Her guilt that she was unable to perform hers as his wife increased.

Silence reigned. The fire popped in the stove. Katherine jumped. Rising slowly, she hesitated, uncertain, in the center of the room. Unmoving, her husband stared at the flickering fire beyond the glass door of the parlor stove.

"Should we not go up, then, Daniel?"

He spoke without turning. "You go, Katherine. I'm not as tired as I thought. I'll be up later on. Don't worry," he added tightly, "I won't disturb you."

She took a step forward, opening her mouth to speak. But she could think of nothing further to say. Nothing at all. Without even a "good night" to her groom, Katherine instinctively gathered up *Our Deportment* and silently left the parlor.

5

Long hours later, Katherine sat upright in bed against a pile of pillows, *Our Deportment* open upon her lap, having just completed reading the most disquieting passage of all under "Requirements for a Happy Marriage," which insisted that respect for each other was as necessary to a happy marriage as affection for one another.

Respect? Affection? Were such feelings possible between Mr. MacCabe and herself? Disbelieving the remotest probability of such a happenstance, Katherine thrust the book away, certain she would never be able to sleep this night, her first as a married woman, were she to continue to search *Our Deportment* for answers to her wifely dilemma. Courtship, romance, affection! What were they but pretty words, lovely fantasies. There was no sense wishing or hoping for them in her life, for such was not her lot married to the rough-hewn Daniel Sean MacCabe.

From the look plainly speaking of need when she left him, there was little doubt in Katherine's mind what would have given her husband happiness this night. And she wondered, in spite of herself, what it would have been like. And if she would ever find out.

Should she go to him now? If she gathered courage in hand, breached the distance between his room and hers through the connecting dressing room, would her husband accept or reject her after the words between them? In her heart of hearts, Katherine knew she hadn't the nerve to find out or learn the intimacies of marriage in his willing, if unloving, hands.

Still, she dreamed of him—her husband—when exhaustion finally claimed her. He came to her through the adjoining room, scantily clad in a garment resembling a toga, with nothing more to conceal the well-muscled proportions of his torso. His hair was wild, begging her fingers to tame it, and so was the passion in his smoldering brown eyes flecked with fire. The sight of her husband awakened a responding blaze within her, leaving her breathlessly weak with desire, strangely unafraid. He crossed to her bed in a stride; she rose up to greet him with open arms. He spoke honeyed words of love, of fulfilling her every heretofore unexperienced desire, then took her into his arms for a long, deep kiss that reached to her soul. He stretched out beside her, taking her down with him, murmuring endearments between feathery kisses. And then . . . and then . . . somewhere from afar she heard herself moaning, and knew, somehow, the sound came from outside her dream world. Before her slumbering eyes, her husband's image clouded and dissolved.

Longing for more, Katherine tossed upon her pillow, awakening abruptly in a tangle of bedclothes. With morning's dawning, the dream faded from memory, leaving an uneasy disquiet she could not name. Nor could she discover the source of her deep melancholy as she washed and dressed and headed downstairs, etiquette book in hand.

"By the Saints, do you even sleep with that damn book?" Dandy greeted her from the hall leading to the kitchen, clearly disgruntled. "Did it warm your solitary bed, Kate?"

His mood was as foul as the words he regretted the moment he spoke them. He watched her pale, then flush with distress, and fervently wished he could take the words back. How could he fault his reluctant bride for not wishing to couple with himself, a virtual stranger although he was her husband? He should be grateful she was willing to take on the likes of him for the sake of his kids—he and she had little else upon which they agreed. Especially, and must unhappily, their views on married bliss.

Sleep had been hard to come by, the massively carved mahogany bedstead in the master bedroom more uncomfortable than the lumpiest cot in camp. Or maybe it'd been his conscience telling him he'd been too hard on his virgin bride the evening before. In any case, the lack of sleep and the impassioned, unfulfilled dreams of his wife when at last he slept had him as cross as a cornered wolverine, probably the nastiest beast in the north woods. If he was going to get any kind of sleep at all, he'd best find a way to woo and win her to his way of thinking.

But that blasted book of hers set his teeth on edge each time he saw her with it. He could imagine her comparing every move he made with the dictates within its covers, and finding him lacking in comparison, though it'd given him the devil's own pleasure to tease her with his uncivilized behavior at dinner last night. He rather enjoyed raising her dander; at least then she was not all stiff and prudish. Indignation brought a sparkle to her eyes and color to her cheeks, and left her looking quite beautiful. Like now, until she fought for composure and won, self-command sapping the life from her fine, fair features.

"You are not dressed for church, Mr. MacCabe." As he persisted in calling her Kate, so she would refrain from addressing him as Daniel.

"Likely because I'm not going, *Mrs. MacCabe.*" He stuffed knotted fists in the pockets of his gray woolen pants.

"And the children?"

"Outdoors. Exploring."

"Without breakfast?"

Her cool, distant tone gave no clue to her real feelings. Dandy kept his own as cold.

"We ate an hour ago. In the kitchen. With the Tillits."

"In the . . . With the . . ." On the tip of her tongue lay the reminder of the impropriety of his breaking his fast elsewhere than at the formal dining table with his wife and children. Certain she'd only enrage her husband further, Katherine bit back the retort, attempting congeniality. "Oh?

Oh, well, then, what will you do with your day?''

Surprised—and rather disappointed—at the lack of spunk in her this morning, he answered, ''Something outside. A long walk with Thomas and Celia likely. Maybe chop a few cords of wood to keep in practice.''

''That is Mr. Tillit's . . . Perhaps you . . . and the children will join me for luncheon, then?'' Suddenly she hated the thought of another solitary meal. Even a repetition of last night's mannerless supper would be better.

''Probably not. Hannah's packing us some sandwiches to eat by the pond I saw out back.'' As an afterthought, he added, ''Would you like to join us?''

An invitation so reluctantly given, Katherine could not think of accepting. ''I have my reading to do.'' She held up her book and saw his forehead crease with displeasure. ''Besides, it is rather cold outside for a picnic, is it not?''

Her damned book means more to her than time spent with myself and the children. Some loving wife I've got this time. At least Annie was willing to warm my bed.

''Not as cold as it is within these walls, Katherine. Damned if it's not downright freezin' here where we stand.'' Turning on his heel, Dandy strode down the hall and shouldered his way through the swinging kitchen door.

''Daniel, I did not mean . . .'' But the hallway was empty, the door swinging to a slow stop. Katherine stood alone. Just her and her precious book. A single tear dripped down upon its blue leather cover. A second fell upon her hand.

In the late afternoon, Katherine passed through the hall to find Daniel, newly returned from outdoors, removing a rich vellum envelope from the calling card tray on the hall table. His tall, muscled presence dwarfed the high-ceilinged entry and the dainty, marble-topped table of ornately carved walnut he stood beside. Scenting the room with an intoxicating combination of fresh air and wood shavings, cheeks ruddy and mane curling damply at forehead and nape from exertion, he took her breath away. An unaccustomed warmth heated her cheeks. Distressed that she should find his phys-

ical appearance so compelling, she took a single step toward
the stairs and escape.

Catching a movement out of the corner of his eye, Dandy
glanced up, missing nothing, noting the flush to her cheeks,
the flustered look in her face, the way her glance quickly
shifted away from him. Ah, what had his bride been thinking? Had her thoughts been on him? *Not danged likely,* figured Dandy with regret. She'd sure as hell filled his mind
all day; he wished she'd taken him up on his invitation to
join him and the kids for lunch. He'd chopped half a cord
of kindling attempting *not* to think of her, and failed. Seeing
her now, her face all soft and vulnerable, he wondered just
when it was he'd stopped looking at her as care-giver to
Thomas and Celia and a convenient bed partner for himself,
and recognized the woman she was. Kate, his wife.

Dumbfounded, Dandy shoved the thought into a far corner of his mind for later examination, holding up the envelope for Kate to see.

"Someone's written to the both of us."

In a fine Spencerian script someone had written *Mr. and
Mrs. Daniel MacCabe*—the first time their names had thus
been joined in black and white.

"Who has written so soon?" Surely not a well-wisher
already offering congratulations on their precipitous marriage. She had anticipated none at all.

Dandy slit open the envelope and withdrew a single sheet
of heavy ivory paper. He unfolded it and read aloud, growing anger putting a harsh edge to his voice as he noted the
writer's signature, then the content.

"My Dear Mr. and Mrs. MacCabe,
    Due to the serious nature of the business at hand,
and in order to expedite the conclusion thereof, please
expect both Mr. Grissom and myself to call upon you
at teatime Thursday, the 26th day of April, 1883.

" 'Cordially' . . . ha . . . 'Cordially yours, Mrs. Winston
Stewart.' "

He slapped the paper against his thigh, dropping both envelope and letter onto the tray, dusting his hands against each other as though soiled, his face tight with rage.

" 'Twould seem her majesty's plannin' a royal inspection."

"It is obvious your mother-in-law intends this visit to afford her the opportunity to determine the sincerity of our commitment to the children, and to each other."

"Then the first order of business, Katie, is to give every impression we're happily and thoroughly married."

"You cannot be suggesting we . . . ?" Katherine's cheeks flamed as she left her comment unfinished.

Damning himself for thinking she might be mellowing, Dandy put in bluntly, "I'm suggestin' a few kind, maybe even affectionate words spoken between us, Kate, nothin' more. Old Lady Stewart's expectin' to prove we've failed to provide a happy home for Thomas and Celia, and it'll be up to us to show how wrong she is."

Katherine nodded. "I feel the best way to demonstrate to her we have made them a good home is to help the children improve upon their manners, as evidence of their adaptability."

"I agree."

"You do?"

"You needn't raise one eyebrow at me—the Saints only know how you do that—but as a matter of fact, I do have a very good idea what would most likely impress that harridan and her henchman." A slight smile came to his lips and a wicked light to his warm brown eyes. "A tea party the old woman's requestin', and a tea party she shall have."

As a dog was trained to fetch a stick, Dandy informed his wife, surely a child even as backward as Celia could be taught to curtsy when presented to guests, then sit quietly out of the way. As for Thomas, the boy had only to be coached in a few polite responses to questions he'd most likely be asked.

Katherine merely raised that single eyebrow at Daniel and held her silence. She knew how much more there was to an appropriately executed tea party, especially one with children present; *Our Deportment* corroborated what she suspected. To educate Thomas and Celia in the finer points of teatime etiquette required far more time than was afforded them. Still, the effort must be made. Their lessons began that very afternoon, with Hannah and Andrew Tillit performing their duties as maid and butler, replete in formal attire.

Thomas immediately understood the seriousness of the training and quickly threw himself into the challenge as though it were great fun. Little Celia, however, seemed incapable of comprehending even the simplest rudiments of the curtsy, no matter how frequent and graphic the demonstration. After an hour the little girl grew flushed and cranky, close to tears.

"I think our Celia's in need of a nap, Miss ... Mrs. MacCabe," Hannah Tillit commented firmly. "And, if I'm not mistaken, a change of nappies."

Katherine sighed in frustration, distractedly brushing wisps of hair out of her face with both hands.

"I believe you are right, Mrs. Tillit. I could use with a bit of refreshing myself."

"Go on, then," responded Dandy. "We'll give it another try this evenin'. I think I might have an idea how to make these lessons a little easier on our lassie." There was a decided sparkle of secret amusement in his eyes, but when asked he would give not a single clue concerning his plan.

Katherine and Hannah climbed the stairs with Celia between them, matching their steps to hers, both reluctant to take the damp child into their arms.

Hannah spoke up. "An effort must be made to train Celia out of her diapers. She's far too old and, I'm beginning to think, far too smart to be messing herself."

Speaking over Celia's head, Katherine asked, "Do you believe she is educable, then? In spite of this afternoon? It would please Daniel so—and myself, of course—if she were."

"Can't hurt to try. Maybe it was only her mother's illness and her inability to take care of the little mite that's kept her sort of backward all this time."

"Of course, Mrs. Tillit. Of course, that has to be the reason. See how brightly she looks from one to the other of us as we speak. I am sure there is intelligence locked away, if only we could find the key."

"We'll see to it she gets an education, you and me, if it can be done. Can't say I'd relish changing the little miss's diapers when she's a woman grown. Come along now, Celia. We'll get you all cleaned up, then a little nap before dinner and you'll be fresh as new."

After one of Hannah's tasty meals, they reassembled in the formal front parlor with the notable exception of Dandy Dan MacCabe.

"Where is your father, Thomas?"

The boy shook his head, shrugging.

Katherine opened her mouth to protest his unseemly absence, only to be interrupted by a strident knock at the front door, followed by a *brrring, brrring, brrring* as the doorbell was twisted with obvious impatience.

"Whoever could that be?" The fashionable hour for making calls had long since passed.

"We'll see in a moment, madam." Hannah hastened out into the hall, with Mr. Tillit, Katherine, and the children following behind. She opened the door cautiously, peering out into the early evening gloom, then swinging the door wide as she brought her hands to her cheeks, shaking her head. "Well, I never." She began to giggle like a girl.

Giggling from the unflappable Hannah Tillit? "Who is it? . . . Oh! Oh, my!"

An extremely wide and tall matronly figure with a red-plaid flannel chest now the size of two bed pillows made an auspicious, sweeping entry into the vestibule, replete in a flopping flowered hat of another era and one of Mrs. Tillit's enormous white aprons for a skirt, beneath which protruded two large, moccasined feet. The beard-shadowed face and russet mane, as well as the roguish brown eyes and wide, dimpled grin, were clearly those of Katherine's husband.

"Mr. Mac—"

"Good evening, Mrs. MacCabe," responded a falsetto

voice. A rough, work-toughened hand extended in her direction. "Mrs. Beatrice Stewart, here to partake of your lovely tea party."

The room exploded with laughter. Thomas doubled over, hands on knees. Mrs. Tillit's high-pitched giggles accelerated; she wrapped her arms around her generous waist as if to keep from bursting. Behind a fist over his mustached mouth, the usually dour Andrew Tillit chuckled silently. Katherine put two hands to her own lips, not quite covering her unladylike grin. Celia's large-eyed stare went from one to another of the hall's occupants without comprehension, but when her da winked at her, she smiled, her face crinkling in soundless humor.

Glancing at the little girl, Katherine quickly understood her husband's attempt to lighten the mood, to make the lessons fun, especially for the child for whom the world was such a puzzle. Her heart swelled, and she blinked back sudden, happy tears that a man of Daniel's obvious masculinity would allow himself to present so ridiculous an image for the sake of his daughter's education.

The impostor Beatrice Stewart placed a large paw over her pillow-stuffed shirt, feigning indignation. "Well, I never. Is this any way to treat a guest come for a visit?"

Regaining some composure, Katherine stifled a smile to apologize. "Where are our manners? Please, come into the parlor. Mrs. Tillit, you will see to tea, won't you? Come, Thomas, bring your sister. We have company. This way, Mrs. Stewart."

Demonstrating impeccable manners, Katherine ushered her guest to a seat of honor on the sateen-upholstered settee beside the fireplace. With a flourish Mrs. Stewart daintily settled her considerable bulk, then spoiled the illusion by hiking her apron thigh high to reveal woolen pants and knee-high moccasins while crossing ankle to knee.

Katherine gently but pointedly cleared her throat.

"What? Oh!" Dandy uncrossed his legs and smoothed down his skirt. Directing his attention to the children, he insisted, "Thomas, Celia, come say hello to your granny."

Thomas rushed forward to throw himself into his father's

arms and would have had not Katherine stopped him with a hand on his shoulder.

"As we practiced earlier, Thomas."

The boy came to an abrupt halt and screwed up his face in concentration. As he remembered his lesson, his expression cleared, and he offered a friendly grin, bending slightly at the waist in a bow.

"Hello . . . er . . . Grandmother. It's nice to meet you. You're lookin' . . . lookin' . . ." He thought a moment longer, smiled and added, "Lookin' swell."

"That is 'well,' Thomas," said Katherine, "but otherwise perfect."

All attention turned to Celia, who, judging by her expression, strived mightily to understand what was going on around her. Katherine stepped to her side, taking Celia's chubby hand into her own, tugging slightly to bring the child to Dandy's side. The little girl regarded her da in his ridiculous outfit and grinned. Dandy struggled to keep his face passive, though his eyes shimmered with fun like twin pools bathed in sunshine.

"Show Celia how, Katherine," Dandy encouraged. "Curtsy right along with her. Make it like play, and she'll learn. You, too, Thomas. Give your old granny another bow or two, or as many as it takes for Celia to catch on."

It took considerably more than a bow and a curtsy or two to teach Celia what was expected of her. Everyone grew warm and frustrated, but no one was willing to quit. Finally, after a couple of false starts, when they had about given up hope, Celia crossed her pudgy little legs, bent one knee down and the other out, spread her skirt in an arc, and dipped her head as she made a perfect curtsy.

Thomas and Dandy cheered, Katherine cried, "Well done, darling," and from the doorway to the hall came jubilant clapping. Celia looked from one ecstatic face to another, and curtsied again, her face wreathed in smiles.

Mrs. Stewart rose and swept Celia into his arms, planting a smacking kiss on her flushed, cherubic cheek.

"Ah, little lass, you make your old da proud," he said, his voice choked with elation.

Katherine wiped moisture from her eyes, smiling until she felt as though her mouth might split at the corners. Thomas danced a jig around his father and sister, while a tearful Hannah and a sniffing Andrew brought in silver trays laden with cups of hot chocolate and hearty oatmeal cookies.

"This calls for a grand celebration," boomed Dandy, and Katherine hadn't the heart to reprove his loudness. He tore off the oversized hat and flung it on the nearest chair, whipping Hannah's apron after the hat. "By the Saints, I'm sweatin' like a pig. How you ladies wear so much gear, I'll never be understandin'. Took not one but two pillows to fill out my bosom to resemble that Old Granny Stewart and—"

"Daniel," Katherine said, but her warning turned into an uncontrollable giggle when he released the middle buttons of his flannel shirt and one of the pillows plopped out onto the floor at her feet. Knowing *Our Deportment* would not encourage a lady's unseemly laughter did little to stem her soft chuckles. Much of the family's behavior this entire evening did not follow the rules of proper etiquette, but, for once, that didn't seem to matter. Celia could curtsy, and that was all that was important.

Dandy pulled out the second pillow, tossing it down with the first, and shook himself like a wet dog. With his left hand splayed dramatically over his plaid shirtfront in the vicinity of his heart, he declared, "With all the blessed Saints as my witness, I will never . . . never . . . don female fluff again."

"I am in full agreement with that pronouncement, Daniel," said his wife with a bright smile, "for you are the most singularly unbecoming 'lady' upon which it has ever been my misfortune to gaze."

Dandy turned a startled, incredulous look her way. By damn, Katie was attempting a joke! Who'd've guessed? What's more, she looked downright pretty when she smiled like that, with her full, rosy lips and lovely blue-gray eyes. Her cheeks glowed pink, and a few strands of honey-colored hair had escaped to caress them as Dandy suddenly longed to. She was his wife, dammit, and he wanted her. Despite her prickly, pious ways, Katherine was all woman—irresistibly all woman. Though he vowed he would not take her to bed unless she was willing, Dandy figured there must be a way to make her agreeable. He had only to find it. And soon.

Daniel had a hungry look Katherine could not mistake in spite of her inexperience. Though she had no practical knowledge of men's carnal urgings, the expression on her husband's face spoke as clearly as words of his desires, needs she alarmingly discovered matched her own. More startling still came the discovery that she was growing uncommonly fond of the blustering, handsome brute who was her husband. Who loved his children so dearly he would do anything—including making an utter fool of himself—to ensure their well-being in his most capable care.

His heart-stirring gaze evoked a delicious, responsive warmth within her. Feigning interest in the dregs of cold chocolate in her cup, Katherine forced herself to turn away from Dandy's scrutiny, knowing full well that someday—soon—he'd press his husbandly claim to her. Would she respond to him? Could she? The sudden heat coursing through her dared her to wonder, and to wish.

Thursday afternoon found the new family dressed in their best and nervously awaiting the real Mrs. Stewart's arrival.

Katherine felt justifiably proud as she surveyed her young charges, resplendent in the outfits she and Hannah Tillit had worked day and night to complete: Celia's, a pink-flowered dimity tea dress that Katherine's mother had once worn, recut and sewn into a fetching frock, and Thomas in knickers and crisp white shirt fashioned out of garments gleaned from her father's wardrobe.

There was no need for the guests to know that beneath Celia's lovely new dress her only two petticoats bore shaggy hems and a dingy color no amount of soaking in bleach and airing in sunshine could remove, and Thomas's knee-high stockings sprouted darning on both heels and toes.

The children had been outfitted in new high-buttoned shoes as well, though it had cost Katherine two of her favorite Dresden figurines for Mr. Tillit to procure them.

Dandy donned his navy flannel wedding shirt over woolen pants and moccasins, as usual, having not possessed a suit since his teen years. Katherine slipped on the best of her black gowns, the satin, her female vanity sorely tested that she could not wear something new and decidedly not black, were it only a gown made over from one of her mother's. Had there been time to sew up something new for herself and her husband, Katherine was sure she would not feel quite so apprehensive.

Promptly at four, Beatrice Stewart arrived, attended by the turncoat attorney, Gilbert Grissom. The disgruntled matron gave him little chance to speak, however, stating, "Let us dispense with the unnecessary pleasantries. We all know we have gathered together to see how poor Annabella's children are faring in your questionable care. Shall we begin?" She swept ahead of the rest into the formal front parlor.

Katherine shot Dandy an anxious glance, distress mounting when she saw the glowering glare he directed at the pair.

Under his breath he told her, "I thought this was supposed to be a friendly visit, not a danged inquisition."

"And so it shall be," Katherine returned in a low tone, "if you will behave yourself." Turning to their guests, Katherine suggested, "Won't you have a seat?" She led the dowager to the most comfortable chair in the room. "Mrs. Tillit has gone to bring down the children. Ah, here they are now. Thomas, Celia, come say hello to your grandmother."

Thomas performed his bow and rehearsed greeting manfully, though stiffly. His expression remained wary; perhaps he recalled his grandmother's intent to have him placed in a military school should she win custody. Celia, clearly overwhelmed with the stern-visaged strangers confronting her, clung to Katherine's skirt, her face pressed into its folds, and would not release her death grip either at her father's command or Katherine's whispered request.

"Celia's feeling a bit shy today, Mrs. Stewart," Katherine offered.

"Nonsense." Mrs. Stewart snapped a brittle retort. "There is certainly no need to be shy with one's own blood relation. Come here, child. Let me have a good look at you." When Celia made no move, she asked, "Can she understand me at all?"

"My sweet, darlin' daughter has intelligence equal to your own." Dandy's voice trembled with effort to control the anger hidden just beneath the surface. "Had you welcomed my daughter with a friendly smile, she would have offered a very pretty curtsy by way of greetin'."

"So, bring her to me, then," Mrs. Stewart ordered with obvious skepticism. "Allow me to observe what little tricks you have taught her." She attempted to stare down the angry father and, failing, turned her haughty gaze on poor defenseless Celia.

Standing guard behind the dowager's chair, Grissom, while remaining silent, had the decency to look chagrined over his employer's lack of sensibility and caustic tongue. Mrs. Stewart extended one heavily ringed claw of a hand in Celia's direction, beckoning with a talonlike finger.

"Come to your grandmother, child, so I may see you curtsy."

With enormous reluctance, Katherine drew the quivering little girl out of the folds of her skirt, and with hands on both Celia's shoulders, she gently nudged her forward, murmuring encouragement. Clearly frightened, Celia hung her head and slipped her fingers into her mouth, refusing to look into her grandmother's seamed, imperious face.

Mrs. Stewart caught her granddaughter's plump arm with one dry-skinned hand and pulled the child's fingers away from her face, making a disapproving moue with pursed lips.

"Nasty, nasty habit. One which must not be encouraged."

"Now, just one gol-danged minute—"

Katherine shot Dandy a warning glance and interceded. "Celia is only three," she offered, watching tears gather in the child's eyes, then spill over.

Unexpectedly, Thomas darted forward, planting himself

before his grandmother, his face pugnaciously mirroring his fury.

"You leave my sister alone. Yer scarin' her!"

The dowager drew back, clearly displeased. Over her shoulder, she informed her attorney, "As you can see, Gilbert, we have intervened none too soon by requesting custody of these hapless children."

Mr. Grissom merely cleared his throat nervously, but Dandy very nearly exploded, so enraged nothing came out but a strangled expletive.

"Mrs. Stewart," Katherine spoke up quickly before he could find his voice, "the children are anxious over the uncertainty of their fate. Perhaps we had best let Mrs. Tillit serve tea. A more congenial atmosphere can only help set their minds at ease, I am sure."

Gilbert Grissom cleared his throat, speaking up at last. "I believe we might as well dispense with further amenities, Mrs. Stewart, to inform Mr. and Mrs. MacCabe of the arrangements that have been made for an interview with Judge Hardman in his chambers on the morrow."

Beatrice Stewart stood abruptly.

"As you have already so informed them, Gilbert, we will make our departure. I have seen all I came to observe—"

"It's been somethin' of an eye-opener for us, too," blurted Dandy in spite of Katherine's slight warning gesture. "Now get the *hell* out of this house before I do somethin' we'll all regret."

The grandmother and her attorney departed post haste, much to Katherine's mingled relief and dismay—relief that the enemy had left at last without any further explosions from her husband and dismay because she knew that before the Honorable Judge Abel Hardman acquired his judgeship, he and her father had often been on opposite sides in one business deal or another. As a judge, his reputation suggested he frequently favored wealth over poverty, power over humanity. It was not difficult to guess why he had allied himself with Mrs. Stewart, and she with him. The choice did not bode well for themselves.

6

The portly Honorable Abel Hardman in his expensive three-piece suit strode to a prominent place in the center of the lush Oriental rug in his chambers. Rocking heel to toe, with hands clasped behind his back, he cast a speculative glance from Mrs. to Mr. Daniel MacCabe and back again.

"I have been asked by Mrs. Stewart to expedite a decision as to the guardianship of the children, Thomas and Celia MacCabe. If all parties are prepared, I suggest we commence."

Sitting with her spine scarcely touching her chair and hands entwined in her lap, Katherine hid her growing apprehension behind downcast eyes. Calm restraint was required if she and Dandy were to keep the children, and both calm and restrained she would be at all cost.

For his part, Dandy, too restless to sit, clutched the back of his wife's chair, holding on to his self-control by concentrating on Kate's. It was the only way he knew to get through what was to come.

Judge Hardman leveled his cold gaze upon Katherine, asking, "How long before your rather precipitous marriage had you known Mr. MacCabe, Katherine . . . er, Mrs. MacCabe?"

Lifting her chin, Katherine looked unwaveringly into his

eyes, replying, "Approximately one week, though I fail to see—"

"And what would you say motivated this hasty, decidedly . . . unusual union between you and your husband upon such short acquaintance?" His Honor continued, scarcely giving her time to respond. "Let me caution you that I have been advised of the unchaperoned night you spent in Mr. MacCabe's home . . . and your rather, ah, disheveled appearance the following morning."

From his position behind his employer's chair, Gilbert Grissom murmured, "Mrs. Stewart and myself can certainly attest to that," though the judge was clearly in charge.

Riding over Katherine's "Nothing untoward hap—" Judge Hardman queried, "Are you claiming then that this was not a marriage of necessity?"

Katherine's chin rose a notch higher. "The only necessity was that Daniel's children had become very dear to me in a relatively short time. I desired to make a home for them, contribute in providing both father and mother—"

He remained unimpressed. "As a matter of fact, were it not for the children, you would never have undertaken joining your life with that of Mr. MacCabe. Is that not correct?"

Knuckles white with his grip on Katherine's chair back, Dandy interjected, "Give her a chance to speak, dad-blast it."

Katherine leveled her gaze upon the pompous, offensive magistrate, replying without hesitation. "Were it not for Thomas and Celia, my husband and I most likely would not have met. The circumstances are as they are, Your Honor. We wed out of concern for the children and a mutual willingness to love and care for them. Our joined commitment to that end has made our unconventional union a satisfactory one, however inauspicious its beginning."

"Ah, now we arrive at the crux of the matter," Judge Hardman concurred, rolling back on his heels, "providing for the welfare of the children." He cleared his throat, two fingertips against his lips, studying the pair under his inquisition, deliberately taking his time. "According to the information that has been brought to my attention, Mr.

MacCabe, there has been some doubt about your ability to oversee your children's upbringing in the past. In fact, when your first wife was alive, you were absent from your home for several months of the year—''

"I'm a shanty boy, for chrissake." Dandy spread his arms wide, then let them fall, hanging on to his temper by sheer will. "I have to go where the job takes me. There was never any trouble between us because of that. Annie understood—''

"Annabella." Mrs. Stewart broke her self-imposed silence, staring down her long nose, her thin lips pursed as though smelling something distasteful. "My daughter's name was Annabella, and she was an innocent young girl with little knowledge of the real world before you seduced her away from her family and into a most inappropriate marriage.''

"Annie," Dandy spat out tightly, piercing Mrs. Stewart with his glare, "was not livin' at home when I met and married her, and she was most willin' to accept me as her husband." He refrained from saying more only with the greatest difficulty.

His mother-in-law's face expressed incredulity, then scorn. "Which was an obviously regrettable mistake on her part, was it not?" Her aged, imperious voice choked with what sounded suspiciously like crocodile tears. "She wasted away and expired with no one to care for her but a pair of helpless children scarcely out of infancy, while you"—now enraged, her pale, seamed face splotched red with righteous wrath, she pointed, arm extended—"were off chopping down trees in some godforsaken wilderness. You deserted her in her time of need as you had each and every year of your marriage for—what was it?—seven years?"

"Seven years we were man and wife, yes," Dandy retorted with ill-concealed anger, "but if she hadn't kept how sick she was from me, I wouldn't've signed on for another season and—''

"Did you know Annabella mailed a most informative letter to me," Mrs. Stewart abruptly interrupted to tell him, grim triumph on her face, "advising me of the—shall we say—less than desirable relations between the two of you from the beginning?''

"The bloody blue blazes she did!" Dandy's voice became ominously low.

"Indeed, but she did. Written on her deathbed, stating that you had left her alone once again, and ill, asking me to come take care of her children."

"Annie'd *never* lie about me like that. And she'd sure as *hell* never to her dyin' breath be wantin' you anywhere near Thomas and Celia." Realizing he was shouting, cursing, Dandy fought for some last shred of restraint, insisting, "You'll have to show me that goddamn letter before I'll believe one exists. You don't happen to have it on you, do you?"

The old dowager harrumphed, uncowed. "Most certainly not, not when there might be the slightest possibility you would try to get your hands on it. You can be certain Annabella's letter is securely locked away in my safe at home." She appeared inordinately pleased with herself, offering her challenger a self-righteous lift of the head.

Dandy turned on Judge Hardman, demanding, "Have *you* seen this supposed letter?"

"No, but I have no reason to doubt Mrs. Ste—"

"Have you?" Dandy glared at Gilbert Grissom to ask.

"Why . . . no . . . but . . . I—"

"Yet you're both willin' to take only *her* word concernin' its existence? If you knew . . ." He stopped himself by clenching his teeth until his jaw jumped. "Damn you all, and your—"

"Daniel, please—" pleaded Katherine.

"Mr. MacCabe!" Judge Hardman's stern voice broke in. Had he his gavel with him, he would have been pounding it upon his massive desk. When all parties fell silent, he suggested, "Let us adhere to the subject at hand. The fact of the matter is that Mr. MacCabe's ability to provide financially for his children clearly depends on his continued forays into the woods to cut lumber, and to that end, he has acquired a new wife to care for his children in his absence. The question remains, is this an appropriate arrangement for

the children, Thomas and Celia MacCabe? Further . . ."
Dandy seemed about to say something at this point, but the
judge silenced him with a glance. "Further, it has come to
my attention that both Mr. MacCabe and the new Mrs.
MacCabe are, ummm, each currently rather strained for sufficient funds, whereas Mrs. Stewart—"

Dandy snapped, "If you think money and all the worldly
possessions it'll buy are more important than blood ties and
a lovin' home—"

"I think, Mr. MacCabe, that should you continue interrupting, you will only impede a swift and satisfactory conclusion to this matter."

"The conclusion to this matter is obvious," said Mrs.
Stewart. "The children belong with their grandmother, who
can provide everything they will ever need or want."

Sliding forward on her chair, Katherine could no longer
hold back. "Excuse me, Judge Hardman, but I must ask if
it has also come to your attention that Mrs. Stewart intends
to place Thomas in a military school and Celia into an asylum for the mentally incompetent? Do you feel that even to
consider such recourse is in the best interests of children
who have so recently suffered the loss of their mother?"

Dandy flashed her a grateful glance. Judge Hardman
cleared his throat pointedly.

"Yes, Mrs. MacCabe, Mrs. Stewart has made me fully
cognizant of her intentions, should they be warranted. She
will, of course, assess the situation once the children have
arrived in Boston. In Celia's case, and with the assistance
of the best authorities in the field, she shall make appropriate
arrangements given the child's limited capabilities. As to
military school for the boy, he has clearly led an undiscip-
lined life up to this point. Military school might be the most
suitable recourse—"

"You bastard," Dandy bit out, taking a threatening step
in the judge's direction. "You blitherin' bastard. You made
your decision in the old lady's favor before we ever set foot
in this room, didn't you? How much is she payin' you, *Your
Honor,* for your rulin'?"

"Daniel!" Appalled and frightened, Katherine rose from her chair.

Judge Hardman's face flushed magenta. "I will not listen to such outrageous accusations."

"It's the truth. You never had any intention of lettin' my children stay with me where they belong, damn you. Nothin' any of us could've said or done would've made any difference, isn't that right? *Isn't that right?*"

The judge met Dandy's stare, but his gaze slid away first. "Whenever and however I came to my decision, it has been made clear to me by your foul language and displays of uncontrolled temper that it was the right one. Mrs. Stewart, shall we conclude—?"

Dandy's hand clamped over the judge's arm, reinforcing his threat. "By all that's holy, you will not take Thomas and Celia from me."

Judge Hardman stood his ground, though he obviously quelled under the larger man's fury. "It is not I who will remove these minors from your questionable care, sir, but the court of law in this land once the papers are filed come Monday. I would suggest you avail yourself of the time left to you this last weekend by packing your children's possessions and saying your good-byes. I will see to it that an officer comes for them as soon as the proper documents have been processed, no later than four o'clock Monday afternoon. Now, sir, if you will release me, you may depart. This hearing is over."

Dandy's hand dropped to his side, his expression stunned, unbelieving. Taking his arm, murmuring a few inadequate words of reassurance, Katherine led her husband out of the judge's chambers. Silently they made their way home, and just as silently entered the house. Removing gloves and hat at the hall tree, Katherine began, "Daniel . . . ?" She sought his reflection in the mirror before her, but he was gone. Devastated, she stood alone in the hall.

She put the children to bed without having told them the grim reality of their fate. Time enough tomorrow, after a last worry-free night's sleep. When Thomas asked where Da was, she fought her scruples and offered up the fib that he was helping Mr. Tillit with some necessary chore, assuring them they'd see him in the morning.

Much later Katherine sat alone in the back parlor, waiting for her husband's return, listening to the crackle of the fire, having given up any pretense of sewing a second dress for Celia. There didn't seem to be much point to it now that the little girl was leaving.

Nor did there seem much point to her sham of a marriage to Daniel MacCabe, she reflected morosely. For all their good intentions, they had failed to keep Thomas and Celia safe from their cruel-hearted grandmother.

What was to become of her and Daniel once the children were gone from their lives forever?

Divorce?

Unthinkable. Her good name, already in question, would never survive the scandal.

Dandy Dan MacCabe would most assuredly return to the woods as he did each new logging season. More than a livelihood, being a shanty boy defined the man. His work would eventually bring him solace.

And herself? She would resume her solitary, spinsterish existence, with diminishing finances as well. Without Daniel and the children to make an adventure of every day—albeit an unwelcome one upon occasion—how empty and dreary the future suddenly seemed. Katherine's throat constricted with an ache that had begun somewhere in the region of her heart, and she feared the pain might never go away.

Katherine sensed Daniel's presence before she saw him, and turned her head to face her husband as he hovered in the doorway to the hall. Quick, unexpected tears flooded her eyes. Tears came far too easily, and far too frequently, of late, but she seemed to have lost the ability to stem their flow.

"Daniel, I am so sorry. If only—"

He came to her, kneeling beside her chair, covering her hands with his. Surprisingly he did not appear to share her dejection. His dark eyes sparked with emotion, not tears of regret like hers, but with excitement, anticipation. His words resounded with hope.

" 'Tis too late for 'if only's, Katie. I spent long hours going over everythin' this afternoon, and I'm more convinced than ever there was nothin' we could've said or done to change the decision Judge Hardman had already made. But all is not lost." He flashed his wife an encouraging smile. "I've come up with an idea for savin' Thomas and Celia from their grandmother's clutches . . . and I want you to hear me out before sayin' anythin'. Will you do that for me, Katie?"

His compelling Irish lilt cast its spell. At her bewildered nod of assent, Dandy launched into the plan he'd obviously worked out, down to the last detail, during his solitude. True to her word, Katherine did not interrupt, though she wanted to do so every time he paused for breath, his scheme sending her senses reeling. By the time he finally stopped speaking, however, awaiting her response, words all but failed her. The expectancy on his face turned to keen disappointment.

"Come on now, Kate, what do you say? You got any better idea?" he challenged.

"I . . . no, I . . . but, Daniel, running away with the children? Possibly never coming back? Where would we go?"

That she had not said "no" flat out revived his enthusiasm. "I told you, I own a farm about fifty miles southeast of here—"

"So far? And a . . . farm? What do you know of farming, Daniel? I myself have not so much as visited a—"

"We'll learn, Kate." He leaned closer, grabbing up her hand. "And the kids'll be safe, that's all that's important. No one knows about the place. I inherited it from the parents of a friend of mine who was killed by a widow-maker." At her puzzled frown, he added, "Widow-maker's a limb snagged high in a tree, fallin' in some evil breeze onto a poor unsuspectin' fool standin' beneath, maimin' or doin' him in. Was left to me to go and tell Andy's folks his sad fate. Spent the summer with them that year . . . and a couple of summers after that, until I got married to Annie. Learned more'n a few things about farmin' helpin' them. The rest will be a snap, you'll see. What do you say, Kate? For Thomas and Celia?'' He openly pleaded from his raised russet brows to dark eyes liquid with emotion, to his encouraging half smile.

Katherine's mind spun with indecision. "Can we possibly get away? What if Mrs. Stewart hired someone to watch us, who sees us leave?'' Though one hand lay captured in his, the other trembled at her collar, fingering the pulse fluttering there.

His grin widened hopefully. "I've thought of that, too. If it seems we're but havin' ourselves a Sunday picnic, no one would dare deny a father his last outin' with his children, Katie.''

"A . . . a picnic? It is only April, far too cool—''

"The weather's been mild, and there's even a few wildflowers in bloom. Besides, May's only days away.'' Dandy's excitement grew. "We'll have Hannah fill the hamper to the brim with enough food to see us through 'til we get to the farm, three or four days worth. And we'll dress in as many layers of clothin' as we can without arousin' suspicion, so there won't be any luggage should that old hag have someone keepin' an eye on us. Then we're on our way out of town, headin' for my farm. I've worked out every detail, Kate. There's no chance we'll fail.''

Katherine retrieved her hand from his clasp and rose, pacing two steps across the rose-flowered carpet before turning back to her husband still squatting beside her chair, regarding her with eloquent, pleading eyes. A battle raged furiously within. How could she leave behind all she'd ever known for a man with whom she had nothing in common save his children? Having come this far, having given her word to him and them, how could she not? Letting the three of them go on without her was an impossibility; a sense of overwhelming loss flooded her to her very soul at the mere thought. She did not even want to imagine a future without the children. Or, she realized with shocked amazement, their rogue of a father.

Would she do it? Would she go along with his plan? Dandy anxiously watched his wife's somber, unreadable face for some clue to her thoughts. A knife-thrust knot clutched his gut at the thought that she might choose to stay behind, stunned to discover he couldn't imagine leaving without her. Damn, if only she'd give him some idea what was going on in her head and her heart. Even a single raised eyebrow would be welcome now. This waiting and wondering was pure, unadulterated hell.

A small, resigned sigh escaped her lips as Katherine raised her gaze from the tips of her shoes to him, offering the slightest, most hesitant smile.

"We entered into this marriage for the sake of the children, Daniel. I do not see how we cannot do all in our power to continue to protect them," she said, her hands clasped at her waist. "After all, we did promise 'for better or for worse' . . . and I believe circumstances could not be much worse than they are right now-w-w-w. Ohhhh, D-D-Daniel."

Her husband bounded to her side and swept her into his arms, and now spun them both like a top. He planted a hearty, impetuous kiss on her parted lips to smother her protest. The spinning slowed and ceased, the kiss deepening as Dandy held Katherine suspended above ground. Slowly lowering her until her feet found purchase, he traced a question on her lips with the tip of his tongue. She made an indistinguishable sound like the mewl of a frightened kitten. With that as his answer, he released her from his embrace. He left Katherine feeling strangely bereft, and more confused than ever as to her true emotions toward this large, exuberant man.

Wordlessly they moved away from each other, she to return to her chair and pick up the neglected sewing with trembling hands, he to spread his before a warming fire.

By the gods, he wanted her. Now! Here on the flowered carpet before the flames that matched the one blazing inside him. His need was great to express with action what words could not say, to show his gratitude, make her understand how important her decision was to him and his. A few words of thanks and a quick, unsatisfactory kiss were not nearly enough to release his bottled-up feelings. Tension grew like a log jam about to break. His breath came out ragged; his heart thudded so loudly beneath his shirt that Dandy gave a quick, furtive glance in his wife's direction to see if she could hear it, too. Her face was turned in profile, a face that never gave her away, never let on to what she was thinking. He'd give a year's pay to know what was going through her mind right this minute.

If only he'd stop watching her, thought Katherine. It was taking every ounce of her willpower to keep her features impassive so he wouldn't know how terrified she was. Terrified of the decision she'd made, knowing she would never go back on her word once given. She was terrified of him. Because of the way he made her feel. *Because* he made her feel. She hadn't been afraid with him before—not like this—not until his kiss. The insistent pressure of his lips upon hers awoke something . . . something overwhelmingly strange and wonderful within her. For those brief moments she had felt love, loved. In the next instant he released her, leaving her alone and lost without his embrace, a decidedly unwelcome, frightening sensation. By the powers that be, what was happening to her?

Dandy was the first to break the silence when it became unbearable, glancing over his shoulder in her general direction.

"If you're agreeable, we'll set out around eleven Sunday, after all the good people are safely settled into their pews for another long-winded sermon."

Choosing to ignore his irreverence, grateful that its distraction interrupted her tempestuous thoughts, Katherine concurred. "But Daniel," she spoke far more calmly than she felt, surprised her voice sounded so normal, "there is one additional problem. All of us will never fit into the rockaway. We will have need of a wagon if we are to—"

"A wagon would attract too much attention . . . might make the wrong people suspicious. The rockaway will suit just fine for the four of us."

"The four of us? What of the Tillits?"

Stubbornly he faced her. "They'll need to stay behind, Kate—"

"But, no—"

"To throw off the suspicion that we'll not be comin' back. And to see to the upkeep of your fine, fancy house."

Dandy waited for further arguments. He saw the questions, the indignant retorts, mirrored in her gray eyes as clearly as if she had spoken, watched her lips pull into a tight line, holding back ... who knew what. When after a long minute she had still said nothing, he retreated to his leather chair in the shadows, unable to face her look of grave contemplation. From his corner he watched her silently struggle with the thoughts she had need to put voice to, knowing full well she'd have much to say once she recovered sufficiently. He was startled by her query when it came, having had no inkling such an idea had entered her mind.

"I do not mean to appear ... to pry, but I must ask. Thomas is not your own true son, is he, Daniel?" she asked quietly with obvious reluctance.

He leaned forward in his chair, elbows on widespread knees, hands clasped.

"Why would you ... ?" Seeing she meant to have the answer, he admitted, "Not flesh of my flesh, but son of my heart nevertheless. What put it into your head to ask *that*, of all things?"

She relaxed against her chair back, apparently satisfied. "To prove to myself you are the honorable man I believe you to be, that you would take a child you knew was not yours and love him as a son ... enough to risk all for his welfare." Watching his face diffuse scarlet with embarrassment, and finding her husband tongue-tied for once, Katherine continued. "I suspected almost from the first that Thomas was not yours. His appearance is so unlike your own and that of the picture of your wife I saw on your nightstand. Mrs. Stewart's comment that you were married to Annie for seven years merely confirmed my suspicion. Thomas is already seven, and even as inexperienced a lady as myself is aware a birth takes nine months to ... " She floundered over such intimacies and trailed to a stop.

Dandy lifted his arms from his knees to thread his hands through the hair at his temples. Sighing heavily, he admitted,

"The truth of the matter will test your sensibilities even more, Kate. Annie . . . Annabella . . . was not the flawless young lady her mother thought she was. Nor me the villain. She came here supposedly to visit a cousin, but in reality to escape the rigidity of her mother's iron rule. And escape she did, though not to the freedom and excitement for which she had hoped. Cousin Rosie—a whorehouse madam, though the family never knew—introduced her to men, many men, and a . . . a less than honorable way of life. Annie—she found herself with child, Kate, and not knowin' who the father was, came to me beggin' for my help. I guess she thought I was the most upstandin' of the so-called gentlemen of her acquaintance—"

"One of her best customers, I presume." Katherine's voice came out tinged with something akin to jealousy, surprising them both. She felt her cheeks color.

"A customer, yes," Dandy admitted, having the good graces to look ashamed to confess it. "But not one of the most frequent. We met just before I took off for a season in the woods. When I came back, she was in a family way. I had my winter's pay in my pocket, hadn't spent it all on drink or other entertainments like the others fresh out of a winter in camp. I guess she took me to be more reliable than most. It was her tears that brought me down. I . . . I promised I'd marry her, be a father to her child—"

"And you have kept that promise over and above what any other man would have done, Daniel. You are a good and loving father to both children. Not only that, but you did not betray your wife's . . . colorful past to her mother. It would have caused Mrs. Stewart a great deal of discomfort, perhaps some real suffering as well, to learn that her Annabella was not the young lady she believed her to be."

"I had no desire to shame Annie's memory. She suffered enough in her short lifetime, especially in her mother's hands—"

"Had you told Judge Hardman—"

"He wouldn't't've believed me," Dandy concluded bluntly.

Katherine had to agree with her husband's pronouncement. Had he spoke of it before the judge and Mrs. Stewart, he'd simply have been taken for a desperate liar.

Bringing to conclusion one subject, she reluctantly broached another. "You must have loved Annie very much . . . to have married her under those circumstances."

Tiredly he responded, "Katie, what was between Annie and me is one subject too many for me tonight, but if it'll set your mind at ease, the best thing to come out of our union was Celia, who is indeed my child, conceived one hot summer between loggin' seasons." He hesitated. "You know, Kate, I've answered every question you've asked of me, and then some."

"I . . . I suppose," she agreed reluctantly, though she suspected what was coming.

"How about answerin' a few of mine, then, Katie? Fair's fair!"

She'd given up requesting that he use her proper name. Too apprehensive to respond verbally, she could only offer a slight nod.

"What became of your money?" he asked without preamble. "I can plainly see there once must have been quite a fortune." He waved his hands, palms upward, to take in the entire room and beyond.

"My father was well-to-do, yes," she responded, uncomfortable with the subject, but determined no secrets remain between them. "Until one of his junior partners, a young man named Braxton Howard"—she faltered over the name—"embezzled a considerable sum, leaving us virtually penniless once all the financial obligations were met." With a soft cough, Katherine attempted to clear the growing lump from her throat. Unshed tears prickled behind her lids. "My father and mother both took ill with *la grippe* soon thereafter, and . . . and passed away within days of each other. I strongly feel they had lost the will to live after what Braxton—" Katherine could not go on.

"The junior partner?"

"Braxton Howard . . . yes—"

"You and he were courtin'?"

"We . . . that is, we were keeping company . . . though no

commitment had been made." Her cheeks went hot. She could not meet her husband's steady gaze.

"You weren't jilted, then?" Dandy persisted.

She stared up into his chestnut eyes, glaring. "Of course not! That you should suggest—"

"Now, don't get your dander up, Kate—"

"Katherine! My name is Katherine."

"I was just tryin' to work out in my head," he said, his voice becoming soft, cajoling, "why it is you never unbend . . . never give any clue to what you're thinkin' or feelin'. I figure this Howard guy hurt you pretty bad—"

"He didn't—"

"Didn't he?" he said even more softly.

Katherine turned her face away and refused to answer.

Dandy rose in one fluid movement, taking a single, angry step forward. "If I had that . . . dad-burned bindle-stiff here right now . . . I'd . . . I'd knock him from here to tomorrow for what he did to you and your family."

In view of his gallant need to champion her, Katherine's heart raced with unexpected happiness. The agony Braxton Howard had caused faded and all but disappeared. She offered her husband a tentative, faintly mischievous smile. Speaking most vehemently and fisting her hands, Katherine raised them, ready to do battle.

"Were the scoundrel within the vicinity, Mr. MacCabe, I would take the greatest pleasure in witnessing your doing just that, for I have frequently had the same desire myself."

Startled, Dandy looked at her a moment, then threw back his head and barked a laugh. Catching his breath, he covered her small, tight fists with his large, warm hands. His brogue went playfully thick.

"Ahhh, Katie, me darlin' girl, may I never be forced into hand-to-hand combat with the likes of yourself, for you'd be the winner for sure."

Flushed and flustered, Katherine gently withdrew her hands from his. "Please keep that thought firmly in mind, Mr. MacCabe," she responded tartly, "should we, in the future, come to a point of major disagreement."

He watched the spark go out of her—as if she realized

how open she'd almost become—studying her guarded expression, dismayed at her hasty emotional withdrawal. At last he spoke.

"That I will, Katherine, that I will."

Silence fell heavy between them. In the hall the grandfather's clock struck eleven times. Rubbing the back of his neck, Dandy flexed his shoulders in a futile attempt to relieve the tension building there.

"This day has left me more done in than any spent swingin' an ax in the pine woods from dawn to dusk. And tomorrow's a bigger one yet. We've much to do before Sunday. Best hit the sack before daylight's upon us, Kate."

Keeping her profile averted, Katherine agreed. "Perhaps you are right, I . . . I am weary as well, but I think I shall need to sit here quietly before the fire for a while before sleep will come. Until morning, then, Daniel, good night."

He walked slowly to the doorway, his thoughts as heavy as his footfalls. A glance showed him his wife was already far away in her own deep thoughts, her expression somber and somewhat sad.

"Good night to you, Kate. May your sleep be as peaceful as a night spent with the angels," Dandy whispered, certain she could not hear, but needing to say the words. With new tenderness he watched her a moment longer, then walked away into the shadows of the hall.

She waited until his tread sounded on the stairs before shifting her gaze to where he had stood watching her. "May your sleep be blessed as well, my husband," she replied in a whisper still softer than his.

7

"Oh, Miss Katherine," exclaimed the unflappable Hannah Tillit, nearly beside herself in tearful distress.

His handlebar mustache bobbing, Andrew Tillit sniffed, blinking rapidly. "You take care of yourself, and the mister, and them kids, Miss Katherine."

Katherine and the Tillits stood in the deep shadows of the hallway, far from possibly prying eyes, to say their difficult good-byes. Dandy tactfully waited outside with his children.

"I will. You two take care of yourselves as well. If you run short of supplies or cash, feel free to dispose of anything in the house you think might fill the need." Her voice choked off. She cleared her throat. "If you require professional advice for any reason, go to Judge Meyers. He will help you, I am sure. Do not attempt to enlist Mr. Grissom's help. His loyalties are obviously with Mrs. Stewart now. Oh, and—"

"Kath-er-ine," her husband bellowed from the open front door, his broad-shouldered frame blocking the light. "Come on along now, Kate. Time's awastin'."

"Only a moment more, please, Daniel."

He came toward her along the hall, sympathetic but insistent. "Partin' won't get any easier with postponin' it, Kate. And we've miles to cover before nightfall."

"I know . . . I know . . ."

With effort, Hannah regained her calm efficiency. "It's time, Miss Katherine. Go on with your husband, as well you should. I'm sure this will work itself out in the end, and we'll all be together again soon." She awkwardly patted Katherine's arm, then fisted her hands in her voluminous apron pockets.

Taking his silent, resigned wife's elbow, Dandy led her down the hall, knowing full well how difficult this parting was. He'd said heartrending farewells of his own when he left Ireland some ten years past. Guiding Katherine along the wide, painted floorboards of the porch, Dandy dipped his head close to her cheek, whispering encouragement into her ear.

"Plant a smile on your face, Kate. If the old lady has someone keepin' an eye on us, like I suspect, we want him to see us havin' a good time leavin' on our picnic."

Drawing a steadying breath, Katherine offered a tremulous, if somewhat grim, smile. "A happy Sunday outing it shall appear, then, Daniel. Let us proceed."

"That's a good lass."

With his firm, warm hand reassuringly under her elbow, Katherine allowed her husband to lead her across the veranda to the carriage. She settled into the rockaway between Thomas and Celia. Hannah's enormous covered hamper lay safe and secure under the seat. As Daniel pointed out, they couldn't chance the basket getting wet if there should be an afternoon shower like those they'd been having most of the week. The boot in the rear held blankets for bedrolls wrapped around Daniel's precious dulcimer. "Nourishment for the soul," he had proclaimed when Katherine raised a single, questioning brow. She could not argue with him on that score, though it was probably just as well her husband did not know she herself had secured *Our Deportment* in oilcloth and placed it in the bottom of the picnic basket.

The morning proved mild, the only clouds in the blue sky moving low across the horizon as their journey began. Beside her on the narrow, padded seat, the children squirmed under the bulk of double layers of clothing and sturdy woolen coats; and while Katherine felt like squirming as well for the same reason, she did not. On the seat up front, her husband had already discarded his mackinaw jacket and released the collar buttons on the two shirts he wore. Perspiration beaded along the angle of his jaw and dampened the curls at his nape. A picture came unbidden to Katherine's mind of a night not so long ago when fever's heat had dampened those same wisps, and how her ministering fingers had tangled in them. She found herself experiencing the same disturbing sensations now and struggled to quell them, with only modest success.

"All set?" Dandy turned his head to ask.

Hot with embarrassment, Katherine only gave him a curt nod.

Dandy threw her a curious, probing stare. Attesting the flush in her cheeks to the layers of clothing she wore, he turned his attention to leave-taking.

As they pulled out from under the carriage porch, away from the only home, the only life, she'd ever known, any thoughts other than those of loss and longing fled Katherine's mind. The panic she'd experienced on the porch surged through her tenfold. She wanted suddenly to cry out, "Stop! Let me out! I cannot do this!" Instead she tightened her clasped hands on her lap, looked straight ahead over her husband's right shoulder, and offered fervent prayers for the successful outcome of this desperate venture.

Settling back upon his perch, reins lying lightly across callused palms, Dandy turned the rockaway toward the picnic grounds some five miles down the road. There they would eat a noon meal and spend as much time as necessary—maybe the better part of their first day—making their trip appear to be nothing more than an outing. Though Dandy was positive a spy on horseback followed at a distance, his spirits remained high. Everything was going along right on schedule, and in spite of roasting like a trussed-up rabbit on a spit, he felt pretty danged pleased with himself and the world in general.

"Along with you, Bess." Dandy flicked the reins over the mare's rump. "There's a carrot and an apple, too, waitin' for you if you get us to the picnic grounds before noon.''

Bess picked up her ears and her pace appreciably. Thomas slid forward in his seat.

''Looks like Bess understood you, Da. Do you think she did?'' he questioned eagerly while working two fingers around inside his coat collar, scratching ineffectively at the prickly heat.

''Don't doubt it for a minute, son. Bess's a most understandin' kind of filly. We ought to be reachin' the picnic grounds before you know it.''

Dandy selected a likely spot and tethered the mare for grazing. Alongside the park a river ran wide and deep, swollen and flowing swiftly with spring runoff. Katherine cautioned Thomas to keep an eye on Celia and stay well back from the water's edge as the children tossed their coats onto the carriage seat and scampered off.

Dandy chuckled. ''Now you've gotten the hang of it, Kate, you're becomin' a regular little mother hen.''

Katherine overlooked his remark to discuss a more pressing matter. ''Do you think we have been followed?''

''Sure of it. And so close behind, he'd be eatin' our dust for his lunch if it wasn't for the rain we've been havin' of late. No, now don't go lookin' around for him. He's hidin' off in that stand of willows down by the river. Just forget the man's spyin' on us and spread out some of Hannah's good victuals for our lunch, Kate. Enjoy yourself as much as you can. He won't be creatin' a problem much longer.''

Katherine threw him an apprehensive glance. ''What do you mean?''

Dandy reached over to push a wisp of Katherine's hair off her cheek and out of her eyes. ''Don't be worryin' yourself about it, Katie. I know just how to handle things.'' Quickly he changed the subject. ''Here, let me help you out of that heavy coat. You must be boilin'. I'll go check on the kids while you set out lunch.'' He strode off toward Thomas and Celia at water's edge, whistling.

Reluctant to let the matter drop, but having no other

choice, Katherine spread a generous picnic feast on a blanket in a grassy patch of sunshine, wondering and worrying over the drastic steps her husband might take to deal with their bothersome observer.

Dandy returned, children in tow, as Katherine set out the last dish. It had been his idea to sit in full view of their spy; and he gnawed on his fried chicken drumstick with exaggerated relish just for the sequestered man's benefit.

Later, satiated, Dandy stretched out on his back, forearms crossed behind his head, eyes closed to slits, secretly watching his bride pack up leftovers. He enjoyed the economy of her movements. Never a wasted gesture as, with spine straight as always, Kate wrapped bread and cheese and meat, shook out cloth napkins and folded each one precisely, then brushed crumbs from her black woolen skirt. She frowned, as if irritated that crumbs should dare settle upon her person, and Dandy nearly gave himself away by laughing aloud.

If only she'd find it in her heart someday to treat him with the same consideration she gave to the details of her task, he'd call himself a happily married man. Not that he was beginning to care for his high-born, prim-and-proper wife, he assured himself. A man had certain needs. Or . . . if forced to be honest with himself, maybe it *was* something more . . . something he wouldn't or couldn't put a name to . . . sure as hell not love. She didn't seem to be falling head-over-heels for him. Still, she did love his kids, and that was a beginning. Lulled by that thought and by the warm sunshine, Dandy felt himself grow sleepy, and he dozed.

Katherine picked up and packed, pointedly ignoring the blatant virility of the man at her side, and the errant emotions his proximity aroused. His quiet snoring assured her he was most certainly asleep and not surreptitiously regarding her under half-closed lids as she'd first suspected. Thus comforted, she fell to watching the steady rise and fall of his broad chest straining under the fabric of his two shirts. Familiar with every ripple, every hollow from waist upward, she'd memorized as well the rugged angles of his jaw, the full sensuality of his lips, the golden hue of his skin, the texture of which her fingers still recalled. Merciful heaven, there were precious few hours since that fateful day she'd nursed him that her thoughts hadn't brought forth images of her husband's glorious features and form.

It pained her to the depths of her being, believing he could not help but find her undesirable. Not pretty enough. Not soft and full-bodied enough. Lacking in humor and congeniality—and, yes, femininity. Unshed tears burned behind her lids; self-pity welled in her heart. What a poor bargain Dandy MacCabe had made, taking a plain, parsimonious spinster for his bride. How soon might he regret his hasty decision, if he hadn't already?

Nonsense, her practical nature chided. Daniel had agreed to the pact between them with eyes open wide. They'd married to protect the children, nothing more. The upheaval of their departure had simply turned her maudlin. She most certainly was not succumbing to the man himself, she was almost positive of that fact.

Closing the hamper with firm finality, Katherine felt a chill breeze lift the loose hairs at the back of her neck as the sun disappeared. Looking up, she was dismayed to see that a bank of ominous clouds had rolled across the sky toward them.

"Daniel. Daniel, wake up. It is soon going to rain."

He winked one eye open to confirm her pronouncement, then sat up cross-legged, dusting his hands off on his knees.

"What are we to do now? Our guard is never going to believe we choose to continue picnicking in the rain."

"Time to put the second part of my plan into action, Kate. Here, let me take the hamper to the buggy. I'll be back in a minute. You go round up Thomas and Celia." In a single fluid movement he rose and grabbed up the picnic basket.

The first big droplets fell on them as Katherine gathered the children from their play. They scurried to the rockaway to find Dandy there ahead of them, breathing hard, his hair disheveled and a smudge—or a bruise—high on his cheek.

"Daniel, whatever—?"

"Hurry, Kate, before the downpour hits. Thomas. Celia. Climb aboard. We're off on our great adventure."

The three were scarcely seated in back before Dandy

slapped the reins smartly over the mare's flanks, and Bess took off at a surprising fast trot. The sound of her hooves on the hard-packed clay of the roadway echoed a companion sound at the rear of the carriage. Peering out the back window, Katherine saw a second horse trailing very close behind; in fact, it appeared to be tethered to the rockaway in some fashion. She turned on her husband.

"Daniel, you stole that man's horse." Indignation snapped in her tone.

Dandy chuckled. "Just borrowed, Katie. I'll turn the beast loose a few miles down the road." He pulled a pair of boots out from under his seat and held them aloft, declaring triumphantly, "You might be sayin' I also did a little shoe-nappin', as well. That sneaky fellow back there will be havin' a painfully long, wet walk back to town to report us to Old Lady Stewart. I made sure of it." Over Katherine's further protest, Dandy urged the mare out of the park and down the road to freedom.

A mile or so later Dandy was forced to stop to light the coach lamps and pull Mr. Tillit's slicker and hat out from under the driver's seat against the relentless onslaught of rain slanting under his inadequate roof. Katherine tied down the isinglass back and side curtains. Even so, gusts of wind blew rain in on her and the children, making them uncomfortably cold despite their multiple layers of clothing. Katherine could only imagine how her husband must be faring on his damp perch, and worried about a recurrence of his recent illness. They were all dependent upon him now, for only he knew the direction to their new life and freedom from prosecution for having broken the law—possibly many laws—by their flight.

Evening came early with no relief from the rain, but luck was with them that first night. As a blanketing darkness descended, Dandy managed to make out an old barn standing rickety and alone amid the rubble of other outbuildings and the burned ruins of a farmhouse.

There was no sign of habitation anywhere nearby, and that was good. They were still far too close to town to welcome questions, however innocent, about their travels or their destination.

The barn proved surprisingly sound; and a pile of dry, if musty, hay would serve nicely as their beds, Dandy declared. Thomas and Celia romped in the hay until they resembled a pair of scarecrows. Loath to spoil their fun, Katherine reluctantly suggested an early bedtime was in order. Dandy heartily agreed.

"But I'm hungry, Da," Thomas protested.

"Aren't you always, son o' mine? How about a little supper, then? I'm as hungry as a bear myself." He enfolded Thomas in a hug, growling, pretending to nip Thomas's ear, then offered his wife a rakish grin and a wink. A multicolored bruise decorated his cheek, and he winced, but his smile did not falter.

They supped on bread and cheese and ham, watching the rain pour down beyond the doorless opening in the barn, listening to its heavy patter upon a surprisingly sound tin roof, instinctively moving closer together for warmth. Katherine fell to studying Celia, who nibbled halfheartedly on a piece of buttered and jellied bread as though it held no interest. She and Dandy exchanged worried glances when the little girl issued a volley of three sneezes in a row. Dandy reached over to feel her forehead.

"Is she feverish?"

He shook his head. "Not so's I can tell. Hope she's not comin' down with somethin' out here in the middle of nowhere. Celia doesn't get sick much, but when she does she seems to take it real hard. One time Annie had to send for me to come home midseason, thinkin' our babe wasn't goin' to live to see mornin', her fever was so high. But, Saints be praised, she pulled through . . ." His voice faded off as he felt her forehead again. "Nope, she's cool as can be." He threw up his hands in exasperation. "How can the lass be perfectly fine when she's out in the cold and rain, and sick as a pup when she's nestled in a dry, warm barn full of hay?"

An idea surfaced in Katherine's mind. "Perhaps it is the hay that causes her to sneeze, Daniel. I myself find chrysanthemums distressful when in bloom.''

"Kate, you're a wonder, comin' up with the answer so quick. Makes sense to me," Dandy agreed with a grin. He grabbed her by the shoulders and kissed her heartily on the cheek.

Their gazes locked and held, but only for an instant. She grew red-faced, and he looked flustered. Turning from his wife, Dandy lifted Celia off her feet, giving her a smacking kiss as well.

"No more sleepin' or playin' in the hay for you if we can help it, sprite. When we get to the farm, you're to stay out of the barn and out of trouble." He caressed his daughter's plump, rosy cheek. She looked somberly, intently, into his eyes as if trying to understand what all the concern over her was about. He smiled encouragement, and she responded with a grin. "That's a good lass. You're lookin' a little perkier already. You just keep on improvin', and we'll all make it to the farm in good shape."

"How long will that take, do you think, Daniel, with the weather as it is?"

"Couple of days more'n I planned if it keeps comin' down like this. If the rain stops soon, we might just make it there by tomorrow noon."

Despite Dandy's hopes to the contrary, it rained steadily all night and was still raining when they awoke early in the morning. Katherine stood in the opening where once the barn doors had hung, looking out upon the dismal scene of burned-down house, fallen outbuildings, and a yard awash with the seemingly endless deluge from above. She'd been striving to keep overwhelming thoughts of home and their plight at bay, but that resolve was beginning to erode as had the furrows in the fields beyond. If only the weather would improve. She did not relish the thought of at least another day's travel in the wet, drafty carriage.

As if sensing her mood, Dandy spoke behind her. "Had we made better time yesterday, I'd say we should stay here until the weather clears some. But we need to put as many miles between us and them today, Kate. We should be heading out soon—''

"Surely our trail has been obliterated by the rainfall,'' Katherine suggested. "Could we not assume—?''

"Can't go assumin' anythin', Katie,'' Dandy said as he shook his head. "There aren't that many roads headin' out of town. If Old Lady Stewart's henchman saw the direction we took . . .'' He shrugged. "We'd best have a quick breakfast, then move on out.''

The thoroughfare had become a quagmire of muddy puddles and hidden ruts, making travel not only uncomfortable, but also dangerous for man and beast alike. Instead of miles, Dandy measured their progress in yards—sometimes feet— often quitting the roadway altogether to traverse its grassy edge for a safer, if bumpier, ride.

They lunched without stopping, Katherine feeding the children from the hamper between her feet and passing a sandwich of bread and ham forward to Dandy on his perch.

Dusk was upon them before Dandy consented to look for someplace to shelter them for the night—and found nothing along a desolate stretch of logged-over swampland that seemed to go on forever in all directions. He drove on through the endless night, while Katherine and the children dozed fitfully in the drafty confines of their questionable shelter. In the dark before dawn, the headlamps ran out of oil and sputtered out. Dandy called a soft "whoa,'' and weary Bess stumbled to a halt in the center of the roadway, stretching her neck toward tender shoots along the berm. Beyond exhaustion, Dandy slumped on his seat, rubbing bleary eyes with the heels of both hands.

"Are we there yet, Da?'' asked a small, querulous voice from the rear.

"Afraid not, son,'' Dandy replied quietly so as not to wake Katherine and Celia. "Near's I can figure, our journey's little more than half over. All this rain has . . . Listen . . . listen to that, Thomas—''

"Them's birds singin'. An' it's not rainin' no more, Da. It's not rainin'.'' His voice rose in a joyous shout.

Katherine started from sleep, jostling Celia who slept on her lap, waking her as well.

"Katie. Celia. The rain's stopped. And look there. I think that's the sun comin' up."

"What a magnificent sunrise, Daniel. I believe I have never seen a more beautiful or welcome one. Look at the sky, Celia." Katherine drew the child's gaze with a pointed finger, and Celia responded with a face that glowed with wonder at the color display spreading out before them in the morning sky.

"It's bound to be a better day today, Katie."

"That it is, Daniel, that it is."

But the glorious sunrise and the sunny early hours of the new day proved to be only a brief respite as the small family completed their ablutions and broke fast with the dwindling supplies in Hannah Tillit's basket. The puddles in the roadway scarcely had time to sink into the mud before thunderheads rolled in once again midmorning. The sky turned ugly, and distant rumblings boomed closer and closer. Wind whipped up, wet and cold.

"We'd best find shelter as quick as we can, Kate. That's a bad storm brewin'." He lashed the reins over Bess's flanks.

They outrode the storm, but barely, finding shelter in a large, three-sided shed at the far edge of some farmer's field. Meant as temporary storage for hay, it was now virtually empty except for loose chaff mounded in the far corners. The MacCabes found room for Bess and themselves, but not the rockaway. Dandy and Katherine unloaded the carriage as wind lashed at their clothing and rain, slanted sideways in sheets, soaked them to the skin.

They huddled with the children in the driest corner, rough wood planking at their back, casting worried glances between them. Thomas quivered with fear he tried manfully not to show, and jumped with each subsequent crack of thunder, but Celia simply sneezed twice, then curled on her side, her head pillowed in Katherine's lap. Oblivious to the storm raging around her, the child fell asleep. Brushing the hair from Celia's fair, rosy cheek, Katherine pondered this oddity as well as others in the past. Celia apparently failed to fear the thunder, though clearly she appreciated a colorful sunrise. She'd been ill as a baby, with a high fever. If there was a connection, a solution to the puzzle that was Celia, it evaded Katherine's comprehension as the force of the tempest outside continued to mount.

Thomas finally fell into a restless doze, then slept soundly as the fury of the storm abated, leaving behind a steadily falling rain. As one, Katherine and Dandy eased their charges onto their crude beds and covered them with blankets retrieved from the carriage. There was no help for it but to let Celia sleep on the hay, but well protected from direct contact, her head resting on her father's folded jacket.

Feeling trapped in the confines of the small building, Katherine sought its opening, staring mournfully into the steady downpour. Tonight it seemed as though the rains would never end, that they would never reach their destination—a destination so alien to her nature, she wondered if she'd ever be able to call it home. Overwhelmingly homesick, she inexplicably longed for the comfort of her husband's arms around her, lending his strength to her own, now waning. She ached to shed the tears lodged tightly in her throat with her head pillowed on his sturdy chest. But, of course, that could not be. She and Daniel were little more than strangers joined together in marriage for the sake of the children. Side by side, each undertook this journey alone.

Dandy kissed Thomas and Celia good night, then joined Katherine in the open doorway. Though her back was ramrod-straight as always, her shoulders angled downward in a disheartened slump that cut him to the quick. She'd given up so much by marrying him. Her privacy, her standards, her home. Gratitude and more swelled Dandy's heart to near bursting. He longed to pull his wife into his arms, comfort her, feel her comforting warmth against his rain-chilled body. Hold her until the unhappiness went out of her eyes. He lifted his hand to touch her and, unsure of its welcome, let it fall before reaching its goal.

"I'm sorry, Katherine, that it's come to this."

She acknowledged his presence with a slight inclination of her head in his direction. The serenity of her features was broken only by the sadness in her eyes. A small sigh caused her chest to rise and fall, though no sound escaped.

"There was nothing we could have done otherwise, Daniel," she replied, grateful he had chosen her proper name by which to address her. "It is only that"—she bit her trembling lip briefly—"I am finding it harder to break ties with home than I anticipated."

Lonelier now than before he joined her, Katherine retreated into the enfolding dark interior of the shed on the pretense of checking on the children. Finding them sufficiently covered and sound asleep, she glanced toward her husband now regarding the rain alone. Her regret was keen.

Dandy damned himself a million times over for not saying or doing the right things to comfort her. He wanted to, the Saints only knew. But as self-contained as Kate always seemed to be, how would she welcome him? With a closed expression and sharp retort, most likely. Still, she was homesick, hurting. Who else but he should attempt to give her solace, and possibly find warmth enough in her embrace to sustain him for the remainder of their journey and the uncertain future ahead? Summoning his courage, Dandy went to his wife.

As Katherine stood over the children, watching them sleep, he came up behind her, slipping a blanket around her shoulders and crossed arms. She turned her head to look into his dark eyes, not fully understanding the questions in their hungry depths.

"You were shiverin'," he responded, the color high on his cheekbones, his words hesitant and soft. But he did not withdraw, nor did he release his hold on her blanketed shoulders. Instead he rubbed his hands up and down her arms, briskly at first, then slowly, rising from her shoulders to her neck, resting there, kneading the tightness out of her sore muscles.

Katherine offered no resistance. His hands upon her, an answer to her unspoken longings, evoked responses from the tips of her toes to the depths of her innermost being. Awareness ceased of all but the sound of rain and the sensations coursing through her. When he turned her around to face him, she made a small sound of protest at the loss of his touch, until he lowered his lips to hers, offering a tentative, feather-light kiss. Katherine's lips parted in an ecstatic sigh. Taking the invitation, Dandy's kiss deepened, and he pulled her to him until the lengths of their bodies pressed together as one.

Dandy knew he should ease off before he scared her to death with the hardness growing between them, yet he wanted to go on kissing her until she was as hot and bothered as he was. Damn, he wanted—no, needed—to bed his wife. But if he went too far too fast tonight, she might never let him touch her again. Groaning inwardly, his groin throbbing with exquisite pain, he gently withdrew his lips from hers; gently he pushed her away to arm's length. Keen disappointment swam in her gray eyes.

"Daniel, did I—"

"It's late, Katie," he told her, a catch in his voice. "We need our sleep even more'n the kids."

"But, Daniel, did I do—"

"Good night, Katherine. Sleep well." He leaned toward her, but only kissed her forehead. Releasing her abruptly, he strode to a far corner, grabbing up a blanket from the floor. Locating a spot as remote from her as possible, Dandy wrapped himself in his woolen cocoon and feigned instant sleep, leaving his bride to wonder what she'd done wrong.

Upon arising from a restless, mostly sleepless night, neither could meet the other's eyes. Dandy wondered if Kate's delicate, maidenly sensibilities had been injured by his lusty advances; Katherine longed to know what, in her inexperience, she'd done to turn her husband away.

Shaking her head to clear it, Katherine forced her futile ponderings aside in favor of the far more practical concern over their diminished food supplies as she passed out bread and cheese.

"Will we reach your farm today, do you think?" she

asked Dandy with shy restraint when he returned from checking to see how the carriage had weathered the storm.

He could not meet her eyes. "Late today, most likely. We're a full day behind thanks to this damn...dang weather. But the buggy's in fine shape, except for wet seats and an inch or two of water underfoot. Bailed it out as best I could. Good thing we brought the hamper inside, or our supplies would've been spoiled for certain."

Katherine bit her lip to keep from telling him how few food supplies remained, and guiltily held to silence.

Morning fog gave way to intermittent showers lasting from dawn until near dusk. The rockaway rolled mile after soggy mile along the rain-rutted roadway. Farmland turned to woodland, woods to farms, with disheartening consistency. No towns appeared anywhere along their arduous route. Surely Daniel's property was not this far from civilization. Until now Katherine had not fully comprehended how isolated their destination might be.

Relief blossomed when, late in the afternoon, a white church spire appeared beyond the trees no more than a mile ahead, nestled in the rolling hills, surrounded by clusters of shops and homes. Katherine's expectations quickly plummeted when her husband chose to skirt the town in favor of a less traveled route, at last jolting down a trail narrowed by overgrown weeds and saplings. She found little comfort, only rising distress, when Dandy called out, "Farm's just around the next bend. Ahhh, there it is. Thomas. Celia. Look there, that's our place. We're home at last, Katie."

8

Katherine slid forward on her seat, her heart thumping heavily with uneasy anticipation. Hoping for the best, instinct warned those hopes might prove unfounded.

Through the misting dusk of shadow shapes, she beheld acre upon acre of land long left fallow, sprouting scrub growth like an infant wilderness, set off on three sides by trees—gaunt, spiked silhouettes yet to unfurl with spring— and in the center, an oasis of buildings, mere silhouettes as well. Even at a distance, Katherine observed the sag of the barn roof, the dangerous listing of a corn crib, and the flattened ruins of several other outbuildings. Her stomach in knots, she scarcely dared look to see if the farmhouse itself survived, though she could not avoid that inevitability.

Alone in a yard as wild as the fields, their long-awaited sanctuary from the dark, the cold rain, and detection wore a look of neglect Katherine found not in the least comforting.

"How . . . long has no one . . . lived here?" Katherine willed her voice not to express the enormity of her disappointment.

"Guess I've let the place go unattended longer'n I should've, Kate," a contrite Dandy appologized, hastily adding, "but it's good land. I'll have it back in shape before you know it. Let's just head on up to the house, then, and see how it fared.'' With a slap of the reins, the buggy rolled over a rutted lane, rocking to a stop at a wide wraparound porch.

The dwelling, though structurally sound, badly needed scraping and painting. Windows, clouded with grime, gave no view of the interior. Keeping the children close beside them, Dandy and Katherine cautiously trod up three creaking board steps; at a turn of the knob under Dandy's hand, the front door slowly swung open on protesting hinges.

Layers of thick dust covered the well-worn runner that carpeted the small entry and a steep flight of stairs to the second floor. Cobwebs draped like gossamer from railings to the framed pictures on the walls to ceiling moldings and back again. In the rooms immediately to the right and the left, furniture hid shrouded beneath dustcovers gray with age.

Bunched together and silent, the MacCabes stood just inside the door.

Thomas recovered first. ''Kinda dirty, ain't it, Da?''

Dandy offered a halfhearted chuckle, ruffling his son's hair with one large hand. ''So would you be if you hadn't had a lick of cleanin' in five years or more. With water and soap and a bit of elbow grease, we'll have this place spotless in no time. Right, Katie?'' A pregnant pause. ''Right, Kate . . . Katherine?'' He glanced her way and found her giving him a look that'd kill flies at twenty paces.

''It will require a *great deal* of hot water and soapsuds to set this place to rights, Mr. MacCabe.''

Dandy inwardly flinched. *Uh-oh, so she's back to callin' me MacCabe, is she? I'm in big trouble now, for sure.*

''Katie—''

She ignored the plea in that one word, rubbing gloved hands up and down her arms. ''What we need first is a fire to take the chill out of the air and chase away that awful musty odor. There appears little else we can manage today beyond cleaning a spot in the kitchen to prepare an evening meal and making the bedrooms habitable. I assume they are upstairs?''

Maintaining civility by willpower alone, Katherine stepped away from her husband, glancing up the narrow flight of steps. Furious with him for bringing them to this filthy, rundown excuse for a farmhouse in which to live, she still, in all honesty, had to admit he'd done the best he was able, given their present circumstances. Despite the disaster the house and the farm had proven to be, for the moment she and her family were safe and out of the endless rain. All else could be dealt with in the morning.

"There are two." Dandy broke through her musings.

"Two?"

"Bedrooms. Upstairs. One for the children and one for ourselves." Anticipating her protest, Dandy countered, "It's time we shared a room, you and me, especially startin' a whole new way of life in our own home." His words came out bluntly and sincerely. How was he to warm her heart, steal kisses like the one in the shed, and more, unless they bedded down together?

Leaden silence hung between them. Behind Kate's furrowed brow, Dandy could almost hear the arguments building. She astounded him when she finally spoke, her words measured, her tone even.

"For propriety's sake, I believe I must agree with you, Daniel." Even *Our Deportment,* though subtly to be sure, extolled the virtue of cohabitation. Little doubt remained in her mind about the rightness of sharing a bed with her husband. It would not do, however, for him to sense the near terror and anticipation warring within her breast at the thought of sleeping with Dandy. Assuming a ruler-straight posture, her chin upraised, she insisted, "Bedroom arrangements notwithstanding, before any of us can go to bed this night, there is much to do. We had best discover the condition of the kitchen at once." Heading through the swinging door at the rear of the hall, she left her gape-mouthed husband to follow on his own.

Ah, lass, ye're amazin', he mused when he'd collected his thoughts. *Just when I believe I've figured ye out, ye come up with somethin' to throw those beliefs out the window.* At least life would never be dull with the wife he'd once mis-

taken for a staid, parsimonious prude. Shaking his shaggy
mane in wonderment, Dandy shouldered his way through
the swinging door to find Kate making a slow turn about
the kitchen, knuckles fisted on hips, lips drawn thin with
displeasure. She arched one brow at him, acknowledging the
worst of the mess with a nod. The remains of a bag of flour
left upon one counter had spilled onto the floor from a
mouse-chewed hole, with tiny animal footprints spreading
off in all directions. Mouse leavings dotted every surface.

"If this is an indication of what we can expect to find
everywhere else, I would say we have our work cut out for
us, Mr. MacCabe." She unbuttoned her sleeve and rolled it
to the elbow, followed by the other.

Born and bred in a privileged world, his bride nonetheless
proved to him by the minute there was more spunk to her
than he'd ever imagined. Impressed anew by this down-to-
earth, no-nonsense side of her, Dandy offered, "I'll go see
what kind of kindlin' I can scare up, Katie. We'll have hot
water for scrubbin' in no time." With a reassuring grin, he
escaped out the back door.

Evidence remained of raccoons having recently nested in
the cookstove. While Dandy set to work cleaning out the
stove and building a fire, Thomas brought in endless buckets
of water from the well to fill the reservoir for heating. Katherine set to scrubbing everything within reach with a rag
and suds made from a bar of lye soap found in the cupboard
under the zinc-lined dry sink, Celia both helping and hin-
dering wherever and whenever she could.

The hour grew late. They labored by firelight from an
open stove door and weak lamplight from behind an age-
clouded glass chimney. Finally Dandy stretched his arms
overhead, his hands fisting, then flexing. Yawning widely,
he announced, "Enough for one day. How about a sandwich
and some of Hannah's good oatmeal cookies, Kate?" Dandy
grabbed up the hamper from just inside the door, plunked
it down on the freshly scrubbed worktable, and lifted the
lid. Expectation turned to puzzlement as he looked inside.

Katherine's heart doubled its pace with apprehension.
"Daniel, I . . . I meant to tell you how low on supplies we

had become, but you had so many other worries . . . with the weather and—''

''I understand, Kate. Didn't figure the food to last forever. Besides, there's still half a loaf of bread, a heel of cheese, and this packet—''

''Daniel, no. You see, I . . . I . . .''

But he'd already untied the twine and thrown back the oiled cloth protection to reveal, not an overlooked round of smoked ham or some other delicacy but *Our Deportment,* Katherine's food for thought. Forseeing his ire, she was unprepared for his rage, fueled perhaps by exhaustion and hunger, uncalled-for in intensity nonetheless.

''If that's not the damnedest, dad-blastedest, foolhardiest thing you've ever done, Katherine, I don't know what is.'' He sputtered, red-faced. ''There'd've been room enough for more fried chicken, or cheese, or . . . a . . . another loaf of bread . . . if it wasn't for that . . . that—''

''Daniel, the children. Your language . . .''

He hesitated, his fury unabated. Searching for more acceptable expletives, calling none to mind, he took great satisfaction in slamming the offending volume onto the table with all the force he could muster before leaning toward her, big hands splayed wide on either side of the book in question.

''What were you thinkin', damn it all, Kate? Were you plannin' on spreadin' bread and jam between the pages of that . . . that gol-danged book of yours and servin' them for our supper?''

Her chin came up. ''I was merely affording it the protection its subject matter warranted. We may have been forced to flee civilization, but there is no call for our manners to be reduced to those of barbarians. Besides . . . I had expected our rations to go quite a bit fur—''

''H-h-hogwash . . . and . . . and h-h-horse feathers!'' Avoiding his most colorful epithets left Dandy severely limited.

Silence descended. Katherine tipped her head at an angle, regarding her spouse's florid face.

''Hog-hogwash?'' she queried, fighting an almost uncontrollable urge to giggle. "And . . . and—"

"And horse feathers . . ." Dandy stammered, laughter exploding. "By the Saints, Kate, listen to what you've got me sayin'," he accused when he caught his breath.

Stifling her chuckles, Katherine opened her mouth to respond in kind, only to have Thomas interrupt.

"Da? Da, I need to . . . aaaa . . . errr . . . Where's the privy, Da, do you know?"

Grateful for the distraction, Dandy picked up the single lamp. "Can't be far off, son. Shall we have a look-see?" He spirited the boy out the back door, disappearing into the dark of night.

In spite of sharing a moment of humor, Dandy figured Kate'd have a whole lot more to say about that damned book, and just about everything else in this world and the next. All of it the direct opposite of his way of thinking. Dandy didn't have it in him to spar anymore tonight; he was too blamed tired. And he hoped like h . . . heck Kate was, too. He was looking forward to a far friendlier, more intimate ending to the day. The dull, not unpleasant ache swelling to an exquisite anticipation in his lower regions had him all but wild to begin sharing a bed with his bride of a week, and he prayed to the Saints one and all that she'd be willing at last to welcome him.

He found her sorting through their bedding stacked on the table with something akin to desperation. She glanced up, her cheeks scarlet either from their run-in or her task.

"I am very much afraid we will have to sleep here on this floor tonight," she told him, her eyes over-bright. "Goodness knows what awaits us in the rooms overhead, and quite frankly I simply haven't the energy to find out." Her voice trembled to a shaky halt.

Dandy's hopes fell lower than the soles of his mocs. He had to clear his throat twice to get the words to come.

"A dusty kitchen floor can't be any worse than where we've been sleepin'. Let's call it quits for now and get some shut-eye, all right?"

Katherine nodded, blinking hard. Dandy patted her awkwardly on the shoulder.

"Things will look brighter in the mornin', Katie. Maybe the sun will even shine down on us for a change." What more could he offer?

"I hope so," she whispered so low he had to bend toward her to hear. "I truly hope so."

How could she let him know it was not their argument or the deplorable state of the farm and the house that had her in tearful turmoil, but something else altogether? Something she could not clearly define even in her own thoughts. Preposterous to imagine she might be disappointed to the brink of weeping because she would not be sharing her husband's bed this first night in their new home. Simply preposterous.

Somewhere not too far away, a rooster crowed. Katherine gave up the last vestiges of sleep and unwrapped herself from the cocoon of woolen blankets that had been her bed on the linoleum floor. Rising gingerly, she acknowledged all the sore spots from hip to shoulder, noting that her husband's blankets lay in a neat roll on the kitchen table. Fortunately, he himself was nowhere in evidence. She knew she must appear a grim sight to behold. The black cashmere dress she'd worn for countless days and nights bore stains and wrinkles impossible to remove. Her hair . . . Katherine's hands went to her hair; she was relieved she'd had the foresight to work it into a single thick braid before retiring. Smoothing down her dress as best she could, she stood in the center of the kitchen, wondering what to do first when there were so many things requiring equal attention.

It occurred to her this might be an ideal time, while her husband was elsewhere, to consult her little blue book. She seemed to recall it contained a chapter entitled "Home Life and Etiquette," surely the most appropriate place to commence a day's labor. Settling herself at the porcelain-topped worktable, her book open before her, Katherine flipped through the well-worn pages and found herself stopping at "The Duties of the Wife to Her Husband" instead. The words "She [the wife] should strive to the utmost of her ability to do whatever is best calculated to please him [her husband]'' caught her attention.

From the look of need he'd given her that first night as husband and wife and all the lonely, loveless nights since, there was little doubt in Katherine's mind what would have given Daniel the greatest happiness. And she wondered, in spite of herself, what it would have been like. She wondered, too, if she would ever find out.

Her head came up, cheeks flushed and warm, half expecting that Dandy might have come in unannounced to catch her guiltily poring over such suggestive material. As if summoned by her thoughts, she heard a cheery whistling and his steps outside the door. Katherine scarcely had time to thrust her book under his bedroll on the table before Dandy came in.

''Mornin', Katie. I see I'm not the only one up bright and early. Been outside yet? The birds are singin', and the sun is shinin'. Took a dip in the stream, and I feel like a new man.'' He shook his shaggy wet mane, and droplets of moisture splattered her like spring rain.

Katherine made a sound of protest. ''Daniel, I prefer to bathe firsthand, if you do not mind.'' She found her words held little sting as she stared at him. He looked so magnificent standing before her.

His large, long-fingered hands came up to slick wet, mahogany curls behind his ears, bringing into prominence his high cheekbones and the strong angle of his jaw. Clear brown eyes under bold, winged brows sparkled with enjoyment of life; weather-bronzed skin glowed with the stimulation of cold water and robust good health. The fact that this tall, muscled, broad-shouldered, virile, handsome man was her husband quickly brought to mind Katherine's reading of moments before: ''. . . the intimacy of marriage . . . the maiden becomes a wife.''

''I—I—'' she stammered. ''I—should perform my own ablutions. If you will excuse me.'' Like a coward fleeing in terror, Katherine all but ran out the back door and down the worn path to the absolute privacy of the privy.

Through the clouded window over the sink, Dandy watched her hike up her skirts and scurry off. Unable to fathom her changeable moods, he shrugged and gave up trying, turning his attention to the bedrolls on the floor wherein his children still slept.

"Wake up, hug-a-beds. A new day's dawnin'. Up and at 'em, there's work to be done."

Thomas blinked and yawned and complained. Sitting and stretching, he nudged his sister awake. While Thomas and Celia struggled into wakefulness, Dandy grabbed up the blanket from the table, causing something wedged beneath to land on the floor with a smart slap.

"What the— That blasted book again!"

He reached down to retrieve it, then paused halfway, hands on knees. It had fallen open face up, to a page that appeared recently creased. Curiosity got the better of his dislike for Katie's little volume when he caught sight of a page filled with words like devotion and love and phrases like "the affection they have possessed and experienced as lovers must ripen . . ."

Squatting down, Dandy took the open book in hand, reading as he slowly rose, continuing to read as he placed the book on the table and, hauling a chair out, straddled it backward, still reading, until emotions too heightened to be borne stopped him cold.

"Ah, Katie, my sweet. What wicked readin' my virginal bride is dwellin' upon so early in the day!" He spoke softly aloud, lifting his head to gaze in the direction in which his wife had disappeared, smugly smiling. Playin' coy when found out. Proper as she was, no wonder she took off at a run . . . So she wanted to have her little secrets, did she? Well, that was all right with Dandy. For tonight, in the privacy of their bed in their own room, his pristine wife would no longer be a virgin. Anticipation surged, tightening the muscles in his groin. *Patience,* he reminded himself. *Patience.* There was an entire day ahead of him to be gotten through. Night, and bedtime, would come.

When his wife reentered the kitchen, she appeared her serene, restrained self once again, but her cheeks flushed prettily, and her normally level gaze slid away when she caught him staring. Her skin was moist, he noted, and wisps of hair that had escaped from her braid clung to forehead and cheek like spun honey. The bodice of her severe black dress damply molded itself to her upper form in all the right places. Like himself, Katie had bathed at the stream, and Dandy wondered if it was not so much for the sake of cleanliness as to cool down feelings her morning reading might've aroused.

"What's for breakfast, Da?" asked Thomas.

"Whatever's left in the hamper, son, washed down with cold, fresh water from the stream. After that, we'll help Katie get those bedrooms upstairs cleaned. Don't want to spend another night on the hard kitchen floor, do we now, Kate?" He offered her a roguish grin and a wink.

"C-certainly not, Daniel," Katherine agreed, rosy-cheeked. "I . . . will welcome your assistance. The children's as well, of course."

"Of course!"

They set about cleaning and airing the two tiny dormer bedrooms, and even Celia helped, once she'd been shown how to shake and punch fluffiness back into feather pillows. Thomas swept floors with such vigor that small dust tornadoes rose up around him. Then he and his father hauled mattresses outside for a good going over with the rug beater.

Katherine made a thorough search in both rooms for enough linens for the double bed she was to share with her husband and the single bed with trundle in the smaller room for the children. She found a veritable treasure trove besides the required bedding: colorful patchwork quilts, embroidered tablecloths, tea towels and pillow shams, and seasonal clothing—both men's and women's—to remake as garments for them all.

She shook out a serviceable linsey-woolsey Mother Hubbard in a deep blue with self collar and cuffs. Jumping to her feet, Katherine held it up to her shoulders, finding the garment just cleared the toes of her shoes, for which she blessed Providence. The shapeless, waistless dress, along with a generously sized bibbed apron in a rose calico, meant an immediate change of clothing for her. At last her husband would see her in something besides the unrelenting black. She felt as giddy as a schoolgirl with pleasure at the thought. Throwing caution to the wind, Katherine closed the bedroom door and quickly stripped down to her underthings, slipping into the Mother Hubbard, topping it with the brightly flowered apron. Lifting her braided hair, she draped it over one shoulder to button the two collar buttons at her nape.

"Why's the door shut? Open up, Kate, this blasted mattress is heavy." A muted thudding indicated Dandy kicked at the door with one moccasined foot.

"There, the door is open. No need to stir up such a ruckus, Daniel."

Katherine swung the door wide and admitted her husband struggling single-handedly under the weight of their double mattress. He staggered past her without notice, throwing his burden down upon protesting springs. Swiveling toward her, he immediately pursed his lips in a slow, appreciative whistle.

"D-danged if you don't look all fresh and pretty, Katie," he declared heartily. "That blue turns your gray eyes the color of a summer sky."

She flushed crimson at the praise, her heart fluttering with pleasure. "Why—why thank you. I—I found the dress, and many other things as well, while searching for bedding."

"Anythin' for the rest of us?" He held the fabric of his shirt away from him, declaring, "It'd sure be good to get out of these duds. They're about ready to stand alone."

"I—I am sorry, no. There's nothing for you or the children, I am afraid, until I can do some alterations." Her voice turned prim, for a sudden vision had come to her of Dandy stripped of his soiled clothing to bathe . . . or to bed his bride. Their bedroom became hot and crowded and much too stuffy. Panic rose in her throat, and she wanted nothing more than to be alone until her treacherous thoughts were once again in hand. "In the meantime, perhaps you could bring up the other mattresses? We might possibly finish this chore before noon so we can give our attention to searching out foodstuffs now that the hamper is empty."

Bewildered, Dandy watched her expression change from pleasure to irritation. Now what had he said or done to get her dander up? Maybe he should've mentioned how her bright and flowered clothes made her appear younger, her figure softer. Probably should've told her that her hair, braided in that rich honey coil over her shoulder, gave her the look of a woman meant to be loved. But, hell, he wasn't about to share his thoughts with her now she'd gone all prim and prune-faced on him. Again.

"Whatever you say, *Mrs. MacCabe.*" He gave her a mock salute and strode furiously out of the room.

Katherine sat down hard on the edge of the bed, wrapping her arms around herself at the waist, fervently wishing she could take back her sharp words. Why was it always her way to say the wrong thing, some tart and prissy thing, whenever she was distressed or frightened? Why must they always quarrel? She rested one hand on the mattress, fingering a worn spot on its ticking cover. Most importantly, what if he didn't want to bed her tonight?

It might just break her heart.

Near noon by the position of a golden sun in a cloudless, turquoise sky, Katherine paused, elbow-deep in sudsy water in a dishpan in the dry sink. She glanced for the hundredth time out the now sparkling panes of the window before her. And for the hundredth time her hands stilled in their labor, her attention shifting to the yard near the watering trough as she watched her husband chop much needed wood for the stove.

He'd tied his chestnut mane in a queue with a leather thong and placed a blue bandanna around his brow, now beaded with perspiration. As he continued his work, she watched him discard his flannel shirt, then strip the top half of his long johns down to a trim, narrow waist. His golden torso glistened, muscles rippling, knotting, and stretching under every blow of the ax, as with feet widespread he split log after log into manageable wedges.

Weak in the knees, her insides quivering with desire, Katherine could not force her gaze away though her wash water grew cold, and she fervently longed for bedtime, when, please Providence, he'd make her his own. Belatedly, guilt replaced desire, causing her to wonder if she should beg forgiveness for her abruptness earlier. But pride kept her from saying "I'm sorry."

At a safe distance, Thomas sat on a stump, watching his father with hero worship imprinted clearly on his face, occasionally laughing at something Dandy said. She heard snatches of song, sometimes Dandy alone, sometimes with Thomas, though she couldn't quite make out the tune. Were it not so obvious, she'd open the window to hear better.

Resolutely Katherine returned to her chore. Her stomach grumbled loudly with hunger, the meager meal of stale bread and cheese that morning no longer anything but a memory. She cast a guilty glance at Celia, who contentedly played on the floor beside her, making a pile of pots and pans. Was Celia as hungry as she was? If so, it was not readily apparent. No one at all had complained about the scanty breakfast rations. Still, the responsibility weighed heavily on Katherine's conscience, certain that Dandy, if not the children, blamed her as she did herself. Perhaps indeed she should have packed the book elsewhere. But nothing—and no one—could convince her that her little missive on social manners was unnecessary baggage.

Approaching voices alerted Katherine to Dandy's and Thomas's return, and with regret she noted her husband had slipped back into his clothing. Arms laden with kindling, the pair headed for the house, talking and laughing and singing snatches of song. As they reached the back stoop, Dandy pressed a warning finger to his lips, and Thomas clamped his own tightly together, nodding in silent agreement. They stepped through the doorway to deposit their loads in the woodbox, Dandy winking conspiratorially.

"Now, what are you two up to?" Katherine forced herself to ask lightly.

They spoke as one.

"We heard some chickens . . . might be eggs in the barn, Kate," said Dandy.

"Da made up a funny song."

"Song?"

"Eggs. Just think of it, Katherine." Dandy quickly attempted to distract her, using the name she preferred. "Fried eggs and scrambled eggs and—"

"I want mine over easy, Da—"

"And so you shall have them, son, if we can manage. I'll go see how many I can find for you to cook up, Kate."

"But, Daniel . . ." She paused, and he turned from the open back door. "I cannot cook."

"Can't cook?" he repeated, incredulous.

Ashamed, she could only bite her lip and shake her head.

"You clean house well enough. Didn't Hannah teach y—"

"She did not, but there is little to learn about cleaning. If something becomes soiled, one uses soap and water." She shrugged eloquently, sniffing back the urge to cry. How was it tears had not come easily through the loss of her parents, her income, and her fiancé, but flowed so readily over mere trifles in the presence of this man?

Wishing he dared pull her into his arms, knowing he did not, Dandy smiled encouragement. "It's nothin' to shed tears about, Katie."

"I am not—"

"If there are eggs to be had, I'll cook them myself. Took my turn as cookie—that's cook's helper—when I was a greenhorn in camp, same as many another shanty boy. I'll teach you all I know. It's easy, Kate, you'll see. Come along, Thomas, help me look. We'll be back in two shakes. Scare up a clean skillet, will you, Katie?"

Soon they were back, Dandy with a folded gunnysack cradled against his stomach containing more eggs than Katherine could count at a glance, and Thomas with tales to tell of chickens gone wild.

Raising a single brow, Katherine asked Dandy, "Wild chickens?"

He shrugged. "Just rambunctious. Likely haven't had much human contact for a while . . . the younger ones maybe never. Then there's an old rooster, thinks he owns the place. Can't blame him, he's had the run of the barn and his brood for years. But there's a dozen or more good layers, and some old biddies about ready for the stewpot. We won't be goin' hungry, Kate, for quite some time."

Broken into a frying pan with a scant inch of boiling water since there was no bacon fat or butter, the eggs appeared more poached than fried. Without salt and pepper, the meal tasted decidedly bland, but Katherine and the others relished each and every morsel of their portions. Dandy rocked back on two chair legs, rubbing his full stomach and sighing appreciatively.

"A man never knows how good food can taste until he's deprived of it for a time. Right, Kate?"

Immediately Katherine bristled. "Do you intend to bring up my having given valuable food space to my book forever, Daniel?"

"I didn't say—"

"But you were thinking—"

"Now, Katie, I—"

"Don't you 'now, Katie' me. I will not have you—"

Thomas clapped his hands and chortled, "Just like the song you made up, Da, just like your song . . ."

He kept repeating the phrase though his father tried to hush him. Katherine turned on the boy, demanding, "For goodness' sake, Thomas, what song?"

Thomas looked from one adult to the other, suddenly afraid this wasn't the joke he had thought it to be.

Sparing the boy further distress, Katherine turned on his father, her pale eyes snapping icy sparks.

"Tell me about this song you composed. Does it happen to refer to me? Perhaps you should sing—"

"It's nothin', Katie. Just a little nonsense rhyme I thought up to amuse the lad and make our work go faster . . . I— I've forgotten the words," stammered Dandy, flushing hotly.

"I know, Da. I know." Earnestly eager to rectify whatever wrong he'd done, Thomas cleared his throat in preparation.

"Never mind, never mind, son. It just came back to me. Let the punishment fit the crime. 'Tis my foolish song," he

told Katherine, "and more the fool I'll be taken for after
you hear it. Remember now, Katie, you asked for this." As
Thomas had done, Dandy cleared his throat and rendered
the sprightly tune and silly words with more zest as he proceeded.

> "Katie did,
> Katie didn't,
> Katie could,
> But she won't."

> "Katie, Katie, Katie,
> Won't you smile at me?
> Katie could if she wanted to,
> But she doesn't, *so she won't!*"

His song rang to a resounding finish.

"See, Da," cried Thomas, clapping, "you did remember.
Every word."

"By the Saints, of all times to be havin' a good memory." Dandy rolled his eyes ceilingward. He hazarded a
brief glance at his inscrutable wife, guilt etched on every
feature of his face, before grabbing his son up off his feet
and hauling the child and himself outside at a run.

"Daniel . . . Thomas . . . *Mr. MacCabe.* You—you come
back and—and—face the music."

But the pair was long gone. When Katherine realized the
folly in her own words, she slumped back into her chair,
crossed her hands over her mouth, and rocked in silent
laughter.

No matter how exasperating he was at times, no one else
amused her as her husband did.

Somewhat surprised at that self-revelation, Katherine rose
to resume her chores, still smiling.

9

Katherine tackled the topmost cupboards last, standing on the sturdiest of the four kitchen chairs. She discovered several platters and an enormous mixing bowl, likely used only seasonally, and placed each carefully on the counter below for washing. Scrubbing the painted shelf with hot, soapy water, followed by a thorough rinsing, she continued thus from one cupboard to the next, dividing her attention between her work and her young charge.

Celia had found a sunbeam under the west-facing window, well out of the way. She sat cross-legged on the linoleum, quietly twirling the curl at her cheek into a corkscrew, two fingers in her mouth, giving Katherine her undivided attention. Katherine was grateful that, whatever the little girl's handicap, she managed so easily to entertain herself.

The last high shelf held an assortment of heavy, wide-mouthed pottery crocks, which Katherine set on the counter one by one, relieved the first part of her chore neared completion. She'd be laboring hours longer washing everything and putting it back, but the effort was worth it. By tomorrow the kitchen would be as clean as soap and water could make it, and she'd move on to another room, and then another, until the entire house gleamed. A sense of satisfaction swelled within her unlike any she had previously experienced at the thought of the house, her home, restored to its former habitable appearance.

Celia left her puddle of sunshine and came to sit on the floor below Katherine, pulling the pots she'd played with earlier out of a lower cupboard, stacking them into an unsteady tower, as before.

"Celia, darling, please move out of the way."

The toddler ignored her request. Intent on unloading the last shelf, Katherine let her stay where she was.

She stretched precariously far out on one foot, reaching for the last crock shoved deep into a corner. The crock, though small, proved the heaviest of the lot, far too heavy for a soapy, one-handed grip. Katherine felt it slipping, and watched with helpless horror as the crock tumbled out of her grasp and began its descent toward the little girl directly below.

"Celia . . . look out!" she screamed. No response. "Ceee-liaaa!"

Dandy heard her scream, louder than any banshee, all the way from the barn. After a heart-stopping second, he took off for the house at a gallop, bursting through the back door, sending it slamming against the wall.

Katherine stood in the center of the small kitchen, shaking like a leaf, Celia crushed in her arms, her face buried in the child's curls. Around her lay a toppled chair, scattered pots and pans, and shattered pottery—evidence of some calamitous accident. He felt the color drain from his face, certain his baby had sustained serious injury or worse.

"Kate, by the Saints . . ." Anguish choked off his words. He tried again. "Katie, how . . . bad is it? . . . Is she—" The dreaded question wouldn't come. If he didn't ask, it wouldn't be true. Dandy wrapped his hands over the back of the nearest chair, bracing for whatever was to come.

His wife turned, lifting a tear-stained face to him, her cheeks red-splotched, her gray eyes awash with emotion. Her gaze focused, recognizing him at last. "Daniel . . . Oh, my . . . No! Merciful heaven, it is not what you are thinking.

Thank Providence, Celia is uninjured, only frightened.''

He went limp with relief, releasing the back of the chair to run one shaky hand through his hair. With a wave of the other hand, he encompassed the scene of disaster.

''What—what happened?'' Singling out the toppled chair, he asked belatedly, ''You didn't fall? You're all right, aren't you, Katie?''

''Me? Oh, oh, yes . . . I must have knocked over the chair in my haste to reach Celia. The crock slipped.'' She stumbled over her explanation, unsure herself of the sequence of events. ''It narrowly missed her. I screamed—''

''That you did, Kate, loud enough to wake the dead.'' Dandy drew an unsteady breath. ''Scared ten years off my life.''

Tears welled again in her eyes. ''Daniel . . . *Celia* did not hear me. Nor did she hear the crock shatter directly behind her. She was unaware anything was amiss until I gathered her into my arms, so thoroughly shaken I frightened her into tears as well. Oh, Daniel, she did not hear me. Celia's not simple. The poor child is stone deaf.''

The news hit him hard, like a punch in the gut.

''Deaf? My sweet little one . . . deaf?''

Dandy took staggering steps around the table. Extending trembling arms, he enfolded his child into them, stroking her tousled golden curls with one hand, blinking back unmanly tears. He held Celia in his embrace until the child squirmed for release, then set her down well out of the way of the broken crockery. Stuffing still shaking hands into his pants pockets, Dandy exchanged stricken glances with his wife, then gazed upon his daughter, who had retreated to her sunbeam, to sit and somberly watch the adults with puzzled, questioning eyes.

''It would've been better for Celia to be simpleminded, Kate, than to be of normal intelligence and locked away in a world of silence all her life. Look at her watchin' us. She has no idea how near she came to injury . . . or . . . death.''

''Because of my carelessness,'' Katherine injected remorsefully, her tears gathering once again.

''No, Katie, no. 'Twas an accident, pure and simple.''

"Thank you, Daniel, for those kind words. I fear, though, that I was the victim of poor judgment, allowing Celia to play so dangerously close to where I was working. Had she sustained the slightest injury, I could not live with myself."

Dandy took her by the shoulders; she stared imploringly into his eyes, silently asking forgiveness. He pulled her briefly into his arms, planting a kiss on her forehead.

"Katie, you're only human," he said, his cheek resting on her fragrant, honey-colored crown. "It's a relief knowin' you're as apt to make mistakes as the rest of us." He set her away at arm's length, tipping her chin upward with one knuckle, serious and unsmiling. "If this hadn't happened, how long might it've been before we realized Celia cannot hear? How long might we have branded her an imbecile? Though it's no better knowin' the poor babe's deaf, at least now we do know." He let his hands fall away, turning from her to study his daughter sitting in the sunshine, her face lifted to the source of light and warmth. "Poor little lass. How could we have taken such a bright child for simple? I should have known. . . ." His words trailed off; self-recrimination played across his rugged features.

"What is done is done, and there is no going back," Katherine interrupted. "Thank Providence, we now know the truth of the matter and can do something about it." Seeing skepticism on his face, she added, "Daniel, she can learn."

"How?" he demanded bitterly.

"The same as any intelligent child." Katherine forced herself not to snap at his morose resistance. "By example. By repetition. I have read about deaf children—and adults as well—being taught some kind of gestures . . . hand signals representing words. There are even schools—"

"Special schools, I'll wager, costing money we don't have . . . *if* we could chance sending her to one, which we can't with Old Lady Stewart on our trail," Dandy cut in grimly.

"Then we will have to teach her ourselves," insisted Katherine.

She'd captured his attention. He swiveled on a heel to stare at her. "Ourselves?"

"Most certainly. Now that we know what Celia's problem really is, I am certain she will not be a difficult child to teach."

A smile brightened his face, gratitude and more lighting a glimmer in his chestnut eyes. "Kate, you're a wonder," he added quietly. "Thank you for—"

"Please do not offer me your thanks. It was only through a lucky happenstance I did not harm this precious child today, and I shall carry that guilt with me for a good long time. No, let me finish. I realized when I saw what had almost happened how deeply I had grown to care for her, and Thomas as well. Celia can learn, and we shall teach her. It is both our duty and our privilege to nurture such a special little girl."

He crossed the short distance between them, cupping her cheek with one large, callused hand. She felt the roughness and the heat in his touch, poignantly longing for more than words of gratitude from his lips, every fiber in her being ready to respond. With baited breath, she waited to hear what he'd say, discover what he might do.

The moment was lost with the thud of running footsteps as Thomas burst into the room from outside, red-cheeked and breathless. Guiltily Dandy and Katherine drew apart.

"Da, there's a whole mess of fish in the stream out back, can we go fishi . . . Hey, how come there's money all over the floor?"

Following his pointed finger, Katherine and Dandy recognized the soft metallic glint among the broken shards of crockery as coins, and a scattering of paper as bills. Dandy carefully knelt on one knee, scooping up change and gathering paper money while Katherine watched, hands clasped at her waist to still their trembling. Rising, he counted the total collection, then let out a whoop of joy.

"Daniel. Please. How much is there?"

He dumped the cash onto the chipped porcelain surface of the worktable. "Enough to buy much needed food and supplies . . . and seed to plant spring crops, Katie. Must've been Ol' Charlie's nest egg . . . and damn . . . dang lucky you found it, too. Looks like some good has come our way this day after all.''

''Indeed so,'' agreed Katherine exuberantly. ''I do believe this to be a sign of—''

The sounds of wagon wheels and hooves upon gravel, harnesses creaking and jingling, interrupted her words.

''Hello the house!'' called an unfamiliar male voice.

Katherine turned suddenly fear-filled eyes toward her husband, who put a finger to his lips, warning both her and Thomas to be still. She looked questioningly at him, and he shrugged.

''Hello,'' came the call again. ''Anybody home?'' The wagon groaned as someone descended. The visitor headed for the back porch, hesitated, then climbed the two steps to the wide-flung door.

With no time to slam the door and lock it, they waited to see who the intruder might be and what threat he might pose.

''Hello, there.'' A pleasant-looking young man with non-descript features under a thatch of sun-bleached hair, dressed in the coveralls and work boots of a farmer, offered a wide, toothy grin. ''I'm your neighbor, Allen Weatherby. Saw the smoke from your chimney over the tops of the trees and told Martha, my wife, we finally got someone living at the old Martin place. Thought I'd just come over to say welcome.'' His voice trailed off, his gaze going to the pile of money on the table. ''Hope I'm not interrupting something important.''

Katherine watched Dandy's broad chest heave in a sigh of relief, imitating the action as well. Her husband smiled, striding forward, offering his hand.

''Come in, come in, neighbor. We were . . . er . . . just plannin' how best to spend our seed money.'' Seeing the man's gaze go to the broken pottery and overturned chair, he hastily added, ''My wife here dropped a crock and knocked over the chair tryin' to catch it, but too late . . . as you can plainly see. Katherine, come meet our neighbor, Mr. . . . ah—''

"Weatherby, ma'am, but call me Allen." The man extended his hand, taking her offered one into his thick-fingered, work-toughened paw, shaking vigorously. "Martha will be happy to know there's another woman so close by." Turning to Dandy without a pause in breath, he said, "What crop you planning to put in, Mr.—"

"MacCabe . . . Dand . . . Daniel MacCabe." For reasons unknown to himself, his nickname seemed out of place with the start of a new life here on the farm. "What's best to plant? What're you growin', Mr. Weatherby . . . Allen?"

"Soon be putting in corn and beans. I'd suggest you plant the same, though you're getting a late start." Allen shook his head. "Those fields of yours are going to take a heap of cultivating to make workable, Daniel. Be glad to help any way I can . . . me and my family. Say, how about we come on over with our plows and teams early Saturday? Might be we'd have your fields ready by evening if we all work together—"

"Thank you kindly for the offer, but it's too much to ask of you and yours, seein' we're strangers and all—"

"Not strangers, neighbors. What're neighbors for if not to help one another when needed? What condition's your plow in, neighbor? Likely Ol' Charlie neglected it some, and about everything else, those last couple of years. I know he was feeling poorly. Never did get over Nettie's passing. Let's go on out to the barn and have a look-see. Nice to meet you, Mrs. MacCabe."

Before Katherine realized what had happened, their persuasive young neighbor had led Dandy out the door, Thomas trailing, and on across the sodden yard toward the barn. Katherine watched until the small group disappeared into the sagging structure. Uncomfortable with the proprietary way their neighbor had taken over, Katherine lifted her skirts and, kneeling, began to gather broken crockery into the apron tied around her waist. In her opinion, Allen Weatherby took much too much upon himself. There were several obvious breaches in his conduct she'd noticed, and probably several others were she to refer to *Our Deportment*. Perhaps she had better suggest to Daniel—

''Katherine. Katie. Come on outside to say good-bye. Allen's headin' for home now.''

She went to the open back door to find the two men lifting a large, rusted plow into the back of Allen's wagon. Seeing her there, Dandy grinned.

''Allen's good enough to take this back to his place for cleanin' up and sharpenin', Kate.''

''Oh, Daniel, we should not ask Mr. Weatherby—''

''Allen,'' the cheerful young man corrected. ''And you're not asking, I'm volunteering, Kate.''

He climbed onto the seat and gathered the reins into his hands. Before Katherine could correct his use of the diminutive of her name, his words rolled on.

''I'll be back bright and early Saturday morning with my wife, my brothers and brother-in-law, and any others who'd care to tag along. We'll have those fields of yours ready for seeding in no time flat.''

With words of protest on her lips, Katherine could only bite them back in view of Allen Weatherby's cheerful persistence. Dandy offered the young man his hand, and after an attempt to thank him that was only bowled over by Allen's good-natured refusal to accept, he stepped away from the wagon to watch their newfound, self-appointed friend drive off. Dandy headed for the back door and Katherine, shaking his head, grinning his dimpled grin.

''Never saw anybody so eager to help, or anyone who could talk faster and longer than myself, Kate. But that Allen Weatherby's got me beat by a mile, and then some. 'Bout the friendliest fellow I've ever met, shanty boys included. Says he'll even send over a book he has on farmin' so I can read up before Saturday. Had to confess to him how little I knew. Said he'd help all he could 'til I could manage on my own. Real friendly fellow, isn't he, Katie?''

She hadn't the heart to say she found Allen Weatherby more than a little too friendly. With a sinking heart, she recalled he'd be returning Saturday with countless others in tow.

''How will we ever get the house ready for guests by Saturday? Daniel, it cannot be done.''

Dandy wrapped his arm around her shoulders, pulling her against his chest in a hug, pecking her cheek with a kiss.

"We'll do as much as we can, Katie. I told Allen how we found the place. He'll understand, and his family as well, if there's still a bit of dust in the corners when they arrive." He pecked her cheek again and released her to grab up his mackinaw, heading for the door. "Rest easy. Everythin'll work out, you'll see. Soon's I finish with the scrawny stewin' hen I was pluckin' when you screamed, I'll set the old biddy to cookin' with some of the wild onions and parsley I found sproutin' behind the barn. We'll feast tonight, Kate, and celebrate our new friend and good fortune."

And feast they did.

After supper, while Katherine washed and put away dinner dishes, Dandy hauled a wicker rocker in from the parlor. He dusted it well, shook out the cushions, and took up residence in its bountiful arms, comfortably close to the cookstove, a child on each knee. Celia snuggled contentedly against her father's chest.

Thomas begged, "Sing us a song, Da. A shanty-boy song. I like those the best."

Dandy looked from his son to his daughter, his insides tightening with profound sadness. How many times had he sung to the pair of them, told countless tall tales of Paul Bunyan and Irish fairies and leprechauns? Celia had not heard a one.

"I don't feel in the mood for singin' tonight, Thomas," he said sadly, stroking his little girl's tousled golden curls.

It broke Katherine's heart to see him suffer so—and her sorrow mirrored his own—but she could find no words to express the depth of her feelings, nor to ease his pain. If their marriage had been truly one of love and companionship instead of convenience, they would have sought solace in each other's arms. As it was not, they could not.

Quietly so as not to disturb the three in the rocker, Katherine disposed of the dishwater, then pulled a chair close to the lamp on the porcelain-topped table and picked up her mending. Since Allen Weatherby's departure, she'd worried over Saturday's visitors. Not only was the house not presentable, but, more importantly, she had nothing suitable to wear. The blue Mother Hubbard and apron she had on were much too . . . too common . . . for entertaining, and the black mourning dress too stained and damaged. So, while Dandy prepared supper, Katherine had gone through Nettie Martin's clothing once again, discovering a serviceable navy wool day dress she was certain could be altered to fit in time for the expected company.

"Tell us a story, then, Da . . . 'bout when you were a little boy far, far away," Thomas persisted.

"Thomas lad, what good are songs and stories your sister cannot hear?" his father demanded bitterly.

"Well, *I* can hear them." Thomas seemed not all that surprised or disturbed when Celia's deafness had been explained to him. "Besides, she likes them, too."

"Now how would you be knowin' that?" Dandy's voice rose in disbelief.

As if in answer to his question, Celia pressed her small hand hard against his chest to get his attention, then offered him a tentative smile, patting his bewhiskered cheek consolingly.

"She seems to have ways of understanding and communicating to which we have never before paid heed, Daniel," Katherine encouraged.

"So it would seem." He studied his child in wonder. "My little lass must be a most intelligent babe indeed to have managed as well as she has so far with no help from those around her." He kissed his daughter's forehead. "You're capable of a sight more'n we give you credit for, aren't you, sweetlin'?"

Celia gave him a huge, angelic smile, and reaching up both pudgy little arms, she pulled his face down for a smacking kiss on the cheek. She puckered her nose, rubbing her lips with one fist.

"So you say my whiskers prickle, do you?" Dandy asked conversationally, and laughed. "I'll have to be rememberin' to shave more frequently after this."

"A most excellent idea," Katherine said impulsively. "I

am sure there is quite a fine-looking gentleman under all that stubble.''

Her husband threw her a teasing, challenging glance. ''I had not thought you'd noticed, Kate. . . . Tell me more. What else attracts your attention about my person? I'm eager to know.''

Katherine found herself backed into a corner from which there seemed no retreat without embarrassment. Inspiration born of desperation brought to mind Thomas's earlier request.

''Perhaps, Daniel, you might favor us with a tale of your youth after all. You have such a natural affinity with your children—did you come from a large family?'' As an only child, Katherine had always felt the lack of sibling camaraderie. Nor had there been a plethora of aunts and uncles, grandparents and cousins, only herself and the Tillits when her parents were off on one of their many European travels.

Knowing full well that his wife attempted to sidetrack him, Dandy let himself be led away from a subject she apparently considered intimate enough to be dangerous.

''Ah, Katie, there isn't an Irishman or woman alive who doesn't cherish children above all else. As for myself, I come from a family of nine, me bein' somewhere in the middle. 'Twas narry a day I wasn't chasin' after the younger ones, or watchin' them while my mother was attendin' to some chore or another . . . at least 'til I grew big enough and strong enough to have chores of my own, tendin' the sheep or helpin' my da in the potato fields.''

''Then you know all about farming,'' Katherine said, much relieved.

Dandy laughed shortly. ''Sheep and potatoes aren't exactly corn and beans and chickens, Katie. Besides, I soon had my fill of farmin' on rocky hillsides and givin' all but a few pennies of the profits to English landlords. By the time I was eighteen I'd run away to America.''

Katherine's hopes crumbled. So her husband had no liking for farming. Where did that leave them all when their only income was to be earned off the land? What was to become of herself and the children when Dandy left for the logging camp come fall? The prospects were too disturbing to be examined, and Katherine forced such thoughts out of her mind.

"Tell us about Grandda an' Grandma an' the olden days, Da," Thomas encouraged. "Tell us about when they were children like Celia an' me an' almost starved to death in the Big Potato Fa-Famb-Fambin. Sing the potato song. I like those funny words."

"The words are Gaelic, Thomas, proud language of the emerald isle of Eire . . . and the song from those times you mentioned." Dandy's voice took on a singsong, storytelling quality, and his son settled down to listen.

"In those days the farmers raised mostly potatoes, and so their families *ate* mostly potatoes. Which gave them good strong teeth"—Dandy showed his own in a Cheshire grin— "and rosy cheeks," he said as he gently pinched Celia's pink one. "But, oh, how the children tired of potatoes . . .

> "*Pratai ar maidin, pratai um noin,
> 's da n-eireochainn i Meadhon oidhche,
> Pratai a gheobhainn!*

> "Potatoes at mornin', potatoes at noon,
> And if I were to rise at midnight,
> Potatoes I'd get."

Thomas grinned up at his da, who winked in return and ruffled his shaggy brown hair. Dandy's face sobered. Katherine listened quietly and did not interrupt.

"The famine swept across a land where many years and countless crops of potatoes had used up all the nourishment in the soil. Your grandda, whose name is Patrick by the way, was just a lad not much older than you, but he remembers roads clogged with people fleein' the land they never thought they'd vacate except in a pinewood box. Takin' only the clothes on their backs and maybe a single treasured memento, sometimes nothin' more'n a piece of whitewashed plaster broken from the outside wall of their home to remember it by."

"Where were they goin'?" Thomas asked in a hushed voice.

Dandy shrugged. "Most had no place at all to go after bein' evicted from their farms. Hundreds—nay, millions—died, huddled in alleyways or in ditches by the roadside. Or if they lived, 'twas likely in a hole dug in the earth and roofed over with sticks and pieces of turf, survivin' on nettles and cabbage leaves."

"Yuckkk! Did Grandda Patrick starve, too?"

"He did not, as well you know since you've heard this story a hundred times over. Patrick was lucky. Even as a lad it was evident he had a special gift, *cogar i gcluais an chapaill* 'tis called—"

"Tamin' the fiercest wild horses no one else could. Right, Da?"

"In some secret, magical way, that's so. The English landlord his father worked for knew of this and kept Patrick's family on so Patrick could work for him—"

"An' when Grandma Bridget an' her family came along the road," interrupted Thomas, "Grandda Patrick's da felt sorry for 'em an' let 'em move right in with his family."

"Right you are, son. It was mighty lonesome with kith and kin dead or movin' on, and it was good to see neighborly faces. They begged them to stay."

"An' even though Grandda Patrick an' Grandma Bridget were just kids like me, Grandma Bridget was so pretty an' so nice, Grandda Patrick tol' her they were gettin' hitched as soon as they were old enough. An' they did."

"Ah, lad, you know the story well an' tell it almost better'n myself. As you know, they were wed when Patrick was eighteen and Bridget sixteen, and in two years time your uncle Michael was born, then Ian and Mary and—"

"An' when you grew up, you came here to be a shanty boy an' marry Mama. An' then me an' Celia was borned," finished Thomas triumphantly.

"Aye, *Gonadh e sin mo sgeal-sa go nuige sin*—and that is my tale up to now."

"Tell us about the lep-lepre—the little people. Or why there are no snakes in—in—"

''Eire. Another time, Thomas, another time. Celia's sound asleep, and so should you be.''

Tired from his day of work, play, and exploration, the boy made no protest, but followed his father as he carried Celia out of the kitchen and up the steep stairs to their bedroom.

Katherine sat with her sewing neglected before her, pondering the story just told, gaining a clearer picture of Daniel MacCabe from the tale of his ancestry and youth. His had been a lifetime of hard work and hardship, both in the old country and the new. Adversity had honed him into the man he was today, strong and resilient, yet warmhearted and optimistic. Such a man was a prize of a husband any woman would desire. In spite of herself, desire him she did. Later, in bed, had she the courage, she would show him how much.

10

So lost in thought was his wife, she didn't hear the swish of the swinging door opening, then closing behind him. Dandy took the greatest of pleasure in watching Katherine when she was unaware of his presence, for then she let down her guard, no more the proper lady of the manor—cool and distant—but all woman, warm and desirable. And his.

Instead of laboring diligently over her sewing as she had throughout his storytelling, now she sat with her hands spread flat across the dark blue fabric, her chin tipped upward, her eyes unfocused with thoughts turned inward. A smudge of dirt followed the swell of her cheek, and faint shadows of weariness accentuated the pensive look in her expressive gray eyes. The thick honey-brown braid lay precisely down the center of her spine. Dandy smiled to himself. He bet she'd be darned annoyed to know stray wisps stuck out in all directions from the evenly spaced twists plaited by her delicate, yet oh-so-competent hands.

It amazed him to see how quickly and skillfully she'd managed to set the kitchen to rights, going by instinct apparently since she confessed Hannah Tillit had taught her so little. Though out of her element from the moment she left her fine, fancy mansion, Kate had rallied like a champion. She'd traveled through four miserable, rain-soaked days without complaint. She unhesitatingly tackled the filth-iest house a body could imagine. She'd willingly embraced his children as his own—in spite of Celia's problems. She tolerated a rowdy shanty-boy husband, totally unsuited to her dainty, well-bred self. As much the lady in homespun and calico as silk and satin, Kate was a wonder, all right, and damn lucky he was to have her for his bride.

Dandy walked silently across the room on moccasined feet and sank into the rocker to the protest of creaking wicker. Kate glanced his way, a startled doe look in her eyes. Her features relaxed for just an instant at the sight of him, then almost immediately tensed, her gaze sliding guilt-ily back to the sewing she quickly resumed working upon.

Was it having been caught idling that put that look on her face, or something she'd been thinking when he came in? Maybe something concerning himself—an intriguing thought he wished he dared voice.

Figuring she'd never answer him anyway should he ask, Dandy reached for the dulcimer lying on the floor beside him and began stroking its strings the way he longed to stroke his wife's soft, pliant flesh. Desire so keen it pierced his heart like a knife blade all but drove away the lust in his loins and gave the unfinished tune of his own creation a haunting, melancholy air.

Katherine lifted her head, tilting it at an angle, the better to listen, recalling that he'd claimed this particular melody for his own.

"Your tune is so lovely," she said after a few moments. "You should put words to it."

He answered over his strumming, "Can't seem to find the ones to fit."

"I don't recall it sounding quite so . . . sad before."

"Then it's happier songs I'll be playin', Katie," he as-sured her with false joviality.

Picking a livelier rhythm, he played through several fa-miliar songs, humming along with some, singing a phrase or two to others, his heart not really in his music.

Katherine listened as she sewed, finally setting aside her handwork to lift her shoulders in a shrug and rub the back of her neck with massaging fingers. Holding up the altered dress, she shook out its voluminous folds.

"At least I shall appear presentable though nothing else does," she commented with a certain amount of self-satisfaction.

"As I told you before, no one's expectin' everythin' to be perfect, Kate, or us to be all duded up. They're comin' here to help with the work, not take tea." Dandy's tone mirrored a growing irritation.

Katherine replied in kind. "One *cannot* be too presentable for any given social occasion, Mr. MacCabe." Fearing he intended to argue the point, she reached into her apron pocket for *Our Deportment,* adeptly thumbing through the pages to the proper section. Finding the passage she desired, Katherine cleared her throat in preparation.

Dandy groaned and grimaced.

She gave him scarcely a glance, but her one eyebrow rose in skepticism. "There is valuable information between the covers of this little volume, Daniel, information from which both you and I—and certainly that—that—uncouth Allen Weatherby could derive benefit."

With great care, Dandy set his dulcimer out of harm's way; with equal caution he rose.

"What the hell has Allen got to do with any of this, Kate?" he asked evenly.

Profanity aside, her husband's rigid self-control bore an ominous air. Still, if he was willing to listen, Katherine felt she should press her advantage before the moment was lost.

"Mr. Weatherby is a perfect example of how one must not conduct one's self upon first acquaintance, of course. To arrive unannounced—sweaty and soiled straight from work—to assume his welcome—"

"Kate—"

"Not to mention inviting himself and his entire family—"

"Kate—"

"Only listen to this . . ." She ran her finger halfway down the page. " 'A person who pays a visit without invitation need not be surprised if he finds himself as unwelcome as he is unexpected—' "

"Katherine Augusta Bradshaw MacCabe," Dandy bellowed, ripping the book out of her hands, shaking the offending volume in her face. With sinking heart, Dandy realized she'd probably been looking through a dad-blamed deportment section and not the one on sexual love when he caught her at it this morning. Disappointment left a bitter, acrid taste in his mouth. "Damn your blasted book to hell, Katherine. When are you goin' to learn to rely on good old common sense instead of the meanderin's of some goldanged fancy-pants so-called authority? This damn book has become your—your Bible—"

Katherine jumped to her feet. "Daniel, that is blas—"

"You can't make a move without it—"

"There is a great deal of valuable information—"

"Information, my ass. Bunch of rules and regulations that don't have a blamed thing to do with real life. I've a good mind to get rid of this—this crack-brained hogwash—" he roared, taking two steps toward the glowing hot cookstove.

In horror, Katherine watched him hook the hot handle of the firebox door with the toe of his moccasin, wrenching it open.

"Daniel MacCabe, you wouldn't. You couldn't . . ."

But he could, and he did. Without hesitation, Dandy tossed the offending book into the fire. Tongues of flame wrapped around its blue cover, melting the gold lettering, curling white pages into black ash.

"Noooooo!" Katherine wailed. With a strength she did not know she possessed, Katherine shoved her husband aside and reached into the fire for her precious book.

Uttering an oath, Dandy grabbed her by the waist, hauling her bodily out of harm's way. "Dammit, Kate, you might've been burned."

"Like you burned my poor book?" she demanded furiously, pulling out of his grasp. "How—how could you do such a thing? How could you?" Her words trailed off in a dry sob; her body quivered with rage and hurt.

Dandy ran both hands through his forelock, suddenly as appalled as she at what he'd just done.

"Katie, I can't say how sorry I am. Sometimes my hot Irish temper gets in the way of my good sense," he confessed, conscience-stricken and contrite. "Silly as that little book of yours was, it wasn't my place—"

Katherine's hands doubled into fists at her sides.

"Silly book?" she cried, her self-control shattering. "Silly book? You . . . you . . . mannerless barbarian. What would you know of the importance of the rules of deportment contained in that little book? How dare you deprive me of my most valuable tool for survival in this wild, uncivilized . . ." She gasped for breath. "How could you do this to me . . . after all . . . after all we've been through together?" Afraid she could say no more without bursting into tears, Katherine pressed her lips together to still their quivering.

"Kate, I . . . I'm—"

"Don't . . . don't you speak to me," she whispered harshly. "There's nothing you can say in defense of your despicable act."

He reached out for her. "Now, Katie—"

"Don't touch me," Katherine warned, taking a backward step. "After what you've just done, don't you ever lay a hand on me again." Realizing the enormity of what she had just said, Katherine spun away, fleeing the kitchen for their bedroom overhead.

She reached the top of the stairs, the corset stays cutting into her ribs leaving her breathless. Hearing Dandy coming upward behind her, Katherine desperately flung herself into their room, slamming the door, barring it closed with a chair under the knob.

"Katie . . ." His voice was soft, persuasive. The doorknob rattled, but the door did not give. "Katie, let me in. We need to talk. Katie?"

Heavy fists pounded, shaking the door in its frame.

"Kate, you let me in . . . or else," Dandy warned.

Assured he could not enter, Katherine backed toward the bed until her knees touched the mattress, and sat. She could scarcely take in enough air; she gasped like a drowning person, and spots swam before her tearing eyes. A whimper came as if from afar, until she realized the sound came from her. With a shuddering sob, she pressed both hands to her lips, crying soundlessly.

Dandy had stopped calling to her through the door, but Katherine was uncertain whether or not he remained on the other side. If not, where was he now, and what was he up to?

Merciful heaven, how had this evening, so eagerly anticipated, gone so horribly wrong?

Tonight was to have been the beginning of something deeper, something uniquely special, between them. Tonight she would have given herself body and soul to her husband, and she believed he would have taken her willingly. Tonight they were to share the intimacy of a single bed for the first time, her nightgowned body pressing against the hard length of his possibly—probably—naked torso. The image had lingered in her thoughts, her fantasies, throughout the long, busy day; the anticipated bedtime reward of his touch through gossamer linen kept her going on when she thought she could not complete another chore. She'd imagined honeyed words in his seductive Irish brogue, or perhaps the magical, mystical Gaelic of which she had no understanding, but the mere sound of which sent shivers of delight shimmering through her. She'd imagined a wide, cajoling dimpled grin and laughing warm chestnut eyes—or eyes grown black with passion, only for her. Now her dreams, her fantasies, her desires, might never be fulfilled.

What was any book, even one as valued as her small volume on deportment, compared to the tentative kinship that had grown between them? Now what little companionship and understanding they'd gained in recent days lay shattered around them like so much broken crockery.

Bitter tears trickled from beneath shuttered lids and coursed unheeded down her cheeks, evidencing the powerful hurt in her heart. Though she had once believed being unmarried was the loneliest state in the world, now Katherine clearly understood that nothing in this world or any other was as lonely as a deep, seemingly unfordable chasm between husband and wife.

The squeak of boards shifting underfoot broke into her sad reverie. Then the silence, she was certain, of a listener at the door. When that silence became almost unbearable, she heard the quiet knock of knuckles on wood.

"Katherine?"

A long pause stretched between them. Another knock.

"Katherine? Let me in, Kate. Please?"

The plea in his voice tugged at her heart, but shame and self-recrimination held her to silence and immobility. She could hear his harsh breathing, assuring her of his continued presence, though he waited an interminable length of time before speaking again.

"Katie, I'll buy you another book—a whole shelf full— if it takes every last cent of Ol' Charlie's nest egg. I'm takin' Bess and headin' out for the nearest town right now so I'll be at the door waitin' when the shops open in the mornin'. Be back as soon as I can." His footsteps retreated toward the stairs.

Katherine flew across the room, tore the chair away from the knob, and flung the door wide.

"Daniel Sean MacCabe, don't you dare do anything so foolish with the only money we have in this world," she cried.

At the head of the stairs, he paused and turned, his face, his very stance, displaying a wretchedness as keen as her own.

"What would you have me do, then, Kate, to make amends for the terrible thing I've done?"

Her reply came at a whisper. "Only stay, that we may put right this rift between us."

In two strides he reached her. He enfolded her in his arms, pressing her cheek to his hammering chest, laying his own atop her silky crown.

"Buying you a new book would've been worth every penny we have to our name had it gained me your forgiveness. 'Twas unpardonable of me to have so heedlessly destroyed your most cherished possession, Katie, and for that I am truly sorry."

Katherine spread her hands against the flannel of his shirt

and reluctantly pushed away from his comforting embrace to look into his face. The light had gone out of his eyes, leaving them dark with self-condemnation.

"I am sorry as well," she granted softly, "for making it appear I valued a book on manners over all else." She spoke the truth. *Our Deportment* was but a book, not a living thing. With acknowledgment came release so profound that she felt as if a physical weight had been lifted from her shoulders.

His large hands came up to cup her cheeks, his eyes searching hers. Bending, he brushed her lips with his. When she offered no resistance, and instead welcomed him, his kiss deepened. Her hands slid upward to his shoulders, then circled his neck, burying themselves in his lush russet curls. With a low groan, Dandy lifted Katherine into his arms and carried her into the room they had yet to share.

He held her so effortlessly, as if she were no more than a feather, Katherine marveled as she gloried in their intimate proximity. She felt the steady thud of his heart, the heat given off by his body; she breathed in the scents of wood smoke and the outdoors she always associated with this virile man. Now she also picked up the subtle, masculine musk that was his essence alone, and found it the most intriguing scent of all.

Just inside the doorway, Dandy paused. "Over this threshold you're officially my bride, Katie," he reminded her in all seriousness.

Katherine dipped her head, responding softly, "Yes, Daniel, I know."

"Is this what you want, too, Kate?" Dandy persisted. "I'll not force myself on you. Not now, not ever," he vowed.

A rosy flush spread over her cheeks, but her gaze never faltered, locked trustingly on his. "I . . . wish to be your wife . . . in . . . in every way."

"In every way? You're sure?"

Without hesitation, Katherine nodded.

Dandy crossed the small room in two strides with Katherine in his arms. Placing his wife gently on the mattress, he pressed his bride back against the pillow, sitting beside her, one leg cocked, his thigh snug against her hip. His gaze locked on her dove-gray eyes grown smoky, his own dark with desire. He dipped his head to touch his mouth to hers in another hungry kiss.

When at last he reluctantly withdrew to take a breath, he was rewarded with Kate's blissful sigh.

"Daniel, I—"

"Katie—"

"I feel . . . I feel . . ." She searched unsuccessfully and tried once more. "I feel—"

"I know, Katie. I'm feelin' a number of things myself," he responded in a husky whisper.

He kissed her yet again, sensing a willing welcome in the slight parting of her lips. His questing tongue touched her teeth, prodding until she opened for him, gasping at the unfamiliar intrusion, but allowing the invasion without pulling away. He drank more deeply of her sweetness, his loins quickening when, to his surprise, she responded in kind, but tentatively, learning as they went along. If she continued mastering her studies so swiftly and so well, he feared the tension building at his core would explode before he had time to teach her more.

He dropped light kisses along her jaw, down to the pulse point in her throat. Her heart fluttered like a trapped bird beneath her soft skin. Dandy lifted his head to gaze into her eyes, searching for fear he did not find, discovering instead longing and need to match his own.

His hand slid under her braid to caress her neck; the other slipped beneath her waist, flicking the knot out of the bibbed apron she wore. She lay absolutely still as he freed her from the serviceable garment, tossing it away from him while releasing the two buttons of her Mother Hubbard at the nape. Again he paused, waiting for her assent. Finding it there in her steady gaze, he peeled her dress down from her shoulders to her waist, then beyond with a lift of one strong hand on her derriere. The dress slid free of her body to join the pink flowered apron on the floor.

Katherine's arms instinctively crossed high over her chemise, hands splayed protectively over her half-exposed breasts. Dandy caressed her upper arms to her elbows, his fingers closing around her wrists, gently tugging.

"There's nothin' to be modest about, sweetlin'. Before this night is over, I'm plannin' to see all this and much, much more."

"I . . . I find it . . . difficult to lie here before you in nothin but my . . . underpinnings. I have had no experience—"

Dandy held one of her hands in each of his, drawing the pair tightly against his chest. "Ah, Katie me love, I had not expected you had. 'Tis my privilege and my pleasure to be your first—and only—teacher. And 'tis well past time for lessons to begin in earnest."

Gently she resisted. "But, Daniel, how will I . . . please you if I do not know how?"

Dandy nuzzled her neck just below her left ear. "Only let me pleasure you for a while first, Katie, then I'll be informin' you of all you need to know about satisfyin' your husband."

Unhurriedly he unbuttoned her corset cover and released the metal hooks of the corset itself, exposing the soft swell of her breasts with only the fine lawn of her chemise between them. Dandy slid his hands upward over her ribs. He felt her take a deep breath and hold it.

"Relax, sweetlin'. There's a lass." As her chest rose and fell once again, Dandy's hands circled the fullness of her breasts, letting his thumbs roam over twin rosy tips already firm and taut against sheer fabric.

She moaned and arched.

"Patience, Katie . . . we've only just begun."

He pushed a wide lacy strap off her shoulder, the other hand continuing his exploration. When one snowy mound lay exposed, he bent to kiss its peak with lips and tongue, to tease with his teeth, to suckle.

"Oh . . . oh, Daniel."

Her cry of need echoed his own. *Slower,* he reminded himself. *Slower. For Katie.* This, her first experience in lovemaking, must prove to be an awakening she'd remember with fondness all her days, not the lusty pawing of an impatient husband. He sat away from her, his hands leaving only to seek the buttons on his shirt. Her hands followed his.

"Please . . . let me," she begged shyly.

Heart hammering, Katherine began working the buttons of his blue flannel shirt out of their holes one by one, as he had done with hers. She encountered his red woolen undershirt and freed its buttons as well. Her hands slipped beneath the layers of his clothing, making contact with the hard ripple of his massive chest, soft, springy hairs entangling her fingers. Her hands moved upward, each encountering a small, hard knob high up, and she prodded and massaged as her husband had done, to be rewarded with a prolonged groan. Instantly she retrieved her hands, locking them together high between her breasts.

"I've hurt you. Oh, Daniel, I'm sorry."

He caught her fists and brought them to his lips.

"No, Katie, no. 'Tis only a man in need you're hearin'. And it's you I'm so desperately needin'. Do—do you understand what I'm sayin', Kate? Do you know where all this is headin'?"

Her cheeks grew hot, but she nodded, her gaze never leaving his brown eyes, shadowed and dark with desire.

"Then be patient, my love, for we've got all night." He kissed her on each cheek, each temple, her chin.

"All night." Katherine sighed in ecstatic agreement, her hands following the contours of the corded column of his neck upward. Eagerly she pulled his head down for another deep kiss.

A drawn-out wail reached them through the wall between bedrooms. Jumbled words, half understood. "Noooo, noooo more . . . potatoooes . . . Hungry . . . Hungrrry . . ."

"Thomas—"

"Nightmare!"

They spoke as one, both immediately attempting to straighten their clothing. While Dandy fumbled with shirt buttons, Katherine somehow managed to scramble off the bed, retrieve her shapeless Mother Hubbard, and pull it on.

Still buttoning her dress in the back, she was out the door and across the tiny landing to the children's room before Dandy could follow.

Katherine made her way around Celia's trundle in the center of the room without stumbling, to sit on Thomas's bed and scoop the thrashing child into her arms, murmuring consoling words the child finally heard and comprehended. He fell silent and returned to deeper sleep without having really awakened.

From the doorway Dandy watched his wife soothe and comfort his son, marveling anew how easily mothering had come to a woman who, until recently, had spent next to no time at all in the presence of children. Kate gave to Thomas and Celia all the caring and affection their own mother would have given had she lived, and she gave unstintingly. It was obvious to all who had eyes to see that Katie loved his son and his daughter as her own. He need never fear for his offspring in her care.

And care for them she would one day in the not too distant future. Alone, here on the farm, she would be responsible for every aspect of their well-being when logging season rolled around in November. Praise be to the Saints, his bride had the fortitude to do whatever needed to be done.

Watching Kate perched on the bed beside his son, giving him much needed comfort, conjured up another similar scene. The image of a younger Thomas and a very pregnant Annie formed in his mind, and with that picture came a chill as cold as the ground poor Annie now rested in. He realized how close he'd almost come to condemning Katie to the same fate. Like Kate, Annie'd been a lady born, never meant to be left on her own to bear children and perform back-breaking labor day in and day out. A lady wasn't prepared for that kind of survival. Childbearing and never-ending hard work, as surely as consumption, had taken Annie's young life.

Now, God forgive him, he was about to make the same mistake again with Kate—bedding her, leaving her with his two kids and possibly another on the way, hiding out far removed from all she knew and understood. It'd be hard enough for a lady like Kate to manage his kids and the farm in his absence without endangering her health carrying his babe.

No! By all that's holy, I'll not let it be happenin' again, Dandy vowed. Though his new wife seemed to be made with stronger mettle, still he didn't dare take any chances. If he *never* bedded his bride, if Kate went to her grave at a ripe old age still a virgin, Dandy Dan MacCabe would not, could not, in good conscience allow Annie's fate be Katie's, too.

Katherine placed the boy back upon his pillows and covered him, rubbing his back for a few moments to assure herself he slept. Finally she rose to join her husband, a mere silhouette in the doorway. Following him into the hall, she closed the children's door all but a crack.

"Thomas is all right now, Daniel. Your story tonight set him to dreaming . . ." Her voice trailed off, sensing his withdrawal, a change in the man who had so very recently held her in his arms, promising to make love to her all night. His face wore a closed, shuttered look; his stance, with feet widespread, was stiff, unapproachable.

"Nightmares come to the boy sometimes," Dandy responded. "He's had them since he was little." He heard how cold he sounded, though all he really wanted to do was enfold her in his arms.

Katherine took an uncertain backward step.

"I am sorry. I should have let you go to him. I did not mean to intrude."

Dandy reached out both hands to grasp her shoulders, kneading them. "No, *I'm* sorry. It isn't that."

"Then *what?* What did I—"

"Nothin'." He gave her a small shake. "You've done nothin' wrong. It's me, Katie. I should never . . . I shouldn't have—" There was no course left to him but to tell her the truth. "Come back to our room. We have much to talk about."

The hope that had risen in Katherine's heart at his suggestion to return to the scene of their tentative lovemaking plummeted with his last words and grim expression. But once inside their private chamber, with the door firmly closed against intrusion, he stood in the center of the room on a braided rag rug, eyeing the rumpled quilt on their bed with an expression of keen regret.

"Daniel, please tell me what is wrong," she prodded softly. "You say I have done nothing, and yet you no longer seem to want to . . . to . . ." Embarrassment brought her words to a stumbling halt. Tears of bitter disappointment prickled behind her lowered lids; pain squeezed her heart with a crushing grip.

He took a step toward her. "No, Katie, no. Never think I don't want you." Resisting the urge to wrap his arms around her, he fisted them at his sides. "But even more I don't want you to suffer—ever—for anythin' that might happen should we—"

"What could possibly—"

"A baby—"

"A baby? Surely not the first time—"

"First time, second, or third, or any other of the countless times I'd be wantin' to bed you between now and sign-up in the fall . . . makes no difference, Kátie. I won't go off for a winter in the woods leavin' you in a family way."

The matter was settled in his mind, Katherine understood from his blunt words and determined expression. As sure as her husband was that he was correct in his thinking, Katherine was as certain there was nothing she could say or do to change his mind. And was he not right, after all? In her inexperience, the thought of an inopportune confinement with child had never entered her head. Now, the idea seemed both frightening and intriguing.

"Time for bed now, Kate. Another busy day ahead tomorrow." He left her to sit on the bed, bending to loosen his moccasins' hide straps crossing from ankle to knees.

Watching him undress proved far too provocative. Katherine found herself growing uncomfortably warm in spite of her resolve to comply with her husband's decision, difficult though it might be—especially sharing his bed as a virgin.

For modesty's sake, Katherine quickly gathered her nightgown and sleeping corset and slipped behind the dressing screen in the far corner. Minutes later she emerged to find a bare-chested Dandy sitting up in bed, pillows at his back. In one hand he held a stiff-backed photograph, and he studied the image intently, his face sad. She did not have to see the picture to know whose it was, but somehow it had not occurred to her that he would carry with him the likeness of the first wife he had professed not to love.

Jealousy stabbed at Katherine's heart. Then she felt sorrow so deep she wanted to weep as she saw him grow aware of her presence and tuck the photograph out of sight beneath his covers.

Crawling in beside him, turning her back as she extinguished the lamp on the table beside her, Katherine mumbled a "good night" in response to his, but nothing more. No questions, no recriminations. What more was there to say? she thought wearily, hugging the edge of the mattress, her damp cheek buried in her pillow.

Though he had declared it not so, he loved his first wife, Annie after all, and still mourned her passing only a few short months ago.

How could she have expected him to feel otherwise?

How could she have dared hope—wish—he'd begun to care for her for herself? Was she not simply his children's care-giver, her marriage no more than a desperate, futile sham?

Any thoughts she might have had otherwise were nothing more than . . . than the fancies of a spinster's foolish heart. A foolish, broken heart.

11

From the back porch Katherine watched until Dandy and Thomas disappeared from sight, uttering a hasty prayer that the rickety wagon resurrected from the barn would take the pair safely to town for much needed supplies. Although they had most sensibly agreed not to appear in town as a family until they were certain it was safe, Katherine keenly regretted being left behind. She would not admit, even to herself, that the stillness and the isolation of the country made her city-bred soul more than a little uneasy, and that she loathed being separated from her husband of a mere two weeks even for a few short hours. His strong, steady, good-natured presence—though he might not love her—gave her cause to wonder how she had survived so long without him and his offspring.

At her side Celia clung to her skirt with the tenacity of a burr, two fingers of her right hand in her mouth. Katherine feared the child did not understand that her father and brother would return once their errands had been completed. Lifting Celia into her arms, she placed a comforting kiss on the little girl's warm, rosy cheek and gloried anew at the natural fit of the toddler's small body against the curves of her own, fighting mightily the desire Daniel had awakened in her to bear a child. Since last night she had thought of little else save the ecstasy of their brief intimacy, longing from the depths of her being for Daniel to take her to bed, liberate her from unwanted virginity, and plant his seed within her. No matter what the consequences—except giving birth here alone during one of his lengthy seasonal absences. The mere thought of that caused terror to explode in her chest. She felt an almost overwhelming regret that she might never give birth to a baby, hers and Daniel's.

Nor was the thought ever far from her mind that he had already fathered a daughter, with a woman he professed not to love, but obviously mourned sufficiently to carry her picture wherever he went, even into his marriage bed. Likely it mattered little to him whether or not she gave him offspring as well. Better all the way around if she did not. If only—

A reassured Celia squirmed to be let down, interrupting Katherine's musings, then ran into the house to play. Katherine lingered on the porch, basking in the gentle warmth of spring sunshine on her face until a movement in the distance caught her eye. A solitary figure approached on horseback. Fighting the constant fear that someone sent by the children's grandmother had discovered their whereabouts, Katherine watched the stranger ride into hailing distance, certain Daniel would never have permitted the man to pass him by and proceed to the house unattended had he perceived a threat. Forcing a small smile, she awaited her guest.

"Hello, Mrs. MacCabe. Good morning." He led his steed into the dooryard, dismounting at the back steps, offering a firm handshake. "Met your husband a ways back, and he said you'd be home. I'm Richard Wilder, Allen Weatherby's brother-in-law, delivering the book he promised Daniel."

Dressed in chambray and denim, he appeared to be a bit younger than herself, lean and well muscled, skin permanently tanned. Crisp brown curls framed superbly chiseled features bare of mustache, beard, or sideburns. A rakish scar bisected his left eyebrow, disappearing into the hair at his temple; his eyes, the same grayish-blue as his shirt, crinkled at the corners, indicating he found much to enjoy in life, and probably took it none too seriously.

Suddenly realizing she was staring at her guest, Katherine belatedly recalled her manners. "May I offer you a cool sip of water after your long ride, Mr. Wilder?"

He reached into a pouch draped over his saddle horn, producing the promised book. "Thanks, but no, ma'am, can't stay. Spring's a busy time on the farm. Allen'll be needing me to get back."

"Of course, I understand."

"Nice meeting you, though, Mrs. MacCabe, and Mr. MacCabe and your boy. Be seeing you at the plowing tomorrow." He handed her the book and remounted. With a friendly grin and a brief salute, he wheeled his horse and galloped off down the weedy, two-track lane, quickly disappearing behind a copse of budding maples.

Book in hand, Katherine entered the kitchen. More than a simple volume on farming, *The Home & Farm Manual* professed to be *A Pictorial Encyclopedia of Farm, Garden, Household, Architectural, Legal, Medical and Social Information.* Curious, Katherine flipped through the pages until she located the chapters under the heading "Deportment and Society." In modified form, every rule found in her own little volume seemed represented here as well, not irrevocably lost with the burning of her book after all. How odd that it no longer seemed to matter!

Thoughtfully setting the volume squarely in the center of the table for Daniel to find, Katherine picked up a pile of dustcloths and proceeded through the house to the parlor.

After the to-do she had made over something that no longer seemed of so great importance, perhaps it was wise not to mention to Daniel she had found the deportment section in the back of his borrowed book. The less said on the subject, ever again, the better.

Toward noon, Dandy and Thomas came into the kitchen with the first load of parcels from the wagon. Dandy had managed to buy everything on Kate's list and his own, and then some, including a book of poems for Kate. There'd been none on deportment to replace the one he'd burned. Quiet and remote since last night, obviously in need of cheering up, Kate accepted the peace offering in the spirit it was given.

He'd also been unable to resist an assortment of penny candy after watching Thomas's thin, serious face brighten at the sight of the row of candy jars atop one long counter in Wilder's General Store. The boy stood first before one, then another, mouth gaping, his tongue shaking across his upper lip as he focused his big-eyed gaze on licorice whips, horehounds, gumdrops, jawbreakers, chocolate babies, Gibraltars, lemon drops, cockles with their colored paper mottoes rolled up inside, zanzibars, strings of rock candy, and stick candy in assorted flavors. Impulsively Dandy asked the clerk behind the counter for ten . . . no, twenty cents worth, warning his son, "You divide those half and half with your sister, hear? One piece for now, and the rest given into Kate's safekeepin' so the pair of you won't end up with the bellyache."

Even now as they unloaded, Thomas worked a huge yellow jawbreaker from one cheek to the other, obviously relishing each sweet swallow. Little reward for a boy who'd taken on a man's job many a time when he himself was unavailable. What more could he give his son in repayment, with precious few pennies left after buying supplies? He preferred to leave him the legacy of a prosperous farm by the end of the season. If the sweat of his brow and the strain of his back bent in labor insured a future for Thomas and Celia safe from Mrs. Stewart's clutches, then for this one short summer he'd give his all to safeguard their security. And Kate's.

Praise be to the Saints he had not bedded her, though it had taken endless prayers and a midnight dip in an ice-cold stream to cool his aching need. It was his good fortune that Katie had turned out to be a warm and caring, purely desirable woman, but an unexpected pregnancy must not be risked with him heading for the woods in a few short months. Common sense told him abstinence was for the best, but danged if merely thinking of Katie and himself in bed together wasn't causing his loins to stir here and now.

Throughout the long, lonely night after Katie said her

abrupt "good night" and turned her back on him, and on the equally long and lonely journey to and from town without her, Dandy'd thought of little else but Kate . . . the touch of her pale, velvet skin, the clinging honey-gold of her silken hair wrapped around his fingers, the sweet, clean female scent of her love-warmed body pressed against him. He about drove himself crazy thinking of the woman he'd so reluctantly taken for his bride, and he wondered how he could've been so wrong about someone as he had been about Miss Katherine Augusta Bradshaw. If she had once seemed to be a spinsterish prude, rich and spoiled and ornamental, she was a different person now. With fortitude she'd taken on him and the kids; with courage she'd left behind all she knew and loved; with unflagging determination she worked to make a home for all of them from the rubble of his neglected farmstead, and never a word of complaint . . . well, maybe one or two, or, in truth, quite a few, Dandy amended with a remembering grin.

Spunky lass that she was, his wife seldom let him get away with anything, for certain. Ah, the fire in her might've lain banked all these years before their first meeting, but once stirred up, had burst full-blown into a most warming, sometimes blistering flame. Reserved and refined Kate might figure herself to be, but he knew better. The spark in her gray eyes, be it icy or melting, the lift of that one brow in question either playful or tart, the flush of her porcelain skin from embarrassment or pleasure . . . he knew the smallest indications of her humor, good or bad. He welcomed the pleasure of bringing her to life, even if he got her dander up.

He spied the book as he dropped the last of his packages on the table beside it, and rifled its pages from front to back. Just about everything he needed to know about farming lay between the covers—many a long night's reading. Dandy gave little attention to the recipes toward the end, but the section on manners hit him like a blunt ax between the eyes. *Damn!* He thought he'd gotten rid of all those everlasting rules and regulations when he burned Kate's book. Now here they were again. Wait until Kate saw this. He had a good mind to keep it from her, for his own peace of mind and the return of harmony between them. Still, Dandy felt uncomfortably guilty as he placed the volume in the crack between the cushion and chair arm of his favorite wicker rocker. Out of sight and out of mind . . . Kate's especially.

Saturday morning came around far too rapidly to Katherine's way of thinking. Long before the lone old rooster's crow, she crawled from the chaste bed she shared with her husband, quietly gathered up her things, and tiptoed downstairs. Stirring up the fire, she stood in her nightgown, slippers, and robe, a heavy woolen shawl pulled snug around her shoulders, waiting for water to heat for her morning's ablutions. And wishing this day would never dawn, though pink and magenta already streaked a blue-black sky.

"Looks like it's goin' to be warm and sunny, perfect for plowin', Katie. And for willin' neighbors to lend a helpin' hand," Dandy said behind Katherine.

Buttoning a red-plaid flannel shirt over long johns and new blue denim Levi's, he crossed to the stove to spread his hands toward the heat.

Uncomfortable in a state of undress, Katherine pulled her shawl more securely over her breasts, holding it closed with both hands. "How many may we expect to come, do you think?" Apprehension laced her words.

He inspected the coffeepot and, finding nothing but dregs, set about making a fresh batch, good and strong. "Maybe four or five men, as many women, and a half-dozen kids or so, accordin' to that brother-in-law of Allen's."

"Good gracious, have we enough food for so many?" responded Katherine, appalled. "Oh, Daniel, what am I to feed our guests when I have accomplished very little in the kitchen beyond boiling water and scrambling eggs?"

Distress put a quaver in her voice that Dandy couldn't miss. He set the coffeepot on the heat and lifted his hands to his wife's shoulders, squeezing gently. Compassionate chestnut eyes locked on hers.

"Don't worry yourself so, Katie. From what I've been told, Allen's womenfolk'll be bringin' enough victuals to

feed a small army, leavin' you nothin' to do but perform as
their gracious hostess . . . and we both know you're plenty
good at that.''

He offered her an encouraging grin, and Katherine found
herself reluctantly responding, though not completely reassured the problem was as easily solved as he'd like to think.

While Dandy went to wake Thomas and Celia, Katherine
completed a quick wash-up, slipping back into her robe to
scurry upstairs to dress. By the time she returned to the
kitchen, he had spread a hearty breakfast on the work-worn,
porcelain-topped table. Afterward Katherine washed the
dishes and tidied up, ever mindful of the dusty corners and
dirty windows she'd had no time to deal with as yet.

All too soon the visitors came. Three wagons overflowed
with plows and people, exuberant, energetic, noisy men,
women, and children. They poured from the wagons, children running off to play, adults moving toward the back
porch to make the new family's acquaintance.

Katherine tried to keep track of names as each person
greeted her and shook hands, and for the most part she succeeded, a social skill she had learned early on and of which
she was justifiably proud.

Allen's two brothers were easy to remember. Gabriel, the
oldest of the siblings, was a balding, huskier version with
Allen's contagious smile and a crushing handshake. William, the baby of the family, as he was jokingly introduced,
stood a head taller than any man there and bore a family
resemblance in features and mannerisms. Allen's two sisters
were brown-haired, blue-eyed twins, though an obviously
shy Amelia appeared a rather blurred imitation of the more
robust and vibrant Adelaide. Adelaide, with a heavily corseted, yet voluptuous hourglass figure, carried a newborn
infant in her arms. Uncovering his face for Katherine to see,
she proudly proclaimed the child to be her first son after
three daughters.

Cheerfully she added, ''You'll be meeting my girls later
on, when they tire of chasing after their cousins. Gabe's the
father of six—those four strapping lads over there with their
father, they'll be helping out in the fields, and the twins

Lally and Lucy. They're five, and as much a handful as 'Melia and I were at that age. That's my husband, Bert Morrison, there between Gabe and Allen. Oh, and here's Gabe's wife, 'Tilda.'' Adelaide indicated an enormously rotund woman headed toward them with a laundry basket heaped high and covered with a linen towel. "Come meet the new neighbor, 'Tilda. This here's—what's your name again, Mrs. MacCabe?''

"Katherine—''

"This here's Katherine, 'Tilda. What all did you bring? I've got some of them sweet pickles you favor left over from last fall's canning, and Gabe's favorite clover-leaf rolls, and—here, let me help you with that basket. Looks heavy . . .'' Still talking, Adelaide took one handle of 'Tilda's basket, the two women brushing past Katherine to enter the kitchen beyond. Uncertain whether to follow them or to greet the rest of the arrivals, Katherine hesitated.

A dry chuckle rattled at her side. "Leave it to my Adelaide to gabble on like a turkey hen. Not a'tall like my sweet 'Melia here, stayin' close to her mama's side.'' A gaunt, broad-shouldered, gray-haired woman, taller than Katherine by a head, greeted her, the sun-aged flesh of her nut-brown face cracking into a grin over stained, uneven teeth. "I'm 'Phrony Pearl Weatherby, Mrs. MacCabe, and pleased to meet ya. Never you mind Adelaide takin' over like she done. She's older'n 'Melia by five minutes an' come into the world thinkin' she was supposed to be in charge.''

"I—I am pleased to meet you, Mrs. Weatherby, and your family.''

"There's a passel of us, ain't there, girl?'' Her eyes, set deep in leathered skin, sparked with life. "An' always more a'comin'.'' With a nod she drew Katherine's attention to an obviously pregnant young woman clinging to Allen Weatherby's arm beside one of the wagons, her abdomen protruding under a loose-fitting Mother Hubbard and pinafore apron. Smooth, chocolate-brown hair, coiled at the nape, framed a pale oval face; brown eyes luminous with love raptly watched her husband speak with Dandy and the others. He in turn patted her hand occasionally as though the tender gesture had become second nature.

"Newlyweds," commented 'Phrony Pearl. "Married no more'n a year. Was Martha any heavier with child, folks might be puttin' their heads together an' talkin'." She chortled as Katherine flushed hotly.

Amelia, who until this time had gone virtually unacknowledged, gently prodded, "Mama, shall we join the others inside? Remember, the doctor said to keep off your feet as much as possible."

'Phrony Pearl Weatherby turned a loving gaze on her thoughtful daughter. "What the doc don't know won't hurt neither of us a mite, 'Melia. Still an' all, no sense lollygaggin' out here when all the good gossipin's goin' on inside. Find me a comfortable place to sit slap-dab in the middle of things, there's a good girl."

Katherine followed mother and daughter inside. 'Phrony Pearl moved slowly, each step taken carefully as if on eggshells. Amelia held her mother's elbow in a steadying grip, quickly locating Daniel's wicker rocker. Though the older Weatherby woman had first appeared both strong and hearty, now Katherine noted tight lines of pain around her mouth, and a certain grayness under the leathery tan of her skin. 'Phrony Pearl gingerly lowered herself into the chair with a death grip on the arms. Her hands were as knobbed and gnarled as old tree roots; her ankles, under the lift of her skirt as she sat, swollen twice normal size. Disease had robbed the feisty woman of mobility and usefulness in her prime. That the Weatherby matriarch maintained such good humor and cheerfulness in the face of such infirmity left Katherine in awe of her fortitude.

Realizing she was openly staring, Katherine quickly joined the ladies emptying their baskets onto her kitchen table. Baked ham, corned beef, and fried chicken, salads and casseroles, breads and rolls, pies and cakes and an abundance of cookies, covered the scarred porcelain surface, providing little room for any contribution Katherine might have made. Cheerful chatter flowed around the room like a gathering tide, comprised of recipe exchanges and tips on pickling and preserving. An unfamiliar sense of inadequacy threatened to overwhelm her. Katherine longed to slip off to her room upstairs and hide behind a bolted door.

"And what is your specialty, Mrs. MacCabe?" asked the rotund 'Tilda Weatherby, Gabriel's wife.

"Please call me Katherine," she stalled, locking her hands together at her waist. "I . . . I'm afraid . . . well, you see . . . I cannot cook." A hushed silence fell around her. Katherine stammered on in explanation. "The skill was not required until I recently wed Mr. MacCabe . . . But Daniel has been teaching me—"

"Jiminy Christopher, if that don't beat all," exclaimed 'Phrony Pearl, her seamed face crumpling in glee. "The husband teachin' the wife to cook. Now ain't that some-thin'?"

Katherine lifted her chin, clasping her hands more tightly together. "Meal preparation and household chores were not the skills imparted to me. However—"

"Now, don't go gettin' riled," 'Phrony Pearl interrupted bluntly from her wicker throne. "No one's meanin' to twit ya about not knowin' how to cook. Easy to tell just by lookin' that ya've been raised to decorate them high society doin's, not dirtyin' yer hands with work. We'll be pleased as punch to teach ya all ya need to know, Katie."

"That's Kath . . ." But what was the use? "I would cer-tainly appreciate the loan of a cookbook—"

"The best receipts come outta here." 'Phrony Pearl tapped her temple lightly with one crippled talon.

Allen's wife, Martha, came into the room after the men's departure to the fallow fields. "The book your husband bor-rowed has a fine section of recipes. I didn't know any more about cooking than you when we first got married. *The Home & Farm Manual* was my salvation."

She offered an open, friendly smile, neither teasing nor condemning, and something tight loosened within Kather-ine. She responded with a tentative smile of her own.

"Well, then, Kate, can you sew a straight seam?" asked Adelaide preemptorily. "We've all brought handwork to keep us busy 'til it's time to feed the menfolk."

Tension flowed away like melting ice. "If I say so myself,

I am an excellent needlewoman," Katherine assured her guests. "I altered this gown I found in a trunk upstairs." She held the now stylish skirt wide for inspection.

'Phrony Pearl snagged the hem and turned it inside out, exposing several inches of petticoat, squinting myopically.

"Mighty fine stitchin', Katie, mighty fine." Turning to her daughter, she added, "Give her some of them quiltin' scraps to piece, 'Melia. With Katie ahelpin' us, we'll have Martha's baby quilt ready in time for the birthin', which oughtta be 'bout anyday now, right, Martha?"

Martha cupped her belly with caressing hands. "I certainly hope so. Nine months seems such a long time, especially toward the end. If Junior gets any bigger, I'll burst."

"Might be twins, Martha. Run in the family, ya know."

Martha's ready smile faltered momentarily before she responded with forced joviality, "All the more to love, then, 'Phrony Pearl."

Katherine saw fear in the depths of Martha's brown eyes, and spared the girl by speaking up. "Shall we adjourn to the parlor, ladies? The light is much better there for handwork."

"Lead the way, Katie. We're right behind ya," responded 'Phrony Pearl, struggling up from her seat with Amelia's help.

As easily as that, Katherine was accepted into Allen Weatherby's extensive family. The women retired to the south-facing parlor. If anyone noticed dust bunnies under the sofa or windows so grimed over no shades need be drawn against the morning sunshine, nothing was said. Indeed, observing their expressions as they sewed and recounted the latest gossip of home and abroad, Katherine saw nothing but open and honest acceptance on their tanned and freckled faces. Relaxed and contented for the first time since—since possibly forever—in the company of other women, Katherine worked a square of the Dresden Plate-patterned quilt for Martha's baby.

Toward noon, the women spread horse blankets from the beds of the wagons upon the new green grass in the backyard, then set out food and the collection of mismatched dishes, glasses, and utensils each had brought from home. Children came flocking, then men and older boys with hair dripping and faces shiny from a washup at the stream. They sat cross-legged around the blankets and feasted.

Sandwiched between Martha and the quiet twin, Amelia, Katherine ate with relish until the constriction of her stays grew painful, her intake small compared to Martha, who sheepishly admitted to eating for at least two. Through conversation Katherine discovered she had much in common with Martha, whose father owned the local general store.

"We had a hired girl who came in days," Martha confided. "Mother felt our position in town required that I refrain from learning the basics of homemaking. Poor Allen, how he suffered through burned meals and dingy laundry until I happened to look in the back of his *Home & Farm Manual*. There's a treasure trove of information. You'll see."

Katherine offered profuse thanks. "I imagine Daniel and I will have to work out a schedule for the book's use." She would have said more had not Allen slipped an arm across his wife's shoulders to draw her into his embrace. Embarrassed by their casual intimacy, Katherine turned to her companion on the other side.

Amelia sat with her plate half full, nibbling unobtrusively on a chicken wing. She acknowledged Katherine's attention with a shy smile and returned to watching the children who had gone to play tag in the yard.

"Are any of them yours?" Katherine ventured, uncertain at this point which ones belonged to whom.

Two scarlet spots appeared on Amelia's cheeks, and she ducked her head. "Oh, no, I . . . I'm not married—"

"I did not mean to pry—"

"It's an understandable mistake . . . given my age . . . and with Adelaide . . ." Silence fell between them while Katherine searched her mind for a more acceptable topic of conversation.

Surprisingly Amelia broke the awkward silence. "Your daughter seems shy. I know how she feels." She nodded to where Celia sat in the shadow of a massive maple in the dooryard, watching a game of tag in progress, but making no move to participate.

Katherine's heart ached for the longing she saw on the child's face. "We have just discovered Celia cannot hear."

Compassion flushed Amelia's pale complexion. "Poor dear."

"I am hoping we will be able to teach her to communicate, but we have had no time."

Amelia bobbed her head thoughtfully. "I did some seamstress work for a family with a deaf child. There was a sign language they used . . . I learned a bit." Shyly she gestured. "This means 'hello' and this means 'friend.' " Uncomfortable with her sudden demonstrativeness, Amelia let her hands fall into her lap.

Hope swelled in Katherine's heart. "Does this family live nearby? Perhaps they could help us learn—"

Shaking her head, Amelia said, "I'm sorry, they moved some time ago." A sad smile crossed her lips and faded. "I . . . I know how she must feel, being unable to communicate with those around her, how different . . . and isolated." Her ivory cheeks went red again, and she bit her lower lip as if she'd said too much. Carefully returning her uneaten chicken to her plate, she scrambled to her feet, awkward with her skirt and petticoats. "I—I see Mama needs some help getting into the house. Please excuse me."

The men soon dispersed, and the women carried the food inside and washed dishes while 'Phrony Pearl regaled the ladies with stories of early farming days in Michigan, when clearing land meant not only watching out for rattlesnakes and timber wolves, but native "savages" as well.

"Oh, not the scalpin' kind like they have in the wild west, mind you, just the too friendly ones . . . thinkin' nothin' of borrowin' a cow or a few chickens an' not returnin' 'em . . . believin' as they do that nobody owns nothin' an' everythin' belongs to everyone." 'Phrony Pearl pulled out a cob pipe and lit up. She blew a smoke ring, watching it dissipate through slitted eyes, lost in memories of other times. She chuckled. "Once I 'member, some neighbors over yonder—man an' wife both—came tearin' up to the house shoutin' an' screamin' an' carryin' on. Seems the woman was hangin' out the wash, her babe beside her in a basket. She went in for another load an' when she come back outside, baby, basket an' all, was gone. Come to find out after a spell, some Indians—Ojibs, I think they was, maybe Ottawa—come upon the baby under the tree, wet an' hungry an' cryin' an' figured it was abandoned. Returned it, though, without no fuss once they realized it weren't . . . an' it was dry an' fed an' happy to boot—''

"Oh, Mother Weatherby, you're making that up," protested plump 'Tilda as she nibbled on her third piece of cake.

"Cross my heart, it's true," insisted 'Phrony Pearl seriously, but she winked at Katherine, causing Katherine to smile in response, warmed through by the easy camaraderie.

They sewed until the men came in from the newly plowed fields and it was time to serve up thick sandwiches, rich, dark coffee, and frothy, chilled milk. Later, under the trees and on the porch, tired workers, play-worn children, and self-satisfied matrons rested as if loath to call it a day and pack up for home. Dandy slipped into the house and came out again, dulcimer in hand. As was his custom, he fine-tuned with his nameless, wordless melody. Children clustered closer, flinging themselves down at his feet below his perch on the topmost back step, each begging for a favorite tune.

Dandy held up a silencing hand. "My favorite first. 'Tis called 'I Have Worked in the Woods' an' has been sung by shanty boys far and wide since lumberin' began on Maine's distant shores. An' when my song is done, we'll be seein' how many others there's time for." He strummed a few opening chords, then began to sing, mischief alive in his chestnut eyes and wide grin.

" 'I have worked in the woods ten years or more, and slept on a bunk or flat on the floor . . . ' '' The song wound its way through the logging season for a half-dozen short, toe-tapping verses to the end. " 'My songs they are short, but my stories are long. And when I can't tell one, they say somethin's wrong.' ''

Dandy's rich baritone rang to a resounding conclusion amid a burst of applause and a cry for more. Dandy sang requests until his voice began to break and the youngest of his audience had crawled up on a parent's lap to fall asleep. He played and sang "Down in the Valley," urging everyone to join in. Rich voices and rasping ones alike rose into the night sky. Then horses were hitched, wagons loaded, thanks given and received. Silence reigned as the last wagon disappeared around the bend in the road. As she held a sleeping Celia cradled in her arms, Katherine watched until there was nothing more to see. Dandy came up behind her, slipping his arm across her shoulders and giving them a squeeze. Thomas pressed his length against his da's long leg, his eyes heavy, face streaked and dirty, but content. They stood thus for a while, until finally Dandy broke the comfortable silence.

'' 'Twas a fine day all around, wasn't it, Katie?''

Katherine relived quickly the passing hours and answered honestly, "Yes, Daniel, extremely fine."

Silence settled once again, except for spring night sounds. Katherine leaned back contentedly in her husband's casual embrace. She felt the muscles of his arm grow taut, then relax. Dandy cleared his throat.

"Allen invited us to ride to church with him and Martha tomorrow."

"Oh?" She turned her head, the better to see his face.

"I said we would."

She pulled away, facing him. "Is it safe?"

His hand cupped her cheek. "Would I accept Allen's invitation if I didn't think we'd be safe, Katie?"

Katherine went still under his touch. "No, of course not. I am sorry."

His thumb rubbed gently along the soft swell to her jaw, the touch rough with calluses. His eyes, when she sought them, glowed dark with desire. As if seeing something in her steady stare he dared not respond to, Dandy let his hand fall away and took a backward step, taking the clinging, dozing Thomas with him to the boy's mumbled protest. Dandy ruffled the boy's shaggy head. Quiet reigned.

"We've made good friends today, Kate. We need to become part of the community, fit in. I figure church tomorrow is a good place to start."

"I wholeheartedly agree."

He threw her a dimpled grin. "Well, I never thought I'd be livin' to hear those words from ye, wife."

She returned his smile. "Nor I to say them, husband."

12

At the close of worship, people formed small, sociable groups outside, basking in the warmth of a Lord's day glorifying spring with blue skies and a caressing breeze fragrant with tilled earth and apple blossoms. Acting upon kindness and curiosity, one and all came forward, singly or in bunches, to make the newcomers' acquaintances and learn a bit more about the strangers in their midst. They came in an endless stream. Allen and Martha Weatherby would have liked to have protected the newcomers from the most plain-spoken folks, but that wasn't possible. Katherine found some of the boldest queries in questionable taste, though Dandy answered each with unfailing good humor and a wide, welcoming smile.

A burly fellow in a brown suit worn to a polish and too tight for his girth clapped Dandy on his shoulder, demanding, "You a drinkin' man, MacCabe? No bar in this town, but over in—"

"Not me. Can't handle the hard stuff. Gets me here." Dandy placed a hand over his belly. "Even the best Irish whiskey comes back up on me faster'n I can pour it down."

The man, who didn't give his name, wandered off shaking his head at the loss of a potential drinking buddy. Dandy and Katherine exchanged wry smiles. A grandmotherly sort with white hair, glasses, and a tart tongue asked Katherine how long she had been married and just how come a grown woman like herself never learned to cook. Katherine realized just how quickly gossip traveled here, and she longed for nothing more than to go home.

Home! After mere days, the tiny, run-down farmhouse seemed more her home than the grand one in which she'd lived the majority of her life. Until she became Mrs. Daniel Sean MacCabe, took his children as her own, and forsook all others to be with him and them. She felt more whole, and human, than she ever had in her solitary state. Startled by the truth, Katherine flashed a glance in her husband's direction and was rewarded with a wink.

"Not much longer and we can be headin' home." It was almost as if he had read her mind.

Not everyone proved to be caustic or blunt, or rude. Most who bade them welcome were quite sincerely warmhearted. The many Weatherbys found their way over for hellos and to lend moral support, including Richard Wilder, who drew Dandy aside when the last few stragglers had departed.

"Allen and I did some talking after we left your place last night. You're going to need an extra hand for a while, and I'm volunteering."

"But Allen needs you as well—"

"He's got his brother, William. You know, that tall drink of water over there." Richard pointed to Allen and some of his family near the church steps, conversing with Reverend Bates. Gangling young William Weatherby stood tall above the rest.

"I can't pay you. Everything went into supplies . . . and seed."

"I figure you're good for it 'til harvest. With as much acreage as we turned over yesterday, you ought to show a fine profit."

Graciously and gladly Dandy accepted the proffered help. At Katherine's elbow, Amelia, looking like a mourning dove or a shadow in a tailored gray suit and matching bonnet, quietly suggested, "Since Richard will be passing our place every day, maybe I could come with him and help out a bit, too. Free you the time to spend with Celia.'' Her doe-soft gaze never left Richard Wilder's face; the expression in her pale blue eyes shyly spoke of unrequited adoration for her handsome, personable brother-in-law.

Unhesitating, Katherine responded. "I would be most grateful if you could, Amelia. I seem to have my hands full simply trying to make our home habitable . . . much as I hate to delay teaching Celia now that we understand the nature of her problem. Richard, you will be able to bring her, will you not?''

Deep in conversation with Dandy, Richard merely offered a nod and a wave in agreement, oblivious to the importance Amelia gave to the arrangement. Her fair oval face flushed with anticipatory pleasure; and Katherine experienced her first taste of matchmaker's delight, thinking of the hours the single pair would spend alone together on the narrow bench seat of a wagon, traveling to and fro each day. She wondered how she might bring Richard's attention to the bashful young woman's many assets. Excitement built as she mulled over ways of throwing the two of them together at meal-times and with chores of her own concoction. Perhaps, in spite of the obvious differences in temperament, Richard and Amelia might discover common ground between them as she and Dandy had. Had she and Daniel not learned to get along rather well in spite of their inauspicious beginning? In her heart of hearts, Katherine knew now that without a doubt her life had been made better by her decision to marry the rough-hewn logger for his children's sake. She hoped and prayed he was beginning to feel the same.

Fortified with a hearty afternoon dinner largely comprised of dishes left behind by the generous Weatherbys, Katherine went in search of the book Martha promised would teach her how to cook. She had not seen the volume since depositing it on the kitchen table Friday morning. Now, while Daniel and the children were off fishing, was the perfect time to determine what she could learn on her own through the printed word and experimentation. If she could find the book. Finally locating it stuffed out of sight between cushions of Dandy's favorite rocker, Katherine had to ask herself if he had accidentally or purposely left it there. She suspected the latter, for she knew how he loathed her former dependency on rules of deportment.

Be that as it may, the time had come to learn to make herself useful in the kitchen. She settled in Dandy's rocker, staring at the lettering on the cover, willing herself the courage required to embark on this, her first solitary culinary venture.

"Damn, she found it," muttered Dandy, pausing at the open kitchen window. And double danged if she didn't turn right to the back. Couldn't stay away from her fancy rules and regulations to save her life. Plumb foolish of him to hope she'd learn to live without them, that her life here on the farm with him and the kids would be enough for her.

Bitterly disappointed and out of sorts, Dandy caught up the tin pail he'd forgotten and stalked off to the stream where he'd left Thomas and Celia, the fine spring Sunday spoiled for good and all.

The book fell open to a well-used page of bread recipes. Well, why not? They were in need of fresh bread daily. All things considered, how hard could making such a basic, simple food be? Katherine eagerly began to read the section on selecting the flour, thinking that her choice would not be difficult since the only kind available was the one her husband had brought home from his shopping trip to town.

Her forehead furrowed, Katherine continued her search for information on the finer points of bread-making, understanding that in cold weather the flour should not be allowed to become chilled—which seemed self-evident though she had never cooked before, yet scarcely believing the words she read admonishing her that the sponge should at all times be kept moderately warm.

"Sponge? That cannot be right . . . 'and the sponge should . . . ' Merciful heaven, surely a sponge cannot be an ingredient in bread-making." Incredulous, Katherine could only sit and ponder the imponderable. Discarding the idea of baking bread on her own, she flipped to the section devoted to cakes. There could not possibly be sponges in cake! Most certainly she'd be able to comprehend the complexities of cake-making far easier than those of bread.

"Ah, this is more like it." Katherine proceeded to read aloud. " 'General Rules for Making Cake. The ingredients must be of the best, for the best are most economical.' " Nothing at all about blue flour, white, or yellow. Nor—thank fortune—sponges.

Certain of success, Katherine rolled up her sleeves, washed her hands, and began setting out necessary ingredients, grateful to find all she required in the pantry. She proceeded without difficulty, even comprehending the concept of creaming sugar and butter, until she came to "beat the whites of four eggs."

Holding up one fat brown egg fresh from some willing hen, Katherine turned it slowly between her fingers, contemplating its contents. She had mastered the art of cracking open the shell under her husband's tutelage, and she smartly hit the egg upon the edge of a small bowl, letting the contents slide into the bottom. But now, how to get that round, yellow orb out of the clear, rather slimy substance surrounding it? She tried a spoon, and almost succeeded before the yolk slid back into the dish, breaking in the process.

Katherine stamped her foot, catching herself just short of uttering one of her husband's favorite expletives. Blowing a wisp of hair off her forehead, more determined than ever to succeed, she quickly decided it mattered little if white and yolk went together in the cake, and cracked three more into the bowl, with a nominal amount of shell, beating them into what she considered a "froth," whether or not it met with the definition in the book.

The batter reached almost to the rim of the pan she selected, thick and golden in appearance. Proudly anticipating Dandy's and the children's pleasure with the masterpiece she envisioned her cake would be once she frosted it, Katherine added a couple of logs to the firebox and slid her treasured concoction within the heated darkness of the oven. She felt positively smug with success.

Rather than stand over the stove worrying for the required hour's baking, it seemed more prudent to use the time upstairs, sorting through clothing designated for remodeling. As she worked, she frequently lifted her head to sniff the heavenly scent of baking cake, pride in her accomplishment soaring. Wait until Daniel saw what she was able to do all on her own once she set her mind to it. On the heels of this success, Katherine looked forward to others, eager for the day she'd carry her full share of homemaking responsibilities and free her husband of the chore that was rightfully her own.

Sometime later, lost in pleasure over her finds, Katherine became aware of an acrid odor permeating her retreat, and knew immediately she'd tarried too long. Abruptly standing from her crouched position before an open, overflowing trunk, Katherine smacked her head smartly on the slope of the dormer ceiling, yelping with pain, briefly seeing stars. Gathering her skirts, she flew down the stairs to increasingly thick smoke. She covered her face with a free hand, choking and coughing. Billowing clouds of smoke filled the first floor. Fervently praying, *Dear Lord, don't let me have set the house on fire,* she burst into the kitchen from the hall at the same time Daniel slammed in through the screen door, ordering the children to stay outside and shouting her name.

"Where are you, Kate? By the Saints, Katie, answer me! Are you all right?"

"Here, Daniel. Safe," Katherine managed. "Fire! In the oven!"

"Stay back!" he warned, grabbing up a dish towel, throwing open the oven door.

Katherine watched in horror as he disappeared, engulfed in smoke and flames. She cried out. But before she could panic completely and fling herself after her husband, he reappeared, gingerly holding a flaming pan at arm's length, sprinted to the door, and threw it into the yard.

Dandy fanned the back door open and shut, a hand over his mouth and nose, taking his hand away only long enough to say, "Open the windows, Kate, and let in some fresh air."

She did what he asked as quickly as her trembling limbs allowed, dashing into the hall to open the front door as well. Returning to the kitchen, Katherine saw most of the smoke had dissipated. Hands fisted on hips, slowly shaking his head, her husband stared out the open back door at the smoldering black mound in a burnt patch of grass beyond the steps. There Thomas sat on his haunches, poking the charred mass with a stick. At a safe distance, Celia squatted in imitation of her brother, her head tilted birdlike, eyes questioning.

Hearing Katherine enter, Dandy turned in her direction, relieved to see she really was unharmed and unmarked except for sooty streaks on her fair face. He wanted to haul her into his arms anyway until his heart stopped beating like a caged beast and his hands stopped shaking. He dared not chance it. If he took her into his arms now, he'd never let her go and would not be responsible for the consequences. Taking a deep, quavering breath, he spoke with deceptive calm.

"What . . . what was it to have been, Katie?"

She took in the blackened interior of the oven and soot-streaked walls and cupboards she had so recently scrubbed. Then she watched the children curiously examining the remains. Finally she looked into her husband's concerned, questioning face. Her heart plummeted from her throat to her shoes, shamed by the disaster she had nearly brought upon them all.

"C-c-cake. O-o-o-o-oh-h-h-h." Katherine wailed and burst into tears, covering her face with both hands in utter mortification, mumbling into them, "I did so want to . . . cook . . . something . . . all by my . . . mysellllf."

Now that the excitement was dying down, and his heart wasn't hammering in his ears like the breakup of a log jam, Dandy had to ask himself how all this had come about. He was more than a little uncomfortable with the answer. To discover that Kate had attempted to prepare for them . . . by her admission, a cake . . . left guilt settling heavy in his gut. An hour ago he'd roundly cussed her out, thinking she was reading up on some rule or other to hold over his head or his kids' or his friends'. But he'd been wrong. Almost dead wrong. By rights, he owed Kate an apology he'd never dare voice, for then she'd know how he doubted her.

"There now, Katie, 'tis nothin' to cry about."

She only wept harder. "Ohhhhhhh, D-D-Daniel."

Dandy reached her in a stride, encircling her with his arms, pressing her tight against his chest, damned be the consequences. Katie needed him. He waited until the storm had passed, patting her back, offering soothing comfort in both English and Gaelic. At last the flow of tears became a trickle; the sobs became hiccoughs.

"Oh, Daniel . . . *hic* . . . I have failed . . . *hic* . . . so . . . so . . . *hic* . . . miser . . . *hic* . . . ably," she mumbled into his chest.

"Now, Katie. Now, Katie." What more could he say when over the top of her smooth, honey-colored head he could see Thomas poking around in the results of her efforts.

At his lack of gentlemanly denial of her incompetence, Katherine raised a red-blotched, tear-stained face. He offered her a cockeyed grin.

"Well, at least the house's still standin', Katie me love."

Flushing scarlet, she buried her face once again, gathering bunches of his shirt fabric in both hands to still their trembling. She took a shuddering breath, smelling the clean male scent she associated with her husband, and felt her insides quivering, not totally with distress. His fist lightly came up under her chin, forcing her to look into his eyes. There she found no condemnation, only compassion.

"First time the camp cook let me have my hand at makin' slum gullion—that's stew to you—I accidentally salted it twice . . . maybe more. A worse tastin' mess you can't imagine . . . and a hundred hungry shanty boys didn't let me forget it for a month of Sundays, you can be sure."

Katherine sniffed and hiccoughed. "Would you be attempting to make a joke of this, Daniel, had I burned our home down around our ears?"

"It wasn't all that bad, Katie," Dandy was quick to assure her while cold claws grabbed his insides, thinking if he'd only come inside when he saw her with the book, spoken to her, gotten the facts of the matter, offered to help. But he hadn't. If the fish had been biting better, he wouldn't've given up and headed back in time to save the house from burning down with his sweet wife inside. The thought made Dandy weak in the knees. He lifted one trembling hand to her cheek, rubbing the rough pad of his thumb over mingled soot and tears. Saints have mercy, he wanted to kiss her; instead he forced a wide, reassuring grin.

"Cookin' just takes time to learn, Kate. Not that it's hard . . . once you get the hang of it." He thumbed a spot of ash from her chin. "I can teach you some more, and there's Amelia Weatherby comin' over tomorrow. Likely she knows how to cook as good as the rest of her kin."

Longing to lean her cheek into his palm, lift her lips to his in a relieved, reassured kiss, Katherine instead stepped out of his embrace. Pretending to examine the interior of the blackened oven, she remarked, "Anything either of you teach me is bound to be better than my efforts unassisted. The recipes in the back of your borrowed book are more incomprehensible than Latin." She threw a glance over her shoulder at him. "Why it would even suggest putting sponges in bread is beyond me."

Dandy's loud guffaws filled the air. "Not sponges, Kate," he said when he could. "Sponge. It's a sort of yeasty starter used for leavening."

Katherine feigned anger, fisting both hands on her hips. "Well, why didn't they simply say so, for heaven's sake?"

Richard and Amelia arrived early Monday morning, driving up in an old farm wagon that'd seen better days, a brown cow and her calf tied on behind.

Richard leapt from the wagon to circle around and give Amelia a hand down. She blushed furiously, then paled at his touch, her gaze never meeting his. Like a spooked colt she ran up the porch steps and into the house, obviously eager to leave his close proximity.

"You'd think I hadn't had a bath or scrubbed my teeth and didn't know how to mind my manners," Richard mumbled, climbing back on board and heading for the barn. Until this morning, he'd given little thought to the shy one of Allen's pretty twin sisters except that they were related through marriage if not by blood.

His sister Martha's marriage to Allen Weatherby was all right for the two of them, but as far as he was concerned, permanent entanglement of that kind, with any woman, was the farthest thing from his mind. If he was going to be sharing a ride every morning and evening with a single lass, he was damn glad it was Amelia and not some coy, flirtatious, man-grabbing female he'd have a hell of a lot more trouble resisting.

Deep in thought, Richard fingered the scar cutting through his left eyebrow and disappearing into the hair at his temple. He reluctantly recalled the fiery tart who early on in his courting years had taken exception to his advances, even though his intentions had been honorable. He'd been willing, in his youthful inexperience, to take her for his bride; but his persistence as a suitor had gotten him nothing for his trouble but a permanent reminder of the fickleness of womankind.

Greeting Dandy as he came out of the barn, Richard rolled to a stop with a firm tug on the reins and a "whoa."

"What have we here?" Dandy nodded toward the beasts tied on back, rubbing the grime of labor on the seat of his Levi's before offering Richard his hand.

"They're yours. A good milk cow and a calf to fatten up for butchering in the fall."

"Back up, there. Mine, you say? How'd that come about?"

"Partial repayment for the stock the Weatherbys found abandoned and took on home after Ol' Charlie died. Allen says they only intended to care for the animals until the new owners arrived. But after five years. . . ." Richard shrugged and let the rest go unspoken.

"Hope they got some good eatin' and some change in their pockets for their labors. Tell the Weatherbys one and all their honesty and generosity are greatly appreciated."

Amelia found Katherine in the kitchen, her head wrapped in a kerchief, on her knees scrubbing the oven.

"Kate?"

Katherine sat on her heels, swiping the back of one hand across her damp forehead, leaving a black streak. At the young woman's startled expression, she offered a rueful smile. "I tried to bake a cake on my own, with less than successful results."

A gesture encompassed not only the stove, but the sooty walls and cupboards as well. Amelia turned in a slow circle, hands fisted between small, high breasts.

"It . . . it looks like the cake got a bit overdone." Humor sparked in the young woman's eyes and brought a glow of beauty to her face.

If Richard Wilder could only see her now, thought Katherine, admitting, "I do not seem to have the required skills to follow the simplest directions in Allen's book."

"Oh, no, don't say that. I'm sure you can learn. Here. Let me help you clean up—" She shook out the apron she carried draped over one arm and made a move to put it on.

Katherine put forth a staying hand, stopping just short of touching Amelia's sleeve and leaving a mark. "One of us looking like a chimney sweep is enough. You know what I would really like your help with, if you do not mind?"

"Anything. That's what I'm here for."

"I really need you to spend a few hours this morning entertaining Celia, if you would."

Toying with an apron string, Amelia ducked her dark head to admit, "I . . . I'm not very good with children."

"Celia is not like other children," Katherine reminded her. "She has been no trouble at all. You will probably find her in the front parlor, sitting in the sunshine. She spends countless hours entertaining herself that way . . . or following me about as I work. Usually I do not mind, but I certainly cannot have her underfoot while I tackle this chore."

"I—I could take her for a walk," Amelia suggested.

"She'd love that." An inspiration came to Katherine. "Maybe you could take her down by the barn. I believe Daniel said he and Richard would spend the morning shoring up the structure."

"Or—or we could draw pictures to show her daddy when he comes in for lunch."

Clearly Amelia was reluctant to pursue the object of her infatuation, although he was so close at hand.

"That is a good idea as well. You will find brown wrapping paper and pencils in the drawer on the end by the door." Katherine pointedly went back to her own chores, leaving Amelia to find what she needed and locate Celia on her own, thinking that a bond between the deaf, isolated girl and the shy, self-isolating young woman might be the best thing in the world for both of them. Now she only had to figure out a way to open Richard's eyes to Amelia's attributes, as well.

Returning to her dirty chore, Katherine's thoughts filled with plots to bring the reluctant pair together. It was obvious just by looking at Amelia Weatherby how much she'd blossom with the love of a good man, and that Richard Wilder was the man she desired. He himself could only benefit from marriage to a gentle woman like Amelia. As she scrubbed and scraped, Katherine pondered the best way to make each see the light.

The chore took longer than she anticipated, as did washing ground-in grime off her skin and out of her hair. She finished her ablutions in the privacy of her bedroom and hurried down the stairs, braiding her still-damp hair as she went, sure the men would be in from their labors expecting lunch, and the sandwiches she'd planned to serve not even begun. The fragrance of bacon frying and cinnamon buns baking wafted down the hall to her. When she pushed open the swinging door to the kitchen, she was greeted by the pleasant sight of Amelia busy with not only the pan full of bacon, but another of fried eggs. With flushed cheeks, tendrils of curls at her forehead and nape, and an apron competently tied around her slim middle, Amelia Weatherby had the meal firmly in hand.

At the table Celia stood on a chair, wrapping sets of eating utensils in napkins, as she'd obviously recently been taught. Frequently the child looked up at the young woman at the stove, large eyes alight with adoration. When Amelia glanced her way, Celia quickly dropped her latest bundle, raising her right hand to her temple, palm outward, thumb tucked under and fingers extended straight up.

"What is she doing?"

As quickly, Amelia responded in kind, informing Katherine, "She's saying 'hi.' Aren't you, baby?"

Celia grinned widely and repeated the gesture, but to Katherine. Katherine raised her hand to her own temple in response, unexpected tears flooding her eyes. She changed the gesture to a hasty swipe at one cheek, then another, desiring nothing more than to envelope Celia in a hug. She resisted the temptation by clasping her hands together at the waist, recalling how she'd scared the child half out of her wits the last time she indulged in an impetuous embrace, her thoughts filled with joy as she imagined what Dandy's reaction would be when he saw that his precious daughter had learned to communicate. At last.

Dandy had no hesitation in sweeping Celia into his arms in a tight hug once he'd seen her gesture and responded in kind. His eyes glittered suspiciously as he gave her a tender kiss on the cheek and buried his face in the cloud of her golden curls.

"Ah, little lass, little lass," he murmured, his voice choked. "Sweet little lass, we've fooled them all now, haven't we? You can learn same as anyone else."

Regaining some semblance of control, he said to Amelia, "Celia 'spoke.' Thanks to you, Amelia. How'd you manage it?"

Amelia turned bright red with the praise, her discomfort with the undesired attention obvious in her downcast gaze and hands clasped childlike behind her. "She . . . she is eager to learn . . . it took only moments . . . It's . . . play to her."

Katherine spoke, giving Amelia time to compose herself. "Amelia once worked as a seamstress in a family with a deaf child and learned a few of the hand signals with which they communicated . . . The family moved away—I have already asked," she hastily added when Dandy seemed ready to say more.

He looked as crestfallen as she was sure she had upon learning the same news. "We must find out where they've gone, write them and ask for whatever information, whatever help they can give us, Katie. Any idea where the family's gone, 'Melia?"

His intensity caused the young woman to take a backward step, her hands coming together between her breasts defensively. "No . . . I . . ."

"Daniel," Katherine interceded. To Amelia she added her own plea. "You have made such a wonderful beginning for this child, unlocked the door to learning for her. We must persist, for Celia's sake. Any help you can give—"

"I'm afraid I can't do much more. I only know a half-dozen gestures. I wouldn't want to make any mistakes. But . . . I . . . I think Mother has kept in touch with the family. Yes, I believe she spoke of the Chestersons not too long ago. I could ask . . ." Her face came to life, her eyes sparkling at the prospect. "I'm sure I could get their address from Mother and write to them on your behalf. Though it might take some time . . . they've moved near Chicago and—Mr. MacCabe! Oh, Mr. MacCabe!"

Dandy had grabbed her by the shoulders and planted a smacking kiss on each cheek. She blushed furiously and stammered to a halt, but Katherine could tell she was inordinately pleased with this uncommon male attention. Richard and Thomas chose that moment to come in from the back porch, hair dripping, faces shiny. Richard flashed a surprised glance in Amelia's direction, and it was obvious he'd never seen her so animated.

Unable to contain himself, Dandy burst out, "Celia's learned to say 'hi.' Here, Thomas, watch your sister." He gestured, and Celia responded. "Now Thomas!" Dandy pointed, Celia waved, and Thomas imitated the movements to both children's delight.

"That's great, Celia. 'Bout time, I'd say." The matter settled, Thomas eyed the bacon and eggs sizzling on the stove, demanding, "Ain't we goin' to eat? Or are ya goin' to let them burn, too, like Kate's cake?"

13

Katherine straightened, arching, pressing her palm hard against the small of her back, a sense of satisfaction as heady as wine surging through her. At her feet her carefully tended garden swelled with seedlings enough to insure a bountiful harvest for her family and a tidy profit at market as well in the weeks to come.

Resting the handle of the hoe on her shoulder, Katherine shaded her eyes, squinting into the harsh afternoon sun. A cloudless turquoise sky topped an emerald landscape of field and forest. Row after row of sturdy corn seedlings and leafy bean shoots spread outward to meet the rim of woods near the horizon.

Dandy was nowhere in sight, nor were Richard or Thomas. One of them had said something at breakfast about mending fences at the southeast edge of the property—a pasture for the cow and her calf. How proud Thomas was to be included in the repair, and to have been put in charge of the animals' care. Katherine was certain he could be counted on to do a competent job in spite of his youth. As he reminded them, he'd looked after Celia until his father returned from logging camp. A couple of cows couldn't be any harder than one small sister.

The farmyard, too, was shaping up beautifully. In only a

few busy weeks, rickety outbuildings had been torn down or repaired and whitewashed. The barn, now sound and surrounded by a white rail fence, bore a fresh coat of red paint. The house, painted white and trimmed in the same red, wore a border of flowers like a colorful, fragrant garland. To Katherine's delight, beneath five years growth of weeds, she had found lilies, irises, peonies, and countless other perennials showing signs of life. The Weatherby women generously donated additional cuttings and seedlings. Katherine felt justifiably proud of the results of her hard work, and her growing skills, as she was of the vegetable garden in which she now labored. Food for the table, food for the soul, equal in value in her mind.

In the cool shade of the massive oak at the edge of the front lawn, Amelia sat with Celia on her lap, both thoroughly engrossed in finger play that was really not play at all. Celia learned with the voracity of a child starved for knowledge, fast outstripping Amelia's skills. If only a response would come soon from the Chestersons. Maybe it awaited their usual Saturday pickup in the mail slot at Wilder's General Store. Katherine offered up a quick prayer to Providence that it might be so.

Two more long rows until she could join the pair under their leafy canopy, drink deeply of ice-cold well water until her thirst was quenched. She could almost taste it now, wetting her lips, letting the water slide down her throat, cooling her from the inside out. With renewed zeal she attacked the weeds and wild grasses creeping into the neat rows of her half acre, careful not to disturb tomato plants and lacy carrot tops as she completed the day-long, weekly chore. Was there any greater gratification than watching growing things thrive under one's nurturing care? Katherine could think of none, except . . . but she would not think of that one thing and spoil this magnificent mid-June afternoon.

Katherine's hand instinctively came to rest just below her waist, her fingers spread protectively over what was not there and might never be. She thought of Martha Weatherby, her new friend, confidante, and kindred spirit, unable to suppress the wave of jealousy that swept over her like the heat of the sun upon her shoulders. Walking slowly toward the house, her mood of contentment on this bright and beautiful day dampened with her thoughts, Katherine pondered how she could so mourn the lack of one small child as yet unconceived with her husband's two wonderful, challenging offspring filling her days and her life. She resolved anew to be grateful for the many blessings she already had and call them sufficient.

A cloud of dust rising over the treetops beyond the bend in the road heralded the approach of visitors. The now-familiar moment of panic rose and then dissipated as 'Phrony Pearl Weatherby drove her wagon into the yard. Katherine's admiration grew for the pioneer woman who never gave in to her infirmities, nor let it show how they must pain her. Amelia rose, taking Celia's hand, and greeted her mother, head tipped upward to speak with the arthritic woman who made no attempt to get down. Katherine hastened her steps to join them.

Amelia was saying, "And give my sympathies to Aunt Sophie."

"There has been a death in the family? I am so sorry, 'Phrony Pearl."

From her perch the older woman replied, "M' late husband's only brother over in Millbrook. Just got word. The family's all aheadin' out tomorrow for the funeral, an' I come by to ask a favor of ya, Kate."

"Anything I can do, of course." There was nothing she would deny the matriarch of the family who had given so much to her and hers since their arrival.

"Would ya mind astayin' with Martha? She's ready to pop any day now. Wouldn't do to have her traipsin' around the countryside, but we don't want her left alone neither."

"I would be happy to. It has been some time since Martha and I have had a good visit."

Amelia spoke up in a small voice. "I'd stay with her, Mama."

"An' you a single young lady? Not on yer life. What if the baby decided to come? Wouldn't be seemly."

"Then . . . then I'll stay here to take care of Celia while

Kate's gone. After all," she added with some spunk, "she's a single young lady as well. She'd only be underfoot should something happen."

'Phrony Pearl cackled. "Ya got me there, missy. Course ya can stay here, then, leavin' the fellers free ta put in a full day's work in the fields, if ya put it that way. Know how ya hate big gatherin's anyhow. Ya wouldn't enjoy yerself none."

"I . . . I hope you are not assuming," Katherine interrupted, "that simply because I am a married woman I would be able to assist in . . . in the event of childbirth."

The old woman shrugged. "Nothin' to know, Katie. Martha'll be doin' all the work. 'Sides, ain't likely it'll happen all that soon, seein' how the first baby's always late."

"Shouldn't her husband be the one to stay in case—?"

"Now, what good would a man be at a birthin'? I'll tell Martha ya'll be 'round soon's yer mornin' chores is done."

Later, as she helped Amelia with supper preparations, Katherine tried to cast aside her doubts about tomorrow and concentrate on slicing bread uniformly. She had a tendency to make one slice tissue thin and the next as thick as a log— as her husband put it—or at the very least starting off fine at the top only to waver thicker or thinner toward the bottom. Dandy declared to one and all at the supper table last night that the day his wife could cut an entire loaf of bread into ideal sandwich-size slices was the day he'd jump in the chilly, spring-fed stream out back, fully clothed, and dance an Irish jig. Katherine rather enjoyed that image in her mind's eye, and longed to see it in reality after all the ribbing she'd been forced to suffer through since burning up her cake and very nearly the house along with it.

But tonight wasn't to be the night, she discovered with regret, as her daydreaming caused her knife to slide to the left creating another log-sized slice in Amelia's otherwise perfect, golden loaf.

"Oh, drat!"

Amelia glanced over her shoulder from the stove where

she stirred the pot of onion-laden bean soup that had been simmering all day.

"No jig tonight?"

"Not tonight. But soon. I give you my solemn oath."

On the back porch, Dandy grinned from ear to ear, his dimples deepening as he stifled a chuckle. No cold bath in the stream tonight, he congratulated himself as he dipped both hands in the basin that stood on the table beside the rear door. He rubbed his face and the back of his tanned neck vigorously, then dried himself, his gaze once again seeking out his wife laboring over that loaf of bread. Kate's brow was furrowed and her lips compressed with that dogged determination of hers as she tried to master bread-slicing. Dandy saw she'd forgotten to wear her sunbonnet again, and her forehead and cheeks were red, her nose peeling and lightly freckled. The thick braid of honey-colored hair down her back stayed in place better than that old, tight bun she used to wear, but invariably became wispy around her face by the end of the day. In his opinion, there wasn't a prettier sight at day's end than Katie's hair softly framing her face.

She turned her back to him to speak to Amelia, then bent down to hand something to Celia, confirming what Dandy had been suspecting for the last few days. Kate'd given up wearing a corset. Under that loose-fitting apron and dress there was nothing but a couple of petticoats and a lacy top between her and bare flesh. Flesh grown firm and full and strong with unaccustomed daily labor. Firm and full and so damned desirable Dandy had to suppress a groan of agony at the surging need within him as he watched his wife go about her simple mealtime chores. She was more beautiful, more desirable now than ever she had been as a rich and fancy uptown lady. With the Saints as his witness, he wished she *had* sliced a perfect loaf of bread so he could legitimately jump into that icy spring-fed stream. Saints have mercy, he wanted his wife and he wanted her *now*. If only there wasn't a chance of getting her with child. If only he wasn't going off to the woods in a few short months. If only he wasn't pretty sure that in spite of himself he might be falling in love with Kate.

"*Damn* it all. Damn and double damn."

Running both hands, fingers widespread, through his damp and curling mane, Dandy counted slowly backward from one hundred between clenched teeth before heading into the house.

In the morning Katherine tied the ribbons of her blue homespun sunbonnet under her chin, smoothed down the front of her rose calico dress, and surveyed her reflection in the kitchen window over the sink. Her expression appeared grim for someone who was planning a day-long visit to a good friend instead of a day of household chores. But she couldn't get out of her head 'Phrony Pearl Weatherby's suggestion of the possibility of Martha's going into labor with no one but herself in attendance, and she had the most uneasy feeling—or was it a premonition?—that it just might happen.

"Why don't you and Celia come along with me?" Katherine suggested to Amelia as the young woman stacked the last washed and dried breakfast dish in the cupboard with the others.

Amelia threw her a glance over one shoulder. "Would you mind terribly if we didn't, Kate? I promised Celia we'd have a tea party down by the stream today. I suppose we could postpone it until tomorrow . . . but then, who would feed the men when they came in for dinner at noon?"

Her cheeks colored prettily, and Katherine knew immediately of whom she was thinking. It occurred to her, as it most likely already had to Amelia, that this afforded the perfect opportunity for Amelia to more fully demonstrate her housewifely skills to a certain Richard Wilder. She hadn't the heart, no matter what her own trepidation, to deny the young woman this chance to favorably impress the man her heart desired.

"Then, of course you must stay here. I would not want to disappoint Celia." She smiled a secret smile. "Or anyone else."

Their wagon stood in readiness in the dooryard. To Katherine's surprise, Richard Wilder sat upon the seat, reins resting lightly in his palms, elbows on knees, his genial grin firmly in place.

"I thought Daniel would be driving me to Martha's." While she liked the personable young man, his too familiar friendliness sometimes made her uncomfortable. She wished he'd save it for Amelia, who was in a better position to appreciate his attention. She had been so looking forward to time alone with her husband.

Richard jumped down to come around and bow before her. "You're stuck with me, m'lady. Think you can live with second best?" He interrupted her murmured acquiescence to explain, "Thomas needed his pa's help with the calf. Seems she wants only her mother's milk and'll have nothing to do with drinking from a pail so mama can nourish us instead." He assisted Katherine up onto the high board seat.

Looking past Richard as they rolled out of the yard, Katherine spied Dandy standing in the open barn door, staring after them, mopping his brow with a large blue bandanna. Auburn hair curled damply at his forehead and neck. Darkly tanned, his Levi's and flannel shirt clinging like a second skin, her husband set her heart to beating wildly, her insides becoming deliciously quivery, even from this distance, as they did more and more frequently of late when in his presence . . . or when thinking of him . . . or dreaming of him. Almost as if she were falling in love with the rowdy, robust rogue—a silly schoolgirl notion she refused to acknowledge even in her most private moments.

She couldn't be sure from here, but Daniel seemed to be frowning. Perhaps he was troubled by the calf. Perhaps she should have stayed home to . . . to what? Helping with a calf refusing to wean was as foreign to her as baking a cake. She did not flatter herself into believing he was reluctant to see her go away for the day. For weeks now he'd kept his distance, quitting the house early, working late, gulping meals in between. She suffered no delusions that he might miss time spent alone with her as she did him. Most likely the frown at her departure only stemmed from her imagination, or her longings.

For Dandy's part, his frown deepened, watching Richard grab Katherine around the waist to help her onto the wagon seat, then say something to make her smile. Seemed like there'd been all too much of the pair of them putting their heads together of late. He'd best keep an eye out for trouble. Might have to give the cocky fellow a bum's rush off his property for good and all.

Katherine and Richard rode in silence for a time. Katherine attempted to think of a way to introduce conversation about Amelia, to try to get a sense of his feelings for the smitten young woman. She finally chose a roundabout approach.

"Daniel and I are most grateful for your help this summer. In truth, we could not manage without you . . . and Amelia."

Instead of picking up on Amelia's many contributions, Richard denied his own. "Actually you're doing me a favor," he admitted. "I'd much rather be working out in the fields or mending fences. Anything's better'n clerking for Pop in his store. Wants me to be a merchant like himself— Wilder and Son. But that's not what I have in mind for my future." Richard stared straight ahead out over Bess's broad rump, his expression both stubborn and brooding.

"What do you have in mind? A farm of your own? Wife and children?" Katherine asked hopefully.

He gave her a sidelong glance. "Something like that." He didn't elaborate. Land of his own was his dream. A woman he could do without. Single young ladies pursued him relentlessly, each one with the same goal in mind. They scared him to death. Richard shifted the reins into one hand, and his right index finger traced his scar from brow to temple. The only females he cared to talk to, and harmlessly flirt with, were married ones like Kate here and his sisters-in-law. And shy, unassuming, undemanding Amelia, of course, since he saw her every day. But she was different. No threat there.

Reaching their destination, Richard pulled the wagon

around back, helping Kate down, reminding her, "Either Daniel or I will be back around dusk." When Martha came to the door, he said, "Hello there, sis. No time today, but I'll drop by for a visit soon." With that promise, he lifted the reins, gave a light slap, and was off.

Martha stood on the single step, holding the screen door open, her belly so large Katherine couldn't imagine why the mother-to-be didn't simply explode. Still, seeing her looking as well as always, Katherine's apprehension diminished appreciably.

"Good morning, Martha. Beautiful day, isn't it?" she greeted. "You cannot imagine how relieved I am to see you up and around. 'Phrony Pearl had me half believing your baby might arrive today. She fully expected that simply because I am a married woman, I would be able to assist." To her dismay, no sooner were the words out of her mouth than Martha burst into tears.

"Ohhh, Kate . . . I'm sorry . . . But I . . . I was just down to the privy . . . and . . . and . . . my water broke . . ." Her words came out breathless and trembly.

"Water—?"

"Kate, I'm having my baby."

Panic spread with the quickness of a wildfire. "Now? Oh, Martha, you mustn't. Wait until your family returns. Or if you cannot, let me call Richard back to—" She spun on a heel, but there was no sign of the wagon on the road. She turned back to Martha, incredulous. "Richard would have helped—"

"I . . . I couldn't let my own brother see me . . . this . . . way. Richard's a man . . . and a single one at that—"

"He could have gone for a doctor—"

"*No!* No. Doctors are for dying—"

"A-a-a midwife . . . then—"

"'Phrony Pearl's the only mid—owwwww . . ." She doubled up, gasping in pain.

Katherine caught her by the elbow, for Martha seemed about to collapse. Any fears or reservations on her part seemed of little consequence with Martha in such distress. "Let me help you into the house—"

"In . . . in . . . a . . . minute—"

"Then I'll go find someone to—"

Martha grabbed her wrist, the grip so tight Katherine winced. "No . . . Stay . . . here . . . Please . . ." Martha took several panting breaths. "I . . . need . . . you."

The desperation in her friend's tone brought Katherine up with a start, realizing the truth. There was no one for her to run and fetch. The Weatherbys were the only neighbors for miles and miles in every direction, and they were all gone, not expected to return until early evening. There was no choice but for Katherine to see her friend through her time of travail.

An inevitable calm settled over her. When Martha's contraction passed, Katherine helped her into the house where the pregnant woman sought out a straight-backed chair and lowered herself into it, hands braced, palms down, on the table.

"Are you all right? Can I get you anything? Tea?" The kettle steamed on the stove behind them.

Martha shook her head, running her tongue over dry lips. "A cool drink of water, if you don't mind."

Katherine took the kettle off the fire and dipped into the pail of water, pouring a generous cup, handing it to her, unsure whose hands trembled the most. There was nothing left but to pull up a chair beside her friend and cover her hand on the table with both of hers.

"I will help you in every way I can," she promised earnestly, "but you must tell me what to do. I have no knowledge of the process of childbirth—"

"You think I do?" asked Martha, close to tears. "I had expected 'Phrony Pearl . . . or Adelaide . . . or even 'Tilda to be here when my time came."

"I'm sorry there's only me."

"Oh, Kate, I've been so foolish," Martha cried, "so stupid. I've been having pains for days. 'Phrony Pearl said I would. False labor, she called it. But today they seemed stronger, different. I should have told Allen, but I didn't want him to have to stay behind. Family means sooooo muuuch . . . ohhhh . . . owwww . . ."

"Sssh! Don't try to talk. We will manage . . . somehow."

She watched Martha tense up and knew conversation would have to wait. Martha's fingers formed a fist under hers, then withdrew to clutch at the apron fabric covering her distended middle. With every inch of her being she seemed to do battle with the wave of pain rising to its peak.

"Hurts . . ."

"I . . ." Katherine was about to respond with a placating "I understand," realizing how ridiculous such words would be, for, of course, she did not and could not understand.

During the weeks she had gotten to know the many Weatherbys, she'd discovered the candid farm folk, men and women alike, had no qualms discussing any subject, including the workings of the female body, especially its reproductive capacities. Very embarrassing to one such as herself who had grown up without the slightest knowledge of these apparently natural female functions, information her own mother had not been willing, or perhaps able, to impart. It had been Mrs. Tillit, and with a great deal of discomfort herself, who had explained menstruation to the young Katherine once the process began. Putting an arm around the terrified youngster who believed herself bleeding to death, Hannah Tillit briefly told her that without the onset of the monthly flow, a woman could not one day become a mother. When the young Katherine had the temerity to ask if this, then, was why Mrs. Tillit had no children, red-faced Hannah instantly withdrew both physically and conversationally, saying only that some things were best left unsaid until marriage. But Katherine had been married for weeks, and still she knew little more than before. So small was her knowledge, she could only hope and pray she'd help her friend rather than hinder her.

When the contraction ended, Martha rested against her chair's back, clearly exhausted by her struggle, and more than a little scared. Fear gleamed in her large brown eyes as she pushed strands of dark hair off her forehead with shaky hands.

"What . . . what have 'Phrony Pearl and the others told

you to expect?'' Katherine ventured, trying to turn her friend toward constructive thoughts.

"The pain . . . They all said how much it would hurt . . . and how long it might take . . . like each one had to . . . to prove she had suffered the most. Oh, Kate, I'm not sure I can handle much more pain than I'm already feeling . . . not if it goes on and on like 'Tilda's, whose first child took three days to arrive. I'm an awful coward about such things.'' Tears gathered in her eyes and threatened to overflow.

Katherine caught both Martha's hands in her own, looking deeply into the dark and tearing eyes. Someone had to remain calm and in control in spite of their mutual ignorance, and it appeared she'd be the one. She offered a reassuring, if falsely courageous, smile.

"You will do what must be done to see this precious baby brought into the world, for your child's sake and your own. And Allen's.''

Martha seemed to draw strength from Katherine's brave show, even managing a wavery answering smile.

"Now, what can we do to make preparations? Would you be more comfortable in your nightgown? Perhaps resting in bed to conserve your energy . . .'' Katherine's voice trailed off, at the end of her fund of helpful suggestions, her mind alive with questions she dare not ask the frightened mother-to-be.

"I—I think I would like to get into my gown . . . and my bed.''

Martha lifted herself carefully from the chair, bracing her hands on the table for support. With Katherine's steadying hands on her elbow and waist, they made a slow procession to the bedroom, the last of it during a painful contraction. Martha sat gingerly on the edge of the bed, grimacing and gasping until the seizure passed. Then she began undressing, while Katherine uncomfortably turned away, pretending to busy herself sorting through the pile of baby things on the dresser, ostensibly looking for something to dress the baby in when it arrived.

Turning toward the bed, her choices in hand, Katherine

found Martha standing beside it, covered from chin to toes in a modest nightgown, eyeing the colorful crazy quilt spread upon the bed she shared with her husband, to be hers alone while she was in labor.

"I'm afraid the bedding will be ruined," she confessed.

"When I nursed my parents during their final illness . . . and toward the end each became . . . incontinent . . . I covered the sheets first with newspaper, then some old towels, or an old blanket, should you have either."

Katherine readied the bed while the mother-to-be struggled through another contraction. Finally Martha rested on a pile of pillows, the quilt tucked sedately around her. Katherine brought in a kitchen chair and placed it near the bed. She sat, and between contractions they talked. Martha explained what little she knew about what they might expect, and Katherine rose from her chair to gather needed supplies.

Contractions came and went with increasing frequency, but the child made no appearance. It both frightened and worried Katherine to see her friend suffering so, and the niggling worry caused her to wonder what she would do should there be complications with the baby or Martha herself.

Katherine offered her a sip of cold water when she complained her mouth had gone dry, straightened pillows and covers when Martha's pain-racked tossings tangled them, and refrained—with greatest difficulty—from acting upon her growing desire to pace the room, wringing her hands, or bolt out of the house altogether.

The day wore on. Martha labored and Katherine waited and prayed. The pains began coming so frequently that Martha scarcely had time to rest between them, hurting so bad she screamed and fought as if to escape her body. Her head swung back and forth on her sweat-soaked pillows, her flailing legs kicking free of the quilt, sending it to the floor on the far side of the bed. Her nightgown, twisted about her body, rose well above where her waist had once been, exposing her stretched and straining belly and everything below.

Katherine's face turned scarlet at the sight of her friend's nakedness, and she scurried around the bed to retrieve the blanket. Standing with the quilt pressed in both hands against her chest, she watched Martha arch high on her bed of agony, her arms flying up to grab the spindles of the brass headboard in a death grip. Her back came down hard on the mattress, and her legs drew up, spreading wide to expose her most intimate regions. She bore down mightily, and as Katherine watched, too fascinated to be embarrassed now, the first evidence of the child's birth appeared.

Martha pushed until she was winded. Gulping air, she pushed again.

"I see hair . . . quantities of dark hair," said Katherine in awe. She dropped the quilt and went to Martha's side, encouraging her to work harder, harder still, telling her what she was seeing as the birth took place before her eyes.

The head came out first, then the rest slid out upon the bed between Martha's legs, still connected to its mother's lifeline.

"It's a boy. Martha, it's a boy."

Weakly Martha held out her arms. "Let me see him. Please. Let me hold him."

Gingerly Katherine lifted the tiny, slippery infant from the bed. He stirred as if awaking and offered up a bleat, then a lusty wail as Katherine placed him on his mother's belly.

"Oh, sweetheart, don't cry. Hello, darling one. I'm your mama. Oh, Kate, he's so beautiful. Isn't he the most beautiful baby you've ever seen?"

Privately Katherine had expected him to look a little less like a drowned white rat, for the few infants she had seen were red-cheeked and plump. Still, he was a miracle of life . . . the most miraculous Katherine had experienced, and she wholeheartedly agreed with the new mother that her child was perfect.

Martha finally roused herself enough to tell Katherine about tying off the cord. The afterbirth followed quickly and cleanly, and Katherine took it from the room wrapped in newspaper only to return at a run with a frantic scream from Martha.

"Kate, help me. Take the baby before I drop him." She

clutched her still-bloated belly. "Lord, Kate, it's happening again . . . A pain . . . ohhhhhhhhh."

She writhed upon the bed, and Katherine quickly plucked the child from her, holding it close to her own breasts as Martha bucked and arched as if in labor. And indeed she was. The boy's twin made a much hastier appearance.

"You have a daughter as well," she told Martha tenderly and placed another indignantly crying baby in her mother's arms. At the sound of his sibling's wails, the boy took up the cry, eyes tightly closed, fists waving defiantly, shivering. Katherine hurried to wrap both children in warm blankets, knowing instinctively they should be bathed as well, not daring to take the time until she'd seen to Martha's care.

She looked into the mother's ecstatic tear-stained face, raising her voice above the din. "Are there any more, do you think?"

Martha offered a tremulous laugh. "I . . . I don't know . . . I'm not sure I could go through it again. At least, not today."

While Katherine gently bathed and dressed each baby in turn and Martha supervised, they waited. When a half hour had passed with no more contractions, they assumed it was over at last. Katherine helped Martha wash herself and dress in a clean gown, all embarrassment gone after the intimacies of the past hours. She brushed Martha's chocolate-brown hair and plaited it, removed soiled towels and newspaper, and straightened the bedding, finally covering Martha with the quilt and placing a sleeping baby in each of the young mother's cradling arms. Standing back, she viewed the entwined and sleeping trio and was satisfied with her work. She indulged in watching them for long minutes, wrapping her arms around her waist, feeling their emptiness like a deep-seated ache, at the same time very nearly bursting with joy over Martha's accomplishment, and her own. Together they had managed. They had managed very well indeed.

14

I know what she's thinkin', Dandy told himself, driving Kate home from Allen Weatherby's at dusk. She's got that cozy, warm-all-over look about her women get when someone has a baby an' they're wantin' one, too. Hell, he'd probably soon be listening to an earful of Katie begging for a kid or two of her own, and damned if he was up to it.

He arrived at Allen's while a family celebration over the twins' birth was in full swing. Knowing what one drink did to him, still Dandy let himself get talked into a tumbler of hard cider and a second—maybe even a third, he couldn't be sure. How bad could something made from apples be? How could he refuse his friend in light of the man's happiness? Now he was paying the price with a spinning head and a rolling stomach he knew would only get worse. On top of it all, his wife had gone all doe-eyed and secret-smiling on him. Any minute now she'd open her mouth to ask why they couldn't have a baby, too; Dandy was as certain of it as he was of the fact he'd be puking his guts out before morning.

But Kate said nothing, not on the ride home, not as she pulled down the hanging lamp over the kitchen table and lit it. She looked . . . mesmerized, kind of like the folks he'd seen hypnotized at a state fair once . . . except the expression on her face was more like a madonna's, like the statue in the church back home in Ballywae. She turned to him, eyes misty, mouth turned in a half smile.

"Daniel, I—"

"Now, don't go dreamin' up any ideas, Kate," he interrupted. "You know where I stand on your gettin' in the family way with me leavin' in the fall."

"I wasn't going to—"

"And don't go thinkin' you can seduce me into forgettin' about leavin' neither."

"If you'd only—"

"Been a shanty boy since I came to this country, don't know anythin' else, don't wanna do anythin' else. I don't intend to leave a second wife behind pregnant, so you can just blame well get that idea outta your head." His voice rose, his accent thickened, and his words slurred. He swallowed heavily and ran the back of his hand across his mouth.

"Please, Daniel, hear what I—" Her voice came out soft but insistent, her tone hurt and bewildered.

"If you're goin' to carry on an' on about a kid of yer own, I'm headin' on out to the barn so's I can get some peace an' quiet an' a good night's rest." He was sure his wife didn't know how stinking drunk he was; he prided himself on not being sloppy about it. But she'd know for sure if he didn't get out of the house. Soon. He could feel the bile rising.

He crossed the room in a stride, toppling a chair, leaving it. He slammed the door open so hard the knob left a dimple in the wall behind it. Took off at a lope toward the barn. Tripped over his own feet. Went sprawling.

He made it onto his hands and knees before he began to heave up cider and supper. He hung his head, totally helpless to do anything else even after his stomach came up empty and sore, as if he'd been kicked in the gut.

He felt the cool, damp cloth on his face, mopping up the icy sweat that had him shivering. Comforting hands gripped his shoulders firmly and rocked him back on his heels.

"Done?" Her voice held no condemnation.

He nodded weakly.

"Let's get you up to bed. In the morning you'll feel better. Though I understand there is often a headache."

She got him on his feet somehow, into the house, and up the stairs. He was only half conscious of the trip, and of her stripping him down to his long johns and tucking him in under the covers. Mercifully he went right to sleep, or passed out. It didn't matter which as long as he didn't have to feel the effects of his drinking.

With the dawn last night's words and deeds came back crystal clear. The morning sun hit his face like shards of glass slicing through his lids, trying to shatter his eyeballs. He turned his head away from the glare, a cannonball rolling from side to side in his skull. He smelled bacon, and his stomach knotted. He swallowed hard; it settled uneasily. He raised himself up on elbows, slid one leg toward the edge of the bed, then decided to get it over with and swung himself into a sitting position, feet on floor, eyes screwed closed. He clung to the headboard until the room stopped spinning.

The door opened. Dandy smelled coffee, hot and black. Kate came in with a steaming cup and set it on the bedside table under his nose. He breathed deeply of the rising vapors, wrapping both hands around the cup to pull it closer.

"Careful. It is hot."

No condemnation in her voice. A good start. Dandy cautiously threw Kate a sideways glance. Her expression was serene and noncommittal as she stood quietly, her hands clasped lightly at her waist.

"Expectin' some kind o' apology, are ya, Katie?" His voice croaked out roughly over a dry, raw throat.

"No, Mr. MacCabe. Your words were the truth, if rather bluntly stated . . . and I suppose I had grown a bit maudlin with the idea of a child of our own. It was only natural, given yesterday's events, and I can understand why you assumed I would try to convince you of something you already said you did not want."

There was no bitterness in her tone, no self-pity, no nothing. In fact, Kate sounded exactly like the unapproachable prude she'd been when they'd first met. Inwardly Dandy groaned. He'd have to do a lot of fast talking to get out of this one and back to the way they were before he opened his big mouth.

"Now, Kate—"

"Drink your coffee while it's still hot enough to do some good—"

"Katie, we need to—"

"Breakfast will be ready very shortly—"

"Listen here, Kate, I—"

"Amelia and Richard have already arrived. I believe it would be best if you could behave as though you were not recovering from the ill effects of last night. We would not want it to get back to Allen and make him feel bad that you suffered because of his celebration."

"Katie MacCabe—"

"That's Katherine . . . and we'll be expecting you down in five minutes." She was at the door.

Dandy lurched to his feet, reaching Katherine in two strides, catching her upper arm, spinning her toward him.

"Just one gol-danged minute, Kate. Don't go gettin' all prim and proper with me. I apologized, didn't I? What more do you want, Kate?"

"I want noth—"

"The hell . . . heck you don't. You're madder'n all get out 'cause I won't bed you and plant my seed so's you can have a baby like Martha." The pounding in his head had Dandy saying things he knew he shouldn't've soon's they popped out of his mouth, but he couldn't seem to stop himself.

Her one eyebrow raised high—a sure sign of trouble— she gave him a look cold enough to freeze his coffee. "I am neither frothing at the mouth nor blithering like a madman—"

"Huh?"

"However, I am *angry* with you, furiously so. You presume much, Mr. MacCabe, in believing I desire nothing more than to go to bed with you." She refused to blush or look away. "And bear your child." That was a bold-faced lie, though she would die before letting him know. Her chin rose a notch higher. "On the other hand, *should* I so desire,

circumstances would be far different than they were with A
. . . your first wife, for *I* would not be alone in my travail
any more than Martha Weatherby was. We have good
friends who would see to my welfare while you were gone.
Now, if you will release me, thank you, I shall return to my
chores downstairs.''

The door shut quietly behind her. Staring morosely after
his wife, Dandy realized his big mouth had just cost him
the easy goodwill—and, yes, affection—that'd grown between them during the last couple of months. Damned if he
knew how to get it back.

One fact was sure; she didn't want his child. She as much
as came out and said so. Why should she, crude brute that
he was. She didn't love him—never had, never would. Married him for his kids, and for that he blessed her. But now
he wanted her to want—no, need—to be his wife for himself. Was that too much to ask? Seemed certain it was.
Damn, that hurt.

Lord, he was going to miss her. Staying clear of his Katie
was going to be the hardest thing he'd ever done. God only
knew how he'd manage.

In the dreary days following the estrangement between
herself and Dandy, Katherine fervently wished she could
have taken back her biting words and prim, proper retreat
from her husband's attempts to apologize and explain. But
she decided it was too late to tell him how hurt she'd been
by his tirade, spoken in drunkenness and its aftermath
though they were. He seemed relieved by the distance between them, neither doing anything to bridge the gap, nor
allowing her to help.

Once she saw him take out the picture of Annie he kept
in his bedside stand drawer and study it solemnly and sadly.
Katherine could understand that he did not want to cause
her the grief he had his first wife, but she suspected he likely
did not care for her as deeply as he had cared for Annabella
Stewart MacCabe. Though Katherine longed for a child to
carry, to hold in her arms, to love, she knew with growing
certainty that in her heart of hearts she longed even more to

lie with her husband and become truly his in every way. Her heart ached with the realization that this would never be. She wondered how long it took to mend a broken heart, or destroy it altogether.

Two weeks to the day after the twins' birthday the community celebrated the Fourth of July. Katherine fervently hoped the festivities would provide a few needed hours of relief from the relentless strain between herself and her husband. Though nothing had been said in the children's presence, Thomas and Celia knew something was wrong, as did Amelia and Richard. They were all too kind, too helpful, too congenial not to be trying to cover up the uneasy silence that settled around them whenever she and Dandy were in a room together. One and all, they desperately needed this distraction.

By the eve of the Fourth, Thomas's enthusiasm proved unsuppressible. "Johnny-D says there's goin' be races . . . an' contests . . . an' more food'n I've ever seen before in my life . . . Johnny-D says we can eat 'til we bust, if we've a mind to, an' nobody'll stop us . . . Johnny-D says there's goin' be fireworks . . . an' I ain't never seen no fireworks afore . . . Johnny-D says—"

"Whoa, there, lad. That'll be enough bits of wisdom from Johnny-D Weatherby for one night. You'll have us all wishin' you never met up with Gabe's youngster if you continue quotin' the boy like that." A kindly chuckle followed his gentle chide. His son had filled out, even grown taller, and lost the serious expression Dandy thought Thomas would never get rid of after all the misery and responsibilities he'd suffered in his short life. Now the lad was becoming the child he hadn't had the time to be before, and the sight of it warmed Dandy's heart.

Katherine watched the exchanged between father and son, pleasure spreading like a warm fire within her. Thomas was a different child than he'd been before coming to the farm. The wholesomeness of fresh air, good and plentiful food, and carefree pastimes afforded him the chance to be a typical seven-going-on-eight-year-old for the first time in his short life. Celia, too, blossomed, thanks to Amelia Weatherby, upon whom Celia doted. The Chestersons had responded at last, and more generously than either she or Amelia could have imagined. Just days ago, a long letter and a carton had arrived. They found a collection of books concerning deafness and hand signing. The enclosed letter encouraged as only people who had faced a similar fate could convey. Amelia took the material home with her to study and prepare lessons for the child. Any day now, Celia's education would begin in earnest, setting her mind free. The emancipation of both children presented further cause for celebration and fireworks this glorious Fourth.

The day dawned, promising to be clear and cloudless and not too hot, though the past week had been blistering. Katherine thanked Fortune for the cooler weather affording her the opportunity to wear her new dress. She'd combined the fabric of three others found in various storage trunks. A whole other avenue of dressmaking had opened to her with the discovery of an attic door accessing the crawl space between dormers, wherein lay twin hump-topped travel chests of a long-ago era. Inside, carefully preserved in tissue, she found garments of the style worn during the war. One dress in particular caught her eye, a blue-and-white-striped sateen with yard upon frivolous yard—fifteen all told—in the skirt alone. Combined with an almost perfectly matched blue poplin from a second dress, and lace at throat, wrist, and hem from another, she believed she had concocted a garment to place her among the best dressed of the picnicgoers this day.

Celia wore a pink calico dress that put roses in her cheeks and brought out the sky-blue of her eyes; both Dandy and Thomas wore blue chambray shirts fashioned from the best parts of those belonging to Ol' Charlie and a voluminous everyday skirt of some unknown Civil War matron. Due to Katherine's skill with scissors and needle, worn and faded portions had been eliminated or artfully concealed. Her gentlemen and her little lady looked quite stylish, if she did say so herself, causing her husband to remark how fine they all appeared, concluding, ''From that flowery concoction on your head to those ruffles skimmin' the ground, you'll be the loveliest lass at the picnic today, Mrs. MacCabe, and proud I am to be seen with you and claim you for my own.''

Knowing he was teasing, Katherine still blushed and turned her gaze downward so as not to embarrass herself by letting him see how inordinately pleased she was at his compliment. If there seemed to be a long moment while he waited for the return of the kind words, Katherine pretended not to notice. A few pretty phrases bandied about could not heal the rift between them, and only served to widen it with longing on her part for more, so much more.

Finally Dandy cleared his throat. ''Shall we be off, then? There's a fine day and a grand celebration just waitin' for us to begin.'' Katherine agreed.

Following a train of buggies and wagons, the MacCabes arrived at a wide field at the edge of a large, gloriously blue lake. Plank tables draped in red, white, and blue bunting stretched for some distance under a copse of maples not far from the road. Already food contributions covered the boards from one end to the other. Women dressed in Sunday best mingled near the long, makeshift table. Men set up folding chairs; a dozen others gathered on a newly constructed platform, tuning musical instruments. Children of assorted ages ran and shouted and played, or giggled and guffawed in separate groups of boys and girls.

The band struck up a rousing rendition of ''The Glorious Fourth,'' drawing groups together around the bandstand in an attentive crowd. ''The Battle Hymn of the Republic'' followed. Speeches commenced, then a reading of the Declaration of Independence, climaxing with the ''Star-Spangled Banner,'' everyone lifting their voices as one, hand to heart or saluting. The Reverend Bates offered a prayer to bless the day, the bounteous food, and peace and prosperity for one and all, then the captive crowd regrouped in family clusters to fill their plates and eat their fill.

The MacCabes ate off pie tins on a blanket spread in the sun among the many Weatherbys. It appeared Dandy had not slighted anyone by overlooking a single cook's contribution, including a generous portion of Katherine's baked beans and two of her biscuits, promising to return to the serving table to sample her cake as well. The Weatherby women congratulated her on her accomplishments in the kitchen. Fortunately they had no idea, nor did she tell them, that these three items were all she was thus far qualified to prepare.

"What competitions you going to enter, Daniel?" Allen asked.

"Don't know yet. What's bein' offered?"

"There's a wood-sawyer's tournament and a log-rolling contest oughtta suit you pretty good," Allen's older brother Gabe commented.

Dandy leaned back on one arm, rubbing the hand of the other in slow circles over a full belly, appearing to consider his options seriously. Katherine thought she detected a glint of sly humor in his dark eyes and a quirk of a smile around the corners of his mouth.

"Been a feller for a number of years now," he admitted reflectively. "That's my specialty. Don't be after havin' a contest for fellin' a tree on mark, do ye now?"

Gabe and Allen agreed they didn't.

"Guess I'll have to be settlin' for the sawin' contest . . . and maybe the log rollin' as well, just for the fun of it." He grabbed up his tin plate from the blanket. "After I've had me a slice of Katie's fine cake, if there's any left."

Kate rose beside him, her cheeks rosy with his second unexpected compliment of the day. "I'll go with you. I'd nearly forgotten my promise to take a turn helping to serve desserts."

Dandy strolled off casually, his wife walking sedately at his side, letting no one see the wide grin he could no longer suppress. He'd been a sawyer, a chopper, a topper, and finally a feller in his long career as a logger. Hell, he'd even been a white-water man many a spring, herding logs to the mill down roaring rivers, over foaming rapids and falls. He'd broken up a jam or two, dancing across logs stacked like jackstraws two stories high, singling out the key log, getting the heck out of the way when the jam broke free. There wasn't a chore he hadn't tried a time or two in the camps he'd worked, depending on the need. A greenhorn he might be at farming, but not so when it came to logging, as his new friends and neighbors'd soon be finding out, though in the meantime he'd have a bit of fun stringing them along.

Inordinately pleased with himself, Dandy turned his attention to the pretty woman at his side, wishing things were different between them. Some of the brightness went out of the day, some of the gleeful anticipation of showing off, as he studied her serene features, shadowed by her bonnet brim. No longer pale and porcelain as when they'd first met, now freckled and golden with the sun's kiss, her face remained unreadable. To others, she gave her kindness and affection. To him, no more or less than required. Lord, how he missed her.

Dandy escorted Kate to the dessert table. Grabbing a generous chunk of her cake, he asked with exaggerated casualness, "You plannin' on watchin' the competitions?"

She briefly glanced up from serving Sammuel Wilder, Richard and Martha's father. "What? Oh, yes, I'll be there."

Chewing contemplatively, Dandy headed toward the Weatherby men engaged in an informal baseball game at the far edge of the clearing. Only yards away, he turned back to watch his wife as he finished his cake, sucking frosting off each finger, relishing the taste. His Katie was turning into a passably good cook. He watched her hand out slices of cake and pie, a cookie or brownie or two to those waiting to be served, offering smiles and a friendly comment to everyone. He noticed the majority of her customers were men; he noticed, too, how each man chose her especially, though several other ladies were positioned along the table to help. He saw Richard Wilder linger longer than the rest, saw the handsome young rake's hands come up to cover hers as she handed him a plate of not one slice of her own cake, but two. Wilder said something, and Kate tipped her head back as she laughed at him. When finally the lad took his plate and left, Dandy saw Kate follow him with her gaze until he disappeared from view. She frowned, and Dandy would've given almost anything to know what she was thinking, though he was pretty damn sure he already knew, and recalled countless other times he'd seen them with their heads together—intimate-like—in the past. In his very own home.

Jealousy exploded in his brain, turning his anger into cold rage. So, when push came to shove, he wasn't man enough for Kate, but Wilder was. Dandy cursed himself for a fool for hiring the man, feeding him at his own table, treating him like family. Some thanks he got with Wilder trying to seduce his wife, and she letting him. Well, he'd show them both, prove who was the better man, then make Kate his wife in every way so *no one* need ever again doubt where she belonged. Which was with him. Her husband. Like it or not.

At the bandstand the drummer tapped out a roll, drawing people young and old in that direction. Tempering his wrath with difficulty, Dandy followed the crowd, keeping his distance from Kate.

"Ladies, gents, and kiddies, too, it's time for the fun and games to begin," Sammuel Wilder shouted over the murmurings of the crowd. A congenial man, he'd been master of ceremonies throughout the Independence Day festivities, and now explained the rules of the various contests and the order in which they'd be held.

The children competed first. Thomas had entered the three-legged race with Johnny-D. Cheering them on to victory, Dandy felt his fury die down to a simmer. Kate stood at his side, as enthusiastic as himself, and even clutched his arm when it seemed, for a moment, that the boys might lose. She flashed him an excited smile he halfheartedly returned, thinking that maybe it wouldn't be so hard to win her back after all.

When the time came for the wood-sawyer's contest, Dandy found himself pitted against Richard Wilder, one on one. Dandy spit on his hands, grabbed up his bucksaw, and set the blade across his length of log resting on a pair of sawhorses. He glared over at Wilder. Not realizing they'd become mortal enemies instead of friendly challengers, Richard offered a cocky salute. The whistle blew, and the competition began in earnest. It was over before it had half begun, Dandy slicing through his log like a hot knife through butter. Amid the cheering following his all-too-easy win, Dandy sought out Kate in the crowd and found her cheering as lustily as the rest, her attention fully on her husband, none spared for the loser. Even so, when Richard came forward, his hand extended to acknowledge his defeat, Dandy turned away, heading purposefully for his wife, leaving the puzzled young man to drop his hand, unshaken, at his side.

"Didn't you notice Richard coming to congratulate you?" asked Kate first off, frowning and looking past him to Wilder.

"Musta missed it," Dandy replied bluntly, clamping his teeth together, his jaw muscle jumping. No words of praise from his own wife, just worry over another man's tender feelings. "Better head on over to the lake for the log rollin'. You comin'?" he asked over his shoulder.

"Why . . . yes . . . of course."

Confounded, Katherine lifted her skirt ankle high and all but ran after her husband, attempting to keep up. He was clearly out of sorts, in spite of a day well begun, and she hadn't the faintest idea why. Even his easy win over Richard had not lightened his mood as she'd expected. Whatever his problem was, perhaps the log rolling would put him in a better frame of mind.

A half-dozen logs twenty feet long, fully half the circumference of her washtub, bobbed on the placid lake surface. She had heard the mill on the other side had donated their use for the day, even transporting them tied together in a raft. The mill's manager, Ben Hosley, directed the event, saying two men were to stand upon a single log, propelling it around at increasing speed until one of them was dislodged and disposed of into the water. The last undrenched man would be declared the winner.

"Who'll go first?" he concluded.

"First and last, I will," declared Dandy loudly, striding forward. And so the game began.

There were others with logging experience, but none as

quick on his feet as Daniel Sean MacCabe. Katherine watched with growing pride as one after another he dunked opponents into the cool lake water. His feet moved with incredible speed, sometimes rolling the log forward, sometimes back, changing direction on a whim, never giving the other a chance, never so much as losing a step. Every time he dunked a man, he hollered a challenge to all who remained, until a queue of men, young and middle-aged alike, fought for the chance to be next.

"That's some Paul Bunyan," said a voice at Katherine's elbow. "Mrs. MacCabe, I presume? Your husband, isn't he?"

"Yes, he . . ." She turned to face a stranger, a young man in shirtsleeves, banded above the elbows, a pencil behind his ear and another in his hand poised over a notebook. "I . . . I do not believe we've met. Are you a reporter, Mr . . ."

"Selby, ma'am, Matt Selby. Reporter for the *Weekly News* here in town. This is about the biggest event of the summer. Folks love to linger over every detail 'til the next celebration come fall. County fair in October," he explained, peering at her over round glasses that had slid down his short, freckled nose. He looked to be no more than twenty, and harmless, with a beguilingly boyish smile. Katherine found herself answering his questions, although her attention largely remained on her talented husband.

A roar went up from the crowd, following a splash as another beaten man hit the water. Standing stock-still on his log, feet widespread, Dandy fisted his hands above his head, challenging, "Anyone else needin' a bath this fine afternoon?" His head tipped at a cocky, questioning angle, and his grin was wide, dimpled, and a bit smug. No man came forward. As predicted, he'd beaten them one and all.

Ben Hosley, the millwright, loudly declared Dandy the winner and held aloft a trophy and a ten-dollar gold piece as the prize. Dandy casually walked to the butt end of the log and, in the process of leaping to shore, caused the log to flip up, towering above the crowd for an instant as if it might topple among them, then falling into the water, sending a tidal wave up and over the nearest people on shore.

Not even winded, Dandy caught the coin Ben tossed to him, bit down on it with his strong white teeth, declared it genuine, and bowed low before his startled wife.

"How was that, Katie?"

After a moment's silence, she didn't disappoint him. Her face glowing with pride, she declared, "Magnificent, Daniel, simply magnificent."

People crowded around to congratulate him, to express their awe, finally disbursing to find family members for a supper of leftovers from the noontime picnic.

Dandy stretched out in the grass, his hands behind his head, his legs crossed at the ankles. With a satisfied grin on his face, he rested, waiting for the band concert to start, then the fireworks. He'd done what he set out to do—prove himself to Kate and return her to his side where she belonged. Just let Richard Wilder make a move to try to steal her away again.

Kneeling at the edge of the picnic blanket, Katherine shook crumbs off her skirt, giving her husband a sidelong glance under lowered lashes. His victories had left him in a far better mood than earlier, and she fervently hoped that whatever had been ailing him was forgotten.

Beside her on the blanket, Celia napped, totally oblivious to the continued activity around her in her world of silence. Amelia had asked if Celia could come spend the night with her so she could test out some of the Chestersons' material before actual lessons began the next week. Katherine agreed to the plan, as had Dandy when Amelia shyly approached him. It pleased Katherine no end to know her husband had as much faith in the young woman's abilities as she did herself.

Thomas darted out of nowhere and skidded to a dusty stop before them, squirming like an overjoyed puppy.

"Johnny-D's lettin' me spend the night at his house. His maw says I gotta ask my folks. Can I go, can I? Pleeease?"

Dandy sat up, rubbing his palms over his knees, his gaze seeking Katherine's. She looked at him questioningly. A long minute passed.

"Celia won't be home tonight either," her husband reminded her somberly. "Well, Kate, what do you say?"

What could she say but yes in view of the pleading in Thomas's hazel eyes—and the unexpected, irresistible promise in her husband's?

15

Bright shards of red and blue and gold burst and bloomed and faded in the pitch-black sky.

As near to exploding as the sky-bent fireworks, Dandy sat cross-legged on a blanket in the grass beside Kate, about to crawl out of his skin with impatience. Katie had made no protest over the two of them being alone in the house overnight, and his hopes soared high. He was all but certain she had the same idea as he did of what lay ahead, and she was willing. Come hell or high water, tonight they'd at long last be using their shared marriage bed for more than just sleeping.

Made reckless by need, Dandy ignored the small voice inside telling him nothing had changed. His reason for not bedding her weeks sooner had not miraculously disappeared because jealously had fueled the fire of his desire for his wife, and opportunity, with the kids gone for the night, had flamed that fire into an uncontrollable blaze. He silently told the voice of common sense to go to hell. It was past time to take his virgin bride to bed, and dammit, that was what he was going to do before he went clean out of his head with wanting.

Almost without his knowledge, Dandy's craving for his wife, his Katie, had grown far beyond the lusting of his loins, becoming closer day by day to something blessedly and damnedly near to love. It'd crept into his being as silently as the blanketing snows of winter, felled him as surely and as fatally as a widow-maker blown free in a blizzard.

What he wished he knew now was Katie's feelings. A quick glance showed him her serene profile intent on the exploding sky, unaware of the thoughts spinning in his brain. He couldn't've been wrong, could he, earlier reading her look to be meaning she hungered and thirsted after him as much as he did her? That she had found something in him to love, just a little, these weeks they'd been married so their joining would leave her with no regrets?

Unanswered questions knotted the muscles at the back of his neck and gnawed at his insides. If only the dad-blasted fireworks would come to an end so the two of them could head on home. Then he'd gather his courage to find out where he stood. One way or the other.

Sitting quietly at her husband's side, Katherine clenched her hands in the folds of her skirts, determined not to jump at every booming crescendo, every fiery eruption, however much she longed to cry out, somehow release the tension building within. She hazarded a glance in Daniel's direction, but his gaze followed the fire show in the velvety black sky, his features boldly, if briefly, illuminated by a burst of brilliant color. Weakness quivered through her at the mere sight of his handsome silhouette against the luminous heavens, and she found herself trembling with fear as well.

What if she had mistaken the expression she'd earlier seen in her husband's warm brown eyes? What if he had not been silently pleading for her to agree to let the children sleep elsewhere tonight, and he had no intention of freeing her from the bondage of virginity? Suppose the idea originated only from her own deep desire, and not Daniel's—his conviction having not wavered concerning the consequences. Somehow she had failed to communicate to him that it was not just wanting a child of her own that drew her to him. It was simply her needing to be with him in the most intimate way possible, needing *him*. Now and evermore.

Shaken to her very soul by her overwhelming love for the magnificent man beside her, Katherine tried to recall the flaws she had seen in him only a few short weeks ago, and could not. The manners she'd once found lacking no longer seemed of any great importance, merely the trappings of a superficial society thankfully no longer a part of her life. She belonged here now, with this man and his son and his daughter. There was nowhere else in the world she'd rather be, so deeply had she grown to love Daniel Sean MacCabe. But did he return that love? Would he tell her, perhaps show her tonight while they were alone?

All but overcome with her apprehensions, the hopes she scarcely dared put word to, Katherine turned her gaze upward to the last of the fireworks, a spectacular finale.

Darkness fell around the crowd like a cloak. Disembodied voices spoke in whispers as families and couples moved off, seeking their vehicles, homeward bound. Dandy slipped his hand under Kate's elbow, wishing he dared to put an arm across her shoulders and pull her close, not at all sure of his reception if he did. She didn't speak, and neither did he, afraid anything coming out of his mouth might break the fragile peace between them. If only he knew what she was thinking and feeling. But Katie wasn't one to let it show on her face, and he was no mind reader.

"Nice night," he ventured.

She threw him a startled look, her thoughts likely miles away.

"What? Oh, yes . . . lovely."

"Grand fireworks."

The tip of her tongue darted out to wet her full lower lip, making it all the more kissable in the moonlight. Dandy offered up a silent groan, feeling a quivering response below his belt, willing himself to cool off, slow down.

"Most grand."

He'd forgotten whatever he'd said to prompt her comment. To cover his confusion he asked, "You warm enough? Let me give you my jack—" Then he remembered he wasn't wearing one and felt as stupid as a callow youngster fumbling through a first date.

"It is a mild night," Katherine responded, worrying her husband was floundering through small talk because he was so uncomfortable with the prospect of being alone with her, now and later, and felt her throat clog with unshed tears.

With only carriage lanterns to guide the way down the dark road, they sat intimately pressed together on the narrow wagon seat without exchanging a word. The closer they drew to home, the more nervously apprehensive Katherine grew. Her pulse quickened alarmingly, thrumming in her ears until she could no longer hear the crickets and cicadas singing their evening song in the tall grass at road's edge. With every turn of the wheel she was more positive she had misinterpreted her husband's desire to be alone with her. In all reality, little had changed between them. She longed for nothing more than to crawl into bed, pull the covers over her head, and stay there until the children returned in the morning.

Dandy pulled Bess to a stop before the back porch, more certain than ever that what he'd been thinking all the way home was the truth of the matter. Kate was as nervous as all get out at the thought of spending the night alone with her lawful husband. She no more wanted to go to bed with him than dance naked down the main street of town. Hell, she'd probably prefer appearing in the buff, truth be known. As pale as a ghost in the moonlight, she trembled from head to foot, yet she'd claimed she wasn't cold. What a fine mess they'd managed to make of a night offering so much promise. Still, he couldn't let her go on being scared to death of him and what he might do. He forced false good humor into his words.

"Now, don't go tryin' to get down by yourself in the dark, Kate. You might slip and fall."

He climbed over the wire back of the seat into the wagon bed, then balanced on the hub of the wheel, leaping lightly to the ground, silent in knee-high moccasins. He offered up his arms to her, his large hands circling her waist. Putting one foot and then the other where he directed, Kate let him lift her and set her safely on her feet. His hands stayed warm and firm on her waist, hers tight on his shoulders, his muscles bunched, rock hard, at her touch. His bride couldn't seem to bring herself to look into his eyes, and she kept her gaze downcast. He cursed himself for making her afraid. Curling a finger beneath her chin, tilting her head, he willed her to look him in the eyes and understand he meant her no harm.

They stood poised thus, each searching the other's face, seeking to learn what the other was thinking, feeling and, failing, finding only shadows. An owl hooted, breaking the spell. He stepped back, ending the tentative embrace. Her hands dropped to hide in the folds of her skirt, his to fumble for the reins draped loosely on the plank seat, his back to her now.

"I'll rub down Bess. Milk the cow. Be in soon's I can. No need to wait up, Kate. It's been a long day." Plucking the picnic hamper out of the wagon bed, setting it on the ground beside him, he half turned toward her. His gaze avoided hers, looking out and away over his fields instead of attempting to find hidden meaning in her face now bathed in moonlight.

She watched his supple, economical movements as he climbed aboard the wagon and offered a soft "gid'ep." Bess moved into a tired walk, her pace quickening as the barn grew close. Katherine wrapped her arms around herself, shivering, not cold exactly, yet chilled by their brief, unsatisfactory encounter. Had her husband any amorous intents for the evening, surely the cry of some night bird would not have dissuaded him. Only in her fantasy would the end of this day be different from any other.

Lifting up her skirts with one hand, the empty basket with the other, she entered the darkened kitchen. Lighting the overhead lantern did not dispel the dark shadows, except for a stark ring of light on the scarred porcelain tabletop. The bright celebrational holiday, and her hopes for its outcome, seemed but memories. If she went up to bed now, Katherine knew she would not sleep. Better to wait up for Daniel. Offer him a cup of coffee. Maybe talk a bit. Tell him—tell him what? How she really felt? How she needed him in her bed? Only if her courage did not fail her.

The water boiled; and Katherine made coffee. She stood at the window, cup in hand, looking outward, seeing nothing. Waiting. Time ticked slowly by, but Daniel did not return to the house. She waited. Paced. And at last went in search of him before her resolve weakened.

He sat haloed in the light of a single lantern hanging from a nail hammered into the overhead beam. In one hand he held a tack cloth, in the other the harness on which he'd been working. He might have been cleaning, polishing, but his attention had wandered, his gaze far-reaching into dark corners, unseeing. He looked as big and strong and capable as always, at the same time as lost and alone as she herself felt, his face pensive, sad. He turned at some small sound from her.

"Kate, what're you doin' still up?"

"I made coffee. Will you be coming in soon?"

"I was thinkin' I might sleep out here tonight."

"Daniel, have you been imbibing again—"

"Kate, you know I haven't. I just thought . . . well, I thought—"

"Then there is no reason you cannot spend the night in your own bed."

He threw her a sideways glance. "Isn't there, now, Katie?" He dropped the tack cloth into the pail beside him and stood, very carefully hanging the harness on its hook on the wall.

"Or . . . or one of us could sleep in Thomas's bed," she added in a tremulous voice, it suddenly occurring to her he might be loath to be near her, even in sleep.

His expression turned thunderous. "So now you cannot stand to share a bed with me, is that it, Kate?" His voice rumbled ominously.

Her chin came up though her eyes glittered suspiciously. Her hands locked into fists at her waist. "It is you who apparently cannot tolerate me, Daniel, preferring a bed of hay in the barn to . . . to . . ."

He came to her quickly, his chestnut gaze penetrating her eyes of gray, willing her not to look away. He briefly placed two fingers over her mouth. "Kate . . . Katie . . . if we were to climb in bed together tonight, alone in the house like we are . . . I do not think I'd be able to resist—"

A small, relieved sob escaped between her slightly parted lips. "Nor I you, Daniel," she whispered. Realizing she might have made a grievous error in assuming what he intended to say, she held her breath, waiting.

"What're ye tellin' me, Kate?"

She bit her lip, fearing she'd already said too much.

"Are ye tellin' me—Kate, look me in the eye, there's a lass—are ye tellin' me ye want us to share a bed—our marriage bed—that ye want me as much as I do you?"

"Yes, Daniel. Oh, yes," she whispered, scarcely able to breathe.

His head dipped; his mouth covered hers. One hand slid deep into her silken honey hair, his fingers splayed against her head; the other slipped around to the small of her back, pulling her closer. She responded by wrapping her arms around his neck, clinging as though she might never let go. Indeed, she prayed she might never have to, ever again. His lips parted; hers did, too. His tongue darted in, out, in. Hers followed suit.

He knelt, taking her down with him, and laid her back upon a clean bed of sweet-smelling hay, feathering kisses over her cheeks and chin and forehead. Her fingers, wove through the hair at his temples, gently tangling in fiery curls. He groaned; she sighed. Their lips met, the kiss long and lingering. Bodies entwined.

Dandy suddenly withdrew scrambling up off the floor and, gasping, bent forward, his hands resting just above his knees.

Bereft, Katherine rose as well, asking, "What—what is wrong? What did I do?"

"Nothin', Kate," he hastened to assure her, "ye've done nothin' wrong. 'Tis me. I can't be carryin' on like this, Katie, without goin' too far to turn back." Her bewildered, hurt look cut him to the quick. "What if I get you with child?"

Relieved, Katherine asked, "Is it not more likely you will

not?'' He was shaking his head, and quite suddenly anger rose within her. ''Daniel Sean MacCabe, what in the world leads you to believe it is your right to arbitrarily decide whether or not I shall bear children?'' She strode several paces away across the floor, turning, hay swirling around the hem of her skirt, hands on her hips. ''I am well aware you will be off in the woods a good part of each year. Am I to remain a childless virgin forever because of that, never to know intimacy with the man I lo—my husband, because *he* has decided I should never be a mother? How dare you make that decision for m—''

Hearing nothing after that one telling word, though but half spoken, Dandy reached her in a stride, grabbed her, and crushed her mouth under his to silence her, then gently folded her in his embrace.

''I love ye, too, Katie lass.'' His words came out husky with emotion.

Her heart all but bursting with wonder and relief, Katherine pressed her face against his rough shirtfront, arms around his waist, clinging, afraid to let go lest she was only imagining what she heard.

''Can't ye see, lass,'' he whispered against her hair, his breath hot, '' 'tis because I love ye I cannot go away in the fall leavin' ye to face childbearin' . . . maybe worse—''

''Like Annabella . . . your Annie?'' Bitter disappointment and jealousy tainted her words.

''*My* Annie? Meanin' my *wife* Annie?''

''Meaning the *pretty* wife you''—the words came hard—''loved best, and whom I am sure you were perfectly willing to go to bed with—''

Dandy threw back his head and barked a laugh. ''Me an' every man jack around.'' He sobered instantly, seeing how dead serious she was, how wounded. ''Kate, I told you I didn't love her—''

Tears beaded on her lashes, and she blinked. ''You did not tell me.''

''I didn't? I thought I told you everythin'—''

''I distinctly remember you saying we'd speak of it later . . . or something to that effect. The subject was never mentioned again . . . and what else was I to think with you hiding away her picture so you could sneak glimpses of it when you thought I was not looking—''

''Hidin'? Sneakin'? Katie, oh, Katie.'' He shook his head, his face unsmiling.

''You even brought it to bed on our first night in this h-house—''

''I did?'' He appeared thoughtfully puzzled. ''I seem to remember findin' it on the floor. Guess it fell out of my pocket, so I picked it up. Then you came to bed, and I stuffed it under the pillow out of the way . . . I only saved it for Thomas and Celia, so I'd have a reminder of her for them. If I pull it out on occasion, 'tis to help me recall what she was like at her best . . . for the children. You needn't be jealous—''

''I am not jealous,'' she insisted, turning her back, dipping her head so he couldn't see she was lying.

He refused to let her remain that way, saying as he pivoted her toward him, ''Probably no more'n I've been of Wilder. I've no cause, have I, Katie?''

Her head snapped up. ''Richard? Why would you even think such a thing?''

''Because you always seem to have your head together with him . . . talkin' . . . laughin' . . . like today at the picnic.''

''Today?''

''Servin' him cake, holdin' his hand—''

''Pretending to withhold his favorite chocolate cake so he made a grab for it,'' she finished. ''He is a tease, you know that. It means nothing. He flirts with everyone in skirts, except Amelia, who is smitten with him and whom I am trying desperately to get him to notice.''

He saw the truth of her words in her face and chuckled ruefully. ''Ah, Kate, aren't we a pair?''

She smiled her madonna smile. ''That we are, Daniel. Now will you please take me to bed?''

''Are ye sure?''

''Indeed I am. Oh! Oh, Daniel.''

He swooped her into his arms, then blew out the lantern,

throwing the barn into shadowed darkness. "Wouldn't ye rather have a roll in the hay, Kate?" he whispered into her ear. "I'm not all that sure I can wait 'til we reach our own sweet bed. I've been waitin' so long, I'm fair to burstin' with needin' ye."

"As I am you, Daniel. But, please, not here. Not this first time."

"As you wish, m'lady."

His strides long and urgent, he headed for the house, carrying her as though she weighed next to nothing. Unerringly he made his way through the dim kitchen and up the dark stairs, his hot breath fanning her cheek like a caress. For the second time he carried her over their threshold, praying to his blessed Saints this time it'd take. At her request he set her on her feet, pulling her into his embrace, kissing her thoroughly and long until she melted along the curves of his taut body and clung. She felt the hardness of his throbbing manhood, and a responding throbbing surged between her legs and spread through her limbs, making them weak. When the kiss at last ended and their lips reluctantly parted, Katherine spoke in a voice trembling with emotion.

"I shall hurry into my night things."

"Nay, Kate. Ye'll not be needin' them tonight."

His fingers began at the button of her collar and, releasing it, worked their way down to her waist. His hands slid up under the open garment, and the separate bodice slipped off her arms to fall to the floor. He kissed each shoulder, breathing in the warm, clean essence of rose-scented soap she bathed in. He found the fasteners at her waist; with a few nudges on his part, the striped skirt puddled at her feet.

"By the Saints, ye're wearin' that blasted corset again. It's been drivin' me crazy, Kate, knowin' these last weeks ye've been goin' without it."

"You knew?"

"Yes, lass, I knew, and died a thousand deaths with wantin' ye, an' thinkin' ye'd never want me."

"I felt the same. How foolish we've been. How much time we have wasted—"

"Then we'll be wastin' no more," declared Dandy,

swiftly releasing the corset hooks, sliding a hand beneath her camisole, and cupping one velvety white breast with a callused palm. He ran an equally callused thumb over its rosy peak, leaving it hard and so sensitive she groaned in ecstasy. "So ye like that, do ye, m'lady?" He bent and gently nipped her with his strong white teeth through the fabric.

Her head fell back. "Please . . . Daniel . . ." she said with a gasp.

He grinned a wicked, dimpled grin. "Please what? Please stop? Please more?"

"Yes, more. Please."

In one fluid movement he lifted her chemise over her head, discarding it with a toss. He dipped his head and suckled at one soft, firm orb while caressing the other. When this delicate torture became more than she could endure, Katherine swayed toward him, clutching the fabric of his shirt in both hands.

"I . . . did not know . . . it would be like this."

"We've only just begun, Kate." His husky voice whispered against her cheek.

"Then, Daniel, you must . . . undress as well. I need . . . I need . . ."

"You need what, Kate?"

Her cheeks flushed hotly, but she lifted her head to look deep into his eyes. "To see you . . . touch you . . . all over . . ."

With her assistance, Dandy made quick work of getting rid of moccasins, shirt, and jeans, beneath which he wore nothing. Katherine divested herself of three summer petticoats to stand in pantaloons only, glancing up shyly to see her husband most grandly revealed.

"Gracious, Daniel, you are most generously endowed," she blurted.

He chuckled softly, admitting, "No more than most, Kate. Are you frightened?" he added seriously.

"A little, perhaps," she admitted, unable to tear her gaze from his aroused manhood.

He caressed her cheek with a feather touch. "I wish I

could promise not to hurt ye, sweetlin', but in truth the first time is most always painful for a woman. But there's pleasure, too, more'n there are words to tell. Only let me show you, lass—"

"Oh, yes, Daniel. Please do."

He lifted her into his arms once again and carried her to their bed across a room lit only by moonbeams and set her down on the edge. Standing back, he requested, "Take down yer hair for me, Kate."

He watched her hands working slowly, seductively releasing a turn in one plait, then another until at last she shook her head and her honey hair flowed freely down her back and over her shoulders, covering her breasts to her waist. He dipped both hands in the silky stuff, running it through his fingers from her scalp outward to the tips. And again. Pulling fistfuls gently to his face, he breathed in the wholesome cleanness of rose soap. Groaning in happy agony, he pressed her down on the mattress. He released the button to her pantaloons, sliding the fabric downward. Cupping her now bare derriere, Dandy lifted her, discarding her last bit of clothing. When she would have covered herself, he would not let her, pulling her hands away, holding them, kissing each palm. Looking into her eyes, he told her, "There's to be no modesty between us. The good Lord made us as we are, man and woman, gave his blessing to us as husband and wife. There's nothin' wrong with drinkin' our fill with lookin' and touchin' . . . only pleasure, Kate, pleasure ye can't begin to imagine."

"Show me, Daniel," she demanded urgently.

Stretching out beside her on the bed, Dandy placed a large gentle hand on her belly, just below the waist. Beneath the velvet softness of her fair skin, taut muscles quivered.

"Relax, sweetlin'," he murmured.

"I . . . I am trying, Daniel. I want to. Only, it feels so . . . strange. I have never experienced another's touch so intimately before."

He raised up on an elbow, resting his chin on his hand, a bemused smile on his face.

"I would hope that you haven't, Kate, not since your

mother bathed you and dressed you in nappies. Put away your fears now, lass. Think of nothin' but my touch upon you. Here. And here. And here.''

He ran his hand slowly, very slowly, upward, his rough palm sliding around the hardened tip of first one breast and then another. She made a low, throaty sound and lay still under his exploring hand. Propped on his elbow, he looked down at her face gone smooth with pleasure, eyes half closed, her head pressed back against a pillow, feeling instead of thinking. He dipped his head to kiss her on the cheek and forehead and chin, on neck and shoulder and breast, while his hand slid to her waist, rested there, and continued to her belly. He stopped at the faint, involuntary tightening of her muscles. He felt the release of tension, and grew braver. Turning his fingers downward, he buried them in the springy, clinging curls of her feminine mound, reaching farther, finding her moist intimacy with searching fingertips. He withdrew quickly before she could protest. Slipping his hand across her hip, he grasped her buttocks to lift and turn her toward him. Looking into her face to see her gray eyes wide open, staring, a bit frightened but wanting, needing.

He kissed her full, moist lips. Languidly her arms came up around his neck. Her breath against his lips came in short, uneven gusts. His chest against hers, their heartbeats matching, he held her quietly, massaging her hip, her thigh, her long, supple back.

''Are you ready to go on, lass?'' he whispered in her ear.

Katherine nodded silently against his chest and rolled onto her back, gazing unblinkingly into his eyes, willing herself to cast aside fear and modesty, desiring the feel of his hands on her flesh forever. The sensations evoked by his touch enervated her, excited her, left her quivering with delight. Made her want to explore every part of him as he did her. Her hands slid down his chest, capturing curls, skimming over small, hard nipples, delighting in his throaty groan so like the one he'd brought forth from her. Her hands followed the thin line of curls to his waist, then hesitated.

''Go on, Katie, go on. Only lightly, if ye've any mercy.''

He could barely get the words out over his need for release.

Her fingertips brushed his maleness, one hand slipping beneath, one continuing its journey to its tip. So soft it was, yet so unresisting and hard she longed to continue until she had learned all its secrets, and his. There were beads of perspiration above his upper lip and rising on his forehead. His body shuddered under her touch. A growl surged from deep within him.

"No more," he whispered harshly, "I can stand no more 'til ye've had yer turn, sweet love." He lifted her hands swiftly to his lips and kissed them so she'd understand she'd done no wrong.

She understood that he was not displeased with her, indeed desired her so much he was nearly beyond self-control. Reluctantly Katherine left her fascinating explorations. His own gentle, persistent caresses had begun anew, bolder now, reaching sacred, untouched territory, and Katherine quickly lost all sense of time and place, all her puritanical modesty, with the new and overwhelming sensations his seeking fingers brought forth. Every nerve in her body surged wildly to life, while at the same time every muscle seemed to grow weak, completely unresisting. When his fingers touched her triangle of curls, then farther, she had no strength to resist. She felt him touch her, just so, in some mysterious, agonizingly sensitive spot she did not know existed, and heat glowed at the source of his touch, spreading upward, making her half crazed. She thought she heard herself beg, "More, more," but wasn't sure if it were inside her head or cried aloud. Her will gone, she allowed him to spread her legs, to mount himself over her, to touch his manhood against her. He continued to caress with his hand and with his lower body. From a fog she heard him murmur, "This will hurt a bit," but it didn't matter. She felt a small, sharp tearing of flesh, then he slid inside, filling her, fulfilling her, making her his wife, his woman, his love—at last.

He rested, panting, when she would have him go on. When she could stand the waiting no longer, he began the slow, subtle movements as old as man and womankind. The sensations Katherine had believed so overwhelming only moments before waned when compared to those she experienced now. His thrusts grew stronger, faster. Without conscious thought, she began to move in the same rhythm, ecstasy warring with the agony of the building need at her core. Fierce white heat swelled within her, glorious tension building to the peak of endurance—and beyond—and when she could take no more, exploding throughout her body like a rapid volley of fireworks. Her screams rose in exquisite agony as Daniel's thrusts increased rather than diminished. His triumphant shout of release mingled with hers.

Like returning darkness after the last climactic rocket, so did languid contentment spread through every fiber of Katherine's being. Daniel poised over her, his hands braced on the pillows against her cheeks, his head lolling backward, eyes closed. She could see the rapid pulse throbbing in his throat beneath clinging tendrils of russet curls, feel that same pulse deep within her maidenhead wherein he'd left his seed. She found him watching her, searching her face. Apparently finding what he sought, he smiled, dimpling.

"I believe ye liked that, Mrs. MacCabe," he teased, his eyes black with passion but twinkling in the depths.

Her cheeks grew warm, and she didn't care. "You assume correctly, Mr. MacCabe," she agreed, then uttered a faint moan of protest when he withdrew from her and stretched out beside her, one leg cocked up and over her stomach.

"Ah, lass, ye've wearied me." He sighed contentedly. "I've not felt so fine for a good long time . . . perhaps never."

"Nor I, Daniel."

She wrapped her arms around his waist. Together they rested. Katherine's heart slowed to its normal, steady beat, as did his under her ear pressed to his broad, muscled chest. After a while she felt the heat in her groin, that earlier had almost overtaken her, glowing like a hot ember once more.

"Daniel? Daniel, you aren't asleep, are you? Daniel?"

"Mmmmmmmmmmmmmmm?"

"Could . . . could we . . . ummm . . . do that again?"

A long pause. "In a little while, Katie," he said at last. "It takes a bit of time . . . to . . . to . . ." She was uncon-

sciously kneading his backside as if she were learning to
knead bread. Dandy felt his manhood quiver in response.
He waited, unbelieving, for surely he was wrong. He'd
never been able . . . 'til now. Her hands roamed all over his
back, returning time and again to knead . . . "It takes a bit
of time . . ." He tried to remember what he'd been saying,
and couldn't. A sound filled his throat, a growl, a groan.
"Awww, Katie, me love, yer about to have yer way
sooner'n I dreamed possible." With a happy sigh, Dandy
rose up over his wife, slipping his burgeoning manhood
once more deeply within her, to her most vocal delight.

16

"I did it!"

"The *whole* loaf?"

"Every slice identical to the ones before and after," Katherine gloated triumphanty, smugly surveying the stack of even bread slices on the cutting board.

"Then tonight's the night."

"Indeed it is."

"I can't wait to see the look on Daniel's face when you tell him."

Amelia's blue eyes sparkled, and she giggled, so much less the shy young woman of weeks earlier, and Katherine marveled at the transformation. Now, if only Richard Wilder would soon notice as well. Up to now, the young man seemed oblivious to all Katherine's attempts to get him to see Amelia's obvious virtues. Matchmaking apparently was not her forte.

"I am looking forward to the sight of my husband, soaked to the skin, dancing a jig in that cold stream." She chuckled at the image she had evoked.

Once believing laughing aloud unladylike, now Katherine took pleasure in that and so many other things once forbidden. Smiles and laughter and a sense of well-being filled each and every day from sunrise to sunset. Once a lonely

and bitter spinster, now she felt loved, and loved wholeheartedly in return. How could she be anything but totally
happy? She performed meaningful labor from dawn to dusk
and had beloved children to do for and to nurture. And, most
importantly, she had a husband who sought ways to please
her from morning to evening, and through the sweet dark
hours of the night. Just the thought of their lovemaking
brought a flush of expectation to her cheeks, then she realized her thoughts might be transparent enough for Amelia
to see.

Glancing at her companion, Katherine found the young
woman's gaze upon her, an expression of longing—and
envy—in her knowing eyes. With the universal desire of a
happily married woman, Katherine prayed her friend would
one day soon experience the same contentment. If there
were a way on earth or in heaven to make Richard Wilder
aware of the treasure that was his for the taking, she would
see to its doing, Katherine silently vowed.

Amelia roused herself first to break the silence. "I think
I'll ask Richard if we might stay on for a while after supper.
I'm sure he'll want to be here for the dunking, too."

The mere mention of the young man's name brought rosy
color to her cheeks and love lights to her bright blue eyes,
leaving no doubt in Katherine's mind that the two must be
brought together soon.

"A splendid idea, since Daniel took such pride in demonstrating his skill with water sports on the Fourth," Katherine quipped.

Cheerfully they returned to their noontime labors. Amelia
poured milk and set out bread, butter and jam, potato salad,
and ham. Katherine laid place settings of dishes and table-
ware for four, wishing Daniel did not have to carry his lunch
with him into the far fields. She missed him and the casual
meals they and the children had previously shared with
Amelia and Richard, like one large genial family. Wiping
her hands on her apron, she stepped out onto the back porch
to call in Thomas and Celia, savoring another dry, sunny
day in late July and the blessed country silence.

Not total silence, of course. Listening attentively, Katherine became at once aware of the churr of the crickets, the industrious buzz of bees, and the contented cluck of the chickens pecking in their fenced yard. Sometimes it was possible to hear the occasional plop of a frog into the stream nearby. On a breezy day, one could catch the sound of the wind through the cornfields, a whisper without words.

Since today was Monday, drying sheets slapped on the line. On Tuesday, a hot iron would hiss on dampened fabric, followed on subsequent days by housecleaning with its own select sounds, sweeping sounds, scrubbing sounds, sounds of beaters striking rugs hung over the porch rail. Daily in the kitchen, logs snapped and sparked in the cookstove, pans clanged, bacon sizzled, and stews bubbled. The staccato of hammer and nails came from the barnyard and barn, as well as the low of the cow begging for milking. Come evening, shouts of greeting from Dandy and Richard could be heard when they came home from the fields. Thomas never failed to be boisterously loud, no matter what he was doing, including hollering at his sister who couldn't hear him—or any of the other sounds of the land, the season, or the labor.

It occurred to Katherine that she had not heard Thomas's voice in quite some time. Usually this close to a mealtime he and his sister played within calling distance, more often under foot in the kitchen. Certainly no farther away than just out of sight in the front yard.

Quelling her tendency to worry, Katherine cupped her hands to her mouth and called, "Thomas." A pause. "Thomas. Lunch." She listened for a responding "Coming!" but the cry was not forthcoming. She tried again, willing all the summer sounds to cease so she could hear the faintest reply. She received none. Icy fingers of panic slithered up her spine and embraced her heart. The bright, beautiful day dimmed though the azure sky remained cloudless. "Thomas, answer me, please. Thomas? Celia?"

"They probably wandered off farther than they realized," Amelia said from the doorway.

Katherine shook her head, scanning the yard and closest fields with a troubled gaze, silently praying for Thomas and Celia to come running across them, homeward bound.

"I hope that is all . . ." Katherine abruptly stopped herself from revealing her true concern, suddenly all too aware how quickly happiness and a sense of security could be snatched away by dread and growing terror.

Amelia tried again. "You know how eager Thomas is to explore every inch of the farm. And Celia's so determined not to be left behind."

"Of course. You are probably right. Still . . ." Again she could not continue.

Her hands cupped to her mouth, Katherine called out. Amelia added her voice as well, but without results.

"They must be close by somewhere, Kate," Amelia insisted. "Maybe hiding from us—"

"They would not hide from me or go very far without telling me. They've been taken—" All the fear and worry building inside of Katherine burst forth, and too late to take the words back, once spoken.

"Taken?" Amelia repeated the word, incredulous.

"I did not mean to say that. I . . ." But she could not lie to her good friend.

"You don't have to tell me. I know you and Daniel have something you can't share."

"However did you guess?"

"By that look you exchange whenever you hear someone approach the house. The way you keep a watchful eye on the children."

Katherine's shoulders sagged, and she studied Amelia's compassionate face, more frightened than before. "I had no idea we were so transparent," she admitted woefully.

Amelia lightly touched her upper arm. "Only to me, because I'm with you all day, every day," she quickly assured her. "Can I help? I don't want to interfere if you feel you're unable to trust me, but you know I will do anything . . ."

"There is no one I trust more, 'Melia."

In the end, Katherine blurted out everything, emphasizing what Grandmother Stewart intended for the future of each child.

Tears sparkled on Amelia's lashes when her friend finished. "That's the most horrid thing I have ever heard."

She stamped her foot. "Those children must be kept out of that terrible woman's clutches, no matter what. Oh, surely she can't have gotten her hands on them already!"

Having shared her burden, Katherine's spirits lifted a bit, especially in light of her companion's righteous indignation, knowing in her heart of hearts Amelia would not betray them. She would have to tell her husband she had shared their secret with the young woman—but later, when the children were safely home.

"Perhaps my imagination has been overactive," she assured the worried and frightened Amelia. "Maybe we have only to look harder, seek them farther afield."

"They're bound to turn up somewhere nearby," Amelia agreed. "They could be lingering at the pasture. You know what affection Thomas has for the cow and her calf, how seriously he takes his responsibilities."

"The pasture. Of course! Why did I not think of that?" exclaimed Katherine with renewed hope.

They hastened to the clover-filled meadow as fast as their heavy skirts and petticoats permitted, and found the small, enclosed field empty.

"Where are Bossie and Brutus?"

"Look. The fence is broken." Amelia pointed to the far side, nearest the extensive swamp between their property and Allen's.

Closer examination revealed splintered rails and footprints in the muddy soil, two sets of four with cloven hooves, two sets human, one boy-sized, one tiny, toes turned in, heading into the swamp. Her relief that they'd not been spirited away by Grandmother Stewart's henchman pitifully short-lived, Katherine uttered a small bleat of distress, covering her mouth, for the evidence before them spoke as clearly as words of the fate of the youngsters.

"The animals broke out, and the children went after them," Amelia concluded in a half whisper.

Katherine's hands fisted at her sides. "We must follow." She was terrified of the swamp—the snakes, the treacherous ground underfoot, the wild animals. But for Thomas and Celia, she would face anything.

Amelia caught her arm. "We can't find them in there by ourselves. We need help. We have to ring the bell, Kate. Summon Daniel and Richard in from the fields. They'll come at a run when they hear it."

"You are right, of course."

Lifting her skirts, she took off at a trot, Amelia at her heels. Dandy and Richard arrived while Amelia still tolled on the emergency bell set on a post in the yard. Katherine ran to meet them. Dandy caught her by the shoulders.

"Kate, are ye all ri—"

"The cow and her calf got out, and the children followed them into the swamp."

"The Saints have mercy, we must find them, an' quickly."

Richard, the calmest, offered the first practical suggestion. "We'll go out searching, you and me, Daniel. The women can stay here in case the children turn up on their own."

"I will not be left behind," declared Katherine.

"Nor I," added Amelia, and all heads turned toward her at the firm decisiveness in her voice. "If Thomas had heard us calling—or ringing the bell—he'd have brought Celia home by now."

They followed the footprints of beasts and children into the swamp. All too soon, the muck that outlined the tracks became so liquid as to cover them instead. The four stood close together on a grassy rise, searching for some sign of the children's passage.

"There's nothin' to do but split up, Richard with Amelia, and Kate and myself."

No one argued the sensibility of the arrangement. The two pairs set off, choosing the widest openings between trees, the driest bits of land, assuming the children might have done the same. At Richard's suggestion, they marked their trail with a bent branch or uprooted weed to keep themselves from getting as lost as Thomas and Celia.

Katherine's fear became a palpable thing, more thick and smothering with every step. She was afraid of the creatures living in the surrounding underbush and in the stagnant water through which they sloughed their way. She feared for herself—and for Thomas and Celia, who were likely as frightened as she. The hem of her skirt dragged, caked and sodden, impeding her progress. Water had long ago invaded her boots, her feet blistered with the friction of wet stockings against tender skin. Biting mosquitoes and flies welted her face and neck and hands with their stings. Low-hanging branches tore at her clothing and scratched her face. Brambles captured her skirts, like grasping claws holding her back. Daniel, she knew, fared no better, but he never gave any indication, with a word or a look, that he felt anything but the determination to find his children safe and sound. Katherine gritted her teeth and silently vowed she could do no less.

A mere hour or so past noon the dismal swamplands seemed as dark as twilight. Sinister shadows stretched long at their feet. Before long, what small light remained would fade as well. A terrifying place for anyone to lose his way, especially youngsters.

Frequently she and Daniel stopped to call out. Sometimes they heard an echoing call, but in the voices of Richard and Amelia, never Thomas.

Daniel stopped abruptly. "They came this way," he cried out, pointing to small prints in two sizes on a bit of muddy hill. "And look, they're still trailin' those blasted animals." Clearly the bovine tracks angled alongside. "Thomas! Thomas, it's Da. Answer if you hear me. Thomassss!" Desperation echoed in his shout.

He strode off after the prints, Katherine following, only to have them soon disappear. Dandy ran his hands through his hair; his shoulders slumped in weary defeat. Katherine linked her hands around his upper arm, feeling the muscles bunch.

"We will find them, Daniel."

"Aye, that we will, sooner or later. But when? An' how will they be farin' by then?" he challenged, frustrated and angry with helplessness. "There's nothin' more important to me in this world or the next than my children, Kate."

"I know, Daniel." Her voice quavered with the intensity of her emotions.

Daniel pulled her into his arms. "Don't look so scared, Katie. By the gods, we'll find the lad and lass safe and sound. I'm certain of it," he insisted with false self-assurance.

"I am, as well, Daniel," Katherine agreed, only half believing her own words, and his. Should anything happen to those two precious children . . . She could not even finish the thought.

Not far away, Amelia kept pace with Richard, placing her steps in his before they had time to disappear in a swirl of muddy water. She was determined to keep up, to prove she was as capable as the others. Though she wore a light, work-weight corset, she was soon breathless and panting. Finally she was forced to stop, gasping for air.

Sensing Amelia was no longer behind him, Richard glanced over his shoulder. Her cheeks had gone pale, her breathlessness evident in the heave of her chest. He retreated a step or two.

"Are you all right? You aren't going to pass out on me, are you?"

She waved away the possibility with a gesture. "I . . . I'm . . . afraid . . . my legs . . . aren't . . . as long . . . as . . . as . . . yours. I'll . . . be . . . all right . . . as . . . soon . . . as I catch . . . my breath."

Contrite, Richard took her arm and led her to a fallen log, sitting down beside her, elbows to knees, waiting, eyes searching where their feet had not yet tread.

"Never did like this place much," he admitted conversationally.

"Nor . . . nor I." More breathless now at his solicitous touch than the rapid pace, Amelia felt color swiftly return to her cheeks. "We . . . weren't . . . allowed . . . to play . . . here . . . as children." The return to normal breathing was seriously hampered by Richard's close proximity. A new discomfort rose up in her, the shyness that had been her lifelong bane once again taking over. "Shall . . . we . . . go on? I . . . I'm less . . . winded now."

"In a minute," Richard agreed, then searched his mind for something to say to fill the awkward silence rising between them. "I want to tell you I've been admiring the way you've helped Celia."

The flush on her cheeks revealed her pleasure. Turquoise eyes offered silent thanks.

"Celia's such a dear to work with, and so eager to learn. . . . I . . . I think I've made real progress."

He was definitely on the right track now. Inordinately pleased with himself, Richard continued along the same line. "Anyone could learn from you, Amelia. You have a natural talent for teaching." He found himself speaking with real sincerity.

"I appreciate your saying that . . . more than you can know," she confided. "I—I—I'm thinking of going back to school . . . to obtain a teacher's certificate. Possibly help other deaf children."

"*Away* to school?" Unexpected panic flared in his chest. "But I thought you already worked as a . . . a . . ." Richard frantically searched his mind for a forgotten bit of knowledge.

"I found employment as a seamstress for a while," Amelia admitted, "but I wasn't cut out for it. Traveling from home to home. Staying weeks, sometimes months at a time. Living in unheated attic rooms; sewing dawn to dusk . . ." She paused, shuddering. "I couldn't endure it and came running back home to Mama."

"You'd be leaving home to go to school," Richard reminded her a bit desperately.

"But I'll be returning in a year's time with such valuable knowledge. And the right to teach officially."

A year, thought Richard, *a whole year.* For someone he'd scarcely noticed until—when was it? he couldn't recall—he found himself missing shy, sensible Amelia Weatherby already, and he wasn't so sure he'd be able to let her go when the time came.

"Richard?"

"Huh? What?"

"I'm all right now. We can go on."

Tongue-tied for possibly the first time in his life, Richard stammered out, "Which way? You know this area best. I'm a city boy, remember."

Amelia looked around, frowning thoughtfully.

"I hear Katherine and Daniel over to the left. We must be crossing one another's trails, covering the same areas over and over . . . missing others altogether."

Richard jumped up, pulling Amelia to her feet beside him. "I hadn't thought of that, but you're right. We could waste hours without finding those kids unless we come up with a plan to keep us from retracing our steps. Amelia, you're one smart lady for realizing our mistake."

He took a long second look at the flushed young woman before him, her head tipped down and away from his scrutiny, her smooth brown hair auburn in the weak, dappled sunlight. A quiet little thing she was, not bold as brass tacks, too loud, or far too bossy, like her twin. Amelia's voice was always soft, and when she spoke, like now, she had something worth hearing to say. She was good-natured to boot. Every day, without exception, he heard her singing or humming while she worked. And, on second look, Amelia was mighty pretty to look at. Small and dainty and trim-waisted. Fine features. Big blue eyes. Heck, there wasn't much about her that wasn't gentle, sweet, and lovely. She was too darn good for the likes of him to be thinking about that way.

He cleared his throat. "Let's call in the others and see what we can work out."

An hour later, working as a team, they spread in a line a length from each other, scouring the muck and swill at their feet with every step, sometimes finding a clue, more often going on instinct alone. The afternoon passed all too quickly. Though daylight lingered long in late July, precious little of it penetrated the swamp, less and less as early evening progressed. Among the four hung the unspoken fear that darkness would fall before the children were found, and that in the blackness of the impenetrable night, they, too, might fall victims to the swamp.

In the end, good fortune smiled, and prayers were answered. In the last lingering moments of twilight, they found the children beside the stream at the edge of the MacCabe property. At dusk, old Bossie had circled around, heading for her own dry stall, her calf and the children trailing behind. A wet and filthy Thomas dozed on a grassy berm, propped against a tree. Celia curled against his side, mud-crusted but unharmed, and sleeping. The cow and her calf stood placidly by, with Thomas's fist securely around a rope tethering them together.

"Thomas!" Dandy's cry was joyous now.

Thomas woke with a start and dislodged Celia, waking her.

"Da!" Thomas scrambled to his feet. Ever mindful of his responsibilities, he did not let go of the rope. "I found 'em. Dad-burned cow went an' kicked a hole in the fence an' took off with her dumb ol' baby followin'. But me an' Celia, we found 'em." He puffed out his chest proudly.

Dandy, who'd been about to embrace his boy in a hug, stopped in his tracks. Something in the lad's stance told him this was no time to embarrass him with a display of unwanted emotion. Thomas had done what he thought he had to, and succeeded. A man's job deserved a man's praise. Later, privately, he'd give him a scolding. But for now, Dandy swallowed hard and clapped the boy soundly on the shoulder.

"Good job, son." He cleared his throat. "Next time, though, when you've a man-sized task ahead of ye, ye might leave Celia home with Katie."

Thomas scuffed a muddy shoe in the tufted grass. "Sorry for makin' ya worry, Kate. Celia wouldn't stay behind no matter how many times I signed for her to, danged female."

"Thomas, such language," chided Katherine, as much from relief as dismay. She had a fair idea from whom he'd learned the phrase. She arched a single brow in her husband's direction.

Shamefaced, Dandy quickly sought to turn her attention elsewhere. "You ought to see yourself, Kate, all covered with mud. And you, Thomas. And my little lass." He picked her up and held her close until she squirmed. "Ye can't even tell she's kin. The rest of us look no better."

Out of the blue, a wicked thought came to her. "I know how *one* of us can rid himself of a layer of filth, Daniel . . . someone who owes his wife a dunking and a dance."

Glancing at his wife, he then gave her his full attention, not at all sure he liked the mischievous smile playing around the edges of Kate's lips, and the same smug grin on Amelia's face.

"Oh, how so, wife? You tryin' to tell me you sliced an entire loaf into perfect, equal slices?"

"She did. I saw them myself," Amelia spoke up impulsively. "In fact, the loaf's probably still sitting on the kitchen table, if you'd like to go check, Daniel."

Dandy looked from one to the other of the young women and could tell they spoke the truth.

"Then a dunkin' and a jig ye shall have. But with the Saints as my witnesses, I'll never make a bet with me wife again. At least one I'm not positive of winnin'." With a wicked wink, he headed the procession to the edge of the low, pebbly bank of their own spring-fed stream, now little more than a ribbon of darkness disappearing into the night around a gigantic weeping willow standing sentinel.

Taking a deep breath, Dandy plunged into the water to his waist, then flung himself backward, disappearing beneath his own swirling ripples. Coming up gasping with the cold, he stood, dripping, demanding, "Are ye satisfied now, lass?"

"There is still the matter of the jig, Daniel."

"Could we not be savin' that for another warmer time?" begged her husband, wrapping his arms around himself and shuddering mightily.

Katherine gave the matter some serious thought. "Perhaps we might," she agreed at last. "I should hate to miss any of the intricacies of the dance in the dark."

"And with me bein' a man of my word, darlin' wife, ye can be certain someday soon I'll be doin' my little dance for ye, come hell or high water. And now I've another treat for ye, one guaranteed to please ye as well."

He'd risen out of the water as he spoke, caught up her hand, and now pulled her determinedly to the water's edge.

"Daniel . . . Daniel . . . what are you doing—?"

"Just savin' ye the trouble of bathin' tonight and doin' a wash tomorrow." In the dusk, his eyes glittered with devilment, and his grin grew wide as he continued dragging her into the water.

"Daniel, stop. Right now. This is . . . this is . . . cold. F-f-freezing . . ." But delightfully refreshing to perspiring skin abused by biting bugs and clawing brambles.

Certain she wouldn't return to shore, Dandy released her to sit in water to his shoulders, then lay back, dunking completely beneath. He sat up, shaking his copper mane, spraying his wife nearby, and those standing on the bank.

Thomas laughed uproariously, hopping from one caked foot to the other. "Da, you an' Kate're gettin' all wet."

"But cleaner'n before we jumped in. Come on, lad, and bring your little sis with ye."

Thomas complied without hesitation on his part or Celia's. Katherine bent to splash water onto her forearms, then dip her face into cupped hands, commenting to the astounded Amelia and the grinning Richard, "This is indeed refreshing. You should join us." With that, she sat down in the water, her skirt ballooning up around her.

"Can't resist an offer like that." Richard caught Amelia's elbow, leading her, unprotesting, into the water.

Adults and children alike cavorted in the cold, clear water of the stream, washing away the grime and pain of their adventure. Shoes were flung up on the bank. It was a time of relief for tragedy averted, a time to release pent-up tension turned to silent exaltation for the safe return of the children. A time of foolish, happy-go-lucky joy.

Finally, reluctantly, Dandy suggested, "We'd best be climbin' out before it's too dark to locate our footgear and find our way home. But 'twas grand, *clean* fun while it lasted, was it not?"

Katherine, Amelia, and Richard groaned in unison. Kate said, "And a lot more humorous than that poor attempt at a joke, Daniel."

Dandy sobered after a bit. "I've a need to express thanks to ye all for helpin' me find my babes. I'm in your debt, Richard, and yours, Amelia. As for you, Katie, me love," he said as he caught her about the shoulders, pulling her to him, giving her a smacking kiss, " 'twas my good fortune to have met and had the good sense to marry ye. You're a wife beyond measure."

"And you, Daniel," Katherine retorted wryly, relieved he could not see the pleased, if embarrassed, flush to her cheeks in the darkness, "are a flatterer beyond that same measure. Now, may we head for home before we freeze where we stand?"

17

A day that might have come to a tragic end concluded with boisterous, rollicking good fun. Life once again settled into long days of hard work, evening sunsets from the back porch, and nighttimes learning the intricacies of each other's bodies in lovemaking. Except to Katherine, nothing was the same as before. Characteristically, when troubles weighed heavily, she withdrew into herself, unable to share her fears, even with her husband.

Throughout the next day and subsequent ones, troublesome thoughts invaded her mind, whether she was awake or asleep, and simply wouldn't go away, like a nagging toothache one worries with the tongue. In spite of herself, Katherine dwelt on the concern, awakened during the dismal trek through the swamp, over how quickly the children could be snatched from them, through accident *or* the indefatigable perseverance of their grandmother. The inevitability of her taking Thomas and Celia out of hers and Daniel's care became all-consuming in Katherine's mind, until all else paled in meaning.

She grew afraid to let them out of her sight, though in good conscience she could not refuse Thomas the freedom to do his chores and Celia to tag along—no matter what her state of agitation until their safe return.

At night she dreamed she ran through house and barn and field calling their names, never finding them. She awoke crying out, seeking comfort in her husband's arms but unable to tell him, when he asked, what in her dreams terrified her so—as if putting her fears into words might bring them to life, or that to tell him was to question the wisdom of Daniel's decision to move to the farm in the first place. Instead she allowed herself to be rocked back to sleep with an Irish lullaby, hoping against hope in the bright light of morning that her fears would be gone. They never were.

If only she did not feel unwell, Katherine was certain the vagaries of her mind would not be so tormenting. She awoke each morning with a nagging headache, an uneasy stomach, an aching back, and a general tenderness, especially in her breasts, giving cause to the belief she had contracted some illness from the miasma of the swamp.

Exhausted from sleepless nights, ill and out of sorts, she'd also apparently lost the ability to form rational thoughts. A week or more passed before it occurred to her to question her diagnosis, to count back on the calendar, realizing two weeks had passed beyond the time of her monthly flow. She who was always regular month after month since the onset of her menses in her early teens.

"I cannot be with child," she told her pale, drawn reflection in the mirror over her bureau. "I simply cannot."

Daniel's warning against such an occurrence came to mind, but visions of Martha suffering through the labor and delivery of twins took all remaining color from her cheeks and all blood from her head. In a half swoon, she sought the bed with groping hands, and collapsed upon it until black spots ceased to dance before her closed eyes.

Grasping at straws of hope, Katherine tried in vain to recall any other occasion upon which her monthly cycle had failed to complete itself with absolute regularity. Not during the trials of nursing her parents through their last illness, making necessary arrangements, and burying them. Not when learning she was next to penniless. Not upon being forced into marriage with Mr. Daniel Sean MacCabe, leaving everything behind to follow him into the unknown.

Throughout, her body had functioned with repeated, unshakable regularity. So why, oh, why, had it failed her now?

She tried not to let herself think of the prospect of pregnancy, yet the thought, once brought to mind, could not be erased. What would Daniel say if she told him? More importantly, what would he do? As adamant as he'd been about her *not* getting with child, there was every possibility he'd fly into a rage. Or worse, he might leave her. No, not that, not with Thomas and Celia to consider. After all, they were the reason he married her in the first place. He could withdraw from her in other ways just as damaging, however. He could refuse her in bed, deny her his laughter and smiles, treat her like a stranger as he did in the beginning; he could do all those things and destroy her as surely as if he were to walk out the door.

Not knowing what to do, Katherine decided to simply do nothing until possibly forced by nature to act otherwise. Or until she felt better, more able to cope. With a sigh she closed her eyes, knowing sleep would not come even in a short, refreshing nap. She willed the turmoil within her to settle so she could be up and about to do her chores.

Dandy paused outside their bedroom door on his way to the children's room, bent on locating his favorite hammer Thomas had somehow misplaced. He heard Katherine's small sigh and looked in to see her stretched out at an angle on the bed, flat on her back, one foot on the floor, an arm flung up to cover her eyes. At first he thought she was catching a few winks after another restless night's sleep. Then he saw her worry her lower lip between her teeth, clench and unclench her hands spasmodically, and he knew she found no rest.

Something had been tormenting her for days, maybe weeks, troubling her awake, torturing her sleep. Something she wouldn't share with him, declaring it nothing when he inquired. If he persisted, she all but burst into tears or got mad enough to call him Mr. MacCabe for hours afterward. He gave up finally. If she wanted to confide in him, she knew where to find him. But it hurt like . . . like *hell* that she didn't trust him after all this time, after all they'd been through and meant to each other these last few months. He had figured she thought more of him and their marriage than that.

Kate was as much a mystery to him as the day they wed. More. No matter how aroused and responsive in bed, how warm and caring toward him and his children by day, still there was a part of herself she held back, a reserve she never gave up. Tempted as he was every time he found himself in the same room with her to haul her into his arms for a ferocious hug and a smacking good kiss, along with a few suggestive words and an "I love you," he never quite dared. She'd be more likely to turn a cold shoulder than to say the words back to him. Kate was never restrained with Thomas and Celia, lavishing them with love and affection. Sometimes it took all the strength within him to curb his jealousy toward his own dear children. They got from Kate what he so longed for and didn't. He kept telling himself it was only a matter of time. But he wondered of late if that time might never come.

"Kate? You awake?" he ventured softly.

The arm across her face fell away, and she sat up like a shot, looking like a startled doe caught in his gun sights.

"What? Oh, Daniel. Yes, I am awake now . . . I believe I must have dozed off," she lied.

Her face was pale and dewy, her eyes red-rimmed and a bit unfocused. But she hadn't been sleeping. That was as plain to him as the blue sky outside the one small window over their bed. So how come she claimed to be dozing?

"Well, then, ah, Kate . . . I'll not disturb your rest. Know you haven't been gettin' much, what with those nightmares of yours." He left it up to her to speak of the miseries she held so tightly inside.

She brushed wisps of hair from her face with both hands, avoiding looking him in the eye. "No, I . . . it's time to be up and about. I'm feeling most refreshed." She rose, moving to the mirror, fussing with her hair, avoiding him. Again.

Danged if he knew what it was, double danged if he knew how to get her to talk about it. Nothing to do but wait while

Katie took her own good time getting around to telling him. He backed out of their room without another word, stomping downstairs, forgetting the errand bringing him up in the first place. He was as mad as a grizzly, far more worried than angry. *Damn* if she wasn't as ornery as when they'd first met. Or . . . or as skittish as Annie both times she was carrying a child.

It hit him like a poleax to the head. *Hell's fire,* Katie couldn't be in the family way! Well, she could, he amended. Dammit all, what if she was?

From the beginning, when he took her virginity, Dandy had done his manly duty, withdrawing at the last moment to keep the fruit of his passion from entering her. But sometimes, he had to admit, in the mindless ecstasy of release, he couldn't be positive he always did so in time. He tried to recall when she'd last donned the rag, but memory failed. Pregnant? By the Saints, she'd better not be.

He no longer feared leaving her alone for six long months, had already written to Donovan, telling his boss he was quitting the woods for good. It was time, maybe past time, to sink his roots. This farm, with Kate and the kids, was where he wanted to stay. He hadn't gotten around to telling Kate, not with her being so touchy, but leaving her alone carrying his child wasn't what scared him shitless. It was remembering how Annie never really got over that last pregnancy with Celia, easy prey to the illness that'd finally done her in. That couldn't happen with Katie. As much as he'd grown to love her, his broken heart would kill him for sure if she took sick and died.

Katie had darned well better tell him what the hell was going on, and soon, or he'd take matters into his own hands. Dandy stormed out the back door and was halfway to the barn before remembering the hammer he'd gone inside for in the first place.

Katherine knew her husband was furious since Daniel never hid his ire, always making the recipient painfully aware by word and deed. She didn't know why he was angry with her. Did he think she shirked her chores by napping in the afternoon? Whatever it was, she was too tired and too sore of mind and heart to add the reason for his temper to her burdens. Helping Amelia with evening supper and cleanup afterward used up her remaining energy.

Later, when Amelia and Richard had headed for their respective homes, Katherine sat at the table, a cup of tea between her hands. In his wicker rocker, Daniel read from Allen's book. Thomas and Celia sat together on a rug near the back door, a picture book between them, Thomas signing his version of the story to his attentive sister. Katherine found no contentment in the scene as she usually did; in fact, with every tick of the clock on the shelf, her disquiet grew, and with it the fear that their idyllic summer on the farm was drawing very quickly to an end.

Sudden violent pounding shook the door in its frame, rattling the pane of glass in the window beside it.

"Open up, MacCabe. We know yer in there."

Terror-stricken, Katherine leapt to her feet, toppling her chair, nearly spilling her tea. The knocking and the shouting—now in more than one voice—persisted.

"Daniel?"

Dandy rose, laying a staying hand on her arm.

"Fear not, Katie. That caterwaulin's got a familiar ring to it."

Not reassured, Katherine moved toward the children, frantically trying to think of a secure place to hide them. Already her husband had reached for the knob and swung the door wide with a welcoming grin and hearty greeting.

"Buckskin! Doc! Crosshaul Paddy! You're a sight for sore eyes!" he boomed, slapping each burly man on the back, then offered his hand, receiving a hearty shake and a slap in return, amid the babble of rough masculine voices. "What the holy ol' Mackinaw brings you bindle stiffs to these parts, and it nowhere near time to be headin' north?"

Recognizing the logging garb the three boisterous giants wore, Katherine felt weak with relief, gripping the edge of the table, attempting to focus on the conversation rolling over them all like a tide instead of her own giddiness.

''Me an' m' brother an' Cousin Paddy're followin' up on the rumor th't y've gone an' become a blasted swamp rat, Dandy,'' Buckskin bellowed, his Indian-dark features belying his stoic heritage with a toothy white grin. ''How th' hell'd th' best damn feller in camp end up on a gol-danged hard scramble stump stead? Turnin' int' some kind o' shit-kickin' mossback?''

Appalled at the man's profanity, unable to comprehend most of what was said, Katherine cleared her throat, suggesting, ''Perhaps an introduction is in order, Daniel . . . and I am certain your friends would benefit from some refreshments after their journey.''

''Sure thing, Katie. Buckskin, Doc, Crosshaul, this is my wife, Kate.''

He slipped his arm around her protectively. A thought niggled in the back of his mind that his buddies didn't seem surprised he had himself a new bride so soon after Annie's passing. This was no casual drop-by visit. Looking from the two swarthy brothers, Buckskin and Doc—both one-quarter Chippewa and proud of it—to their carrot-topped cousin, Crosshaul Paddy—as Irish as himself—Dandy bit back his questions for later and ushered them into his home.

''Come in, come in. Sit. Katie, how about some good strong coffee? Any cake left from supper?''

Nodding compliance, Katherine released her white-knuckled grip on the table to set out plates and cups, her limbs steady under her once again. These were not their dreaded foes, only her husband's friends, posing no threat. Except—cold fingers of apprehension encircled her heart—except that they might have come for Daniel . . . to take him away with them.

Oh, surely it was far too soon . . . only late July . . . not nearly time for the logging season to begin, Katherine reassured herself in an attempt to quell her panic. November, he had said, and she believed him. She knew with certainty that, come November, he would abandon her.

For now, however, like it or not, Daniel's shanty-boy friends were as much her guests as his, and welcome in their home. She roused herself to serve, her hands trembling only slightly, hoping no one noticed her discomposure.

Dandy and his friends had taken possession of the four chairs around the table. Thomas leaned against his father's leg, wide-eyed, listening raptly to every word of ongoing dialogue. Celia snuggled in her father's arms, simply content to be held by the da she so adored. The one called Crosshaul Paddy took a hearty swig of coffee. Grimacing, he slammed the cup onto the table, wiping a sleeve across his mouth.

"Phaaa! What th' bloody blue blazes is this?" he demanded of Dandy. "Narry a dollup added in o' somethin' with a bit o' bite t' it fer a weary man after his travels? Some Forty Rod or Bald-faced Whiskey, maybe?"

"Hell, I'd be willin' t' settle fer some haywire lightnin' or mule if y've got it, MacCabe," chimed in one of the brothers, Katherine wasn't sure which.

Dandy shook his head. "Sorry, boys. Can't even keep the stuff in the house without goin' queasy in the stomach. Besides, Katie here'd tan my hide was I to take to drinkin' spirits, wouldn't you, lass?" He gave her a cocky grin and a wink.

"Most assuredly, Mr. MacCabe," Katherine retorted promptly, not at all sure she approved of these ribald friends, or his equally rowdy response to their presence. The following rapid exchange of incomprehensible lingo punctuated liberally with vulgarisms left Katherine bewildered, her sensibilities sorely tested.

"Daniel, perhaps the children should go on up to bed. Daniel . . . ?"

He half turned his attention from the tales being spun. "Aw, 'tisn't every night good friends drop in, Kate. Let 'em stay up awhile longer. Any more coffee? How's about another cup all around."

Hating the look of pure, nostalgic pleasure on her husband's dear, handsome face, Katherine quietly served the hot, black beverage, and the rest of the cake as well. Already he had deserted her, if only in spirit, and she raised up a fervent prayer he didn't take it into his head to quit the farm for the logging camp early this year. Had these men come to take him away with them? Seeing Daniel with them like this, she could imagine him picking up and going.

For the first time, it struck her—like a blow—that these friends, and logging itself, were as much—no, more than— a part of his life as this farm, and her, and his children. A shanty boy was what he was, who he was. Ten years he'd been one, having grown from raw youth to manhood embracing the severest of elements, the hardest of labor, the crudest of companions and living arrangements. He'd become the man she loved more than life itself because of those ten years as much as for the eighteen before in Ballywae. She could not, would not, keep him from it. Even if she was carrying his child.

The four swapped stories, then commenced spinning tales about the legendary Paul Bunyan, each taller than the last . . . as much for Thomas's enjoyment as their own. Finally Crosshaul Paddy pulled a Jew's harp out of his pocket, and Doc a mouth organ, demanding Dandy bring forth his dulcimer for some musical entertainment.

The shanty songs proved wilder than the tall tales, and far louder. Dandy and Buckskin sang along at the top of their lungs, and every one of them stamped their feet in tune, including Thomas. Katherine resisted as long as she was able before joining in with foot-tapping and hand-clapping. The songs ranged from ''Once More A'lumbering Go'' to ''Aura Lee.'' With the conclusion of that ballad, Katherine noticed Thomas was falling asleep on his feet, and she insisted he and his sister go up to bed. Taking a child's hand in each of her own, she asked Daniel, ''Will you be coming up to say good night?''

''Not tonight, Kate. Give 'em each a kiss for me . . . Now, tell me, Paddy . . .''

She and the children had been dismissed, Katherine realized, and forgotten. She tucked them in, then took herself to bed, exhausted enough to long for sleep in spite of the recurring nightmares, too worried to drift into slumber before her husband joined her. She waited. And waited. And finally slept. Alone.

Hours later Dandy came in from sending his chums down

to the barn for what remained of the night. Undressing, he gave his fitfully dozing wife a perfunctory kiss on the cheek and fell instantly asleep, softly snoring, leaving Katherine more restless than before. Questions went unanswered, apprehensions unshared. Or perhaps she was simply not as important to him as those three with whom he had spent the last hours of the night and the first of the new day.

All too soon, morning arrived. Heavy-eyed and heavy-hearted, Katherine dressed herself for church. When she suggested at breakfast that Dandy ready himself as well, he waved her away.

"You and the young'uns go on without me, lass. Me and the boys've got a whole lot more palaverin' to do in the short time the lads're stayin' . . . once they've slept their fill." He scarcely looked up from his breakfast of bacon and eggs.

Katherine chewed her lip, but the words had to be said. "Will . . . all of you . . . be . . . here when we return?"

He bit a half-moon out of his toast. "And where else would I be?" he asked. "Though I can't be sayin' about the boys. A roamin' bunch they are come summer . . . Winter arrives all too soon, snowin' a shanty boy in for weeks at a time."

"Weeks . . . ?" Her voice was soft with distress, but he seemed not to hear.

Gulping the last of his coffee, Dandy stood, gave her a quick hug and a kiss, and strode off to the barn as though scarcely able to stay away from the trio who'd so thoroughly invaded their lives. She longed for them to leave, the sooner the better. Without her husband.

"What's so danged important it couldn't wait a couple of hours while I attended church with my family?" Dandy asked without preamble the moment he set foot in the barn.

Crosshaul Paddy, from his perch on a stall rail, thrust the copy of the *The Lumberman's Gazette* under his nose. "Read fer yerself. Page six . . . 'Mighty Paul Bunyan Licks All Comers.' "

"I don't get it." Clearly puzzled, Dandy obligingly flipped to the article.

"Ya will," Buckskin and Doc muttered in unison.

"Ah, here 'tis . . . 'Mighty Paul . . . ' " Dandy fell silent, reading a phrase aloud now and again. "Fourth of July picnic . . . log rollin' . . . *Dandy Dan MacCabe*. What the—How the *hell* did my name—Who talked to a reporter?" He looked from one shanty boy to another, and another, disbelieving.

"Says somewheres in there." Doc pointed. "Fella name o' Selby wrote it up in th' local paper first, then sent it on t' the *Gazette* . . . probably figgerin' t' earn hisself some cash twice over fer the same stuff—"

"But that was only four or five weeks ago—"

"Brand-new issue . . . hot off th' presses—"

"The boss says—"

"What's Donovan got to do with it?"

"He's th' one tol' us t' come on over here. How'd ya think we know'd where t' find ya? Says he got a letter ya sent awhile back, lettin' him know where ya was. Couldn't come t' warn ya himself, so he sends a tellygram t' Paddy here, on account of he can read, an' we weren't too far away—"

"Come to warn me about what?" Dandy interrupted, impatient for the important news.

"Some dude's been nosin' around th' camps since spring, goin' from one t' th' next . . . been back t' Donovan's twice. Lucky fer ya, bein' off season, weren't hardly no one around fer th' punk t' pump fer information . . . Ain't no shanty boy woulda talked anyhow but—"

"Askin' what kind of questions?" Dandy's stomach knotted.

"Like yer whereabouts, mostly. Course, weren't no one 'bout t' tell some fly cop or town clown nothin', 'specially figgerin' it might land ya in th' calaboose . . . Every man jack he collared t' answer his dad-burned questions would as soon put the calks t' 'im as give 'im th' time o' day. One nosy Johnny Newcome, he was. Didn't get nothin' outta nobody, ya can rest assured o' th't."

"And 'tis beholden' I am you three came to warn me. Donovan tell you what the fellow was lookin' for me and mine for?"

Paddy shrugged. "Tol' us t' bring ya th' *Gazette,* let ya know some damn nosy greenhorn was askin' after ya . . . an' bein' danged sly about it . . . Easy t' see he weren't up t' no good."

Pacing, Dandy ran his free hand through his hair, slapping the *Gazette* against the nearest support post. "If he gets his hands on this, we won't be hard to track down—"

"Only if he happens t' read th' *Gazette,*" suggested Doc.

"Bound t', sooner 'r later," snapped his brother, hitting Doc's bicep with a hammy fist. "Anyhow, th't's how come Donovan sent us 'round, t' warn ya. Figured ya'd better be on the lookout—"

"Maybe quit this here cowbell country . . . light out on th' run . . . with th' missus an' them kids?" Doc helped. For his efforts, he took another fist to the arm. "Dammit, cut th't out, Buck."

Dandy ignored the horseplay, his mind going a mile a second, trying to work through all that'd been thrust upon him these last few minutes.

"Can't run. Got corn to harvest, and beans after that," he mulled aloud. "Can't take the chance on stayin', either."

"Won't ask what this slicker's after ya fer, th't's yer business, an' yers alone. But if there's anythin' else we kin do—"

"You've all three done more'n your share, and I thank ye kindly. I'm in your debt . . . If ever you're needin' anythin' I have to give—"

Paddy harrumphed. "Jest helpin' out one o' our own . . . and we'll be on our way after dinner so's ya can do what ya gotta, Dandy boy. Hope t' see ya in camp come fall, with this here trouble far behind."

They wouldn't stay the night, and Dandy was relieved, much as he hated to watch them go once Katherine's Sunday chicken and dumplings disappeared. He and his wife had some mighty serious talking to do, the sooner the better. For

all their sakes. He hated like hell to put voice to the only solution he could think of—to pack up and move on. To Donovan's camp? They'd be no safer there than here with that stranger, probably Ol' Lady Stewart's henchman, sniffing around. Besides, like he said, he had crops to harvest or he'd lose the summer's worth of backbreaking labor, and Ol' Charlie's nest egg, too. Not to mention how the farm had begun to seem like home for all of them. Go, or stay and take their chances. Whatever he and Katie decided, their easygoing days were gone for good.

He went to look for his wife in the kitchen, where he knew she'd be finishing up dinner dishes.

18

Katherine snapped the damp dish towel, hanging it up on the string stretched in the corner behind the stove, before facing him resolutely.

"I will not leave, Daniel. There has to be another solution. I will not tear up the roots we have sunk so deeply into this soil. This is our home now, whatever trials may come our way. We have the truest friends in all the world in the Weatherbys. Celia cannot be without Amelia. And Thomas is looking forward to starting school in September. He absorbed like a sponge the reading and writing skills Amelia taught him, and craves so much more. He wants to be a veterinarian, did you know that, Daniel? As for myself . . . I have been piecing a quilt to enter in the fair. Not to mention all your hard work . . . and harvest so close at hand. We cannot leave. We simply cannot." Katherine voiced every argument that came to mind, speaking quickly, afraid to stop and allow reality to set in.

She stood tall, and Dandy had to admire her sheer determination, no matter how ill placed. He glanced out the window over the dry sink. The children played just outside in the yard, Thomas patiently tossing a ball to Celia, she running on short toddler legs across the grass to retrieve it. For their sake, he quickly decided he had to convince Kate it was time to move on.

"I don't see how we can stay, Katie," her told her, his regret keen. "We've been found out . . . or soon will be. All because of this damned article. We could've gone on hidin' out a good long time, maybe forever, except for some blasted ambitious reporter." He slapped the *Gazette* against his thigh for emphasis, the unfairness causing his blood to boil. "If I ever get my hands on this—this—what's his name?—Mr. Matt Selby—who wrote about me—"

"You cannot blame that young man for doing his job," Katherine hurriedly defended. "I am certain he had no idea—"

"How'd you know Selby's a 'young man'?" His tone went sharp with accusation.

"I . . . well, I—"

Dandy took a menacing step toward her. "Unless it was *you* he talked to to learn my name—and just about everythin' else—includin' where to find us—"

Barely withstanding the full force of his rage, Katherine retreated, bumping up against the porcelain-topped table, the truth of his words striking her like a blow. Paling, hands pressed flat on the scarred surface behind her, she choked out in a voice that fairly wept with remorse, "Then . . . it was I who betrayed us all. I had no idea, truly. He said he was writing for the . . . the local paper . . ."

The stony appearance of his rough-hewn face as he backed away from her broke her heart. She took a single step toward him, one hand upturned in supplication.

"Oh, Daniel, can you ever f-f-forgive m-m-me?" Pride alone kept her from bursting into sobs.

Dandy watched Kate struggle mightily with the pain of her admission. As angry with her as he was, he couldn't keep from pulling her into his arms to ease her suffering. Feeling the familiar fit of her body against his, Dandy's rage melted, and he pressed a kiss onto the top of her contritely bent head.

"You didn't do it on purpose, Katie, I know that." Speaking in a soft, soothing tone, he rubbed the length of her back from nape to waist, his hands circling her waist to separate her from himself far enough to look deeply into her eyes. "Makin' no excuses for that Selby fellow, he couldn't've known his writin' would put us in danger, any more'n by talkin' to him did you think you'd bring this trouble down on our heads. Thanks to the lads stoppin' by, we're warned well in advance," he assured his wife, releasing her to pace restlessly a few steps away, seeking a view of his children playing in the yard, so carefree, so unaware.

"How did your friends know where to find you? The *Gazette?*"

He gave her his attention, explaining, "Nay, 'twas my boss, Donovan, who sent them. I wrote to him a while back to let him know . . . er . . ." Now was not the time to let her in on the letter's true purpose. If he told Kate he'd given his boss notice, that he wouldn't be heading back to work during Kate's first winter alone on the farm, she'd believe he didn't trust her with his property, or kids, especially after today's turn of events. "To let him know I wasn't back in town where I usually summered . . . should he . . . ah . . . need to get in touch with me."

Katherine knew Daniel hadn't told the entire truth, and she couldn't fathom why, for he tended to be most bluntly truthful in most instances. But then, she withheld secrets of her own she was reluctant to confide in him. If she told him of unburdening herself to Amelia, his anger could reach new heights in view of this, her second betrayal in mere days. And if she told him she suspected a possibility of being in the family way, his fury might know no bounds. He'd made it clear from the beginning that he did not want to leave her alone and pregnant when he went to camp in the fall. Contrarily, if he stayed behind should she declare herself with child, she would know with all certainty he did not consider her capable of coping with the farm, her pregnancy, and his offspring without him. She could think of no workable solution to her quandary and so held her silence.

Daniel seemed not to notice, assuring her, "What's done is done, Katie. Now we must decide what to do about it. Stay or run."

''Run to where, Daniel? There is nowhere else. Unless we have more funds remaining than I had thought.''

'' 'Fraid not. There's little left of Ol' Charlie's nest egg. Like it or not, we may be forced to take our chances by stayin'. Try to get the crops in before we're found out. If ever we are. Maybe it'll never come to that after all, Katie.''

Putting voice to the thought that had been just below the surface of consciousness for so long, Katherine suggested, ''We could go back to my family home in the city—''

''Go back—?'' asked Dandy, misbelieving he'd heard right.

Katherine rushed on before her courage failed, passionate in her heartfelt plea. ''Yes, Daniel, we can go back to resolve this matter by confronting Mrs. Stewart with her duplicity. Petition the court to have the judge's decision overruled and put an end to the fear of discovery hanging over us, once and for all, so we can live in peace.''

His long, chestnut mane flared about his head with the vehemence of his refusal. ''You're daft to think of it, Kate. What's to keep Ol' Lady Stewart from buyin' herself another judge, a whole passel of 'em?''

More determined than ever, Katherine insisted, ''I am positive Clinton Meyers, who married us, is above reproach. He would assist us, I am certain.''

'' 'Tis not worth the risk, Katie,'' Dandy interrupted bluntly, offering no compromise.

''We are at risk every day we are in hiding, Daniel, never knowing at what moment the children will be snatched away from us and returned to their grandmother. What if Judge Meyers were to prove us more fit than she?''

''What if he didn't, have you thought of that?'' demanded her husband, striding two paces away and back again, towering over her. ''I will not take that chance with my sweet babies' futures . . . their *very* lives. If I should lose them in spite of your judge's honorable qualifications, I could not bear to be without them, Kate.''

She took an involuntary backward step at his intensity, fighting growing dismay, longing to ease his obvious pain with even the smallest shred of hope, something only she could give. "If the unthinkable were to happen, there is always the possibility of . . . of other children."

His expression went rock-hard, ice-cold. "You can't be meanin' to suggest any other child could replace Thomas and Celia. Were they to be taken from me, I would never father another, Kate. That is both a promise and a vow."

"I had not meant to suggest—"

"What were you tryin' to say, then?" Her grabbed her upper arms in a viselike grip.

Another time, another place, in another gentle and loving way, she'd meant to tell him. Not like this. But what choice did she have with him demanding an immediate answer of her? The words would not rise around the growing lump in her throat.

"Well, Kate? Have out with it!"

"I might already be with child," she blurted in her agitation and watched the color leave his face.

"Dammit, Kate, 'tis not a joking matter." It was as he'd suspected, but a bitter shock all the same.

She pulled back hard against his hands. "I am not joking, Daniel. Please, unhand me, you are hurting—"

Dandy pushed her away so abruptly that Katherine stumbled. He quickly made a move to offer a steadying hand, but she caught herself before falling, instinctively placing a splayed hand protectively across her trim, flat belly. He saw the gesture and glowered.

"You knew how I felt about your gettin' in the family way. Why now, of all times—"

Furious herself now, she lifted her chin high, one brow cocked in silent disdain. "It was not as if I came to this pass on my own, Mr. MacCabe. I believe you made some *small* contribution."

"My contribution be damned. What the blinkin' bloody hell are we supposed to do now?" He ran both hands through his crown until his hair was as wild as himself. "And stop raisin' just one brow at me like that. Ye know it drives me to distraction. 'Tisn't natural."

"*Oh,* and bellowing profanities at the wife you profess to love is? Or . . . or were you simply plying me with sweet phrases and tender caresses to insure yourself of a care-giver for your children so you can return to your true love, that— that logging camp in the winter woods?''

Red blotches of rage stained his cheeks, his eyes narrowed to slits. ''You knew when we wed that loggin's in my blood, always has been, always will be.'' Damned if he was going to tell her now about his intention to quit logging and become a farmer full-time. ''And you were more than eager to take me and mine on in any case. Wasn't like it was love at first sight, was it, Kate? More like a maiden, long in the tooth, lookin' to find herself a man, any—''

He knew he'd gone too far before the words were half out of his mouth; her stricken expression plainly told him he'd wounded her deeply. He knew those words to be a lie; she'd married him for the sake of his kids, nothing more. From that, love had grown between them. And they'd had loving, plenty of it. Now she stood before him, head still proudly high, too wounded for tears, and damned if he knew how to make it right.

''Katie, 'tis sorry I am . . .'' He reached out for her; she turned a stiff back to him.

She cleared her throat. ''I am certain we have both said things for which we are sorry, Daniel, but they have been said. Whether you decide to stay or run . . . or go back, I will abide by your decision and my vows as your wife— for whatever reason they were made.''

''Then we'll be stayin', Kate.'' That should please her. She acknowledged his words with a nod of the head, but did not turn to look at him. ''I . . . er . . . suppose it would be best if I . . . er . . . moved my gear out to the barn—''

She faced him then, features tight, eyes glassy with unshed tears. ''Would you shame me before the children and our friends?''

''Course not, I only thought—''

''Then we will continue to share a room . . . and . . . and a bed . . . Mr. MacCabe, if you do not mind too terribly.''

This whole argument had gotten way out of hand. ''Look, Kate, we've both said a lot of things we—''

''And I wish to say one thing more, so that everything

will be clear between us. I told Amelia how we came to arrive at the farm, and from whom we are hiding. I am certain she has told no one else, and equally as certain she will not betray us.''

''I'm sure you're right, Kate,'' Dandy commented more amicably than she'd expected. ''I can see where you might confide in her, bein' with her day in and day out like you were.''

Katherine had gathered herself together, expecting another tirade, and now consciously relaxed her shoulders and unclenched her hands. Unshed tears dissipated without flowing, thank Providence, but the ache swelling within her only continued to grow. At least she had confided the last of her secrets to her husband, once her lover and her friend, who now seemed no more than a hurtful stranger.

''If you will excuse me,'' she said, ''it is past Celia's bedtime.''

As she made a move to walk away, he caught her arm. ''No, Katie, I'll not have you leave with this misunderstandin' between us.'' She paused, but would not look at him. ''I'll not have the sun settin' with us at odds. Are we to be lettin' foolish words spoken in anger destroy the sweet lovin' that's been growin' these last few months?''

Tears came then, of their own accord, large and silent, wetting her cheeks and his hand upon her arm. Looking up, she saw his pain-filled eyes and realized suddenly his suffering was as great as her own. She lifted a hand to lightly caress his cheek, some of the clutching pain releasing its grip on her heart.

''I'm sorry we quarreled so bitterly, Daniel.''

Vastly relieved, he turned his head to kiss her palm, pulling her into his arms, placing his lips tenderly over her own. When he lifted his head, he cupped her face in his big rough hands, rubbing her damp cheeks with his thumbs.

''By the Saints, may such harsh words never come from our lips again.''

''Never again,'' she agreed, knowing in her heart of hearts that those already spoken had left permanent, painful scars that would not go away soon—if ever. What her husband had let slip during their argument mirrored his true thoughts, she felt sure. That she'd been a desperate spinster, that she might be carrying his unwanted child. Instinct told her things between them would never be the same again, and she would carry this ache in her chest for a good long time.

Alone in the MacCabes' kitchen the next afternoon, Amelia Weatherby glanced up from shelling new peas into a porcelain pan in the dry sink at the sound of a solitary horseman approaching. Her hands stilled, and she watched the stranger dismount at the back porch, his features hidden beneath the shadow of a broad-brimmed hat. Something in the way this man stood and looked over the MacCabe property before setting foot on the back step told her he was the one who had asked questions in the logging camps. The copy of *The Lumberman's Gazette* protruding from his jacket pocket confirmed her worst fears, fears that had been building since Dandy told her and Richard the real reason his friends had stopped by.

Wanting nothing more than to run and hide until all danger passed and the stranger was gone, knowing he would only return, maybe next time finding the MacCabes at home and unprepared, Amelia hesitated, thoughts churning. With Daniel and Thomas off mending fences in the cow pasture, Kate visiting Martha, Celia napping upstairs, and Richard puttering in the barn, there was no one to depend on but herself. Praying the man would not see her trembling from head to foot, she stepped up to the screened back door, fervently wishing it had a lock.

"May I . . . help you?"

He studied her, his eyes shaded, his face, so ordinary and not at all menacing, without expression.

"Mrs. MacCabe?"

"No. She's not here. That is to say . . . she no longer lives here," she responded, perhaps too quickly.

His shadowed eyes slitted with suspicion. "Oh?"

"I . . . I'm sorry you came so far . . . Mr. . . . Mr.?" No response. "I'm sorry you came all the way out here for nothing. The MacCabes moved out a while back . . . sold this farm to myself and . . ." She was trying too hard not to panic completely, trying to sound calm and logical.

"And?"

"And . . . my husband, Mr. Wilder. I'm Mrs. Wilder." Should Richard come up from the barn, his presence would be explained, but how could she possibly let Richard Wilder know he had just acquired a wife? *Please, please, please, Richard, stay in the barn.*

So concerned was she with that thought, she didn't hear the slight sound behind her until the stranger's gaze searched beyond her into the house.

"Your child?" he asked pointedly.

Amelia turned. Celia stood three feet from her, golden curls tousled, big blue eyes a bit unfocused after her nap, two fingers in her mouth.

"Yes, my daughter."

The little girl remained unmoving, except to stare from one to the other of the adults, and back again to the one she knew and trusted.

"How old?"

"Three . . . almost four."

"Can she talk?"

Amelia went cold. He must know the MacCabe child could not. "At her age, of course." She tried to laugh it off. She spoke to Celia, mouthing clearly, "Come here and say hello to the nice man, baby."

Celia silently wiggled her plump little fingers in a wave, imitating the small gesture Amelia made under cover of her full skirt. Swiveling back to the stranger, Amelia explained quickly, "She's shy."

"But bright enough, it seems," he replied coldly.

Knowing to what he referred, Amelia let the comment go without response. She waited to see what he would say or do next, to take her cue from him, feeling calmer now, more in control, for it seemed he accepted her explanations unquestioningly. He turned away from her. Amelia thought, *Thank the Lord, he's leaving,* then quickly decided the man must have eyes in the back of his head, seeing what he obviously did—Richard striding purposefully toward them from the barn, wiping his hands, then his forehead with a red bandanna. She saw the stranger's lips draw back from his teeth in a forced grin. His hand went out for shaking in a nonthreatening gesture.

"Mr. Wilder?"

Richard stopped a couple yards away, still wiping his hands, making no move to take the one extended to him. His expression was wary, but not hostile.

"Been having a chat with Mrs. Wilder, here." He let his hand fall to his side.

To his credit, Richard did not betray her lie.

"Nice little girl you've got there. Shy, though."

Again no betrayal. "She's that, all right. What can I do for you, Mr. . . . ?"

"Smith. Heard the MacCabes owned this place."

Richard surreptitiously glanced past their guest; Amelia desperately hand-signed, hoping he'd understand.

"Did," said Richard with a friendly smile, keeping the stranger's attention on him. "Gone now, though."

"You own the place, then?"

A wider grin. "Lock, stock, and barrel."

The man's face remained impassive. "Any idea where he was headed?"

Richard shrugged. "Said something about going on back to the logging camp, didn't he, dear?" he queried his "wife" with a cock of the head. At her slight nod, he added, "Fed up with trying to make a go of farming, he said." As he spoke, he climbed the three steps to the porch. Amelia opened the screen door to him, but rather than enter, he drew her out beside him, pulling her close with a hand at her waist. "Anything else we can help you with, Mr. Smith?"

"Don't believe so," said Smith grimly.

"A cup of coffee or a sandwich to tide you over for your trip back to town?"

"Nothing, thanks. I'll be on my way." Smith touched the brim of his hat with one finger, descending to the ground, taking reins in hand and mounting. He paused, "If you happen to see MacCabe—"

"Not likely—"

"Or hear from him, tell him Mrs. Stewart sends her regards." He wheeled his animal around, dug his heels in, and tore out to the road as if pursued—or working out his frustrations at the expense of his beast.

Amelia's knees went weak, and she sagged against Richard. Liking the feel of her in his arms, he led her into the house and to the nearest chair. He brought her a cup of cold well water and gave her a couple of minutes to calm down. Soon her color returned, and her hands steadied around the cup.

Knowing from Dandy's explanation what the man likely wanted, knowing, too, how shy Amelia was, he had to give her credit for her courage and presence of mind, and for the story she'd concocted. Husband, hmm? Suddenly that thought had more appeal than he'd ever expected.

"Well, I think we fooled that bast—fellow good," he chortled. "Mighty quick thinking on your part, 'Mrs. Wilder.' And mighty smart, spinning a tale so easily believed."

"*If* he truly believed us, Richard. What if he only pretended to believe . . . what if he comes back when Kate and Daniel are here? What if—"

Richard put two raised fingers to her lips. "He won't be back, sweetheart, don't worry." Then he gave her a feather-light kiss on the forehead, adding, "Lunch ready yet? I'm starving."

She managed to make him a sandwich and pour him a glass of foaming fresh milk without mishap, her thoughts in greater turmoil than ever. Richard had called her "sweetheart." And he'd kissed her again, if only on the brow. What did it mean? Or did it mean nothing at all? Had he only been performing for Mr. Smith's benefit, or dare she begin to hope?

For a time, Amelia indulged in fantasies of being Mrs. Richard Wilder, mother of a darling child like Celia, in a home of her own like this one. Soon enough reality came crashing back. Foolish dreams, for of course the attention and sweet words were for the stranger's benefit, not hers. How bitterly hard reality could be at times!

After supper the four adults sat around the kitchen table while the children played out-of-doors. Four faces looked grim in the lamplight as Amelia and Richard related the afternoon's happenings, and then they each in turn gave an opinion as to what they might expect next.

"I—I think Mr. Smith believed us and will look for you elsewhere," Amelia insisted quite boldly for her, but then she was learning to be stronger day by day.

Dandy shook his head. "You and Richard told him we were headed for Donovan's loggin' camp, but if he's just returned from there himself, he'd likely know that wasn't so. He'll be back, probably when we're least expectin' him."

"Then we must make some plan for that eventuality, Daniel," responded his wife with determination.

"And so we shall, lass. Rest assured I'll not let that woman's henchman chase us from our home, especially when there's every possibility that what Amelia says is true and we have nothin' to fear by stayin'."

"Just in case he comes back," said Richard, "Amelia and I'll stay here day and night to hold up our claim that *we* own this farm now. All we need is a safe place for you and your family to hide out when he appears."

Dandy and Katherine spoke at the same time.

"That's too much to be askin'—"

"You have done so much already—"

Richard ignored their protest. "It's all settled, then. Let's work out all the details."

Less than a week later, at the supper hour, two men rode into the backyard. Amelia, who had risen to refill coffee cups, glanced out the window and saw them, identifying one as Smith. Blanching, she blurted, "He's back . . . and with the sheriff."

Richard slammed to his feet, calmly taking charge. "I'll head them off in the yard. Amelia, get rid of the extra dishes—"

"Where should I put them?"

"I don't know . . . the oven. Daniel, take Kate and the

kids upstairs 'til I can talk our visitors into leaving—"

"Nay, if they search the house, we'll be trapped—"

"Daniel—"

"The root cellar?"

Dandy shook his head. "Another sure trap—"

"Daniel—"

All faces turned in Katherine's direction.

Head up, her gaze steady on her husband, Katherine spoke. "I realize I agreed to abide by your decision whether to go or stay, but, please, Daniel, we cannot continue to run and hide like common criminals. It is time we face our pursuers, if we are ever to resolve this matter and find peace."

Dandy ran a hand through his forelock and tugged, his eyes downcast, his expression thoughtful. His shoulders heaved, fists falling to his side. He spoke to Richard and Amelia, standing side by side only awaiting his word to move into action, resignation in his words.

"She's right. We can't be hidin' like frightened moles forever, nor drag the children from place to place for the rest of their lives, fearing discovery, knowin' someday it'll have to end, and maybe not well."

Coming to him, circling her hands about his upper arm, Katherine reassured her husband softly, "We shall fight Mrs. Stewart in the courts. And win."

His gaze locked on her, his expression grim. One large hand closed over both of hers.

"There's every possibility we may not, Kate. But we'll give it the best we've got, in any case. You're right in sayin' we can't be on the run for the rest of our lives, especially with no place to go and no cash in our pockets."

Richard spoke up with false good cheer. "You'll be back, you and Kate and the kids, in no more than a week or two . . . three at the most. Amelia and I'll keep things running 'til then, and the Weatherby men'll help with the harvest, if necessary. We'll send the profits on to you."

Dandy threw him a grateful glance.

"Be sure to take a share for yourself, and Allen, too, like we agreed upon. We're most beholden to ye, and it's been a pleasure to know ye one and all." He held out his hand for shaking.

Richard clasped it in both of his. "Good luck!"

Amelia softly added, "God bless. You'll be in our prayers."

Fighting tears, Katherine turned to more practical matters. "We must get in touch with Judge Meyers as soon as possible—"

Dandy slipped an arm across his wife's shoulders. "The first order of business, it would seem, sweet love, is to greet our guests. Smith and the sheriff are at the door."

19
❦❦

The hollow *click-click* of her heels on the polished parquet floor made a lonely echo down the empty, door-lined hall and up the wide, carpeted stairs. Old habits died hard. At the ornate hall tree, Katherine reached up to take out her hat pin before realizing she wore no hat, only a faded cotton bonnet over the single braid down her back. Lowering her hands, she looked at their freckled, suntanned backs, so out of place in this austere setting, as was the worried tanned face staring back at her with troubled gray eyes from the hall tree mirror. To hang her sunbonnet on one of its polished brass hooks seemed somehow irreverent, so she simply held it in her hands, swiveling in a slow circle to view every angle of this room in the house she'd once called home. Daniel had called this place a mausoleum when he first saw it, and with new eyes Katherine saw more clearly what he had meant. With no warmth, no light, no welcome, it might well have been a mausoleum or a museum. The Ming vase on an elaborately carved table, a landscape by a well-known artist in an enormous gilt frame, Oriental runner in rich colors and intricate design, appeared so unnecessarily ostentatious. To what purpose? And for whom? The cost of any single item could feed and clothe her family for a year, take the burden of worry off her husband's broad, capable shoulders until the crops came in, or tide them over should they fail. Had there actually been a time when she took such wealth for granted? How long ago and far away that seemed now.

"Miss Katherine. Oh, Miss Katherine, is that really you?"

From the kitchen came the ever-faithful Hannah Tillit, wiping her hands on her apron, her composure slipping badly at the sight of the young woman she'd raised from infancy.

Without hesitation, Katherine ran to meet her, embracing the startled woman with a huge, heartfelt hug and a kiss on her round, rosy cheek.

"Oh, Hannah, I have missed you."

If Miss Katherine had forgotten her place, Hannah Tillit had not forgotten hers. Placing plump, workworn hands on her mistress's shoulders, she gently pried herself out of the young woman's embrace, holding her at arm's length to give her a good looking over. What she observed seemed almost beyond her grasp, so changed was her mistress from the lady who'd left less than four months ago.

"Miss Katherine, what have you done to yourself?"

Katherine ran two rough hands down the faded front of her hand-me-down dress of rose calico, noting the worn toes of her shoes sticking out from a frayed hem. She'd not thought of her appearance at all when she packed a few necessities and grabbed up her reticule for the return to town, and it showed.

"I have been working, Hannah, hard and long from dawn to dusk . . . cooking, cleaning, washing, ironing, planting and cultivating a garden—"

"Planting . . . ironing . . . *cooking,* miss?" Hannah's hands flew to her cheeks, and she shook her head in disbelief.

"And the requirements of my toilette are not what they once were." Katherine spread her shabby skirt wide and offered a whimsical smile. Leaning toward Mrs. Tillit, she stage-whispered, "And underneath, I am not wearing a corset."

Hannah Tillit looked for all the world as if she'd gone apoplectic. "Miss Katherine!"

Katherine patted her arm. "Do not fret, dear. I have every intention of being properly garbed when next I set foot outside this door." All levity went out of her voice and manner. "So much to do, and so little time. First to the jail to visit Daniel—"

"Jail?" squeaked Hannah.

"Then meet with Judge Meyers to enlist his aid in locating the children—"

"Sweet, merciful Lord, where are those dear children?" demanded Hannah.

"Temporarily in their grandmother's clutches, I fear. But do not worry, they will not be for long. Come up with me while I ready myself, and I will explain everything."

How comforting was Hannah Tillit's presence, so steadying, so familiar. Explanations of the recent events tumbled out, the tale unfolding to the growing consternation of both older woman and younger.

"The local sheriff and Mrs. Stewart's henchman, who proved to be a private detective, bound Daniel hand and foot as if he were a common criminal and loaded him into our wagon bed like so much baggage." She plucked a gown from her wardrobe.

Hannah uttered a small bleat of incredulity.

"The children were required to ride on the seat between the two lawmen . . . Nothing either Daniel or I said gave them any true understanding or comfort on that horrid three-day return trip. Both children had grown so accustomed to their life on the farm, I believe they had forgotten our reason for being there, Hannah. It was heartbreaking—" As for herself, she had scarcely had time to gather a few necessities for them all and climb in beside her trussed-up husband, and no parting words for Amelia or Richard. "Daniel was taken directly to the jail the moment we reached town . . . and I have not seen him or the children since." Katherine slipped out of her everyday dress.

"Thank the blessed Lord you weren't incarcerated, too."

"Rest assured I have. I am most grateful no delay will

keep me from seeing to my family's speedy release. And to that end, do you think this outfit will do, Hannah?''

Corseted, layered with petticoats topped with the hated black satin suit, Katherine waited for Mrs. Tillit's approval or disapproval. She couldn't help but notice the bewilderment on the older woman's face for having repeatedly called her by her first name, for having requested rather than demanded what she needed, but she could not do otherwise, not having learned the lessons regarding relationships these last few months had taught her.

"It'll do just fine, Miss Katherine, far more suitable than the one in which you arrived, if I may say so."

"That you may, dear Mrs. Tillit, that you may."

She paced the hall, impatient for Andrew Tillit to come tell her the rockaway was ready. Hannah bustled in from the kitchen.

"Mr. Tillit will be with you directly. He was grooming the horse after its long journey and—"

"That is quite understandable, Hannah, after the arduous labor to which we put poor old Bess these last few days. She deserves a good rubdown and a feed bag of oats. I do not mind the wait. It gives me a few moments to recall old memories of this house and home. Speaking of which"—she hated to bring it up, but the matter must be dealt with—"I . . . I need to have a few words with you and Andrew about . . ." Katherine chewed her lip.

"About selling the house, miss?" Hannah finished.

"Yes, but how did you—"

"Mr. Tillit and I have been hoping and praying you'd decide to settle down with the mister on that farm of his and put this big old place up for sale." She leaned toward Katherine confidentially. "We've been putting some money aside for years to open a boardinghouse . . . for our old age . . . you know. We're so used to caring for folks, we have no idea what else to do with ourselves. Knew the day would come, sooner or later, when you'd move on, miss, and so would we. Glad it's sooner—if you don't mind my saying— while we're still young enough and able enough to start over on our own." Hannah Tillit's burst of words dwindled down, and she waited for a comment from her mistress.

Katherine's mouth opened and shut a few times while she digested this bit of information. "Why . . . why . . . that is a simply wonderful plan, Hannah. That being the case, I will not delay seeing to the sale of both the house and its contents—unless there are things here for which you might have some use?"

"Mr. Tillit and I'll have a look-see and let you know, and our thanks for offering. Ah, here's himself now, and ready to go, I'll wager. Give Mr. MacCabe our best, and tell him our prayers are with him . . . and the children."

Less than two hours later, sweltering in black satin but sporting her mother's best hat of royal velvet at a jaunty, hopeful angle, Katherine grimly followed the guard into a small, dingy room with bars on its single window. He left her alone there, the gray brick walls closing in around her with the shutting of the door behind him. She paced, too anxious to sit in one of the two straight-backed chairs set beside a scarred wooden table. The view outside the barred window was of nothing more than an air shaft between buildings. She prayed Daniel's accommodations were better; she knew he hated confining spaces.

Her wait proved mercifully short. The door swung open, and Daniel stepped in alone, his jailer retreating to provide much appreciated privacy. Katherine had expected to find her husband in chains, handcuffed, something. But he remained unfettered and blessedly familiar, if scruffier, in the clothes he'd worn through his journey back to town and with several days' growth of russet beard shadowing his face.

They eyed each other from across the room, appearing to one another as in the beginning—she, prim and proper in black, her hair twisted in a tight knot under her hat; he, rough and ready and somewhat wild in plaid shirt and Levi's. So many hurtful things had been said, misunderstandings left unresolved, and warily, like strangers, each waited for the other to begin.

"Katie," said Dandy quietly at last, " 'tis grateful I am you came."

"I had thought I might not be permitted to see you . . . that you might not be allowed visitors." Her voice held a desperate note.

"Thank fortune, it would seem that I am. In fact, I've not even been locked in a cell as yet."

Katherine took a single step toward him.

"But I thought you were under arrest?"

"So had I, no one said otherwise, not durin' the trip, nor after arrivin'. I was put into a room much like this, but with a cot, and there I spent the night. . . ." Dandy's words trailed off. Spreading wide his hands, he shrugged, his rugged features mirroring puzzled frustration. "Makes no sense at all to me, Kate, and I'm startin' to think somethin' underhanded's goin' on. We know who's to blame for that." His temper flared, though he fought to control it.

She moved another step closer, reaching out to place a reassuring hand on his arm. "I have sent Mr. Tillit to Judge Meyers with a written message. He should have it by now. We are bound to know something very soon."

With the physical distance bridged between the Katherine saw his features soften and a glimmer of loving light in the depths of his eyes.

"I've missed ye, Katie."

"I have missed you, too, Daniel," she replied unhesitatingly.

"There's been disagreement . . . and harsh words . . . keepin' us apart. But no more, Kate. Not now. If the charges against me prove to be for kidnappin' my own babes, I may never see freedom again in my lifetime—"

"Daniel, no!"

Katherine's grip tightened on his arm. His big hand covered hers. Earnestly he forced her to face the truth.

"Yes, Katie, 'tis more than likely. If that's how this all turns out, I don't want to leave without you knowin' you're the only woman I have ever loved."

"Oh, Daniel. Oh, my dear love." Katherine flung her arms around his neck and pressed her face into his shoulder, heartbroken to realize under what circumstances the barriers had finally crumbled between them even as she exulted in the words themselves.

He wrapped comforting arms around her and let her cry, unmanly moisture gathering in his own eyes. He led her to one of the wooden chairs and took her onto his lap, every angle of his body instantly recalling every curve of hers fitting against him like a glove and a hand.

"There, there, sweetlin', that's enough tears for now. I've missed my arms around you and the taste of you on my lips." Dipping his head, Dandy covered her mouth with his, a kiss of gentle passion and longing, for who knew when or if he'd have another chance.

When the kiss ended, he held her, simply held her, not moving or speaking, memorizing the warm feel of her in his arms for later, when she would no longer be with him in reality. At last he spoke, from the fullness in his heart.

"One thing more you must know, Katie, my love. If from this time forward Thomas and Celia are no longer my own, if that wicked old witch has stolen them for good and all—" Over Katherine's protest, murmured against his chest, he struggled on. "I want you to know—and believe to the depths of your soul—that even without them, were I free, I would come back to you . . . and welcome with all my heart our babe, should you be with child."

"Daniel . . ." But for once in Katherine's life, words all but failed her. With tears streaming down her cheeks unheeded, she lifted a trembling hand to her husband's lips, running her thumb across them. "Oh, Daniel, you could not give me a gift greater than those precious words. I pray to God that child lies nestled within my womb this very moment so I may never be truly parted from you. I love you."

"And I you, Mrs. MacCabe."

The long, miserable day waned, and evening came without word from Judge Meyers. Home and at last alone, Katherine paced the front hall, wringing her hands and waiting, until exhaustion forced her to bed. At dawn she arose, scarcely rested, certain word would be forthcoming soon.

But it was midmorning before the front door suddenly burst open, and in strode Dandy himself.

"Daniel!" she cried out, startled. Then, "Merciful heavens, have you broken out of jail?"

Grinning broadly, he reached her in a stride, giving her a smacking big kiss, lifting her off her feet, and swinging her around and around until she was dizzy.

"No, I've not broken out, lass, though 'twas a temptin' thought through the long, lonely night just passed," he boomed, setting her on her feet. "By the Saints, I'm a free man—"

"I beg your pardon, but I believe I had some small part in that," said a voice behind them.

"Judge Meyers, I had almost given up hope," declared Katherine at the sight of the tall, stooped, Lincolnesque figure in the open doorway.

Of her father's generation, he looked very much as Honest Abe might have had he lived to grow gray and bowed with age. In spite of his years, the judge's blue eyes remained keen, his wit sharp, and his narrow seamed face— not as dour as that of the past president—alight with fatherly good humor.

Loath to put the least distance between herself and her husband, Katherine clung to his arm, asking, "However did you manage this miracle? I feared with the charge of kidnapping against him—"

"The only charge against your husband was for ignoring a restraint order filed by Judge Hardman requesting that he and the children remain in town until the question of custody was resolved."

"He told us he had given custody to Mrs. Stewart."

"So Mr. MacCabe informed me. For that little deception, concocted I am sure by himself and Mrs. Stewart, you can rest assured Judge Hardman will be severely reprimanded, at the very least. Confronted with my knowledge of the incident, he was more than willing to drop charges against Mr. MacCabe, so here we all are."

"Not quite all, Judge, not without my babes," added Daniel grimly.

"Thomas and Celia—where are they?"

The judge patted Katherine's arm comfortingly. "Safe and sound with a kindly couple who will see to their care until this matter is decided."

"Can we be seein' them soon, then?"

"Yes, we must see them at once. Celia will not understand what is happening to her and Thomas." But the judge was shaking his head, and the rest of her words went unspoken.

"I am sorry that it cannot be otherwise, Katherine and Daniel, but until this matter is resolved, the children may not be visited by either the two of you or Beatrice Stewart. Should the matter go to court, and as yet I am not certain it will have to, no one must be accused of exerting undo influence upon the children, in case their own testimony is required. Come, let us make ourselves comfortable in your parlor, Katherine. We have matters to discuss."

Dandy stood with an arm draped along the mantel of the cold fireplace, Katherine perched on the edge of one of a pair of brocade slipper chairs. Only Judge Meyers made himself fully comfortable, settling back on the settee, crossing one long leg upon the knee of the other. He quickly covered again the facts he'd briefly gone over in the hall, answering their questions, asking a few of his own.

"So there was never any need for us to run," Dandy burst out in exasperation, striding back and forth along the length of the hearth rug, "and Ol' Lady Stewart never had legal claim to my kids. All those months of hidin' out, scared of our shadows . . . *for nothin'*."

"Not for nothing, Daniel," Katherine softly reminded him. "Aside from the fear of discovery, I for one was the happiest I have ever been in my life at home on the farm with you and the children."

Dandy's loving gaze locked on hers. "Aye, that's the truth, we were happy there, weren't we, Katie? We will be again, the Saints willin'." Then his chestnut eyes grew dark once more with anger. "But it galls me no end to have let

that woman drive us to runnin' away with nothin' more than
her lies.''

Judge Meyers broke in. "It is my belief the children's
grandmother was hoping, through the intimidation of Judge
Hardman's apparent decision, to get Mr. MacCabe to give
the children to her without questioning the legalities. I can
think of no reason for her to have taken this recourse, unless
she has serious uncertainties concerning her ability to win
by more traditional means.''

Dandy gave a short, triumphant laugh. "Hear that, Katie,
Ol' Lady Stewart has her doubts about winnin' my children
away from me. It'll be a cold day in hell—"

"Daniel—"

"There is still the matter of finances," interrupted Judge
Meyers. "One of the strongest points in her favor is her
ability to see to their physical care—"

"Judge Meyers, excuse my speaking out of turn," said
Katherine, "but finances are . . . rather, soon will be . . . no
problem. I have contacted a broker about selling this house
and its contents as quickly as possible, and to that end, he
sent word this morning of an offer beyond my expectations." In spite of the frown pulling Daniel's eyebrows into
one, she hurried on. "I had expected a rather large portion
of the profits to go toward a trial, but if there is not to be
one—"

"There still may be, Katherine, we cannot be sure—"

"Now wait just one gol-danged minute," boomed Dandy.
"If the two of you will stop makin' plans around me like
I'm not here, I've a couple of things I'd like to be sayin'
myself.''

"Daniel?"

"Mr. MacCabe?"

"That's better. Kate, there's no need to be sellin' your
family home, for I've no intention of headin' off to the
woods loggin' this winter, or any other. Once this little matter's resolved in our favor—and 'tis sure I am it will be—
I'm plannin' on takin' you and the kids back to the farm
and work the land full-time. That is, if you're willin'.''

"Oh, yes, Daniel, of course," she agreed without hesitation, adding enthusiastically, "and with the cash from the sale of my house we can buy more livestock, put additional land into crops . . . maybe even add a pump to the kitchen. I would dearly love a pump in the kitchen, Daniel, and—"

"But sell your house, Kate, when you set such store by this big place and all the fancy things in it?"

"No longer, Daniel. There is nothing here I care for as much as my home and family all together as we were, just you and me and Thomas and Celia and our farm."

Daniel bent to kiss his wife's forehead. "You'll get no argument from me concernin' that lovely picture, Katie, for 'tis my idea of heaven as well."

Judge Meyers harrumphed. "There is one matter as yet unresolved. And to that end . . . Ah, I believe that knock at your front door brings me to my point. I've asked Judge Hardman, Mrs. Stewart, and her attorney—Mr. Grissom, is it?—to meet with us here informally, to see if we might spare an official hearing—"

"You'd bring them into this house after what they've done?" sputtered Dandy, accompanied by Katherine's softer protest.

The judge ignored the younger man's tone, explaining calmly, "As a judge rather than a practicing attorney, it would not be ethical for me to act on your behalf before the court. Here, however, I may be able to bring pressures to bear that will make a courtroom hearing unnecessary. If you trust me to act in your best interest, that is."

Dandy sobered at once. "There's none I'd trust more than myself, save you, with the fate and future of my children."

"Then, shall we proceed?"

Hannah Tillit nervously ushered in the newcomers and quickly withdrew. Judge Meyers lankily rose, Dandy took a step forward, but Katherine remained seated, suddenly weak in the knees. In spite of herself, the dowager intimidated her, not on a social level, of course, but with the evilness of her nature. She offered up a quick prayer that whatever tricks of deception the children's grandmother conjured up, she and Daniel and the judge would be able to soundly defeat.

"Good morning, Mrs. Stewart, Mr. . . . er . . . Grissom," greeted Judge Meyers most pleasantly, then frowned. "And where might Judge Hardman be?"

The ponderous matron in another Worth original, this one in a rusty black, lifted her chin haughtily, causing the black ostrich feather draped over her hat onto her cheek to quiver with equal indignation.

"Judge Hardman felt his presence was not needed here today, so he has informed me." Her nostrils flared with displeasure, as if smelling something bad. It was evident Abel Hardman's decision had not met with her approval.

Judge Meyers smiled pleasantly, if a bit smugly.

"Protecting his ass," mumbled Dandy, and he received a warning glance from his judicial representative, tempered with a half smile of agreement.

"Please take a seat. No need to stand uncomfortably about for this informal hearing," the good judge cajoled.

"No need for us to be here at all that I can see," said Mrs. Stewart, making no move from her imperious stance in the center of the carpet.

"The necessity is in attempting to avoid a trial which might very easily become—ah, shall we say—notorious. I'm sure such a happenstance could not possibly be good for the children in question. Nor, madam, your standing in the community here and abroad should you attempt to take Thomas and Celia MacCabe away from their home and family."

With a glare from his employer, Gilbert Grissom spoke up. "Mrs. Stewart . . . ah . . . er . . . is within her rights and has nothing whatsoever to fear from the likes of . . . of—" On shaky legal ground, at best, the attorney rapidly lost his way.

"That is not strictly true, not according to the counter-accusations made by Katherine and Daniel MacCabe concerning the devious means of intimidation used by Judge Abel Hardman to try to gain custody. Were these accusations to prove true in court, or even if not, irreparable damage to Mrs. Stewart's reputation would most certainly follow.''

Mrs. Stewart chose to respond. "You, sir, are on their side and therefore without impartiality—"

"As was Judge Hardman on yours, madam, when he made his pronouncement a few months back?" the judge countered.

The dowager flushed with livid color, and for the moment seemed incapable of sound. Katherine stood, speaking into the brief void.

"Could we please all sit down and deal with this matter more calmly?"

"An excellent idea," agreed Judge Meyers. "Is it not?" he asked the dowager.

Mrs. Stewart opened her mouth, then snapped it shut into a puckered moue. With a contemptuous wave of one gloved hand, like a member of royalty, she led the way to the cluster of seats before the unlit hearth.

20

Seating herself in the chair Katherine had vacated, Mrs. Stewart gestured for her ineffectual attorney to stand beside her. Katherine and Dandy sat side by side on the settee, her hand securely between his two large, callused ones. Judge Meyers took command before the empty hearth.

"I believe," he said, "that we can resolve the matter of Thomas and Celia MacCabe's custody without going to court. It would seem to me the logical choice would be for the children to remain with their father."

"Sir, I must protest. This is turning into nothing more than a kangaroo court, and I demand—"

"Be still, Gilbert," his employer spoke sharply, then turned her disdainful gaze upon the judge. "I had thought, because of your position, you might strive to maintain some impartiality. As that appears not to be the case, however, one can only hope this farce shall soon come to an end."

Before she could rise, Judge Meyers lifted a staying hand. "Dear lady," he said with surprisingly little sarcasm, "if you will wait a few moments more, I shall clarify." When the dowager settled back into her chair, he continued, "The reasons you gave some months ago for requesting custody are no longer valid. Not only have the MacCabes' financial problems resolved themselves, but a very comfortable and happy home has been created from the union between Katherine and Daniel MacCabe. You no longer need to concern yourself with the MacCabe children's welfare—"

"Sir, there is still the matter of the boy's illiteracy, his incorrigible behavior, requiring a stern military education. And then there is the girl's feeblemindedness—"

"Ah, but we've learned that rather than feebleminded, Celia is deaf, and to that end—"

"Deaf?" bit out Mrs. Stewart, incredulous, recovering quickly to state, "All the more reason the child should have specialized schooling in a hospital setting, and as for the boy—"

"Celia has been receiving special teaching throughout the summer and has learned a hand language . . . signing, I believe it's called. She has become skilled at communicating with her teacher and with her family members as well, so you need have no fears for her welfare. Thomas has taken to life in the country and has learned to read and write so he shall be prepared to start school in the fall."

Undaunted, Mrs. Stewart challenged smugly, "There is still the matter of Mr. MacCabe's periodic abandonment of his wife and family for months on end. Surely it is a criminal offense to have left his first wife—my daughter Annabella—alone, knowing she was dying of consumption—"

Dandy released his wife's hands and slid forward, prepared to bound to his feet and confront the woman's charges. Only Katherine's grip on his arm held him back. His glare fastened on the dowager with an intensity that could burn.

"Annie kept from me how sick she was or I wouldn't've left her, and you know it."

The old woman lifted her sagging chin to look down her nose at him, pale eyes of uncertain color as cold as winter's frost.

"I have no such knowledge, Mr. MacCabe. As you will recall, I received a letter from Annabella informing me of your abandonment, begging me to come to her and take her home to die."

"I'd like to see that letter, Mrs. Stewart," Judge Meyers broke in firmly. "Where is it?"

She turned her arrogant gaze on him. "At home, under lock and key. One does not carry papers so private, and so painful, around with one." She managed a distressed sniff, but her gaze remained chilling.

Shaking off his wife's staying hand, Dandy rose up to tower over his accuser. "That's a damned lie. There is no letter, never was." He took a menacing step forward. "I knew Annie better'n you ever did, and I'd swear on my life she'd not utter or write a single word against me. There never was a letter from her blamin' me, was there?"

"Of course there was, and is," declared the dowager, but her gaze would not quite meet his.

"Then send for it."

She glared openly at him. "I will do no such thing. I will not have anything so private, and so precious to me, soiled by—"

"Send for it," Dandy demanded through clenched teeth. "Judge, make her produce Annie's letter. If there is one. I'm sayin' there's not."

"Mrs. Stewart, I should like to see your letter as well. I believe it might prove pertinent to the resolution of this situation."

The dowager pursed her lips, stubbornly refusing eye contact with the others.

"Mrs. Stewart—" Judge Meyers repeated.

The words burst out, "There *should* have been a letter." Her gaze fell to her hands twisting together upon her lap.

"Could you please speak up, Mrs. Stewart," suggested the judge.

The cornered matron stared at Judge Meyers and Dandy like a trapped animal. "Annabella *should* have written to me in her time of illness and distress. I would have seen she was well cared for, attended to the difficulties she had gotten herself into—"

"Like those other *difficulties* you got her out of?" Dandy sneered. "Annie told me about those other *difficulties* you helped her with—"

"I have no idea what you mean."

"I'm referrin' to the time when she was engaged to be married. Remember that little problem?"

"Perhaps you should enlighten the rest of us, Mr. MacCabe, if it bears on this current situation," suggested the judge.

"Oh, you can be sure that it does, Judge, if you'd like an idea of this . . . this . . . lovin' mother's true nature." Dandy replied without taking his eyes off the old lady. "You want to tell him, or should I?" he challenged.

She said nothing. Her lips compressed until they disappeared. Her body quivered with the strain of self-composure.

Taking her silence to mean she had no intention of telling her side of the story, Dandy launched into the one Annie had confided in him. Loath to expose the horror of it, he knew in his heart it might be the only chance he had left to keep his kids out of the old woman's clutches. He cleared his throat.

"Annie didn't just come to town here, to visit her cousin, Judge. She was runnin' away from the misery her own ma forced upon her, chasin' away the man she was engaged to marry—"

"He was merely a merchant. Totally unsuitable—"

"She *loved* him, dammit, with everythin' in her. Loved him enough to . . . ah, er . . . to take a bit of pleasure in him before they said their vows." He cleared his throat. "And when she got in the family way and told her mama here," Dandy said as he thrust a pointed finger at the red-faced dowager, "about the comin' grandchild . . . *she* took poor Annie to one of those doctors—you know the kind, Judge— down one of those dark, narrow alleys and two flights up? The ones with dirty instruments and dirtier hands?"

"Dr. Collins was perfectly reputable—"

"Annie nearly died." Dandy's voice turned low and harsh. "And by the time she'd recovered, Ma Stewart had paid off Annie's fiancé and sent him on his way to New York or San Francisco . . . one of those big cities where a lad can get lost forever, right, Mrs. S.?"

"I maintain he was totally unsuitable for Annabella. Nor

did she have the age and experience to make such an important decision for herself. She needed my guidance—''

''Just like my kids do, is that it? What with me bein' no more *suitable* than that poor, unfortunate fellow, even though Annie and me were married seven years and turned out two fine kids?'' he demanded, his voice rising. ''Now you want to tear us apart as you had that doctor tear Annie's baby from her womb? Over my dead body,'' Dandy concluded, shouting.

The silently enraged dowager Stewart looked as though she wished she could do exactly that, at the same time having the good graces to appear shamefaced at the accusations made against her.

''I did what I thought was for the best at the time,'' she maintained frigidly. ''I certainly desire no less than the best for Annabella's children.''

''Then you'll be lettin' them grow up sane and happy with a da and mama who love them. I've promised my wife my loggin' days are over . . . that we'll be returnin' to our farm for good as soon as this business is cleared up. With the sale of Kate's home, we've cash enough to last for a good long while, given that we don't require a lot. Had you any conscience at all, madam, you'd head back where you came from to your big house and fancy friends and *leave us the hell alone.*''

''Sir, there is no need for profanity,'' spoke up an ineffectual Gilbert Grissom, but his voice wavered off. He cleared his throat and tried again.

''Perhaps . . . ah . . . Mrs. Stewart might consider . . . ah . . . allowing temporary custody of the children . . . ah . . . in their father's care.''

Dandy turned the force of his ire on the scrawny, bespectacled man.

''Temporary, nothin'. Born mine, and mine they shall remain. *I'll* consider nothin' less.''

Beatrice Stewart rose to her full height, gathering her considerable dignity about her like a cloak. She ignored Dandy Dan MacCabe, casting her malevolent gaze upon the judge.

''I had hoped to offer my dear departed Annabella's children all that my wealth and position would afford them. I would have seen to their upbringing in a manner befitting their station in life, in spite of their questionable paternal ancestry. Throughout this ordeal, I have been thwarted at every turn by this . . . this . . . father of theirs. I believe I have done all I can, and am unwilling to pursue this matter further. Now, if you will excuse us, I have other, more pressing matters requiring my attention.'' Without waiting for the judge's dismissal, she swept out of the room, the house, and their lives.

"Well, I'll be damned," exclaimed Dandy, falling onto the settee beside his wife and taking her hand in his once more. He looked into her face, her stunned, relieved expression mirroring his own feelings exactly. "I'll be double dammed if it isn't over at last. That witch is gone from our lives for good, Katie, and we can go home."

Katherine's heart swelled with happiness. "Home. How wonderful that sounds. Oh, Daniel, let us locate the children and pack up our things at once."

Dandy pulled her to her feet and into his arms, kissing her soundly. "Just as soon as we possibly can, sweetlin','' he promised. "After we thank the judge properly, and sign whatever papers need signin' concernin' the kids and your house, 'tis home we're headin' for sure, Katie, my love."

EPILOGUE

"Merciful heaven, how did I ever get talked into giving a barn dance with the whole town coming . . . as well as every farmer and his family within a day's journey?" demanded Katherine of her husband, pivoting in a slow circle on the dusty, straw-strewn barn floor.

Dandy captured his wife, circling her waist, pressing her back against his hard chest, nuzzling her neck with a kiss.

"Because, sweet lass, 'tis only days away from the hard labor of harvest, and everyone's longin' for an excuse to have some fun. Not to mention the fact that I'm about the luckiest man alive havin' my bit of land and a good crop, the best lovin' wife a man could pray for, and the darlin'est children a man could want. After the worrisome summer just past, I'm powerfully in need of lettin' off a little steam in celebration . . . and I don't mind if the whole *world* joins me."

Katherine turned out of his arms to view Dandy's irresistible mischievous grin and the mirth twinkling in his dark chestnut eyes, loving him all the more for his easy good humor, so consumed with happiness it brought quick tears to her eyes. Gently she chided, "And so you invited everyone within hailing distance to a party without ever considering the work involved to get this place ready in time."

He kissed her forehead, then each cheek, lastly her lips, lingering there until she offered a muffled protest.

"And," she added as if not interrupted, "this tomfoolery is not helping one little bit, Mr. MacCabe."

"So, 'tis 'Mr. MacCabe,' is it?" He kissed her yet again to hush her. When they both came up for air, he offered, "Don't worry, lass, we'll all pitch in and help, the children and myself, and Amelia and Richard, too. Amelia says everyone's bringin' somethin', same as last time—"

"Word must have spread from one end of the county to the other of my lack of experience at the stove."

He circled her slightly thickened waist with his big hands. "Katie, darlin', that's not all that's spreadin'. I've a feelin' word's gotten around we're expectin', and the good ladies are merely tryin' to spare you the hard work of cookin' for so many. What say I haul a few of these tools out of your way so you can start sweepin'?"

"Or what if I leave the cleaning of the barn to you," Katherine offered most sweetly, "while I work at making the house presentable as well?"

"As you wish, m'lady." Dandy gave her a courtly bow and set to work, whistling a cheerful version of his tune with no words and no ending.

Friends and neighbors alike came in droves, from the four corners of the county, it seemed, overflowing the small barn, spilling out into a star-studded summer night. There was food aplenty, and dancing to the music of Dandy's dulcimer, Gabe Weatherby's fiddle, and Rusty Browne's harmonica. On the sidelines, Katherine watched, toe tapping, keenly regretting her husband could not twirl her around the hard-packed dirt floor.

"You look in need of a partner. May I have this dance, madam?" Richard bowed before her, his handsome, boyish face and keen blue eyes alive with unsuppressible joy.

Katherine smiled in spite of herself. "Now, why would you want to dance with a married mother-to-be when there are all these lovely young *single* girls to pursue? Amelia, for instance?" she dared suggest.

The young man's gaze searched out the shy twin standing between her sister and his, holding one of Martha's sleeping babies, and he fairly beamed. Tearing his gaze away, he leaned conspiratorially close to Katherine.

"Guess what?" When she raised a single, questioning brow, he continued, "Thought you ought to be the first to know, you and Daniel." He paused dramatically.

Katherine drew back, chiding, "Now, Richard, please do not withhold your news. It is good tidings, is it not?" She had her suspicions what he intended to confide in her.

He chuckled. "Doesn't appear we've been keeping many secrets from you since the two of you got back. As close as you are to Amelia, I imagine you'll be wanting all the details."

She nodded. "And do not leave out a single one."

His confidences had just wound to a conclusion when Katherine spied her husband bearing down upon them, striding purposefully through the crowd applauding the end of a schottische.

"Unhand my wife, Wilder," he demanded, only half joking, over Richard's and Katherine's combined greetings. "I've a mind to dance with her myself."

He grabbed her around the waist and swung her onto the dance floor to the rhythm of a waltz, in spite of Katherine's protest. "Daniel, that was rude."

"Better to have me rude than fightin' mad over Wilder's flirtin' with ye, Katie." Though he jested, the meaning behind his comment was not.

More than a little flattered, in all honesty Katherine felt compelled to explain, "We spent most of our brief conversation discussing Amelia and himself."

"Oh?"

"It would seem they have found each other at last." Katherine chortled with pleasure. "Richard has told me—"

Daniel's brows came down in a frown. "You been matchmakin' again, Katie?" He twirled her around, so energetic with disapproval, he nearly lifted her off her feet.

"Daniel, a bit slower. Please. Remember I am not the

only one spinning like a top when you twirl me so. And no, I have not been matchmaking, though I must confess I have tried. Fortunately they seem to have found one another, anyway. Richard has promised to wait for Amelia while she completes a year's schooling for her teacher's certificate. They are engaged.'' Her pleasure evidenced by her smile, Katherine nodded toward the other couple, circling nearby.

Dandy had to admit grudgingly that it was far better to have the young man's attention focused on Amelia than upon his wife. ''Who would've thought they'd find each other, Kate, from the way they were actin' these last few months? But, such is the course of true love when courtin','' said Dandy, pulling his wife closer, ''as well we know, don't we, lass?''

''If you are referring to our rather unconventional introduction and inauspicious beginnings—''

''I am—''

''Then I must agree.''

''Well, now, that's twice.'' Dandy beamed.

''Twice?''

''That you've admitted agreein' with me since we've been wed. Three times's the lucky charm.''

''Perhaps. Do not hold your breath awaiting the third, however Mr. MacCabe. It might be a long while forthcoming,'' Katherine retorted tartly, spoiling the effect with a teasing smile.

Dandy pulled her tight against himself. ''Ah, Katie, no wonder I couldn't resist puttin' down my dulcimer to dance with you,'' he said into her ear. ''And there's more of the same to come.''

''The music is delightful. It is a shame, though, you have not yet completed your own song.''

He threw her an odd glance, then shrugged. '' 'Tis not a waltz, in any case, and I'm in a waltzin' mood.'' He spun her through the crowd. ''At least for the moment.''

Katherine pulled back from his embrace. ''Meaning?''

Avoiding a direct response, Dandy paused in the middle of the dance floor, catching the attention of the two musicians. The waltz concluded almost immediately, and as other couples drifted away, Dandy held her where she was.

"Meanin', sweet wife of mine, 'tis time for that jig I promised some time back . . . and time for you to join me, as well."

Katherine's hands went to her hips. "I have no intention . . . You cannot expect me to . . . Daniel, it was *not* the agreement that I . . ." But she could not finish a sentence to save her, not with the utterly wicked mischief twinkling from his eyes, dimpling his cheeks with a wide grin.

"Come now, Katie, don't be denyin' you're dyin' to learn the dance."

"I will be close to death, I am sure, should I try. The baby—"

"Will be fine . . . and lovin' it, you'll see." He held out his hand to her. " 'Tis lucky we are Rusty Browne's knowin' 'The Gold Ring' on his harmonica . . . and Gabe's promised to jump in with his fiddle where he can. Let's not be disappointin' them, or our audience."

Tentatively she placed her left hand in his right, seeing that, indeed, an expectant crowd awaited her decision. As if on cue, Rusty's harmonica commenced playing a tune far livelier than she'd expected, having, until this moment, never heard the music of an Irish jig. Quickly she pulled her hand out of her husband's.

"I cannot dance to that, Daniel."

"Sweetlin'," he responded, "in a few moments, you won't be able to stop yourself." He began the opening steps.

He danced with consummate skill, his left arm curved high over his head, right hand on hip, feet moving with incredible speed and accuracy to the music, and the clapping and foot-tapping from the audience. From the youngest to the oldest, no one could resist the compelling rhythm, it seemed, including Katherine herself. His gaze seeking her out where she'd retreated at the edge of the crowd, Dandy offered her a self-satisfied grin. Before she realized what had happened, he'd descended upon her, pulling her out of the safety of the group onto the dance floor. In only moments the melody captured her completely. Lifting her skirts, mimicking her husband as best she could, Katherine performed a fair imitation of the sprightly dance, much to Dandy's delight and that of their audience. When he saw she'd grown winded, he called the dance to a halt, catching her hand in his, bowing from the waist. She offered a curtsy in response, feeling alive in every fiber of her being.

"Daniel, you are right. That is a *most* delightful dance."

Daniel's russet brows rose high in feigned surprise.

"Why, Katie, me love, that's thrice you've agreed with me."

A bit breathlessly, Katherine capitulated. "And that being the case, dearest husband, does that mean I will never have to agree with you again?"

"Nay, lassie," he replied, "only that ye'll need to continue practicin' agreein', until it becomes natural for ye to be doin' it every time."

"Were I you, I would not wait with baited breath on that account, Mr. MacCabe."

He threw back his head with a great roar of laughter, then looked deeply into her eyes. And winked broadly. "Knowin' ye as well as I do, Mrs. MacCabe, I'd expire and go to my grave first, would I not?"

Katherine nodded sharply. "As long as you remember that fact for future reference, all will be well. And now, I would suggest we afford our guests the opportunity to dance, Daniel. I believe we have made spectacles enough of ourselves for one night."

Resting a hand on his arm, she led him into the crowd, surrounded by good-natured laughter and clapping.

Slipping out the open barn door, seeking the cooling evening breeze, Katherine moved away from others with the same intent, and a pair of lovers kissing beyond the light coming from inside. She found a stump, chair height, at the edge of the yard, and sat, more tired than she'd have believed possible with this early pregnancy, though 'Phrony Pearl had counseled her how it would be.

She sighed, brushing escaped tendrils from her cheeks, and turned her face to the harvest moon, contentment seeping into every corner of her being. So replete with happiness she was certain she could contain no more, so consumed with love for her husband, her home, the children—and children-to-be—it brought joyful tears to her eyes and a smile to her lips. Surely there was no woman in the world tonight more blessed than she. Katherine offered up a silent, grateful prayer, watching wisps of clouds caress the silver orb above and slip on by.

A faint melody . . . barely discernible over the merriment coming from the barn . . . teased her with its familiarity. Turning only her head toward the sound, she saw him step out of the shadows, holding the dulcimer against one thigh, lightly stroking the strings as he had so often caressed her person. He walked toward her until he reached the edge of the moonlight-bathed clearing where she sat, then began to sing.

> "Katie, lovely lady,
>   Does that smile belong to me?
>   Let me make you, oh, so happy,
>   For you've given me such joy.
>   Katie, sweet, sweet lady,
>   Woman warm with dreams of love,
>   When I hold you and you kiss me
>   I thank my lucky stars above.
>   Once I was lost and much too lonely.
>   Now I'm filled with peace and joy.
>   Katie, my lovely lady,
>   Does your heart belong to me?
>   Only tell me that you love me,
>   And I'll give my soul to thee."

Katherine rose and moved toward her husband, her love. With hands pressed over her fluttering heart, happy tears bathing her cheeks, she went to meet him.

"Daniel," she whispered, and fought the constrictions of her throat to continue. "Your song is finished, and so . . . so beautiful."

"Ah, sweet lass, 'tis you who are beautiful with moonbeams and love in your eyes. And though my song may be finished at last . . . happily ever afterin' with you, my heart, my soul, my sweet lady, Katie, has just begun."

The author welcomes letters from her readers. Write to her c/o The Berkley Publishing Group, Publicity Department, 200 Madison Avenue, New York, NY 10016.

Come take a walk down Harmony's Main Street in 1874, and meet a different resident of this colorful Kansas town each month.

A TOWN CALLED
❧ HARMONY ❧

__**KEEPING FAITH**__	0-7865-0016-6/$4.99
by Kathleen Kane	
__**TAKING CHANCES**__	0-7865-0022-2/$4.99
by Rebecca Hagan Lee	
__**CHASING RAINBOWS**__	0-7865-0041-7/$4.99
by Linda Shertzer	
__**PASSING FANCY**__	0-7865-0046-8/$4.99
by Lydia Browne	
__**PLAYING CUPID**__	0-7865-0056-5/$4.99
by Donna Fletcher	
__**COMING HOME**__	0-7865-0060-3/$4.99
by Kathleen Kane	
__**GETTING HITCHED**__	0-7865-0067-0/$4.99
by Ann Justice	
__**HOLDING HANDS**__	0-7865-0075-1/$4.99
by Jo Anne Cassity	
__**AMAZING GRACE**__	0-7865-0080-8/$4.99
by Deborah James	